POLARITY

SUSAN MERAKI

Naomi,
   Thank you for your interest.
   I look forward to your thoughts.
        SMki

Published By
Okada-Zheng USA LLC
Everywhere | Anywhere | Nowhere
www.okada-zheng.com

ISBN: 978-0-9913304-0-9

Printed in the United States of America
UID:477f1416717b1353b2a98313d1163f1f67151

For my sister.

CONTENTS

Chapter 1 – Stalemate

"There is no fate. There is no free will," Father Crane said to his acolyte, Daniel. "There is only something best described as somewhere in-between."

Father Crane scanned the chess board between them and confidently moved a pawn one space forward. He clasped his hands together, placed them calmly over his mouth, and patiently awaited Daniel's next move. He knew Daniel was gifted, but he also knew that Daniel had much to learn. For Father Crane, it wasn't a matter of knowledge, but more of teaching Daniel what to do with the knowledge once he had it – Daniel's strong confidence had always needed constant tempering.

Daniel sat motionless with a steadied breath. Father Crane was pleased to see him so focused, so carefully studying all of his options. Daniel looked up earnestly at Father Crane, as if trying to elicit any information as to what his strategy could be. Father Crane tilted his head to the right and pushed his glasses a little further up on his nose – no clue would be given to help Daniel. Father Crane felt Daniel's struggle through his inaction, but he had no plans to take it easy on him. Daniel was his friend, but Daniel was also his student.

"Your move," Father Crane said, urging Daniel to decide. "If this were not a game, your indecision would have already sealed your fate."

Daniel's eyes stayed on Father Crane for a few more seconds and then returned their attention to the chess board. The room was dimly lit, but it didn't appear to bother Daniel – he had been living there since he was eight years old. Daniel bit his lip, slowly crossed his arms, and let out a deep sigh that boomed through the quiet, austere surroundings.

Daniel's eyes occasionally darted up at him – Father Crane could tell that Daniel wanted to speak, but speaking was strictly limited by rule at the monastery; speaking was only done so under extreme necessity. Father Crane had always given Daniel more latitude on this rule than the other residents because he believed speaking was not just a gift from God, but also a tool that God gave mankind to use. Because of Father Crane's openness towards speaking and Daniel's own insatiable hunger for learning, Daniel had always gravitated towards him.

"Why the delay?" Father Crane asked.

Daniel looked up, "I'm sorry, Father. I want to make sure I make a good move."

"Are you worried?"

Daniel looked down at the pieces he had already captured from Father Crane.

"I've taken six of your pieces. You've only taken three of mine."

Father Crane nodded and gained a curious smile.

"So, you've beaten me?" he asked as he casually placed one of his hands against his cheek.

Daniel sat back in his chair and stared listlessly at the chess board for a few moments. He then leaned forward and rested his elbows on the table. He tapped his fingers a few times and then coursed his hands through his neatly trimmed dark hair.

No one had ever beaten Father Crane before. Daniel had been at the monastery for seven years now and played him many times, but Father Crane had soundly defeated him on each occasion. Father Crane was indifferent – he simply accepted the outcome of the match.

"I haven't beaten you yet. I want to maintain my advantage," Daniel said.

"Oh? I wasn't aware that I was at a disadvantage," Father Crane said as he pushed his glasses a little up his nose.

Daniel looked again at the pieces he'd captured and turned his head towards the few Father Crane had captured from him.

"Father, are you instilling doubt in me as a distraction?"

"Not at all," said Father Crane as he motioned his hand towards the board. "Please, continue."

Daniel grabbed one of his bishops and began to move it.

"Hmm," Father Crane said.

Daniel looked up, still holding his bishop, "What?"

"I'm afraid you cannot move your bishop because my queen will check your king."

Daniel put his bishop back. He then grabbed his knight and started to move it. He stopped himself halfway through the move and put it back; he couldn't safely move it without Father Crane's rook checking his king. He set his elbows on the table and placed his hands against the sides of his head to focus. Disgust canvassed his face.

"I have no move I can make. Is that right?"

Father Crane nodded, "There is no piece you can move without having your king in peril."

Daniel's face grimaced, "I lose again. This time, I lose because I have no move to make."

"Lose again? Technically, a stalemate is a draw. We have tied."

"I lost. Not being able to move is as good as losing. My one hundredth loss against you, Father Crane."

"One hundred times?"

Daniel stood up, calmly reeling, "Yes."

"Daniel, it isn't a loss if you have learned something."

Daniel rubbed his face with his hands and shook his head. He choked up, struggling to speak. "I... I...," he stammered.

Father Crane had a deep respect for Daniel and didn't want to discourage him. He could tell that anger had leeched its way into Daniel's demeanor. He needed Daniel's focus to return to something more constructive.

"What have you learned?" Father Crane asked.

Daniel inhaled quickly and paused. He walked to a nearby window and peered outside looking far into the distance. Father Crane walked over to him and patted him on the back a few times.

Daniel's eyes lost focus and wandered to the floor. His face relaxed into despondency.

"I thought I had you this time," Daniel whispered.

Father Crane remained silent and looked down towards the floor, allowing Daniel to speak freely.

"Not being able to make a move, huh?" Daniel asked rhetorically. "I think you planned the stalemate from the start."

Father Crane turned towards Daniel, "Did you not consider that as a possible outcome? Did you not consider that every move you made was nothing more than a contribution towards creating your own demise? Did you consider that all of my little moves would suddenly result in the only move that mattered?"

"No. I was on the offensive. I was doing everything to make sure you wouldn't have any ability to mount a defense..."

Daniel stopped.

Father Crane could almost see hackles going up on his back.

"Calm yourself, Daniel," said Father Crane. "I did not beat you."

"I beat me."

"Yes."

"I did everything you expected me to do. Everything. And, I let it happen."

"What could you have done about it?"

"I don't know," Daniel said, shaking a little, trying to gulp. "There is no fate. There is no free will... right?"

Father Crane didn't say anything. He did not want Daniel's anger to manifest itself any more than it already had. He wanted Daniel to learn from the experience constructively and Daniel was teetering on a full blowout of unbridled anger.

Daniel narrowed his eyes and asked, "What should I have done, Father?"

"Perhaps... Perhaps trying something that you wouldn't expect yourself to do. You've invested too much of yourself in trying to win when, in fact, with each loss you have gained much."

"I understand, Father, but it still hurts. I'm doing my best to understand your wisdom constructively."

Father Crane walked over to a nearby bookcase. "How well do you know this book?" he asked, holding up a Bible.

"I know it well, Father. As you know, I study every day... as do you."

"Why was it written?"

"For guidance... for understanding God, mankind, and His mercy for mankind."

"I see."

Father Crane paused and asked, "And you've read this book?"

"Yes, Father, many times."

Father Crane was silent for a moment, allowing Daniel some time to reflect on what he said. He then walked over to the table where the chess board was and opened the Bible.

"Then you must know that 2 Kings 19 is identical to Isaiah 37?"

Daniel raised an eyebrow. He rushed to the bookcase, grabbed another Bible, and hurried back to the table. He opened one Bible to 2 Kings 19 and the other to Isaiah 37. He traced his fingers across the texts side by side for about half a page before he abruptly stopped. He looked up at Father Crane briefly and then sat down in his chair. He planted his elbows on his knees and cradled his chin in his open hands.

"Have you mastered the Bible?" Father Crane asked.

"Apparently not."

His monotone voice struck a chord with Father Crane – Daniel sounded hopelessly defeated and Father Crane didn't want that.

"But, up until just now, did you think you had?"

"Well, Father, I thought I was on the path to do so."

"And you were happy with that path?"

"Yes."

Daniel lifted his head, leaned back in his chair, and relaxed his shoulders. He stared at Father Crane and looked him over. His face decompressed and he nodded.

"I need to keep the whole picture in mind. I need to realize there isn't an endpoint. I need to realize that there are many things in play and there isn't always a single path to a goal."

Daniel looked down at the chessboard and cracked a small smile.

"We may have played one hundred times, but the reality is that we never finished anything. Each match was just a continuation of the last. Each previous match influenced our decisions for successive matches. Each time I lost, I had gained knowledge."

"As did I," Father Crane said.

"Yes, but each time I play you, you get better. It's almost as if you've already played the next match before we play it."

"You don't do the same?"

Daniel, wide-eyed, retorted, "Father, there are hundreds of millions of possible combinations of moves. It isn't practical to play out matches in advance to any meaningful level of detail."

"Interesting," Father Crane said with a tone of closure. He looked at the clock. "It's getting late. I better retire for the evening. Please clean up our mess, Daniel."

"I will, Father."

*   *   *

Father Crane left the room and softly closed the door behind him. Daniel stared at the chessboard, still looking at the remains of what he thought he played brilliantly. Just once, he'd like to believe he was at the same level as Father Crane at anything. He began to put the chess set away, feeling as if each piece as was mocking him. He was disgusted with himself.

"I am nothing but a loser," Daniel whispered angrily.

Just then, Father Barrett entered the room. Daniel slowly bowed his head at Father Barrett. Father Barrett returned a nod.

Daniel knew he must not speak, but he could not help it.

"Father Barrett, I know I must only speak when absolutely necessary."

"Go on, child."

"Father Crane... He... He makes it all look so easy."

Father Barrett walked up to Daniel and placed his hand on his shoulder, "Daniel, everyone here at the monastery is very aware of your diligence in trying to beat Father Crane at chess. No one..."

"...has ever beaten him. Yes, I know."

Father Barrett paused for a few seconds and cocked his head back. "Daniel, are you angry with Father Crane?"

"No, Father. I'm angry at... myself."

"Anger should be let go of. It will not allow you to be humble before God."

"You're right, Father. I just... I just wanted to know. I was beating him all along and..."

Father Barrett laughed.

"What's so funny, Father?"

"Oh, Daniel, you know Father Crane's gifts go beyond chess, don't you?"

"Why, yes, of course. His knowledge of sacred texts is unparalleled. His knowledge of foreign language is..."

"Daniel, Daniel, Daniel...," Father Barrett interrupted, shaking his head, "Father Crane has been given many gifts by the Almighty, yes."

Daniel stared blankly for a second.

"Come with me," Father Barrett said.

Daniel and Father Barrett exited the room and began walking down a long, nearly featureless hallway – a few old paintings of Jesus Christ, the Virgin Mary, and John the Baptist were the only décor.

"Daniel, for as long as I can remember, Father Crane has been quite literally free of error. He's never made a mistake, ever. He seems to have every answer to every question. And, he presents answers in exactly the way people need to hear them."

"So it seems, yes," Daniel said.

Father Barrett stopped walking and asked, "And why is that?"

"He's a smart man."

"True, but there are many smart men here and not a single one of them comes close to Father Crane's insight or wisdom – and he has, by far, the least grey hair among all of us."

Father Barrett pointed to a small statue on a pedestal in the nearby foyer.

"You see that statue?"

Daniel nodded.

"It was donated to us by a parishioner several years ago."

Daniel was unimpressed – the statue was unremarkable.

"We were about to throw it out when, all of the sudden, Father Crane emphatically and unexpectedly demanded that we save it."

Father Barrett walked over to the statue and carefully picked it up. He turned it over and revealed markings on the bottom of it.

"You see these markings?" Father Barrett asked.

"Yes. What are they?"

"They are the letters P and M and a date. You can barely read it, but, in Latin, it's January 24th, 817."

Daniel looked up at Father Barrett and cocked his head in wonder.

Father Barrett continued, "These markings were covered with a thick paint. None of us would have known better if not for Father Crane. He immediately recognized it and removed the paint with his bare hands for all to see."

Father Barrett held the statue close to him.

"This...," he said reverently, "...was made by Paschal Massimi on the day before he became Pope Paschal the First."

Daniel's jaw dropped. Father Barrett carefully put the statue back.

"How did Father Crane know of this?" Daniel asked.

Father Barrett smiled, "No one knows. We do not question divine inspiration... Oh, I could go on and on about Father

Crane's connection with God as demonstrated by many other examples such as this."

Daniel was shocked and wondered how he could be so dismissive. "But, Father Barrett, you just can't…"

Father Barrett gently shushed Daniel, "It's time to rest, my son."

Daniel obediently nodded his head. Father Barrett walked away. Daniel stared at the statue.

Father Crane… He just knew. That's it, he just knew. He just knew every move I was going to make in the chess match. He just knew. He just knows everything, he thought.

Daniel narrowed his eyes in envy but then stopped himself. He knew he was being tested by God.

Father Crane does not flaunt his abilities. He uses them with God's grace.

*　　　*　　　*

Far down the hall, Father Barrett was intercepted by Father Crane. The two bowed slightly to acknowledge the other's presence.

"Daniel is as brilliant as they come," Father Crane said.

"Yes, but he is young still."

Father Crane looked towards the foyer, where Father Barrett left Daniel, as if projecting his hope for a good future to him.

"You know, he beats everyone else at chess with little or no problem at all. He's never lost to anyone," Father Crane said.

"Except to you, yes," Father Barrett responded. "Even when I play him, it seems that he knows what to do several moves ahead of me."

Father Crane nodded, but he glanced towards the room where they had played chess. He then looked at Father Barrett intensely, "Father Barrett, he was one move away from beating me this last game. Just one."

"Oh, were you worried?"

"No. I was filled with joy. I couldn't help but feel for young Daniel. Next time we play, I believe he will win."

Chapter 2 – An Accident

10 years later

Father Crane walked with a brisk pace through the hallways of the monastery. He'd never been late for anything and he wouldn't be late for his appointment today. Everyone at the monastery was used to him dashing around, seemingly with never-ending energy. He passed by other monks in haste and he was only greeted with reverent acknowledgements of "Father Crane" as he sped by.

He walked into the foyer and grabbed his fedora hat on a nearby rack and put it on his head with certainty. He paused to look at the statue made by Paschal the First. It reminded him of simpler times, as if there was something remarkably absent from his life.

He closed his eyes and sighed.

He grabbed his car keys from his pocket and walked out the door. The daylight hit him from all angles and caused him to squint a little. The crisp air from the surrounding hills of southern California filled him with some degree of serenity and comfort. Still, he had to keep to a schedule. He walked directly to his car, carefully avoiding discussion with others – he could not be late. His drive to the city usually took about an hour. He already knew he wouldn't hit any traffic as long as he left immediately.

He got in his car and simultaneously started the engine and put on his seatbelt. He rolled down his window while checking his mirrors. His car sped away, passing several people meticulously working in nearby fields. The workers waved their hands at Father Crane and he returned several waves in kind. He turned on the radio.

"78 degrees, partly cloudy," the voice said.

He flicked the radio's tuner and it cleanly landed on another station.

"...and today will be 78 degrees, partly cloudy."

He twisted the radio's tuner again to perfectly land on yet another station.

"...partly cloudy and 78 degrees..."

And another.

"High of 78 with some clouds."

And another.

"We'll be partly cloudy and 78 degrees."

He turned the radio off. His face remained expressionless, evacuated of all emotion. His life had very little mystery or surprise in it. For Father Crane, it was extremely difficult to find any joy or sadness – or to have any emotion, for that matter.

He arrived in the city's downtown area about an hour later, as predicted. There were no parking spaces available, but he did not slow down to look. He took a sharp turn left and quickly turned right. Just at that moment, a parked car pulled out of its spot. Father Crane coolly pulled into the space, parked, and turned off his car.

He looked at his watch. He paused for a few seconds and then grabbed a newspaper sitting on the passenger seat next to him. He got out of his car and began walking along the streets.

"Buy a flower?" a street vendor asked him.

"No, thank you," he replied, smiling.

Father Crane looked around and then looked to the ground with his eyes unfocused for a few moments, deep in thought. He raised an eyebrow.

"Actually, yes, I will have a flower."

"That will be three dollars," the vendor said.

Father Crane drew out his wallet and opened it, revealing exactly three dollars. He gave the vendor the money and received a flower in return. He continued walking down the street. His pace slowed a bit as he approached a central park area. The streets surrounding it teemed with light traffic, pedestrians, and street vendors.

He looked at the street sign and pondered a second or two.

"Hmm."

He began walking again and crossed a busy street. He saw some nearby pigeons, grabbed some crackers from his pocket, and walked towards them. They approached and fed without fear. Father Crane gently grabbed one and petted it.

"Be patient," he said to the pigeon.

He let it go and it flew away.

He continued walking along the perimeter of the intersection and approached a hotdog vendor, but not close enough to elicit a sales pitch. He turned to his left and then turned to his right – debating where he should go next. He paused a few more seconds and walked up to the hot dog vendor.

"What can I get ya?" the vendor asked.

Father Crane put his right hand over his mouth in thought, "Hmm… I guess there's a part of me that thinks it's too early for lunch."

"Heh, to be honest with you, padre, I think everyone else thinks the same thing," the vendor replied. "I haven't had a sale all day."

Father Crane raised his eyebrows in concern and suggested, "You know, maybe it isn't the time of day as much as it is your position here at this intersection."

"Oh?"

"I would move your cart over there," Father Crane said as he pointed diagonally across the intersection.

"Why's that?"

"There's a taxi stand nearby over there," he said, pointing across the street. "People taking taxis are usually in a hurry. I think they'd be a bit more inclined for quick bite and they may go for a dog."

The vendor smiled, "Heh. I don't know about that, but I'll try anything if it works. Maybe this is divine intervention, right?" he said half-sarcastically.

Father Crane smiled back politely.

The vendor folded down the cart's umbrella and began moving it as Father Crane suggested. Father Crane walked in the opposite direction he came. He then crossed another street at the intersection. Before he finished crossing, he intentionally dropped the flower on the street. No one said anything, tried to pick it up, or even seemed to notice. He strolled over to a nearby bench, sat down, and began to read his newspaper.

Birds chirped in nearby trees on this peaceful day as Father Crane read his paper. After a few minutes, he tilted it down to watch the hot dog vendor making his way ever-so-slowly to the other side of the intersection.

At the same time, Father Crane looked over to see a small girl – crossing the street with her mother – spy the flower on the ground.

"Mommy, a flower!" the girl shouted.

"Honey sweetie, you don't know where that flower came from," her mother responded.

The girl started to run to the flower, but her mother grabbed her quickly.

"Samantha! No!" her mother said sternly.

"I want the flower!" she yelled back, flailing her arms.

Her mother ignored her and she tugged the struggling girl along.

"What the…?!" yelled a voice across the street.

Father Crane looked over and saw a pigeon assaulting the hot dog vendor. The vendor tried to shoo it away, but the more he tried the more violent the pigeon became. More pigeons joined the foray on the hot dog vendor.

"Ahhh!" the vendor yelled.

The hot dog vendor ducked to protect his face, bumping his cart and setting it into motion. It headed down the sidewalk, gradually picking up speed. The hot dog vendor moved to grab his cart, but the pigeons showed no quarter. The cart was out of control.

Father Crane calmly put his paper down and looked at his watch. He then looked towards the park at a man who, apart from his yellow shirt, was otherwise just another face in the crowd. The yellow-shirted man was walking along casually, but then suddenly halted and made eye contact with Father Crane. Both of their eyes widened and then narrowed in cold confrontation.

Suddenly, the girl broke free from her mother and darted back to the flower to pick it up. A car swerved hard to miss her, finding itself facing oncoming traffic. Several cars veered away to miss it – one oncoming car jumped the curb adjacent to the park and barreled towards the man with the yellow shirt.

In the same instant, the hot dog vendor's cart rolled into the street. A delivery truck plowed into the cart, causing it to be shoved towards the back of the yellow-shirted man – however, the man was focused on the out-of-control car speeding towards him. He jumped on the hood of the car and tried to jump over it, but his feet were clipped. He shot up a few feet in the air and fell into the path of the hot dog cart. The cart slammed into him with immense energy, severely wounding him.

Father Crane stood up without a hint of emotion, put his newspaper in a nearby garbage can, and walked away.

*   *   *

Sirens were heard quickly and within a few minutes an ambulance had picked up the yellow-shirted man. As he was rushed to the hospital, he went in and out of consciousness. A mask was affixed to his face. Tubes were connected into his arm. Medics were working feverishly over him yelling out numbers related to his health.

"He's dropping! 80 over 50!"

He was rushed through the emergency room and into an operating room. Doctors yelled various instructions with the utmost urgency.

"He's stabilizing!" a nurse yelled.

Night fell. A gurney holding the yellow-shirted man emerged from the operating room. Bottles of fluid, tubes, and monitoring devices canvassed his body. He was being carefully moved to another room.

"I don't know how this one survived," a doctor said.

"A miracle," a nurse said as she stopped the gurney and flashed a light in the man's eyes. "He's still unconscious."

"He goes to ICU 3," the doctor said.

"Yes, doctor," the nurse replied and began pushing the gurney once again.

The doctor put a clipboard onto the gurney; he was finished working on the man for now.

"He'll have quite a journey towards recovery," the doctor said before moving on.

The nurse nodded her head in agreement and continued pushing the gurney. She pushed the gurney down a few hallways, then through double swinging doors, and into the room labeled *ICU 3*. The nurse stopped and looked the room over, trying to find a suitable spot for the man. Another nurse entered the room.

"Oh, Margaret?" she asked, stopping the nurse.

"Yes, Sarah?"

"Where should I put this one? He's strictly here for monitoring."

"Hmm, put him over there," said Margaret, pointing to another man lying in a bed in the area.

"Oh, next to that man in the coma?"

"Yes, that will do. I don't think he will mind," Margaret said with a slanted smile.

Sarah moved the yellow-shirted man into a position a few feet from the man in a coma and took a few steps away for a chat with Margaret.

"You wouldn't believe what this man went through," Sarah said.

"Oh?"

"He was run over by…"

The heart monitor on the man in a coma began to pick up pace. He opened his eyes and heaved his chest up. He yelled in pain. The nurses rushed towards him, but, before they reached him, the yellow-shirted man began to go into violent convulsions.

Margaret rushed to an intercom and yelled, "Two level five patients! Need doctors stat!"

Sarah tried her best to hold down the yellow-shirted man, practically draping herself across him. The yellow-shirted man tried his best to turn away from the man who was in a coma who also tried his best to turn away as well. Both men were strapped down, rendering their efforts useless.

Capillaries began to hemorrhage all over both of their bodies. Their tongues swelled to several times their normal size. Blood began dripping from their ears. Alarms and beeping from the medical machinery filled the room. Margaret and Sarah were doing their best to control the men when doctors rushed into the ICU with medical kits in-hand.

"What happened?!" a doctor yelled.

"Patients Three and Four just started going out of control! I don't know! I don't know!"

The doctor injected something into the comatose man. By now, both men were completely covered in thick sweat. They both began vomiting uncontrollably.

The yellow-shirted man stopped flailing.

"I'm losing him!" the doctor yelled. "His bleeding is uncontrolled! He has no blood pressure! I... I don't know what's killing him!"

The beeps from the yellow-shirted man's heart monitor stopped and went into a continuous din. At that moment, the man who was in a coma went limp and his heart monitor also flat-lined. The doctors and nurses continued in a frenzy of activity trying to bring them back to life.

*   *   *

Just outside the hospital, on the sidewalk below the ICU, Father Crane stood patiently as he looked up at their window.

"Two birds with one stone," he said.

He walked away, without having the slightest emotion on his face. He stopped. He sensed a presence. Across the street, he saw Jill. She was a fair-skinned woman in her mid-30s, wearing sweat pants and a T-shirt. It looked as if she just woke up.

"*You're* late," Father Crane said to her in a raised, almost mocking voice.

Jill's eyes dropped sadly, as if she had suffered a major loss.

"I will leave *You* to ponder *Your* predicament," Father Crane said and then resumed walking.

"*We* will endure in spite of *You!*" Jill snapped back.

Father Crane stopped and turned to her. He removed his hat and held it by the rim with both hands, waiting for Jill's next move.

Jill looked down the street to her right. She scowled and Father Crane knew she had spotted the dark silhouette and the dim glow of a lit cigarette. A switchblade was brandished, glittering in the surrounding street lights.

"You brought help?! Can't do this on your own?!" she yelled at Father Crane.

Father Crane didn't say a word.

"Make it fair and we'll settle this right now!"

Father Crane put his hat on and continued walking, completely ignoring Jill.

"Well?" she asked.

Without breaking stride, Father Crane called over his shoulder, "*You* will be busy for a while."

A few steps later he took out his cell phone. A text message appeared that read, *Focus on Susie.*

Chapter 3 – The Target

"Can I help you with something, miss?" a store clerk asked a young woman, Susie, who was pondering over an endless row of soup cans.

"Oh, no, thanks," she said.

Susie carefully looked over the soup cans. She snatched a can and looked at its label. She would admit that she was perhaps too careful in her shopping, but it gave her a sense of accomplishment, of being responsible. Her weekly ritual of grocery shopping was a careful balance of budget and nutrition; it was a small but important part of her plan in life to make it without anyone's help.

"This one is on sale, but it does have a lot of sodium," she said to herself.

She tossed her shoulder-length dark hair to one side and bit a nail in thought. She grabbed several cans, comparing each carefully – Campbell's, Progresso, Epic – there seemed like an endless number of choices. She closed her eyes, counting the cost of the soup with her fingers, and finally settled on a decision.

"Ok, lunch for the week," she said, adding six cans to her meager collection of groceries. She liked to treat herself at least once a week, but she had to manage her budget wisely. At nineteen years old and having recently moved out of her mother's home, she would gladly eat the same food daily if it meant maintaining her independence. She kept herself to strictly forty dollars per week for groceries, no matter what.

Susie looked down at her cart and realized that she was forgetting something. She tapped her foot unconsciously in an attempt to draw out information deeply hidden in her head. She shifted one hand to her hip and the other on her forehead.

"Pens!" she suddenly said. "That would have been stupid."

She began to move her cart forward and then stopped, considering, "Hmm… Pens are more important."

Susie sighed, but knew she had to do the right thing. She took another can of soup from the shelf, ditching her weekly treat in favor of buying the pens she needed. The wiggle room in her budget couldn't cover both and she was down to her last pen with final exams this week. Susie believed making it on her own meant not depending on anyone else for anything, even pens.

She comforted herself by reflecting on her time at the local university over the past year. She was doing well. She had remained focused on getting good grades so she could get her degree and then a "real job". Susie looked forward to that point as when she would finally be able to help others through tough times, just as others had helped her mother when her father had left many years ago.

She leaned on her cart and stared at the cans of soup – Susie found herself thinking back to long before the university, vividly remembering what being truly destitute felt like. She remembered, as a young child, sleeping in cars and on the floors of other people's homes. Her mother had struggled to make ends meet. When other kids had toys, Susie only had her sister. Christmas was just a day that her mother didn't work and didn't get paid, if she even had a job.

When she got older, she had ignored the common temptations of teenagers because she was too busy studying or working part-time jobs to help her mother with the bills. Whatever spare time she did have, she had usually spent helping younger kids after school with their homework; it was fun for her and it didn't cost anything.

She thought about the endless stream of loser boyfriends her mother had, how all of them had treated her terribly from start to finish. Most recently, Susie had come home and caught her mother's last boyfriend attacking her mother in one of his many drunken rages. Without any regarding to her personal safety, Susie had intervened.

"LEAVE MY MOTHER ALONE!" Susie had screamed.

The man had turned to Susie and recoiled his fist to strike her. Without hesitation, she had grabbed the nearest object, a large mug sitting on a nearby table, and then swung it up in front of her face in defense. The man's fist had made contact with the mug, shattering it and the man's hand.

"Aaaaaa!" the man had yelled, tucking a badly bleeding hand.

Enraged, he had rushed Susie. She had instinctively taken a few steps back, only to unexpectedly fall on the floor. The man had tripped on her, causing him to fly forward headfirst into an end table and rendered himself unconscious. Susie had immediately gotten up to help her mother like nothing particularly unusual had happened.

Susie hoped that those days for her mother were over. She wanted her mother to be safe, but she also needed to live on her own – even though it was a financial challenge. Her mother also wanted it this way since she was finally able to make ends meet;

she had implored Susie to go out and make her proud. No one in her family had ever finished college and Susie was resolute to do so. It was an all-important means to an end and she only needed three more years to finish her degree.

Susie unfolded her shopping list and crossed out *soup* from her list of other basics such as milk, bread, peanut butter, and eggs. She admitted that it was a simple life, but it wasn't without its hardships. There were times when she wished she could treat herself a little more, especially during tough exam weeks like this one. She would like to have just a tiny bit of a social life, too; she wished at least one guy would show real interest in her. Each day seemed just like the last – she was roundly ignored.

Susie casually looked to her right and spotted a familiar face.

"Karen?!" Susie half-yelled.

Susie could hardly believe her eyes because Karen, her sister, rarely goes anywhere without their mother. Karen was holding a shopping basket with a cheap bottle of wine in it.

"Susie?"

"What are you doing here?"

"Oh, picking up some wine. Mom's still a little sick this morning so I thought I'd pick up some chicken noodle soup, too," Karen said as she dropped a few cans in her basket.

"Mom is feeling better, I hope?" Susie asked.

"Yeah, but you know how she is. She doesn't know when to take it easy. She's as bull-headed as ever...," Karen said with a pageant-winning smile, "Just like you."

"Ha ha, very funny," Susie rolled her eyes. "By the way, how's Ken?"

Karen opened her mouth to answer but stopped.

"What? Oh, you didn't break up, did you?"

"Well, he just didn't have the potential I was looking for. I thought if I gave him more time, he would turn his life around."

Susie shook her head in exasperation, "Karen, you dated for, what? Two months?"

"One month and twenty-seven days."

"Okay, okay, one month and twenty-seven days... I'm sure that was plenty of time to turn a life around," Susie said sarcastically.

"I think it was."

"Karen, you chew men up and spit them out like gum."

"Yeah, I suppose...," Karen said, tightening her lips, beginning to grin devilishly, "...but I'm just trying to make up for the boyfriends you don't have," she teased.

"I don't need the drama."

Susie considered Karen to be one of the few people who knew her well enough to give advice that Susie could agree with or at least consider. Karen was with her and her mother through all of the hardships growing up. Their experiences had made Susie strong and independent, but Susie knew they had had the opposite effect on Karen. It was Karen who was always dating – almost speed dating – to find the guy, the right guy, the one who would take care of her. Susie and Karen were very different in many ways, but Karen was still Susie's best friend.

"I know," Karen said, "but sometimes drama is nice."

Karen's life without drama would otherwise be completely boring. Drama was Karen's lifeblood.

Karen looked at her watch. "Well, I gotta run. Hey, are you coming this Friday for dinner with us?"

This decision was easy. After having given up her weekly treat to buy pens, she seized the opportunity.

"Yes. It'll be fun for us girls to have dinner together. But, I could be a little late. I have a test that evening."

"You go, college girl. I'll see you Friday then." Karen walked away, eyeing Susie with a proud smile.

Susie knew that Karen sometimes lived vicariously through her since it was as close to going to college as she would ever get. Karen's ideal world would have Susie living next door to her, if not in the same house.

She watched Karen walk away and then she headed to another aisle to pick up pens. She found them on the end-cap of the next aisle over. She suddenly remembered that she didn't ask Karen if she should bring something for the dinner. She quickly poked her head around the end-cap to see if Karen was still within shouting distance.

She didn't see anyone except a Catholic priest wearing a fedora hat standing about six aisles over. She made eye contact with the priest and smiled at him. He titled his head towards her, causing his glasses to shimmer in the light. He cracked a slight smile back at her and walked away.

CRASH!

A giant light fixture smashed to the floor just behind Susie, narrowly missing her.

She squealed, stumbling to the ground, shocked.

A small crowd of people quickly gathered to investigate. Susie was speechless and panting.

"Wow, that thing is at least fifty pounds," a man said, looking over the wreckage, "Are you okay?"

Susie nodded her head, her heart still pounding.

"One step in the wrong direction and that thing would have killed you," the man said, extending his hand to help her up.

Susie got up and tried her best to collect her thoughts.

"Are you okay?" the store manager asked.

"Yes... Yes, I am, thank you," she said, trying her best to contain a pant.

"Are you sure?" the store manager asked.

"Yes... Yes... Thank you. No worries. I'm fine. It's no big deal."

Susie grabbed her pens and quickly made her way to the checkout counter, minimizing the incident, trying to defuse further attention towards her. She got her wallet out of her purse and opened it, noting her one credit card tucked in its usual spot, which she had vowed to only use in dire emergencies. So far, she had never used it. She would pay with cash, as always, and began counting out the amount.

"Hmm," she said.

"What?" the clerk asked.

"I'm missing a dime."

She fussed with her wallet and began rifling through her purse, hunting feverishly. Quite literally, every dime counted for her.

Fortunately she found it, finished paying for her groceries, and made her way out to her car – which was barely in working condition. She had named it Old Faithful because, as she told anyone who asked, "It's been around forever and it will occasionally make a noise that sounds like a geyser going off." Of course, the part about the geyser was only a guess; Susie had never actually heard one go off. In fact, Susie had never left the state, as far as she could remember.

Regardless, Old Faithful accepted all of Susie's groceries in its back seat. Using the trunk was unthinkable since it was borderline unusable – it was full of random things that, over time, Susie had put in and then more or less forgot about. It was the only part of Susie's life that she tolerated being unorganized and disheveled.

She looked around at the landscape of the surrounding tall buildings of the city. Each structure felt like a lifelong friend that gave her a sense of stability and calm – although she frequently wondered what life would be like somewhere else to help escape the memories of her troubled childhood. Early December in southern California usually required a light jacket, but the weather was a little warmer than usual. The balmy winds were welcomed to help her cope with the stresses of finals at school. She unconsciously smiled – she was content with what she had in life and the promise of knowing where she was going with it.

Susie drove back home and quickly unloaded her car. She left Old Faithful running because she knew that stopping it meant it may not start again, and she was already pressed for time. She thought about her schedule for the night: she had a World History study group at the university in less than an hour; she worked in the computer lab on campus – a part-time job – after that; and, finally, she had her World History final after that.

She rushed towards campus as fast as traffic would allow her to. A light turned yellow and, for Susie, yellow meant red – she didn't take any chances. She stopped at the light and patiently waited for it to turn green. "I'm gonna be late," she said aloud, somewhat disappointed with herself.

The light turned green, but before she could begin moving forward, a pigeon landed on her windshield.

"Shoo! Shoo!" she yelled, having no effect on the pigeon.

At that instant, a car from her left ran its red light. It streaked in front of Old Faithful, barely missing its front end.

"Whoa!" Susie jumped.

The pigeon flew away.

Susie paused, wondering what would have happened if she had been just a little further out in the intersection.

"A pigeon saved my life and it didn't even know it," she joked to herself. "The luck I'm having today… I swear."

A few more traffic lights later, she arrived on campus. She worried that she wouldn't be able to find a parking spot because the parking garages tended to remain full during finals week. Parking on the streets of the metropolis that surrounded the campus would be even more difficult; she knew traffic was bad, but finding a parking spot would be impossible. She drove into the nearest parking garage feverishly looking for any open spot. She shook her head in frustration believing that she was wasting her time in this parking garage and she would have to go to the next one. Finally, on the top deck she found one open spot. She breathed a sigh of relief, parked Old Faithful, and rushed across campus to the library for her study group. She found the study room where her group was planning to meet, but no one was there.

She was relieved. She hated being late. She preferred being ten minutes early than being one minute late. She considered time to be the most precious commodity because time healed all or at least it gave people a chance to sort out any mess that may exist between them.

She opened her history book and began studying on her own. The final was today and she was fighting for another A on her college record. Thirty minutes went by and no one showed up. She looked at her watch and sat back in her chair somewhat puzzled. She stood up and looked around the general area, wondering if, perhaps, her group was somewhere nearby.

There was no one there she recognized. She wondered if she missed something.

Susie gathered up her studying material. She was already well-prepared. This last study session was more of a benefit for the rest of the study group. There were a few of them that were a bit behind in the material and Susie had wanted to help them out. If for no other reason, it was Susie's only real social outlet and she had looked forward to the interaction.

With her backpack slung over her shoulder, she left the library and meandered about campus. She decided to get a coffee as a reward for her diligence – she had time to kill before work. She headed to the Student Union's coffee shop.

The noontime campus teemed with people, even on finals week. Many students lounged on the lawn; some stood or sat in small groups, but most walked about on the sidewalks. Susie didn't know any of them, but she enjoyed the company for what it was worth. The university campus was an enclave within the big city – its smaller buildings and tracts of green lawn made the university feel like a remote island that was unsullied by the imposing urban backdrop.

She entered the Student Union and made her way to the coffee shop. She got at the end of the long line. A few seconds passed and there was a tap on her shoulder. She turned around.

"Hey, Susie," said a tall, thin young woman with dark curly hair.

"Hey, Nicole!"

Nicole was one of Susie's study group members and one of the few real friends Susie had made while in college. She was a year ahead of Susie, but they had had a couple classes together last semester and become friends. It was as close of a friendship that Susie had ever had other than with her sister Karen.

"Uh, Nicole," Susie said, "did we cancel study group?"

"You're kidding, right?" she asked with a puzzled grin.

Susie looked at her blankly.

"Uhh… You cancelled it," Nicole said.

"Me?!"

"Yeah. You sent out an email to all of us."

"Uh, no, I didn't."

Nicole brought out her phone and found the email.

"See that?" she said while pointing at her phone. "You are Susie, right?"

Susie laughed, "Yes, funny girl, but I never sent that."

"Hmm…"

"Seriously, Nicole, it must have been a prank by someone else. I wouldn't have cancelled with the final being today."

"Strange. I wonder who would do that?"

Susie shrugged her shoulders.

"Well, I'm getting coffee for sure. Lots of studying to do," Nicole said.

"You wouldn't believe what happened at the grocery store today...," Susie began but stopped short, suddenly distracted by several guys coming into the Student Union's front door. They paraded inside, instantly taking the spotlight. They were a loud, rowdy, and happy bunch.

"You okay?" Nicole asked.

"Uh... Um... Yeah...," she responded vaguely, distracted by the group.

Nicole turned towards the ruckus, but she didn't see anything out of the ordinary. "What's the matter?" she asked her.

"I... I don't know," Susie said, still in a lucid trance.

She continued staring. She heard them a bit more clearly as they approached.

"Okay, okay, okay... One more time!" one of the guys – the ringleader of sorts – yelled out.

The group stopped and went silent, waiting for him to speak. He said something, but it was inaudible to Susie. The others bellowed out in laughter.

"Okay, I gotta go, guys!" the ringleader yelled.

Susie's eyes shifted to focus solely on him – short dark hair, well-built, tall, and with a confident walk. He passed by her and smiled. She didn't smile back, but she was inexplicably intrigued by him.

"You know him?" Nicole asked.

Susie regained her focus, "Huh? Oh... No."

"You okay?"

"Yeah... I guess I just spaced out from all the studying."

Susie turned back towards the coffee line. There was a large gap in front of her from several people having already moved forward. She took several steps forward and Nicole followed.

"Whoa. I need to go to the ATM really quick. Can you save my spot in line?" Nicole asked.

"Sure," Susie said without looking back.

She perused the menu, determining what she wanted to get by what she would allow herself to spend. She debated for what seemed like several minutes – not knowing why she couldn't make up her mind. She increasingly felt uneasy with each passing second. It was almost to the extent that she just wanted to leave.

I don't need it. I should just go.

She heard someone walk up behind her.

"Do you think getting the bigger cup is worth it?" she asked out loud to Nicole, who she expected was behind her.

No answer. She turned around and, to her surprise, the ringleader of the rowdy group was right behind her.

"Aaa!" she squeaked.

"Hey, be gentle. I may not have showered in weeks, but I still think I'm good for a few more," he said.

His voice was smooth, almost melodious with each syllable. Susie caught her breath and told him, "I'm sorry. I thought you were someone else."

"Wow. First I smell bad and now this," he said with a sideways smile. "Sorry, I can only be me."

"I didn't say you smelled," Susie said, blushing.

"Okay, good. I don't smell. That's one thing down and just this 'someone else' issue left to go."

Susie was puzzled – was he flirting with her? Susie was stricken with shyness and discomfort, rendering her speechless. She wanted to run away but was petrified.

The guy tilted his head slightly and extended his hand, "I'm Dan."

Susie shook his hand in return. His hand felt cold, but strong and confident.

"I'm Susie," she said, her voice shaking a little.

Susie saw Nicole approaching behind Dan, returning from the ATM.

"Hey, sorry for taking so long to get back. The ATM line was long...," Nicole said.

She stopped, looked at Dan, and then at Susie.

"Oh, I was holding her spot in line," Susie said.

"Hey, no problem," Dan responded, backing up.

"Thanks," said Nicole as she stepped in front of Dan.

Dan looked at his watch, "Whoa. I lost track of time. So much for coffee. I gotta run. Take it easy!"

Dan smiled back at Susie as he walked away. She stared vacantly back at him.

Nicole prodded her to move forward in line, "Hey, Susie, you're next."

"Can I help you?" the barista asked.

Susie didn't respond. She was still looking in the direction Dan had gone.

"Earth to Susie! Hello?!" Nicole said. She waved her hand in front of Susie's face, finally catching her attention.

"Huh?" Susie asked.

"You're next in line, if you still have both feet on the ground."

Susie took a step forward towards the counter and glanced up at the menu.

"I'll have a medium black coffee, please," she said to the barista.

She looked back over her shoulder towards Dan's direction again.

"You okay?" Nicole asked.

"Yeah... Yeah... It's just... It's just..."

"What?"

"That guy, Dan..."

"Your new boyfriend?"

Susie shook her head. "No. Never mind. I just get really shy around guys… that's all. Besides, I think he was flirting."

"He was flirting?" Nicole asked.

"You know, I don't know…"

"That's one ninety-nine," the barista told Susie, placing her coffee order on the counter.

Susie dug into her purse and gave the barista exact change.

She picked up her coffee and sighed to Nicole, "I think I'm just nervous about my finals. I don't know what came over me."

Nicole shrugged, "Who knows? Who cares? You'll probably never see him again."

*   *   *

Much later on that day, as the sun was setting, Susie emerged from her classroom after having finished her World History final. She walked alongside Nicole.

"I'm so glad that's over," she said.

"No kidding," Nicole said. "That was brutal. I think school was invented to torture people into believing that the path to heaven leads through hell."

"Don't be so dramatic," Susie countered, shaking her head.

"Yeah? When are you ever going to use World History in your everyday life? Who cares about the War of 1812 or that no one is sure who owns Antarctica? And how about Calculus? When will you ever use that?"

"Calculus? I don't know – I haven't taken that yet. I just signed up to take it next semester."

"You won't," Nicole said flatly.

They started to diverge from each other as they walked.

"Catch you next semester," Nicole said.

"Okay. See ya later."

Susie looked up to see the last remnants of the sunset. She glanced around the campus – it was nearly devoid of students. Susie took in a deep breath, preparing herself for the short journey back to the parking garage where she left Old Faithful. She strolled along casually, her backpack slung over a shoulder. She noticed that her shoelaces were coming untied and she stopped to retie them. When she stood back up, she immediately froze. She felt unsettled, increasingly so with each passing second.

Ahead, she saw a man standing ominously against the shadowed side of one of the science buildings. He was smoking a cigarette. Except for the silhouette of his mohawk, it was hard for Susie to see what he looked like. He wasn't there before, she was sure of that.

Susie didn't move. The most direct path to her car was passed him, but this man seemed to fill her with dread. She was nearly paralyzed and didn't really know why. Her heartbeat increased and her anxiety climbed unexpectedly higher. She felt a rush of negative energy, an extraordinarily strong sense of foreboding.

Someone tapped on her shoulder from behind.

"Oh!" Susie jumped and twisted around.

It was Dan.

"Whoa, didn't mean to scare you," he said, holding his hands up playfully and backing up a step.

Susie, a little disoriented, looked at Dan and then looked back towards the man standing against the wall. The man flicked his cigarette forward and walked away.

"No... No, it's ok," she said, looking back at Dan. She was still extremely uneasy, but felt a little better knowing that man was gone. However, she still felt she wasn't completely safe.

"You look pretty rattled," Dan said.

e didn't say anything. She had a hard time looking at Dan
es. She was definitely rattled.

"Hey… You alright?"

"Yeah, yeah… I'm fine," Susie said.

She finally looked at Dan in the eyes.

"You don't look it," he said, his brow furled.

"No… Really, I'm fine."

The two of them just stood there for a moment.

"You're Susie, right? We met earlier today."

"Yes," she said, trying to smile.

Susie wasn't sure why she had a hard time speaking. She couldn't even get out a single word without extreme effort.

"I'm Dan."

Susie smiled, "Yes, I know."

"Well, okay. Take care."

Susie stood there speechless as Dan walked away. She tried her best to process what had just happened. She looked around and, with both Dan and the strange man with the mohawk gone, it was just like any other night on campus. Susie regained her composure and continued walking.

Susie recalled Nicole saying she would never see Dan again. She laughed a little at the irony that she ended up seeing him again on the very same day. She felt a bit embarrassed at her behavior towards Dan and wished she could take those few moments back. Dan seemed like a regular nice guy. Maybe he was even an interesting guy, but now she was certain she would never find out.

Susie wondered if she was waiting for the perfect guy that would never come along. But she also wondered how many times she met guys who might be perfect but were never given a chance because she was avoiding drama. Susie sighed and accepted this as something close to the absolute truth – perhaps for the rest of her life at this rate.

Dan was a good-looking guy. He seemed sensitive and genuine – or at least genuine enough to worry a bit when things got weird back there. He seemed funny and well-liked. She didn't give him a chance and he just simply walked away.

She cringed and dropped her shoulders. Susie resumed walking to her car and hung her head down in self-pity. She wished she could move on with her life, but she never felt comfortable trusting people for fear of getting hurt. She had never been hurt romantically; no, all of her fear was based solely on what her father did to her family. He had left when she was very young – the enduring pain of this event was deeply ingrained in her because what she had seen happen to her mother. Her mother's ability to function in life had been permanently compromised. In spite of all her boyfriends, her mother seemed to never stop talking about Susie's father abandoning them – forever heartbroken and betrayed.

Susie began to feel sorry for herself, wondering if anyone in the world would ever care about her – other than her mother, sister, and maybe Nicole. She felt she was a nobody.

Chapter 4 – Being Frank

Father Crane pulled his car up alongside a patch of green hills, far away from the monastery and the big city. He got out of his car, buttoned up his black trench-coat, and put on black wool gloves. He grabbed a bag of donuts and a collapsible chair from his trunk. He looked up to his left at the top of a steep hill; it was well over one hundred feet tall. He took a deep breath and walked straight up the hillside, maneuvering around some small boulders along the way. He crested the top and saw Frank curled up on the ground a few hundred feet away. Frank was shivering from the cold, brisk air.

Frank looked up at Father Crane and immediately jumped to his feet, but then he wobbled and fell back onto the ground.

"Take your time getting up, Frank!"

Father Crane slowly winded his way between the boulders of the rugged terrain, approaching Frank. He stopped when he was about forty feet away from him. Frank had finally stood up, but his knees were on the edge of buckling.

Father Crane looked him over. His eyes were bloodshot and heavy-lidded. A little drool was dripping from his somewhat open mouth. His policeman's uniform had the stains of several meals crusted on it. His unshaven face was riddled with confusion. His blond hair was unkempt and matted. He appeared stuck, oblivious, and in a catatonic state of thought.

"You're a mess, Frank," Father Crane said.

Frank looked down to inspect himself and then looked back at Father Crane.

"I... I...," he stammered.

"It's fine," Father Crane said. He unfolded his chair and sat down in it with a commanding posture. Frank took a few steps forward towards him.

"Ah, ah, ah," Father Crane warned, waving his finger as if at a child. "Don't be foolish, Frank."

"Oh. Sorry... I'm... I'm still getting used to... to... this."

Father Crane threw the bag of donuts to Frank.

"Eat those," he commanded.

"I can't keep food down. I've been vomiting for days."

"You'll be fine. Eat."

Franks cocked his head back and hesitated. His eyes lit up a little bit and he ripped into the bag of donuts. Father Crane waited patiently while he ate, not even shifting when Frank eventually closed the bag and waited expectantly for Father Crane to speak. Thunder stemmed from clouds nearby.

"I didn't plan for the rain," Frank said.

Father Crane didn't say anything.

Frank looked up towards the sky, "Oh, wait..."

"It won't rain...," Father Crane said.

"No... No..."

"Not here, at least, until next Tuesday."

"Yes...," Frank said, with a cracked voice.

Frank looked down at the ground and bit his lip.

"I will start," Father Crane said.

Frank nodded his head eagerly.

"How long since you've been one of *Us*?"

"You know... I... I don't know," Frank said.

"Interesting."

Frank shifted his eyes a little and dropped his head. "Everything happened so fast recently... It's just a blur."

"The journey of becoming one of *Us* was a process that started when you were just a child. Since then and through the years – as you got older – you made decisions that allowed you to finally get your full Polarity."

"The past week or so has been exhausting. I could barely think straight. I didn't expect the... the trouble," Frank said, almost gasping.

"No one ever does," Father Crane said, adjusting his glasses. "Many don't live through it. *They* knew you were about to become one of *Us*. *They* came close to killing you during these past few weeks, but *We* prevailed. And now... Now you're one of *Us*."

Father Crane crossed his legs, relaxed his shoulders a bit, and folded his arms.

"What have you learned?" he asked.

"I... I've learned that I know nothing. I've never known anything. I am only starting to learn something. I'm as ignorant as a newborn," Frank said.

Father Crane was motionless, as if he hadn't heard him.

"Does... Does that make sense?" Frank asked, straining his voice.

"Perfect sense. No one convinced you to ignore everything. Now that your eyes have finally opened, you are able to see the torrent of events that you – just like everyone else – never noticed. You will learn much in the next three years of your training. Much of it will be focused on how to deal with *Them*," Father Crane said.

"Yes… They… They are clever."

Father Crane narrowed his eyes with near anger, "*They* are indeed clever. When I say *They*, I stress the word *They*. *They* do not have a name."

"Why… Why not?"

"*We* don't have a name either."

Father Crane gave Frank a minute to ponder.

"Frank, can you see what has happened in the past?"

"Yes, with exact clarity."

"Why?"

"Because it has already happened," Frank said.

"How far can you go back, Frank?"

"As far back…"

"…seemingly to the beginning of time, if you want," Father Crane said.

Frank looked up to the sky briefly and then looked back at Father Crane.

"Does *Cathar Perfecti* mean anything to you?" Father Crane asked.

Frank's eyes went wide.

"Now you know why *We* don't have a name, right?"

"B-b-because… Because it makes it too easy to track *Us*?" Frank asked.

"Yes, Frank. Once *We* give ourselves a name then it makes it all too easy."

Father Crane stood up and walked behind his chair. He placed his hands on the back of it and leaned forward, asking Frank, "How easy is it for you to see into the future?"

Frank closed his eyes. He winced, "It's… It gets more… blurry the further forward I try to see…"

"Choose someone at random. Say, your next door neighbor Joe."

Frank's eyes remained closed, but the strain on his face instantly eased.

"I can clearly see everything about him from this minute until the day he dies twenty-eight years from now. It's easier because I'm just focused on him and nothing else."

Father Crane relaxed back into his chair again.

"If *We* so choose, *We* could have our way with Joe. Every second of his life could be tracked because *We* can easily find him by name. It would be simple to make sure that his future would never happen the way you see it right now," he said.

Frank nodded his head, his eyes still closed, "And, this is why *We* don't have a name?"

"Correct. It's also why *They* don't have one either. It makes it too easy to track down each other. Coming to the end of the first millennium, *We* had nearly wiped *Them* out. *We* were overly confident – so confident that some of *Us* revealed ourselves to the world. *We* quickly had followers. Our followers gave themselves the name Cathar. Our followers gave *Us* the specific name Cathar Perfecti – they believed that they could be like *Us*. Once that happened, the few of *Them* that remained could easily trace our name into the future, find *Us*, and wipe *Us* out one by one, even those who were not yet part of *Us*. Thus, *They* almost ensured that *Our* future would never happen. It gave *Them* the clear advantage. *They* annihilated many of *Us* and, at the very least, distorted the history of the Cathar in modern-day text."

Frank gulped and blinked his eyes slowly.

"Have you killed anyone yet?" Father Crane asked.

"No."

"That will change."

"Yes. Yes, it will," Frank said blankly.

Father Crane nodded once. He leaned forward in his chair, placed his elbows on his knees, and clasped his hands together, "You didn't bring a chair or a coat? We will be here for a while."

Frank dropped his eyes to the ground and then a look of surprise spread across his face. He walked over to a nearby boulder. He pulled out a chair and a bag from behind it. He opened the bag and took out a dingy blue heavy coat.

"Thank you, Father Crane," Frank said.

Father Crane remained free of expression. He had placed these items there a few days earlier, knowing this would happen, and knowing Frank would not realize its existence until this moment. He waited for Frank to sit down and then asked, "Why are you thanking me?"

Frank cocked his head back, "I... I guess it is habit."

"You will lose many habits since you've gained your full Polarity. You will find that everything happens because of reasons, not for them. Thanking is not necessary with *Us*. It is a pleasantry the rest of the world uses. It is a waste of *Our* time."

Father Crane stared coldly at Frank while he ate another of the few remaining donuts.

"*We* have goals. You must help *Us* work against *Them*," Father Crane said.

"I... I don't have a choice?"

"You do, but I highly recommend that you fall in line," Father Crane said. "Your life will depend on it."

Frank looked down towards the ground, "I don't... I don't want... this..."

"You have it," Father Crane said, cutting through Frank. "You have it and you will use it. You will use it every second of your life. You will use it for the smallest action, for the most insignificant issues," he said vehemently, illustrating by nearly pinching his finger and thumb together.

Father Crane rubbed his brow for a moment, smoothing away a trace of impatience. "You will use it in accordance to *Our* goals," Father Crane said. "It is the only way."

Frank's face contorted. He wiped his eyes of fresh tears.

"Why so afraid?" Father Crane asked.

"You are commanding me to do things… horrible things."

"Horrible? Commanding? Neither is true. You must realize…"

"I'm so confused!"

"Are you?! Focus, Frank," he said, pointing at Frank.

Father Crane stood up and turned away. After a moment, he groaned and looked over his shoulder slightly to speak to Frank.

"If so, you're already dead. And dead people are useless. *They* will have no problem killing you. Over the past several thousand years, *They* have learned to be creative in their ways of killing…," he turned towards Frank, "…killing in the most painful ways. Prolonging pain on every level."

Frank shook his head slowly.

Father Crane took a deep breath and continued, "You will spend the next year dying. *They* will make an example out of you."

Frank sniffed a bit, holding back his tears. After a few moments, he regained his composure and looked up towards the sky, as if asking for guidance from above. Frank then tilted his head back down and closed his eyes.

"There's just too much to take in," he said hoarsely, "But there's no going back."

"Frank, *We* have three goals in this world. One, as I talked about, is to stop *Them*. The second goal is to help guide others on the cusp of becoming one of *Us*. The third goal is to annihilate those on the cusp of becoming one of *Them*."

"I understand," he said.

"Good. Now, you know what you must do?"

Frank nodded.

"*We* have a target of opportunity. *We* will need your help. There is the young woman Susie. *We* must take care of her."

Frank nodded again.

"First, let us discuss how you can better use your newfound abilities."

"For the next twenty-one hours," Frank said.

Father Crane gave him a single decided nod.

Chapter 5 – The Movies

"Father Crane has taken an interest in Susie," said Harold as he turned to Jill. "So, now this has become a question of how to get past Father Crane."

Harold could tell that Jill was distracted, consumed in frustration. He waited.

"He was just standing in front of the hospital… Just waiting for two of *Us* to die… So cocky, so…," Jill rambled.

"Patience, Jill," Harold interrupted. "These things take time. This was a minor setback. *We* will recover."

Harold, a well-groomed, slightly overweight man in his early 50's, sat comfortably on a park bench by a lake on the edge of the city. He threw bread crumbs at several pigeons before brushing a few stray crumbs off his tailored suit. Jill was wearing a short-sleeve shirt, shorts, and stood about forty feet away from Harold. The pigeons were noisily cooing, making it difficult for Harold and Jill to talk, but Harold wasn't going to move any closer to her.

Jill nodded her head obediently. "You are always right, Harold. Without fail, you are always right. But Father Crane's always on top of things. Always," she said, biting her lip. "He's very clever."

"Some of *Them* are clever, yes," Harold replied. He closed his bag of bread crumbs, folded his arms, and looked towards the sky. With some remorse, he said, "*We* lost Frank already."

Jill shook her head.

"Will *We* lose another?" Harold asked.

Jill shook her head again.

"What are *We* doing about it? What are *We* going to do about Susie? Are we just going to let Father Crane and the rest of *Them* execute their plans unabated?" he asked.

"I have seventy-four actions in play right now," Jill said.

Harold exhaled a little and closed his eyes in thought for a couple of seconds. "That seems about right," he said. "But it isn't enough, I'm afraid. You aren't creating enough confusion for *Them*."

He leaned forward and rested his chin on his hand to think.

"*They* hide *Their* intentions well. *They* may not even care about Susie. It could be another misdirect," Jill said.

"No, no, no," Harold said, still deep in thought. "*Their* pursuit of Susie is legitimate."

Harold shook his head slightly, then stood up and took a few steps away from Jill. She followed him step for step, carefully maintaining the distance between them.

A bee flew by Harold's face. He grabbed it out of the air by its wings – without any effort – and watched it squirm.

"Honey bees are survivors. They work together without argument. They are coordinated and they sacrifice for the greater good of their hive's cause. They will sting their foe knowing that once they do so they will die. They have not only survived, but they have flourished for millions of years."

Harold let the bee go; it immediately flew away. He looked at Jill and continued, "Nature has a way of teaching us what must be done. It's all around us, yet we, as humans, ignore it. Sacrifice can come in the form of selfless cooperation or self-sacrifice. Both are required to prevent *Them* from moving forward."

"I know, Harold."

"The other night outside the hospital, you had an opportunity to take care of Father Crane. You didn't."

"I was outnumbered. He had Spike with him...," Jill started, but then paused. She averted her eyes. "But, you knew that."

Harold looked at her indifferently. Jill dropped her gaze to the ground in shame.

"You had at least thirty different openings to attack Father Crane. Just simply injuring him would be a huge victory for *Us*, but instead you let him slip away. Now he is free to kill again, free to kill more of *Us*, free to do whatever *They* need." He stopped briefly and then said, "He is free to lead humanity to its demise."

Jill exhaled deeply.

"Now Father Crane has enlisted the full time help of Spike – arguably his top assassin – for his personal bidding. Spike has single-handedly murdered fifty-two of *Us*. To get to Father Crane, *We* must now get through Spike."

"I will take care of Spike. I have his tactics figured out already."

Harold closed his eyes, deep in thought. "You have a chance to kill him, yes. You, like him, have the necessary skills."

"I will kill him," Jill said.

Harold nodded and took out his phone. He began texting someone.

"I will set this up. You will meet him. You will kill him. You cannot fail. A new semester for Susie is about to begin and we

48

need to keep her path predictable. Spike must be eliminated," he said as he typed.

Within seconds, Harold's phone beeped, indicating a reply to Harold's text. He looked up at Jill.

"I'm to go to the movie theater, aren't I?" she asked.

Harold held up his phone and says, "That's what this says, yes."

Jill turned and walked away without saying another word; Harold did the same.

*   *   *

Jill walked along the street adjacent to the lake and entered the busy city. From the start, she ignored her surroundings – she was frenzied with thought. It was just another day for the surrounding populous; cars honked their horns, brakes subtly screeched at every red light, engines revved up at every green, and pedestrians walked by minding their own business. She eventually halted at a bus stop and, within a few seconds, a bus pulled up. She boarded it and sat down. Her eyes were unfocused and she breathed steadily, deeply focused. She heard a voice. It was the man on her left.

"Excuse me, miss?" he asked.

Jill snapped out of her thoughts and responded, "Yes?"

"That newspaper next to you… Is that yours?"

Jill looked down at her right and saw a newspaper. She picked it up.

"A woman already ripped out all of the coupons four hours ago," she said as she handed it to him.

The man jolted his head back with that statement. He quickly rifled through the pages, searching but not finding any coupons.

"How did you know that? How did you know I was looking for coupons?"

Jill was once again consumed in thought. She paid no attention to the man.

"Miss?" he asked. "Uh, miss?"

Jill didn't respond.

"Aw, never mind."

The bus continued on. It pulled up to a stop and Jill got off. Two young men got off the bus with her. They followed her closely. Jill appeared oblivious and completely detached from the world. The streets were largely deserted. One of the young men, lanky and pale, jogged up from behind her.

"Hey, pretty lady?" he said.

Jill kept on walking.

"Hey, you?!" he yelled.

Jill continued walking. He stepped in front of Jill. She stopped, her eyes still unfocused. The other young man, a bit stocky and bearded, stayed behind her.

"How about you spend some time to get to know us better?" the lanky fellow said with a smirk.

He grabbed her arm and dragged her behind a nearby abandoned building. Jill offered no resistance.

"Hey, this one's into it!" the bearded man said.

"She's just retarded or something. Who cares? I go first. You keep a lookout."

The bearded man nodded his head and turned back towards the street while the other looked around for a clear spot amongst the discarded rubbish. He let go of Jill for a moment. She slowly took a few steps away towards the wall of the building.

"Hey, where're ya going?" the lanky young man asked.

Jill stopped and said nothing. The young man stepped towards her. The instant before the lanky man was close enough to reach for her, she bent over and grabbed a piece of glass from the ground. She stood up, quickly turned, and slashed his throat with the glass, dodging to the side to avoid the spray of blood that shot from his neck.

He dropped to the ground instantly. He grasped his throat, gurgling. Blood pumped out from underneath his clenched hands.

The bearded man ran over, drawing a gun. "What did you do?!" he yelled, pointing the gun at Jill.

He frantically looked back and forth from her to his friend who continued choking on his own blood, his shirtfront soaked with it.

Jill, without any emotion, said, "You have forty seconds to call 911 or else he will die."

She walked away without any sense of urgency or fear.

"HEY?! HEY?!" the bearded man with the drawn gun yelled after her.

Jill stopped and turned around.

"You now have thirty-three seconds and even so he will have lost so much blood that he will be brain-damaged for the rest of his life. Stop wasting time on me."

She walked away as the bearded young man got out his phone and called 911.

Jill continued walking as if she was in a trance. She casually dropped the piece of glass down a storm drain and shoved her bloodied hand into her pocket, the only sign on her of the event.

Jill walked along street after street, zigzagging her way through the city. As the sun began setting, she arrived at a movie theater. She sat down on the curb outside its front and waited.

Twenty minutes passed by. Finally, a man in his early 30's emerged from around the corner. He wore a dull black leather jacket, solid black T-shirt, black jeans, and black shoes. His hair was dark, short, but had a spiked mohawk with blond highlights. His ears were pierced and his faced was battle-ridden with various raised and pitted scars.

Spike, Jill thought.

She stood up and walked directly to him face-to-face. They exchanged intense eye contact – predator preying on predator. Neither blinked. No words were exchanged. After a few moments, they walked up to the theater's cashier together.

"Two tickets for *Atomic 2*," Spike said with a strong Australian accent.

He paid for the tickets with exact change and the two walked into the theater. They approached the auditorium with *Atomic 2* on its marquee. They walked by it. They walked all the way to the end of the hall to an auditorium with nothing on its marquee. The door was open and they entered.

As they entered, Jill's urge to kill him was unbearable.

I am prepared. I am ready. I know his weaknesses. I know how he will attack. I know how he will defend. Without him, They will be weakened and We will be strengthened. I will not fail, she thought.

Jill walked down the auditorium's entrance ramp with Spike not too far behind her. They stopped walking – the two of them were about twenty feet away from each other.

"You know you won't win," Spike said, cracking a sinister smile.

Jill shook her head confidently. "One day all of *You* will be gone. *You* won't be able to have your way with people. They will be free to choose what they will," Jill said.

"Ah, Jill…," Spike laughed, "Never givin' up on deception, are ya?"

"*We* have had the upper hand for 700 years now. Mankind needs *Us*."

Spike whipped out his switchblade and exposed its blade, creating a barely audible sha-shing. "Save your breath for dyin'," Spike said.

Jill narrowed her eyes. Spike narrowed his. Then, with perfect synchronization, they charged each other.

*   *   *

Outside the theater's doors, activity continued as usual and patrons passed through without notice or thought of what kind of carnage was taking place in the auditorium at the end of the hall. For everyone else, it was just another day at the theater. For Jill and Spike, it meant the end to one of them.

Within a few minutes, a loud, powerful thud projected from the wall facing the exterior of the theater. The energy put behind it had ended the fight between Spike and Jill. The auditorium's exterior exit doors opened and Spike emerged, his lip badly bloodied but otherwise seeming uninjured. Spike dragged the barely conscious Jill out behind the movie theater. He leaned her against the wall by the door and walked away, leaving her alone.

Jill coughed and coughed, struggling to breathe, but she could not bring herself to move beyond that. Only the dim *EXIT* light above her and a vague glow from the streetlights at the end of the alley broke the darkness. She watched as, in the distance, a man began to pass by the alley but then paused and approached. It was the bearded young man who had assaulted her earlier.

"Well, look what we have here," the bearded man said.

He squatted down and grabbed Jill's chin, tilting her head up towards him. She coughed weakly but said nothing.

"My buddy may not live because of you."

He glared at her for a second more, released her chin, stood up, pulled out his gun, and shot her once in the head.

*   *   *

Across town, inside a tall imposing office building, Harold was sitting at his desk with a troubled look on his face. He typed a text message on his phone, *Jill is gone.*

He sent the text and put his phone down. He leaned back in his chair and looked up towards the ceiling with his hands behind his head.

His administrative assistant walked into his office.

"Mr. McGee, I'll be going home now. Is there anything else you need?"

Harold turned to her and replied, "No, Jane, you've been an enormous help as you are every day. In fact, go ahead and take tomorrow off if you can find someone to cover for you. You've certainly earned it."

"Oh, thank you, sir!" Jane grinned back.

Harold was always good to Jane and took advantage of every opportunity to let her know how much he appreciated her. Harold smiled pleasantly and stood up.

"Actually," he said, "I think I'll be on travel tomorrow. I'll be heading up to our Chicago office."

"I can book your flight for you, sir."

"No worries, Jane. I'll handle it. You go home and rest. Forget about this place for a bit, huh?"

Jane smiled warmly. She turned around and left the office.

Harold returned to a seated position and began to browse the Internet. He went to a news website and noticed a headline: *Dozens Feared Dead in Chicago Fire*.

"Are there any suspects?" he whispered to himself.

He quickly skimmed the text of the story.

"No… not yet," he said, gravely disappointed.

He opened his phone and texted, *Are They suspects in the Chicago fire?*

A few seconds later a reply came back, *No. They evaded us.*

Harold sighed in frustration and wondered what *They* were up to. His phone rang. The caller ID said *Garrett McGee* with a picture of a high school-aged boy swinging a baseball bat. Harold picked up.

"Hello, son."

"Hi, Dad," Garrett responded.

"How are you?"

"Doing okay. I have just one final to go."

"Straight A's, I hope… That would make you a 4.0 college man."

"Should be."

"Good job, son."

"Hey, Dad, when would be a good time to come home?"

"Well, I'm pretty busy, but I can make time for you."

"No, Dad… Not that…"

"What?"

"I just know how hard this time of year is for you."

There was a brief silence.

Harold gulped, "Well, son, your mother's passing was several years ago. I miss her."

"I know. I do, too. I just don't want to be a nuisance," Garrett said somberly.

"Garrett?" Harold asked.

"Yes, Dad?"

"It's okay. I would rather have you here than over there. Even I get lonely a bit. I miss you."

"I wanted to be sure, Dad."

"I know. Thank you, son."

"You workin' late?"

"As always."

"You gotta take a break sometime, too, Dad."

"I enjoy my work."

"I know. I'll let you go. I love you."

"I love you, too, son."

Harold hung up and instantly sent a new text message. It read, *Find a way to attribute the fire to Them immediately.*

Harold clicked to another website.

"Three... Two... One," he counted down.

On saying "one", a news banner flashed on his screen: *BREAKING NEWS - Los Angeles police to go on strike.*

Harold didn't react. He clicked to go to another website and then another and another. He stopped and raised an eyebrow in thought – he smiled a little. He typed *live bees* into a search engine and clicked to find them. He went to a shopping website, made a few more clicks, and hit a button reading, *ORDER NOW.*

He sat back in his chair and settled in comfortably, ensconcing himself in preparation to be there for quite a while. He drew his phone and texted, *Be sure to have a car pick me up at the Chicago O'Hare airport at 3:23 p.m. sharp.*

He tapped his fingers on his desk and said, "Susie, Susie, Susie... What are you doing?"

Chapter 6 – Serendipity

Susie was quietly reading a book in her apartment, trying to relax from the stressful semester. She paused, remembering that she had bought a coffee earlier and this meant she had to update her budget.

She drew out a sigh from the loneliness that visited her often; it seemed never-ending. She looked around her apartment. It was sparsely decorated, but it did have many photographs of people that seemed to dominate the living space; her past was always an integral part of her present. Even if she had more money, she knew she wouldn't spend much on material items because they had no intrinsic value to her. Unlike photographs and memories, they lost value over time.

Susie sat down at her computer and opened a spreadsheet that contained her budget. Among a sea of other numbers, she typed *1.99*. She looked over the rest of her budget. With her electric and water bills, it would seem that coffee wouldn't be in her budget until next month and she wondered what else would have to wait.

She looked at the calendar: It was the 5th of December. Such thrift was going to be uncomfortable with the holidays coming, but she accepted it without question. She had sometimes tempted herself to use her credit card, but this was not one of those times; she knew she already had everything she really needed. Beyond that, she would only buy what she could afford.

She got up from her computer, swiped up the nearby TV remote, and turned on the TV – not caring what show came on. As much as she liked the photographs, the TV was a form of company that broke the monotony of the silence and it seemed more conversational than the radio to her. She also had dishes to do and it always helped pass her through the predictability of the chore.

The TV blared out a report on the fire in Chicago. A newscaster said, "The fire spread from building to building, dominating the first floors of four square blocks of densely populated residential buildings. Residents at the upper floors had nowhere to go. Many are left homeless in the cold weather and it is estimated that the death toll will reach at least…"

Susie turned off the TV, unable to bear hearing more. She immediately began weeping for those who were lost. The sadness and pain of the world gripped her often in a strangely personal way – almost as if she could see and feel them firsthand. She wondered about the children lost, the parents, and the friends. She wondered when tragedies such as this would ever end.

Suddenly, she got a feeling she should turn on the TV, and without thinking turned the TV back on without knowing why.

"The American Red Cross is asking for donations, any amount to help those who've been devastated by this fire," the newscaster said.

Susie immediately went over to her checkbook and wrote a check for five dollars to the American Red Cross. Tears still clung to her cheeks. She took a few deep breaths as she finished the check. She found an envelope and sealed the check inside.

She walked to her computer to search for the American Red Cross's address. Her email popped up first thing, as usual, and she had several messages waiting for her. There were many spam messages and she immediately deleted each, one by one. She saw a message with the subject line: *Address for American Red Cross*. It was sent three hours earlier from a John Doe.

She thought about clicking on it because it seemed too good to be true – it had to be a virus or a scam of some kind. However, the serendipitous nature of having this email appear before she actually needed it made her wonder if it was coincidence or fate.

She finally clicked on it. It opened and there was the address for the American Red Cross. Underneath the address was an announcement of funding-raising activities being held the next day, the midweek break from finals, at her university.

Susie perked up. She was definitely interested. In the stark absence of money, she didn't hesitate in deciding to donate time. She regularly donated her time to various charitable causes and she had some time to spare. She liked that it would give her a chance to meet more people at the university, but it also made her feel good that she would be helping to make a difference – by helping people feel a little more confident in humanity as a whole.

She looked over the pictures in the email – it appeared as if the fraternities and sororities were having a carnival to raise money for those orphaned by the Chicago fire. Anyone was welcome to help. This captivated her. The opportunity to add another little bit of help to a greater cause, especially one close to her heart, brought a smile to her face.

The next day, Susie was up bright and early to go to campus. She walked instead of driving Old Faithful. It was a couple of miles away, but she saved gas and – more importantly – money. Plus, she saw it as a way of staying in shape. There wasn't a cloud in the sky, but it was a little chilly so she wore her light jacket.

By the time she arrived on campus, the carnival was already set up and opened for business. A few patrons were already wandering about. Susie looked around, trying to figure out exactly who she needed to talk to about helping out. She passed by the man who tried to guess everyone's weight.

"105?" he asked with a broad grin and raised eyebrows.

Susie smiled at the clear flirtation. She knew that it was just how he reeled people into his game. She kept walking, but now she was feeling shy – she didn't recognize anyone.

She passed by the shooting games, the bottle knock-over games, and similar booths, but still saw no sign of who to see about volunteering. Then, a familiar face: it was Dan. He was locked up in a wooden pillory, his head and hands bound by heavy wooden boards and locks. He looked up at the passers-by and playfully yelled minor insults at them.

Susie was intrigued. She walked up closer.

Dan yelled out to a man who was walking by, "Excuse me, sir! I'd ask you what time it is if I thought your arms were strong enough to carry a watch on your wrist!"

The man stopped, fetched his wallet, pulled some money out of it, and marched over to a nearby table. He gave the money to the attendant and, in exchange, he received three very overripe, soft tomatoes. He hurled them one by one at Dan's head.

SMACK! SMACK! SMACK!

Each narrowly missed Dan's shackled head. Dan laughed without a smidgen of fear.

"I'd say that was an excellent try, sir, but that'd put you in the same league as the four-year old girl who went before you!"

The man tried to contain his laugh at the playful insult. He got out more money, got more tomatoes, and hurled them at Dan. This time, one of them hit Dan squarely in the face.

SPLAT! Tomato juice and pieces covered Dan's face.

The man grinned at his hit.

"I'd say you throw like that four-year old girl, but I don't want to lead you to believe you can throw that well!" Dan yelled back.

The man paid more money, got three more tomatoes, and this time all three hit Dan squarely on the head.

"Thank you, sir! Can I have another?!" Dan laughed.

The man laughed with him and yelled back, "You've had enough!"

"Thanks... for... your... support!" Dan yelled, spitting out tomato between words.

The man got more money out of his wallet and gave it to the attendant.

"Keep it," he said and walked away smiling.

Susie watched as Dan pushed the top board of the pillory up far enough to pull his head and hands out. She realized that he had never truly been locked up, but simply played the part very well.

Dan snatched a nearby towel and wiped his face. He took a sip of water from a bottle sitting next to his discarded towel, stretched a bit, and then put himself back in the pillory, ready for the next patron who may walk on by.

Susie was captivated, as if everything Dan was doing was in slow motion. She could not think about anything other than Dan, who was graciously donating his time and body to charity. She took a few steps forward.

"WHO WILL SHOW TO THE WORLD HOW WEAK THEY ARE?!" Dan bellowed. "WHO WILL PAY THREE DOLLARS FOR THREE TOMATOES TO THROW AT ME?!

COME ON, PEOPLE, I'M NOT EVEN A MOVING TARGET!"

Dan stopped yelling. He made eye contact with Susie. She looked the other way. But, she then realized that Dan was the only person she knew there and perhaps he could tell her how she could volunteer. She looked back at him and gave him a cross between a smirk and smile – she knew her timing of the smile was a bit off, so she felt a little awkward and had to fake it a little.

She took a few steps towards him but stopped. An obscure uneasiness set in and she looked blankly at the ground for a brief moment. Was she nervous? She wasn't sure. She just felt out-of-kilter. Realizing that the sudden stop probably looked awkward, she forced herself to continue walking towards Dan. He watched her, but broke away a few times to greet and taunt people as they walked by.

More people were gathering around Dan's booth as Susie approached – it was practically a crowd. Several people were lined up, ready to hurl a torrent of tomatoes at him.

"I'VE SEEN MORE POWER FROM A HAMSTER IN ITS WHEEL!" Dan playfully jeered.

SPLAT!

A tomato hit him squarely between the eyes.

"MEH! SMILE IF YOU WILL, SIR, BUT I SEE THAT GAP IN YOUR FRONT TEETH. I DON'T KNOW IF I SHOULD SMILE BACK OR KICK A FIELD GOAL!" he yelled.

The man who Dan was jeering at laughed back, bought more tomatoes, and hurled them at Dan. More and more people lined up to have their shot at punishing the affable Dan. Susie couldn't help but break a smile – everyone cheered Dan and many were even clapping. She decided to get in line.

Patron after patron, Dan took hit after hit. He never missed a beat with his playful insults.

"Sir, do you work out?!" Dan yelled at a patron.

"Yes, I do!" the patron yelled back.

"You need to work out more! Would it help if I threw the tomatoes for you?!"

Finally, it was Susie's turn.

"Three dollars, three tomatoes," the booth attendant said to Susie.

Susie knew that she didn't have that kind of money to spare. A little startled and unprepared, she didn't know how to react. Susie was petrified.

"I'm gonna take a break!" Dan said.

By now, well over fifty people had gathered around the booth. Applause erupted for Dan as he removed himself from the pillory. He bowed with a dramatic flourish at the crowd, pieces of tomato still clinging to him.

He grabbed his towel again, wiping off his face, neck, and his short dark hair. He then walked towards Susie with a confident, square-shouldered strut. His blue eyes locked onto Susie's eyes.

"Hi, Susie," Dan said.

She cocked her head back – her mind went completely blank. No response came to mind. Susie was never like this around anyone. Even in the most stressful situations, she had been able to comport herself with an even keel. She took a deep breath and tried to compose herself, reminding herself that all she had to do was say hello.

"Hi… Dan? Right, it's Dan?"

"Yes," he said, smiling. "I'm taking a break, so you'll have to throw tomatoes at me some other time."

Susie smiled slightly but didn't say a word.

Dan threw his towel down and picked up another off of the attendant's table.

"That…," he said, looking at the used towel, "…is a lot of tomato."

"Yeah," Susie agreed, just to say something – anything.

"Three dollars?" the booth attendant said again.

"Huh? Oh!" Susie said.

She had forgotten where she was. Another guy had already put himself in Dan's place in the pillory and she was still in line to throw tomatoes. Susie stepped out of the way so the next patron could pay.

"Not wanting to throw tomatoes?" Dan asked.

Susie realized that she was caught. She had never really wanted to throw tomatoes and now that was obvious. She had really only wanted to meet Dan, although she didn't know why. Now, here she was, standing stupidly before Dan, making him wonder why she had stood in line all that while for no apparent reason.

"I guess not," she said softly.

Dan finished wiping himself off and tossed his used towels in a nearby basket. He had a poise and finesse about him that made it almost seem like he belonged in a commercial or movie. His movements were somewhat mesmerizing.

"I do believe," he said to the booth attendant, "that she just wanted to get a few hits on me."

Dan gave her a wink. Susie's mouth cracked open in surprise. She didn't know how to react; his comment felt fast and unwarranted to her. If she wasn't so unwilling to make an even bigger fool of herself, she would just walk away. But Dan had done nothing wrong. Being unnerved by him made no sense. He was a good guy.

She asked herself what her sister, Karen, would advise about this. She could easily imagine Karen saying, *Go for it, sis!* But, she couldn't imagine "going for it" with Dan and wasn't entirely sure why. She realized that she was directing her uneasiness towards Dan. She didn't know what to do.

"Hey, you okay?" Dan asked, sounding concerned at her silence.

Susie had been simply standing there like a tree stump. "Oh, yeah. I'm sorry... I just have a lot on my mind," she said with a forced smile. "I'm actually interested in volunteering time here at the carnival."

"Wonderful! Let me bring you over to our coordinator."

Dan and Susie walked side by side across the carnival. Dan said hello to a number of people along the way. He knew many people; his popularity amazed her. Everyone – from child to adult – knew his name. Everyone greeted him with big, star-struck smiles.

He connects with people so well, she thought.

She turned briefly at one point to look at his face as they walked: it was focused and had a kind demeanor.

"We've run into each a few times in the past couple of days," Susie said.

"Yeah, I've been stalking you. I'm really bad at it, though," Dan replied.

Susie laughed a little.

"So, what year are you?" she asked.

Immediately, she regretted the unoriginal and juvenile question.

"Second year," he said.

Susie looked at him oddly. He seemed a bit old to be just a sophomore.

"I know, I know... I'm kinda old to be a sophomore. It's a long story. Let's just say that I'm here finally, and I'm thrilled to be here."

"Great answer," Susie thought.

They walked up to a foldout table with a young woman sitting at it, busily talking on her cell phone.

"This is Brenda. She's the volunteer coordinator," Dan told Susie as they stood there, waiting for the woman to get off the phone.

Brenda was oblivious to them. They waited another minute and still no Brenda.

"Well, we will get back to you," Dan said to Brenda, who still didn't acknowledge him.

They walked away.

"Sorry about that," Dan apologized. "She's usually right on top of things."

"Yeah, that was a little surprising…," Susie said, trailing off.

"Don't mind Brenda. But, if you don't mind being an unofficial volunteer, I do need some help getting more tomatoes from our truck."

"I'd love to help," Susie replied.

"Let's use that," Dan pointed to a nearby flatbed cart.

Dan grabbed the cart and pushed it forward. The two of them walked down the sidewalk, through campus, and to a nearby parking lot where a large truck was parked. They went to the back of the truck and opened it up.

"Wow, that's a lot of tomatoes," Susie said, seeing several crates of tomatoes on the floor of the truck.

"Yeah, the local farmers were very gracious to donate these. Of course, they're past the point of ripeness where people will buy them anyway, so it works out for them too."

Susie looked at all of the other random equipment farther inside the truck. There was a wide variety of items.

"Why is there a motorcycle in here?" Susie asked.

"You know, I'm not sure," Dan replied.

He stepped up into the truck and took a closer look at it.

"To be honest, we just loaded a bunch of random stuff that each of us thought could be used for the carnival. But, I'm not sure why anyone would bring a motorcycle," Dan said.

Dan hopped down and extended the ramp from the truck. He went back up and wheeled the motorcycle down.

"What're you doing?" Susie asked with surprise.

"I like bikes. I've only ridden them a few times. I wish I had one, you know?" he said with a hint of exhilaration.

Susie nodded with indifference. She had never cared for motorcycles, but she was curious what Dan would do next.

Dan sat on top of the motorcycle and smiled.

"What?" Susie asked.

"Oh, I just can't help myself. One day I'd like to go on a long road trip on one of these. The fresh air, the sun, the winding blowing…"

"…the rain, the bugs, the sunburns," Susie finished with a smile.

"Completely worth it," Dan replied without hesitation. "I'd gladly go through that pain to experience the pleasures in return. Wouldn't you?"

"I guess so…," Susie said.

She had always thought of herself as a very positive person, but she was having difficulty finding any positive thoughts at the moment. She felt a little out of her element in the presence of Dan and his thinly veiled flirtations.

"Everything has that kind of tradeoff. Nothing received should be unearned," Dan said while he gripped both handlebars with authority.

"Not a statement I'd expect from a charity volunteer," Susie responded.

"Oh, let me be clear: I gladly donate my time to help those who are in need – gladly. There's a difference, though, between wants and needs. I draw the line there."

"Fair enough," Susie nodded.

Dan started the motorcycle.

"What are you doing?!" Susie yelled over the noise of the engine starting.

"Anything in this truck is fair game to be used here! I just wanted to see if this baby would start!"

Dan rode the bike around Susie once and stopped.

"Nothing wrong with this baby," he said. "You wanna hop on?"

Susie stalled, pausing but not knowing why.

"Don't we have to bring tomatoes back?"

"We will. We have a few minutes."

Susie balked, "Well…"

VROOOM!

In an instant, Dan had sped off without her. He didn't look back. He pushed the bike full throttle towards a busy street about a hundred yards away.

"Okay…" Susie said, watching him speed away.

She thought about yelling to him, but his departure was so bizarre. She watched as he accelerated at full speed. She was alarmed and wondered what he was doing. He was going so fast that she wondered if he was going to stop.

After getting within thirty feet of the street, Dan slammed on the brakes, turned the bike so that it braked at a right angle to its momentum, and lowered it down into a slide. Dan jumped off the bike and scooped up a small child about to wander unattended into the busy street.

Susie jumped a little, realizing what Dan had just done.

Dan held the child in his arms, looked around – presumably for the kid's parents – hesitated, and then walked back towards Susie. The little girl seemed calm and simply held onto him. Just as he got close to Susie, a woman ran up to Dan and reached out for the child.

"Caitlyn!" she yelled, "I was worried sick about you! I thought I lost you!"

Dan gave the child to her mother.

She turned to Dan, "Thank you! Thank you, sir!" and then she walked away, tightly hugging her child.

"Sorry about that. I didn't have any time to explain," Dan apologized to Susie. "I looked up and saw that little girl wandering towards the street, and it wasn't worth the wait to find out if her parent was nearby to stop her."

Susie was dumbfounded and completely taken by Dan's casual heroics.

"I've gotta go get the motorcycle," Dan said, gesturing behind him and walking away as if nothing had happened.

Susie was still frozen. She watched Dan as he walked and could not take her eyes off of him. Dan picked up the bike and wheeled it back to her.

"I think this baby is done," he said.

Susie could see that the bike was badly damaged on the side that scraped along the ground.

"Ugh," Dan grunted upon further inspection.

He squatted down, looked at the bike, and pondered what to do.

"You know," he said after a minute, "I bet the engineering shop here on campus can fix this thing. Maybe even redo the paint job. I think I'll go wheel this thing over there."

Dan stood up and looked at Susie standing by the flatbed cart. "Wait… We still have tomatoes to deliver," he said.

He looked over her shoulder and shouted, "HEY, PHIL!"

Phil was a couple of hundred feet away, but he turned around. He had long, unkempt hair and was clearly out of shape, his belly hanging out of the bottom of his too-small black T-shirt.

"YEAH?!" Phil yelled back.

Dan motioned Phil to come over to them.

"Phil's a good guy," Dan reassured Susie. "Don't let the way he looks scare you. He's helping with the carnival."

Phil was slowly walking to them – painfully slow – taking his sweet time.

"His sense of urgency leaves much to be desired, however," Dan commented.

"It sure seems like it," Susie said.

Dan, getting restless and a bit impatient, yelled, "Can you help my dear friend, Susie here, bring back some tomatoes?! I've got to get this motorcycle to the shop on campus!"

Susie tingled a little bit at hearing Dan call her a dear friend.

"Sure thing, man!" Phil hollered back.

Dan began to walk the bike away from Susie as he told her, "I'll catch up with you guys later."

"Okay…," Susie said.

Susie stood there all alone for a few moments as Phil was still slowly coming to her and Dan was going away from her. As Phil got closer, she saw piercings covering his face and ears. She spotted a tattoo on his neck of a devil in bright red. Susie tried her best to keep her eyes averted from the piercings and that tattoo, but they attracted her attention so much that they seemed to occupy every inch of him.

He looked menacing – even Phil's face looked like it was full of anger. To Susie, Phil looked like the kind of guy who the police would eventually arrest for hideous crimes that would make headlines for weeks.

She realized she was scared of him. She found herself imagining what it would be like to defend herself from Phil if he attacked. Usually, she easily adhered to the principle of not judging people based on their looks and getting to know people for who they are now, not for who they were or how they look. This guy, however, simply gave her the willies and was practically advertising trouble. In any other circumstance, she would be running for dear life away from him.

"Hey," Phil said as he walked up to Susie, his voice and face blank of expression.

"Hi."

She didn't know what else to say. She just wanted him to go away, but she didn't want to be rude or make him angry.

"So, are we going to move tomatoes?" Phil asked flatly.

"Oh, um, yes. Thank you," Susie said with some hesitation.

The two of them loaded the cart with tomatoes without a word between them. She got the vibe from Phil that he, too, just wanted to get this over with.

"How do you know Dan?" Phil asked, breaking the uncomfortable silence.

"Well, I don't really. We kind of just met."

Phil's mouth twitched into something like a slight smile, but it died almost instantly.

"Dan's a good guy," he said quietly.

"You guys seem kind of like opposites of each other," Susie blurted playfully.

Phil stopped loading crates and stared at Susie coldly.

She stopped what she was doing. All she wanted to do now was run away.

"I... I didn't mean it that way... I didn't mean to sound offensive... I...," she stumbled.

Phil shrugged his shoulders and moved to load the last crate into the cart.

Phil was without a soul or so it seemed. Susie shivered a little. She had never been around anyone like Phil before and found it hard to believe that people like him existed in everyday life. It was as if he was from a movie set but didn't need a makeup artist. His hair, long enough to be resting on his shoulders, even reminded her of the mane of a wild animal.

She realized what she was thinking and stopped herself. Reminding herself that it wasn't right to judge people without getting to know them, she recanted her assessment. She reminded herself that he had done and said nothing wrong.

They got to the tomato booth and unloaded the crates.

"Well, Phil, thanks for your help," Susie said.

He just stared at her emptily for a moment, and then his face suddenly filled with contempt.

"I'll be honest with you: I don't like you at all," Phil said to her face, making direct eye contact.

With that, he strolled away.

Susie was stunned. She wanted to cry, but she didn't know why exactly. She looked down at the ground in reflection and confused shame. She looked up just in time to see Phil before he left her field of view.

"Hey!" Dan said as he walked up behind her. "How're you doing?"

Susie turned to him, "Phil... Phil said he doesn't like me. I..."

"Hey, hey... It's okay. Phil's a little... a little, well, strange."

That didn't help Susie. She had met strange people but never anyone who just said they didn't like her so directly.

Dan explained, "He's had a tough life. Phil's kind of testing you. I've known him for a long time. If there's a drawback to Phil, it's that he's too honest in what he tells people. The best part is that he's real and doesn't have any hidden agendas."

"With all due respect, Dan, you can be honest but you don't have to be mean."

"True," Dan nodded.

Susie didn't want to sound sanctimonious – she knew that Dan was trying to help her through an awkward situation. She worried that she sounded like a downer to him.

"It's okay, Dan. I can't please everyone," she told him with a faint smile.

"Yeah, I know. I just wish that Phil wasn't being Phil today. If you're a friend, he treats you like a brother. He buys you stuff for no reason. When we go out, he pays for everyone."

Susie shrugged at Dan, "Let's change the subject."

"Not a problem," Dan conceded.

Dan's phone beeped. He had apparently received a text message. He quickly typed a response and pocketed his phone.

"Sorry about that. I'm really a South American drug kingpin and I have twenty tons coming into Miami tonight," he said with a convincing Latino accent.

Susie laughed.

"You've got a good laugh," he said, smiling brightly, almost beaming.

Susie smiled back.

"Let's sit," Dan said, pointing to the verdant grass lawn under their feet.

He grabbed two bottled waters from a nearby cooler and handed one to Susie. Dan sat down on the grass and Susie followed suit.

She liked that Dan didn't get hung up on the little things, like sitting directly on the grass instead of a chair. *Karen would never do that. She'd be consumed with the notion of someone's old gum or spit being on the ground, there could be glass, bugs...*, she thought.

Susie laughed a little.

"What?" Dan asked.

"Oh, I was just thinking that my sister, Karen, would never sit on the grass."

"She's too high-strung," Dan replied.

"What?"

"She's too high-strung, right?"

"Yes, but you say that like you know her."

"Anyone who has a problem simply sitting on the grass has to be too high-strung."

"Yeah, I guess."

The conversation hit a sudden end. She struggled to think of a new topic; she had to conclude that if she didn't share a class with someone then she had nothing to talk about. She was boring.

"What are you majoring in?" she finally asked, resorting to the most generic question she could think of.

"Oh, I'm on the fence in deciding between majors. Either math or engineering. I'm taking all the base classes for those now, so I'll decide next semester I guess."

"Oh," Susie said.

"What about you?"

"Physics."

"Physics?" Dan asked, lifting an eyebrow.

"What?" Susie shyly asked back.

"You're a smart one," Dan said with a smile as he took a swig of water from his bottle.

Susie glowed from the compliment.

Chapter 7 – The CEO

Harold sat in his spacious first class seat, wearing headphones and watching the TV on the back of the seat directly in front of him. He sipped a glass of wine slowly, savoring each drop.

"The fire in Chicago is gone, but its destruction will remain with us forever," a newscaster reported somberly.

He set his glass down, took off his headphones, and turned off the TV. He loosened his tie a bit, settled back in his chair, and closed his eyes, tilting his head back slightly to relieve the neck tension built up from the past couple days. Trying his best to relax, Harold went through his mental to-do list of everything that needed to be done once he landed in Chicago.

874 actions to be taken, he thought.

"What brings you to Chicago?" a voice on his right asked.

Harold opened his eyes and turned to face the owner of the voice. A man was staring at him, awaiting an answer to his question. The man was in his late fifties, had a wiry frame, a greying beard, and a short ponytail. Harold briefly squinted in thought.

Hmm... Tom Sullivan. Net worth: $198,789,344. Started in ranching and expanded to plastics and investing. Sits on the board of three companies. He likes to be called Sully by his friends. He is devoted to his wife, but she constantly accuses him of cheating on her, Harold thought, briefly looking the man up and down.

He instantly knew everything about Tom Sullivan since his birth and knew the exact moment when Tom Sullivan would die, even though he didn't know a thing about him a few seconds ago; as usual, such an advantage lightened his mood.

Harold grinned back. "Business...," Harold answered at first, then added, "Well, partially. The fire weighs heavily on my mind."

"Oh, yeah. Terrible, terrible. Those poor people. How many dead now? Thirty?" Tom Sullivan said.

"The death toll... It's... It's just horrible. It breaks my heart," Harold responded. "The damage to the survivors seems unrecoverable."

"For me, I'm heading home there," Tom Sullivan said.

"Chicago's a great town," Harold replied.

"I'm Tom Sullivan. People call me Sully."

"I'm Harold."

The two shook hands.

Halfway through the handshake, Sully tilted his head and recognized Harold.

"Hey, you're the CEO of Beytern, right?"

"I am."

"Good to meet you, sir," Sully said with a bright smile. "You guys do good work. I think I've got about ten thousand shares in your company."

9,724 to be exact. He gave a few to his two kids as birthday presents three years ago, Harold thought.

Sully continued, "Think you can give old Sully here some ideas as to where Beytern's going next?"

"Well, I think we're at a point where we want to focus on taking care of our family of consumers. The economy has hit everyone hard. The last thing anyone needs is for a family member, including us, to be distracted with acquisitions, shipping jobs overseas, and whatnot."

Sully smiled and slapped his knee once.

"Well, that's the sound bite I'll give CNN," Harold chuckled.

"Heh, heh, heh," Sully laughed and slapped his knee again.

"But, seriously, at least for today, I'm going to Chicago to assess the damage from the fire and see what we can do. It's become one of those catastrophes where things like earnings per share don't mean anything right now. Not with this."

Sully's face softened with graciousness. "Dangerous words you're using, especially if you're on CNN. No CEO should trash earnings per share."

Harold wobbled his head slightly with indifference. He already knew exactly how Sully would react to anything he said and did – everything was intentional and deliberate.

"I don't care about CNN's opinion or any shareholder's opinion with this. It isn't about opinion. It's about doing the right thing. If shareholders have a problem with this then they don't have the long-term picture in mind, and they can drop their money somewhere else."

Sully took a sip of his drink.

"Not caring about what others think is a good formula," he declared, holding his drink up a little, as if he were toasting. "I've done well with it."

Retired at thirty-eight, Harold thought. He then said aloud, "I agree. Everyone has an ulterior motive and it becomes hard to see through the smoke."

"You didn't get to be CEO of Beytern because of indecision," Sully said, shaking his finger at Harold.

Harold smiled a little, "I don't think anyone can be a leader if they are constantly bowing to everyone else's demands. You're basically conceding that other people somehow know more than you do about how to solve a particular problem."

"Agree," Sully said with a single nod.

"Why be a leader if all you do is parrot back what others tell you to do? Isn't that, by definition, a follower?"

Sully grew a huge smile – so huge that his eyes narrowed. "You know what? I'm going to buy more stock in Beytern."

The intercom interrupted their conversation.

"Ladies and gentleman, this is your captain speaking. We are beginning our final descent into Chicago. Please remain seated and we'll be down on the ground in a few minutes."

Sully extended his hand, "Well, Harold, it certainly was a pleasure to meet you."

Harold shook Sully's hand.

"You, too, Sully," Harold responded and handed Sully his business card.

"Thanks," Sully responded. "Sorry, I don't carry business cards. I'm more of an independent investor."

He will gain fifty-seven million dollars in the next six months.

*　　　*　　　*

The plane landed on a bright, sunny, clear day in Chicago. Sirens were heard in the distance. Harold walked through the airport with his suit coat draped over one arm and toting his bag with the other. He walked out the exit door of the airport and got into a parked car.

"Right on time," Harold told the driver. "Thank you."

The car drove off.

Harold got out his phone and dialed a number, "This is Harold. I'd like you to take good care of a major stockholder of ours named Tom Sullivan. He should have just-under ten thousand shares with us. Send him a nice care basket. Invite him to our quarterly social as well. Pay for his expenses."

Harold paused while he listened to the voice on the other end of the call.

"Thanks," he said and hung up his phone, knowing his driver was about to ask him a question that required his attention.

"Sir, the traffic ahead is terrible," the driver told Harold. "The fire has caused all kinds of problems."

"Not a problem. I know this city. Get off on this exit."

"Yes sir," the driver replied.

The car exited and Harold continued giving directions down to the finest details.

"Keep in this lane until you pass the car in the lane next to us. Then switch lanes and take the second right."

The driver obeyed.

"The light up here is yellow. Go ahead and stop for it. Take a left there instead of going straight."

"Sir, your hotel is right along this street."

"I know. But, I heard there was an accident ahead that will keep us tied up. We'll circle around."

At that moment, an SUV sped by them and darted through the yellow light at high speed. Harold's car stopped in the left turn lane, just as he demanded. The SUV weaved through lanes, well ahead of them now. A car parked along the side of the road pulled out and the SUV broadsided it, spun out of control, and headed into the opposite lane, hitting on-coming traffic.

Harold's driver looked up in his rearview mirror at Harold, wide-eyed. Harold didn't move a muscle. He had known it was going to happen with as much certainty as he had that the sun was going to rise the next day.

The car eventually pulled up in front of the hotel. Harold got out and thanked the driver.

Harold's phone beeped – he received a text, *Hotel security cameras disabled.*

Harold didn't react. It was planned; everything was tightly and precisely planned, and every plan was tightly and precisely executed. He carried his bag into the lobby, refusing the help of the bellhops. He checked in at the front desk.

"Oh, also, Mr. McGee?" the desk clerk asked after checking him in.

"Yes?" Harold asked.

"This package arrived for you literally a few moments before you got here."

The desk clerk handed a package about the size of a pillow to Harold.

"Uh, it seems to be making some weird buzzing."

Harold took the box and put it to his ear. He knew it was the bees he had ordered online, but he had to pretend he didn't know what it was. He needed to constantly remind himself that he must pretend to know less than he did so that he would not draw too much attention to himself. He had his full Polarity for such a long time that he couldn't always delineate what normal people should know anymore.

"Hmm," Harold said, shaking the box a little bit.

The buzzing got a little louder. He set the box on the check-in counter, grabbed a pair of scissors sitting on the other side of the front desk, and sliced the box open. He already knew that the danger wasn't from the bees but from the man sent to kill him – the man who was directly behind him.

The man was still walking up towards the front desk; Harold, even with his back turned, knew every step he took, every nuance of movement he made. Within five feet of Harold, the man shifted his right hand, revealing a large knife. The man began to cock the knife up into the air, ready to come down into Harold's back.

And... now, Harold thought as he yanked open the box.

Bees poured out of the box as Harold immediately ducked under the check-in counter to avoid them. The man with the knife cried out in deathly fear. He dropped his knife and flailed his arms at the bees as he began to fall backwards in panic.

"Ahhhh!" he screamed.

He fell to the floor. He grabbed his throat, his breathing hampered. Dozens of stings quickly covered his face, neck, and hands, puffing up and turning red. Everyone else ran away in fear of the swarming bees – except Harold, who knew that not a single bee would sting him.

Harold calmly walked away. He opened the door to the hotel's lounge and sat down next to a man hidden behind an open newspaper.

"Father Crane sent you after me?" he asked, barely raising his voice above a whisper.

The man's arms trembled but kept holding the newspaper. Harold pushed the newspaper down. It was Frank.

"I can think of 117 ways to kill you right now, Frank," Harold said confidently. "But there are too many people here. It's a bit inconvenient."

Frank was silent and shook in fear. He looked at Harold and tried to maintain eye contact.

"You're out of your league attacking me with, what? A knife in the back?" Harold asked, with a mocking tone. "That's a bit cliché."

Frank remained petrified, only his eyes shifting away from Harold from time to time.

"Oh, poor Frank. So confused, so lost, so unknowing... You are so new to your Polarity and you've come to play with the big boys," Harold said derisively, as if talking to a small child.

He patted Frank on the shoulder in a gesture of patronizing superiority.

"Oh… Can you feel that Frank?" He leaned towards Frank and softly asked, "Can you feel that urge to kill me? Being so close to each other makes it unbearable. It makes it sweet, doesn't it?" Harold whispered inches from Frank's ear, closing his eyes, savoring the thought.

Frank nodded his head quickly and wiped the sweat from his brow.

"You're shaking?" Harold said with a smile. "I guess opposites do attract."

Harold squatted down to look at Frank, eye to eye.

"You want to kill me so bad. You've never been so close to one of *Us* before, have you?" Harold whispered, "I had the security cameras disabled to obfuscate that little bee incident. Perhaps you want to take advantage of it, too, hmm?"

Frank didn't move.

"Come on, Frank, you know how this is supposed to go: I mock you and you mock me. It's feeling a little one-sided so far…," Harold paused, "but I guess Father Crane either sent you off on a training mission or he just wanted to see you dead."

"Father Crane is a smart man. He would never send me off to my death," Frank answered nervously.

"Really, Frank? Really?" Harold said, shaking his head in disbelief.

Harold stood up and looked down on Frank with regret.

"*We* will deal with you at another time." He then walked out of the lounge and back down the hall towards the elevators.

By now, the general panic had passed and nearly all of the bees had flown outdoors. Harold could see a couple of people had gathered around the man attacked by the bees; they were trying to keep him breathing. Harold knew the paramedics would arrive too late to help. He stopped and looked back towards the lounge once more. Frank had left.

Harold made his way up the elevator and to his hotel room. He pulled out his phone and texted, *Go forward with the plan.*

He sat down at the room's elegant Victorian desk. The room, as a whole, was opulent from floor to ceiling. There was a huge flatscreen TV with a leather sectional, a fully-stocked bar, tasteful statues and artwork, and a very large bed in the adjoining area. Harold ignored these items as well as the spectacular views of Chicago through the windows. He had been in these environments many times as CEO of Beytern.

He opened his wallet to look at a picture of his wife, who had died in a car accident while he was rising through the ranks of Beytern. He thought about how, shortly before she had died, she had already left him because he had seemed to lose interest in her overnight – he became fully consumed with work once he got his full Polarity. He had known, once he got his full Polarity, that he would lose all his previous personal relationships in one way or another.

"All that matters are *Us* and *Them*: what *We* and *They* will do next, how to guide those who will become *Us*, and how to eliminate those who will become *Them*," he said to the picture – a ritual of sorts that he practiced whenever he had a moment alone.

Harold had enormous influence in his circles, but he also knew that Father Crane did as well. He considered what might have been intended in sending someone as inexperienced as Frank.

He texted, *Frank was sent because he is so new They thought We wouldn't have picked up on it.*

The reply asked, *Kill Frank?*

Harold sat down in a large leather chair, closed his eyes, and thought for a few seconds.

He wrote, *Not yet. His time will come in a year or so.*

He put his phone down and pulled some papers out of his bag. He put them on his desk and flipped through them. They were covered with thousands of handwritten notes, written in both large and small hand and with different colors of ink. To others, they would look like random gibberish. To Harold, they represented his to-do list.

He selected a particular paper, whipped out a pen, and wrote a few lines of words, snaking between and around other words on the paper.

"Ah!" he said mutely with a smile, as if he came up with the most brilliant idea.

He picked up his phone and dialed a number.

"Buy out North Central Mining Company...," he commanded, "...at $3.22 per share from all angles. Now, please."

He hung up. He turned the TV to the business news and poured himself a soda from the room's stocked refrigerator.

The newscaster announced, "Stock prices of North Central Mining Company have been dropping all day long, ever since the government released its preliminary investigative report that found it negligent for last year's mine explosion and subsequent collapse. Right now, it's selling at $6.77. At the beginning of today, it was almost fifteen dollars. I don't think this company will exist tomorrow."

Harold took a sip of his soda and sat back with zero anticipation, as if he were watching a movie he had seen a million times. He loved flash crashes in the stock market such as this. He knew everything would be okay, as he had in all his business decisions for the past six years since gaining his full Polarity.

"At Beytern, we manufacture everything from prescription drugs to lawn chairs... Now to include mining," he said to the TV.

He picked up his phone and wrote a text message, *Susie???*

A moment passed.

As planned, read the return text.

Harold returned to his desk and continued to write notes on his many pieces of paper. Hours went by. Dozens more texts and phone calls were made along with several hundred scribbles and notations written in various colors. As the sun began to set, he returned his attention to the business news.

"Beytern Industries, the behemoth Fortune 25 company, now owns North Central Mining Company, apparently. We've just received word that they have bought up 57% of the common stock in the past few hours at rock bottom prices. I, for one, would like to know the wisdom in this buyout. Beytern has positioned itself to be liable for the unimaginable lawsuits from the disaster last year."

Harold shook his head in certain disagreement, with no emotion.

"Wait a minute," the newscaster said, briefly pausing. "We're now being told that the preliminary government report that was released was an earlier draft that wasn't meant for release. The government has corrected its statement and says that the disaster was ultimately caused by a small earthquake. North Central Mining isn't at fault for the disaster. Wow. And, just like that, the stock is certain to rise."

It will close at $22.37 tomorrow. Another $180 million earned, he thought with a smile.

Harold picked up the phone and made a call, "I want to sell our stock in North Central Mining tomorrow to the point where we are still plurality holders. Sell at no less than twenty-one. Donate half of that money to the American Red Cross for the victims of the Chicago fire. Thank you," he instructed and hung up.

He laid down on his bed, feeling good about himself and what was to become of his actions. He reached for the hotel room's phone and dialed a number, "Room service, please send me my usual dinner if it's no trouble," he said and then hung up.

On his own phone, he texted, *I want to run into Sully again.*

Consider it done, the response said.

Harold looked at his watch. He knew that he had 11 minutes and 12 seconds before his food would arrive. He got up, went downstairs, and walked through a door marked *Employees Only* that had been left ajar. He entered a large room full of pipes and other mechanical equipment; he stopped just inside the door. He waited.

Within a few seconds, another figure appeared on the other side of the room.

"Hello, Jennifer," Harold said.

Jennifer, a young, good-looking, dark-skinned woman appeared in his view.

"Hi, Harold," she said in monotone.

"You are lost?" Harold asked, almost yelling to be heard over the ambient noise from the surrounding equipment, but he made no move to get any closer than the forty feet between them.

"It isn't clear how I can be of best use to *Us* since I finished my last assignment," Jennifer replied.

Harold said nothing. He folded his arms and looked off to his left and then up towards the ceiling in deep thought. A full minute went by as Jennifer waited patiently.

Finally, he spoke, "You've done well for *Us.* You will be needed to help with Susie. She is getting increased interest from *Them.* We cannot fail. Keep yourself in the background."

"How many do *We* have working on her directly?"

"Directly… Just one right now," Harold said, holding up one finger.

"Oh, right," Jennifer replied, averting her eyes in thought.

"Father Crane has someone else who is trying to get close as well. That's where *We* need the upper hand," Harold said.

"Father Crane? If this has his attention, Susie must be…"

Harold interrupted, "Be patient. All will be taken care of. I will add more of *Us* to guide Susie if *We* need to. Just await instruction and do as you are told."

"I will," Jennifer nodded.

Harold checked his watch. "I must go now."

He left without bothering to exchange pleasantries. He made his way to his room, arriving just as room service knocked on his door.

"Perfect timing," he told the room service attendant.

Harold lifted up the covering of one of the platters.

"Ah, yes, perfect indeed," he said.

"Peanut butter sandwich, sir," said the attendant.

"Every time. Why ruin a good meal with something different?" he asked rhetorically with a warm smile.

"Yes, sir."

Harold gave the attendant a hundred dollar bill.

"Thank you, sir!" the attendant gasped, barely containing himself.

Harold wheeled his meal into his room. He uncovered the various dishes. Other than the peanut butter sandwich, there was also plain tap water, two apples, and a few slices of cheddar cheese. Harold dug into his food, considering it a well-deserved meal after a long day.

Harold went to bed shortly afterwards. But, before he could fall asleep, his phone rang. He didn't look at the phone number and he wasn't expecting a call, but he knew who it was.

"Ah, Father Crane," Harold answered the phone, his voice dripping with disdain. "Have you called to wish me luck?"

"There is no luck," Father Crane replied without emotion.

"Yeah, there is no fate, there is only the in-between, blah blah… I got it," Harold replied, sitting up in bed.

He wanted, indeed, needed Father Crane dead as much as he knew Father Crane needed him dead.

"Let me conjure your memory of 23 years, 144 days, 15 hours, and 12 minutes ago," Father Crane said like an automated speaking clock.

"There was a car commercial on TV," Harold responded.

"Twenty-three seconds after that," Father Crane replied. "*You* know what I'm talking about. Mock me if *You* will, but your plan will only end in disaster. *We* have the advantage."

"I'm not mocking *You*. I'm getting *You* worked up."

"Oh, I'm worked up," Father Crane said in a quiet, monotone voice, demonstrating to Harold that he wasn't worked up at all.

Harold paused and then asked, "If *You* are so sure of yourself, then why are you calling me? Are you afraid that *You* will lose Susie? *We* certainly don't need your warnings. It's best that…"

He heard Father Crane hang up. Harold released his phone; it had been pressed firmly against his ear. Father Crane had worked him up and he was disappointed in himself for letting that happen. Harold knew everything that would happen long before it happened; his Polarity granted this. The only exception was when one of *Them* interfered; *Their* actions could not be foreseen easily and could not be compensated for until after they had taken place. In this case, Harold hadn't known Father Crane was going to call and hadn't known the call would work him up. He knew this little demonstration by Father Crane was a reminder to Harold that there were many factors that he couldn't foresee.

Harold laid down in bed again and squeezed his eyes tightly shut, trying his best to erase the frustration of knowing that he may not have complete control over the fate of Susie. She was important to him. He knew that she was important to Father Crane as well. Harold was preparing for this to be an all-out fight for Susie, even as she was kept clueless about it as long as possible.

Harold was up bright and early the next morning. Eschewing his suit, he donned jeans and a t-shirt and then took a cab to the area of Chicago stricken by the fire. He wanted to see the damage for himself so he could better advise how donations should be used. He could reach deeply into his company for both money and supplies, and he intended to do so. He acted without question from anyone; no one had challenged him for a long time because he had always been right. He had the golden touch – or so was the belief of those who worked for him.

He arrived at the scene of the fire and took a look around. There were many news crews around, but he didn't approach them. He preferred to seem as random and anonymous as possible. Harold looked over the scene with a distraught look on his face, shaking his head sadly. About two minutes later, he felt a tap on his shoulder.

"Excuse me? Excuse me, sir," a reporter asked Harold.

Harold turned around – there was a camera on him.

"We are live and I wanted our audience to get your thoughts on what you see."

Harold acted as if he was caught off-guard, but he had known this was going to happen long before it actually had. There were no surprises – unless, of course, *They* intervened.

"My heart is broken. I'm not from this area, but I wanted to see the reality for myself. I want to know if there's anything more that can be done. I see destroyed families, destroyed lives. I see pain everywhere."

A tear formed in the corner of one of his eyes with perfect timing.

"What's your name?" the reporter asked.

"Harold."

"Harold, I'm sure you can find a way to help the people of this neighborhood."

Harold furled his brow in sadness and said, "That's what I'm here for."

"Are you retired?"

"No, I'm just taking some time off work. That's all. It really isn't much to sacrifice when it's compared to what the people here have had to deal with," Harold replied.

"Harold, you're a good man," the reporter said while firmly patting his shoulder with approval.

The newscaster turned to the camera.

"There you have it: random people looking to perform random acts of kindness. I'm Tim Bishop, WHQA Evening News."

Harold walked around the area some more. He squatted down and picked up a piece of cindered wood.

Complete destruction, he assessed. *It was predicted down to the smallest ember.*

Harold returned to his hotel and immediately turned on the news again.

"You never know who you'll find in Chicago. Earlier this evening, a reporter from a local affiliate unknowingly picked out Beytern CEO Harold McGee and interviewed him at the scene of the great fire."

Harold didn't react. As always, he had known this would happen and he had already seen this newscast word for word even though it was a live broadcast. There were no surprises and very little joy when he already knew specifics of the future; Harold's joy at this moment came from the confirmation that everything was going as planned.

"...locals are shocked at his heartfelt concern for the welfare of ordinary people," the newscaster continued. "A CEO of a megacorporation, taking time off and intentionally trying to hide his identity, ends up showing the world what a big heart he really has..."

Harold picked up his phone and texted, *Done here.*

Chapter 8 – Distraction

Susie's alarm woke her. It was a new year and a new semester. She opened her Bible and read a few passages. She said a small prayer, "Dear God, please guide me today. Please help those in need. Please help me find those whom I can help."

She firmly held to the pay-it-forward mentality that helping someone created a chain reaction for that someone to help someone else, and so on. But, the chain of good deeds must be started with those of an individual, and Susie prayed this morning, as she did every morning, to be just that sort of individual. Susie believed in the good in people, but she had to remind herself of her beliefs daily since she had met Phil: That no one was born evil, but that people were led into it. If they could not get out of their predicament, it was because they were so overwhelmingly distracted by it. But, if they could be led into it then they could also be led out.

She got into the shower and closed the door behind her. While showering, she liked to sing. Her preference was The Beatles – mostly because her mother raised her with them playing constantly. She knew she was a terrible singer, but she didn't care. It made her happy and it was part of her daily routine. She found joy in singing, especially when she was nervous – like today. It was the first day of the new semester.

Susie emerged from her shower and got dressed. She felt energized and ready to tackle the challenges ahead of her. After grabbing her bag to make sure she had her notebook and pens. She looked her house over one last time before departing to make sure she didn't forget anything she didn't think of.

In the middle of her final check, she got sidetracked by some of the many pictures she had on display. She walked up to them and held a few of them individually, as if these people were seeing her off to school in person. Last of all, she picked up the only photo that she had of her and her father.

She gripped it – hard – holding it with deeply mixed feelings. The photo was somewhat faded, but it clearly showed a very young Susie, perhaps three years old, being held by a man in his late twenties. In this freeze-frame of time, one could have easily mistaken him for being a caring family man. In Susie's mind, however, here was a man who left his family shortly after this very picture was taken. She frequently wondered why he did.

Even though she had been only three years old at the time, Susie still spent time trying her best to convince herself that she was good enough, worthy enough for him to have stayed with the family. After he left, she grew up feeling very much alone, especially since she was the younger, more studious sister. She had always felt there was a huge hole in her life. Although she was not sure her father's absence had caused this hole, she would like to know if part or even all of it would still exist if he had stayed. She knew it was a little silly for her to think this way, but the subject had eaten away at her for as long as she could remember. Susie was all too aware that her only truly negative feelings persisted solely from this event.

She looked closely at the man's face in the photograph: clean shaven, neatly trimmed dark hair, kind eyes. She felt offended by his smile: This was a man who was about to abandon his family. This thought repeated in her head as it did whenever she looked at this picture; it kept Susie angry.

She didn't remember him, but she did remember the pain that his departure caused their mother. For many years afterwards, her mother struggled to make ends meet: She had to accept government assistance, she took vile jobs, and she worked the oddest hours – she had done anything she could to make sure her two girls would be okay. Now that her two girls were out on their own, her mother had more stability in her life, but it was painfully clear to Susie that the many years of coping as a single parent had caused significant aging. She could not forgive her father for what he did to her mother when he left. Sometimes she felt like burning the picture, but she kept it – in plain view – as a form of motivation for her each day. The pain he caused her was fuel that drove her to finish school and help her mother. She put the picture back on the wall and frowned at it.

Her mother meant everything to her. She tried her best to be a good daughter and she felt guilty that she didn't have more time to spend with her. She was glad Karen was with their mother quite a bit, but she wished Karen would do more with her life – it seemed to her that Karen had so much more potential. Susie noticed that Karen frequented their mother's home more and more – she pretty much lived with her. If it wasn't phone calls at least twice a day, it was visits lasting several hours. Holidays were just more of the same lengthy visits but with extra food. However materialistic Karen seemed at times, Susie knew her sister's heart was in the right place.

Susie flung her backpack over her shoulder and walked out the door. She walked through the city to the campus today, as she did whenever she could. The bustle of the city was a familiar voice and the tall buildings were like inanimate siblings. As she walked by different places of business, she waved at the various employees.

"How are you today, Susie dear?" one shopkeeper asked while sweeping his storefront.

"Fine, thanks! How are you?"

"Doing great," he responded with a grin.

Being the first day of the semester, traffic was a lot heavier than usual and she was glad that she had decided to walk. She heard the loud roar of a bus approaching from behind. It passed her up, but it stopped about fifty feet ahead of her to drop off passengers. A few people got off. One of them was Dan.

Susie's eyes lit up. Dan didn't notice her – he was reading a book while he walked. Susie picked up her pace a little bit to catch up to him. He wasn't walking very fast, and Susie caught up quickly. She tapped him on the shoulder.

Dan looked back.

"Susie? What a pleasant surprise," he said.

"Hey, Dan, I didn't think I'd see you again so soon."

"Well, you know, this whole stalking thing is much easier than I thought at first."

Susie laughed a little. She couldn't help but beam a smile at him. They began walking together.

"You taking many classes this semester?" she asked.

"I've got five classes – some pretty tough ones. I take as many as I can every semester. I really want to get through school as quickly as possible. What about you?"

Susie answered, "I only have a few, just enough to be a full-time student. I work part-time on campus in the computer lab, but I also do little jobs here and there to help with the bills… I'm pretty busy."

"Workaholic," Dan said with an accusing smile. "I'm taking out student loans so I can focus on school. I thought about getting a job, but I just want to get through, ya know?"

"Yeah. I don't want to take a loan for any reason unless I absolutely must. So far I've never had to. Besides, I'm not really in a hurry to finish."

"Why's that?"

"I like to take an average load of classes so I can do well in all of them," Susie said.

"Yeah, but don't you get tired of eating soup for lunch and dinner every day?"

"Ha! I eat soup for lunch every day."

"I think every student does... Take away Ramen noodles and half the student body will die," Dan said. "But, I would also like to be able to travel to see the world. We only have this one life and I want to know more about people and other cultures."

"I don't leave the city much. Never even left the state..."

"Yeah, I know."

"You do?" Susie asked in bewilderment.

"Yeah... You told me that."

Susie briefly tried to remember telling him that. She didn't remember at all, but wrote it off and said, "Oh... Oh, well... I feel fine here anyway."

"You never want to see the rest of the world?"

"Yes and no. I guess it depends on why," Susie said.

"I'd like to join the Peace Corps for a bit. Then I'd like to be able to start my own business centered on the elimination of neglected tropical diseases."

Susie was about to speak but stopped when she fully processed what he had said, "I... Wait... What?"

Dan stopped walking and replied, "There are many diseases out there that the world simply pays no attention to. The big ones like malaria, AIDS, and tuberculosis get a lot of attention, but millions more children are stricken with so many other ailments. It blows your mind away."

"Wow, I never thought of that," she said with concern draping her face. "It makes me a bit sad to know that very few people do."

They continued walking. Susie pondered what he had said and was impressed. At first he seemed like the stereotypical popular guy: good-looking, well-dressed, high school quarterback-type with no real depth. Yet this was the same guy everyone genuinely liked, who had saved that little girl and also let people fling tomatoes at him for charity. Apparently, Dan was much deeper than she thought.

"I think people can learn a lot from you, Dan. I already have," Susie said.

"Thanks," Dan replied, looking a bit embarrassed.

"I mean, I try to do my part to help those in need, but you're going for goals on a much larger scale," Susie remarked.

"I don't look at it that way. I look at all goals, big and small, as being as equally important," said Dan, gesturing with his arms as he talked. "I believe we are all interconnected."

"True, but it seems like your goals are pretty, well, lofty."

Dan stopped and looked at her earnestly, gaining a strictly serious demeanor.

"Susie, name any movement, ANY movement, that didn't start with just one person. It's always just one person who then gets a following. It's always one person who drives forward the momentum of entire populations. Great actions, both good and bad, never start with action by committee. Civil rights, Martin Luther King; gravity, Isaac Newton; Soviet Revolution, Lenin; antibiotics, Fleming... The list goes on and on. It always starts with one person and the rest follow."

Susie stared blankly at Dan, dazzled by his words. She had never met anyone like him before. Here was a guy who lived and breathed without limit. He was either delusional or a genius. He would either be great or he'd be laughed at.

"I do realize that people may laugh at me, by the way. I don't care. I don't think any of the people I listed cared either. Many of them put their life on the line for their beliefs, so being laughed at is nothing."

Susie looked directly into Dan's eyes. His blue eyes returned her gaze steadily, drawing her in. Dan was so serious about his beliefs and conviction that Susie couldn't believe that she was talking to a college sophomore, even if he was older than most.

"Sorry," Dan smiled apologetically. "I'll get off my soapbox. I get carried away sometimes."

"It's okay to have passion."

"It's not passion; it's compassion. I realized this many years ago."

Susie was once again pleasantly surprised. Dan was indeed a great guy – a really great guy. She noticed that she had lost track of time and looked at her watch.

"Whoa, I'm going to be late for my Calculus class."

"Calculus? Really? I have it at 8 a.m., too," Dan said.

"You have Gomez?"

"Yes," Dan said and chuckled a bit, "Heh, guess I'm going to be late too. Looks like we have the same class."

"How cool!"

Susie couldn't be more thrilled. She was finally feeling more comfortable around him, even if she still couldn't go so far as to readily admit that she was starting to like him. She would admit that she liked his ideals, though, and felt lucky that they have a class together so she could get to know him better.

The two of them picked up their pace and made their way through campus. They headed straight for the Math Building, found their room, and sat in chairs next to each other.

"Whew, just made it," Susie said.

"Oh, we could have hung out for another... what, thirty-eight seconds or so," he responded sarcastically.

Susie laughed a little, quietly. She readied her notepad and pen.

Professor Gomez, a heavyset man with a graying beard and thick glasses, entered the room. He walked to the front of the class with authority and adjusted his papers. He looked the classroom over, holding a ruler in one hand and methodically smacking his other hand with it like a metronome. He smiled broadly – as if he was looking at his newborn child for the first time.

"This is Calculus 1. If you don't intend to take Calculus 1 then you should stick around anyways because it's a lot of fun," he said in a poor attempt to make a joke.

No one laughed. Professor Gomez was notoriously difficult, but he also had a reputation for having a sense of humor that no one understood.

"Okay," he continued, "let's go ahead and start with asymptotes and limits."

For the next hour, Susie took notes as diligently as she could. Every word, graph, and hand gesture Professor Gomez used was immediately recorded. Occasionally during the lecture, she glanced at Dan, perplexed – he didn't even have paper in front of him. He just sat there, leaning back in his chair listening intently to the lecture. He slightly nodded his head from time to time, indicating that he got the concepts.

The hour went by in what seemed like a few minutes. Susie had cramps in her hand from feverishly trying to keep up with Professor Gomez's lecture.

"Okay, that's enough for today," Professor Gomez said after a quick glance at the clock on the wall.

Susie finished writing out her last few notes. Out of the corner of her eye, she could see Dan sitting patiently. He was genuinely confident, almost as if he had been through the class many times before; he was completely unfazed by Professor Gomez's onslaught of information. Susie looked towards Dan and noticed that he was now just staring at the ceiling and seemed a bit out of it.

"You okay?" she asked him.

"Yeah, I'm fine. Just thinking a bit."

"You didn't take any notes."

"Nope," he said as he stood up and stretched a bit. "I usually don't. I find I do better if I just pay complete attention during the lecture."

"What about studying later?" Susie asked.

"Sure, I'd love to study later with you," Dan quickly replied.

"No, I meant how do you study later if you don't have any notes?" Susie asked.

Suddenly, Susie realized what just happened and was mortified. Once again, she was acting like an idiot and messed everything up. Not only did she misstate a question and ask Dan to a study group that didn't exist yet, but she basically rejected an easy opportunity to spend time with Dan. She gritted her teeth but kept her overall composure.

"Oh. Yeah, sorry… It's never been a problem for me," Dan replied with indifference.

"But, let's get together sometime and study, sure," she said, struggling through her shyness.

Susie was relieved. She had finally crossed a line that she really wanted to cross. Dan interested her on many levels and the uneasy feeling around him was less intense than when she first met him, although she was still a little far away from wanting to date him. She wanted to learn more about him first. But, she was also afraid that taking too long to show interest might turn him away, especially since she had already had many chances and screwed things up every time. She was just glad that somehow he was still sticking around.

"Tuesdays or Thursdays work best for me," Dan said.

"Great."

"Here's my email address," Dan said as he wrote on a scrap of paper.

She would have preferred a phone number. She always preferred talking versus a cold, unemotional email. But, she decided this was good for now and gave him her email address in return.

Dan pocketed her email address and walked away briskly, without another word or gesture.

Susie watched him go, too surprised at the speed and manner in which he left to say anything.

She didn't expect him to leave so abruptly; she was sure they'd talk a while longer or at least walk out of the room together. After puzzling over it for a minute, she decided to just move on with her day.

With another three hours before her next class, Susie made her way to the university's health and fitness club, which gave free memberships to students. Free was always a good price for her. Susie had discovered its indoor rock climbing wall earlier last year and had instantly fallen in love.

Before, she never would have guessed that she could have both the physical strength and mental fortitude to climb a sheer four-story wall. Each step up the rock climbing wall always gave her a slight boost in self-confidence, a boost that she was already looking forward to. There was something about facing fear and weakness head-on that reinforced her determination and focus. Going as frequently as she did had also put her in good physical shape and, over the past year, it had become a complete workout on all levels. Susie had become so good at climbing that now she usually timed herself. "Simply getting to the top is easy; getting there faster than last time is the challenge," she thought with a smile as she entered the gym.

Her climb went a little differently today. She was about halfway up, making her way over an underhang, when she found herself thinking about the exchange with Dan earlier. She lost focus and slipped. She was snapped out of her descent by her safety harness.

"Darn it!" she shouted, staring at the ceiling as she gently swayed on her rope.

Over the next hour, she tried again and again but to no avail. Dan had squarely distracted her and she was mad at herself for letting that happen. Rock climbing had to wait for another day. She showered, changed back to her regular clothes, and continued with her day.

She still had a couple of classes to attend and then she had a work shift in the computer lab on campus. She tried her best not to re-evaluate how she had interacted with Dan, but she couldn't stop herself. Why did he leave so abruptly? She re-hashed all of the things she said, all of the things she did – just trying to think of what she could have done to make him do that.

Her thoughts kept circling the topic throughout the day, obsessing her. She tried her best to take notes in her remaining classes, but she had a hard time focusing on anything but Dan. She argued with herself about him, about her reactions to him. Her fixation on Dan frightened and fascinated her, and she was torn between confidence and doubt about wanting to get to know Dan better.

She didn't eat anything all day until she arrived at work in the computer lab late that afternoon. She ate the soup she had brought with her from home that morning and then stared into the distance, devoid of any coherent thought. Few people were in the computer lab since it was the beginning of the semester, so she really had nothing to do.

"Hey, Susie," Nicole said as she entered the lab. "I thought I'd find you here."

"Oh, Nicole, how are you doing?" Susie replied, her face lighting up – Nicole was a welcome distraction.

"Just thought I'd swing by and see how the first day of class was treating you."

Susie hesitated. She wanted to say everything was fine, but she couldn't lie to her. Susie hated telling even a white lie. She believed it was best to tell the truth or nothing. Not wanting to hurt people's feelings or tell a lie, Susie had developed a knack for pointing out the good in every aspect. But, right now, she was having trouble finding a silver lining.

"I suppose things could have gone better," she admitted.

"Oh, what happened? That Professor Gomez making life tough on you?"

"Have you had him?" she asked.

"No, but I hear he's sadistic."

"Well, no… It's not him, actually," Susie said. "Really, I just need some time to myself to think."

Nicole plopped down in a nearby chair as if to declare she wasn't going anywhere for a while. "Go on," she told Susie, gesturing with her hands.

"About what?" Susie looked away from her.

"Oh, come on…," Nicole leaned forward, put her elbows on her knees, and rested her head on her hands, "Who is he?" she asked.

"Who?" Susie responded, hoping she would take the hint and change the subject.

Nicole raised her eyebrows, declaring that she knew Susie heard exactly what she said.

Susie relented, "You remember that guy, Dan, from the coffee shop at the Student Union? At the end of last semester?"

"Oh, yeah. Mr. Creeps," Nicole bluntly said.

Susie stared at Nicole, shocked, "Mr. Creeps? I thought you said he seemed okay in the coffee shop."

"I thought at first he was okay, but then he kinda struck me as artificial... You know, a little creepy."

"How so?" Susie asked.

"I dunno... He just seemed too perfect."

"But you don't even know him," Susie said.

"Yeah, but I can tell."

"How so?"

"He just seemed like he was flirting too hard," Nicole said.

That relieved Susie a bit. If Dan liked her enough to flirt too hard, she didn't see anything wrong with that.

"Is that all?" Susie asked.

"He didn't do anything to you, did he?" Nicole said with a firm, serious voice.

"No, no, no. He didn't. It's stupid, really," she said.

Nicole folded her arms – she wasn't going anywhere.

"Well, I thought we were becoming friends... in a close way, if you know what I mean," Susie said.

Nicole didn't move a muscle.

"We exchanged email addresses because we're going to study together and, well..."

Nicole leaned forward a little, as if waiting for a climactic ending to a story.

"...he just took my email address and walked away without saying anything. No goodbye or anything."

Nicole continued leaning forward, still waiting for more information. She gestured her hands for her to keep going with her story.

"That's it," Susie said, chagrined. She could see that Nicole expected more, but there was no more to give.

Nicole leaned back, "Wait. That's it? He just walked away? That's what's bothering you?"

"Uh… Yeah…," Susie replied.

"Susie, that's nothing. The guy just went on with the rest of his day. You're reading into it too much," said Nicole, writing it off.

"Really?"

"Really," Nicole said.

"I mean, I think everything else is fine. I just got weirded out with that," said Susie.

Nicole laughed.

"What?" Susie asked.

"You're smitten," she said.

"What?!"

"Smitten: S-M-I-T-T-E-N." Nicole stood up. "Give me his email address."

"What for?" Susie asked.

"I want to look him up online. I want to see if this guy's a mass murderer or something."

Susie handed Nicole the piece of paper with Dan's email address on it.

"I'll be over there," she said, pointing to a nearby computer.

Susie looked around and noticed that, other than the two of them and the thirty-nine empty desks with computers on them, the computer lab was empty. Now that she was talking about Dan, Susie decided she wanted to get Karen's advice on the matter.

"Nicole, do you mind watching the lab for me for a few minutes? I'm going to step outside and call my sister," Susie said, already halfway to the door.

Nicole had filled this role before during last semester.

"No problem. I'll text you if anyone comes in."

"Thanks!"

Susie left the lab and, feeling a bit thirsty, she took a right down the hallway, heading towards a water fountain at the end.

She took only a few steps that direction before she saw a man drinking from the fountain – a man who looked a lot like Dan's friend, Phil. Susie hid behind a pillar in the hallway. The man stood up from drinking. It was Phil. Susie instantly decided she was not thirsty enough to deal with him. She tiptoed back, past the computer lab, and turned a corner to the side exit of the building.

It was a little cold outside, but she preferred being cold than being near Phil. She called Karen.

Karen picked up, "Hey, lil' sis! Can I call you right back? I'm helping mom with the groceries."

"Sure," Susie replied.

Susie hung up and waited. She paced back and forth a bit, wondering how she would engage in conversation with Karen. The problem was that they thought very differently from each other. Susie knew Karen's first questions about Dan would be about how much money he had and whether or not his major would lead to even more wealth. Susie couldn't care less about that and thought about how she could explain to Karen why money didn't matter.

Ten minutes passed. Finally, Susie felt she couldn't wait any longer for Karen to call back. She had already been gone longer from the lab than she intended. She rushed back.

Nicole was gone.

"Nicole?!" she called out. "Nicole?!"

Susie checked the hallways, calling her name. She called her phone, but it went straight to voicemail.

"That's weird," she said to herself.

She walked over to her computer to look for any sign of what had happened. There was a note sitting on the keyboard:

Something came up. I had to go.
    -Nicole

Susie shrugged, "Well, I guess I'll catch her later."

Chapter 9 – *Them*

There was deep silence in a dark, heavily wooded forest. Only the sounds of wild animals and birds could be heard intermittently. In the distance, the ambient light of a nearby city dimly lit up what night sky could be seen through the branches. A figure emerged holding a hanging lantern – shielded so that the light faced outward, keeping the figure's face dark.

"Lingchi!" he shouted.

"Lingchi!" a chorus of unseen people shouted back in monotone, returning his greeting.

"Slow slicing… Death by a thousand cuts!" he shouted back.

This was *Their* greeting when *They* met as a group, which was very seldom and only held for very important, complicated circumstances.

"It isn't good having these get-togethers, but there is too much at stake!" the man yelled.

Many voices from all directions said "Aye," in near unison.

"Susie… Susie is becoming a problem for *Us*," the shadowed man said. "She is well-protected, but *We* must finish her!"

Silence filled the air for a moment.

The man squatted down, sighed in frustration, and wiped his brow.

"By my count, she's avoided her demise eleven times in the past week. No matter what *We* do, *They* have a correcting response. There isn't enough complexity to *Our* approach. It is too simple for *Them*. Her fate must be made more subtle. *We* are being too overt."

The shadowed man stood up and began pacing. He stopped.

"Why?... Why?" he asked the unseen audience.

Only a handful of silhouettes could be made out in the dark. They were spread apart, some sitting in trees while others sat on the ground. He looked around in all directions, beyond and between the shadowed figures nearest him to the many invisible others gathered there.

"*They* are protecting her more than the others in the past!" a woman's voice yelled.

"Yes, that's obvious," the man said. "Now what are *We* going to do?"

"Just put a bullet through her brain!" a deep-voiced man yelled.

The shadowed man pulled out a gun and quickly fired off several shots in the direction of the deep-voiced man.

"YOU MEAN LIKE THAT?!" he yelled.

Silence.

"ANSWER ME! YOU WANT ME TO PUT A BULLET THROUGH HER BRAIN?!"

"No," the deep-voiced man responded.

"Why not?"

"Because *We* will never have a chance."

"Because *We* will never have a chance," the shadowed man parroted back loudly. "That's right: *We* will not."

The shadowed man dropped to his knees and covered his face, rubbing it in frustration, then chuckled hoarsely and said, "What's so funny is that the dumb whore doesn't even know about any of this."

He clenched his fists tightly.

"Susie...," the man said, spitting, "...is too close... She is way too close. Time is getting shorter."

"What more can *We* do?" a voice in the forest asked him. "She is too routined... too easy to predict and protect."

"*They* have been protecting her with more diligence than anyone else – more than anyone for at least the past 12 years. This alarms me."

The audience shouted back in agreement, "AYE!"

"EACH! OF! YOU! Each and every ONE of you will put forth no less than thirty actions against Susie immediately. She would already be dead many times over if it wasn't for *Them*!"

A woman started laughing.

"What's so funny?!" the shadowed man yelled.

"You are," she said. "*They* work too subtly and are unnoticeable by anyone – even more so than *We* are. *We* should do more with less. *They* expect that *We* will brute-force Susie, that *We* will throw everything at her."

"More with less? Interesting...," the shadowed man said while tapping the side of his cheek.

"*We* are already close to her. *We* could just kill her straight up... have her get killed in a random mugging," the female voice pointed out.

"No, no... That has been discussed. *We* cannot afford it. *We* would never get away with it. *We* cannot afford to lose any more people. The police would be all over *Us*, crippling *Our* future efforts for an unacceptable time frame. *They* would make sure of it."

The shadowed man pulled at his hair in frustration and then went into deep thought. Silence engulfed the area.

He slipped into a brief trancelike state and then suddenly snapped out of it.

"No. There isn't a way for *Us* to kill her directly without taking substantial losses. *We* would be too exposed."

The female voice spoke up again, "It isn't as if *We* haven't been successful before."

The shadowed man agreed, "I can see a lot of potential coming into play here. Perhaps the best path is one of distraction and not one of direct intervention."

Several voices yelled "Aye!" and "Yes!"

"*We* will keep on her periphery then; that is, most of *Us* will. *We* will carefully select who interacts with her. *We* will take from her those who protect her. *We* will leave her vulnerable and alone."

He paused, and then yelled out, "Bring the prize forward!"

A person with a sack over their head and tattered clothes emerged from the shadows – barely walking and unescorted. The person struggled with each step, weak-kneed, as if all will to live was gone. Hundreds of cuts, burns, and bruises covered what was visible of the arms, torso, and legs.

"Keep walking," the shadowed man instructed.

The "prize" lurched forward very slowly, finally reaching the shadowed man.

"Here is someone who was unknowingly sent by *Them* a year ago to help guide Susie." He ripped off the hood, roaring, "A FULL YEAR AGO!"

It was Nicole. Her badly beaten face was barely recognizable and vaguely sad – lost and irretrievable.

"Kill her!" a voice yelled out.

Just loud enough for all to hear, the shadowed man said to Nicole, "You poor sap. You didn't even know you were set up by *Them*, did you?"

Nicole didn't respond.

"One year ago, almost to the day, you ran across Susie and you became friends... And now you are here because of it!"

Still, nothing came from Nicole.

The shadowed man turned, facing his unseen audience.

"Here is an example of how *They* plan! Guiding Susie through puppets, such as Nicole here, for at least a year! A YEAR! AND *WE* DID NOT SEE IT!" he yelled, flailing his fists.

He turned to Nicole and calmly asked her, "Tell me, Nicole, doesn't it bother you that you were used for the past year and didn't know it? Doesn't it bother you that *They* could not rescue you at the computer lab? Doesn't it bother you that *They* are seven minutes late in rescuing you right now?"

The man gripped his forehead in vexation and talked to himself, "Susie... God, I hate that name. I loathe her. I spit on her. I wish I could be there to see the look on her face when she knows she's dying."

Chapter 10 – Opposites

Father Crane was back on the hilltop with Frank. Traces of snow scattered the ground. Father Crane wore a heavy black trench-coat and black wool gloves to stave off the frigid cold. Frank wore the same dingy blue coat that Father Crane had given him before. Once again, they sat in chairs about forty feet away from each other.

"What did you learn about Harold?" Father Crane asked, narrowing his eyes.

"He makes it seem effortless," Frank said, sighing.

"The bees were clever."

"Yes. *He* ordered them far in advance of anything I did," said Frank. "*He* knew what I was planning almost before I knew what I was planning."

"You will find that those who have their full Polarity all have the same ability to see the past as well as into the future. However, as we are all still human, we are limited by distractions, lack of focus, and other flaws. The most powerful of *Us* and

Them are those who can most quickly isolate what's important and then act on it."

Frank averted his eyes from Father Crane in shame.

"Since the beginning of time, it's never been the most powerful who survive," Father Crane added.

"It's those with the ability to adapt, right?" Frank asked.

"Not quite," Father Crane responded. "It's those who can adapt the quickest to their circumstances. Those who come to the solution first will always have the advantage over those who are slower. Always."

"Then, *We* are in a battle of who is fastest with influence?"

"Yes."

"I look back at Chicago now and realize how clumsy I was with my plan. It was easy for Harold to nullify it."

"It's easy to look back at the past and to appear as a genius if you could do it all over again."

"Father Crane…," Frank struggled.

"Yes?"

"When Harold was near me, I wanted… I wanted to kill him right there on the spot."

"Why didn't you?" Father Crane asked.

Frank's eyes lit up. He looked surprised.

"You have your Polarity, Frank. Why is it so difficult? Think about it. Don't use emotion. Rid yourself of it. It is useless," Father Crane said.

Father Crane stood up and began to pace. He continued, "The only reason why you shouldn't have killed him on the spot was because you wouldn't have gotten away with it. And neither would he. You are, by far, too valuable of a resource for *Us* to have been captured or killed."

Frank regained his composure a little.

"He mocked you… Why didn't you mock him?"

Frank raised an eyebrow, "What?"

"Mocking is mankind's most effective tool for making others act stupidly... even if you have your Polarity. *We* use it. *They* use it. If you say or do it just right then you will distract *Them* or, if you're really effective, you will get *Them* to act without thinking."

"I... I... couldn't focus."

Father Crane sat down again and pointed at Frank asking, "How much damage will Harold cause over the next year? And the next month? The next day?"

Frank's face flushed. He inhaled quickly and then deeply exhaled.

"Harold being gone would have been quite the coup in terms of *Our* progress, true? It would be quite an upheaval for life as *We* know it, right?" Father Crane added.

"Yes," Frank answered sheepishly.

"The feelings you had towards Harold were because you have opposite Polarities. He felt the same towards you. There would have been nothing better for Harold than to see you dead, right there, in that hotel in Chicago," Father Crane said coldly.

"Before all of this...," Frank reflected, "...I remember feeling anger at many points in my life. I remember hatred. I remember so many things, but they seem so useless now. What I felt towards Harold was vile... I think that's the word I want to use. I could not think of anything else but killing him."

Father Crane smiled slightly.

"It wasn't vile – it was natural. You're learning, Frank. You managed yourself well in Chicago. Harold would have killed you in a heartbeat if you had tried anything on him. Think about it."

Frank closed his eyes and, within a second, stood up in shock, stammering, "I... I see how... how close I was to dying."

Father Crane nodded his head once.

"But, you lived to serve *Us* another day," Father Crane said.

"Yes."

"Frank, let's get back to Susie. *We* have instructions. *We* have a plan to follow. She must unknowingly follow *Us*. We cannot push her."

"Oh, Father Crane, I really don't think I can help with such a high profile target. I'm still too new at this. I will mess it up."

"Frank!" yelled Father Crane, bolting up out of his chair. "Snap out of it! Focus! You're one of *Us* now! Your past is gone. Focus on what must be done to serve *Our* future. Mankind's future is *Our* responsibility!"

Frank's face went blank and he sat back down in his chair.

"Are you mad at me?" Frank asked with a slightly anxious tone.

"No. I never get mad, happy, or anything else. I only project emotions for efficacy," said Father Crane.

"It worked," Frank said, wide-eyed.

"Frank, go check in on Susie."

The two of them got up from their chairs, folded them, and left in opposite directions off of the hilltop.

*   *   *

Harold sat in his office continuing his diligent scribbling, taking thousands of notes on a single sheet of paper. Blue, red, green, and black ink completely coated its surface. With every stroke of his pen, Harold doted over his handiwork like a proud father. His pen moved continuously – barely able to keep up with his thoughts.

His phone vibrated. He had received a text that read, *Frank is on the move to Susie.*

"Oh, Frank… What are you up to? Why is Father Crane forcing me to kill you?" he said aloud to himself.

Stand by, he texted back.

Harold sat back in his leather office chair. He briefly cupped his hands over his mouth and then rested them over his slight pot-belly, thinking about how he should take care of Frank.

I will deal with Frank, he texted.

Harold looked at the clock. It was a little after 9 p.m. He had another 14 minutes and 22 seconds before he needed to leave. He calculated he could have at least another thirty-one things done by then.

Harold continued scribbling notes on his sheet of paper. Once the sheet looked like it was completely plastered with ink, he whipped out another sheet. He put the fresh sheet of paper flush against the edge of the used one and continued his note-taking.

"The freezer won't be cold enough… The sun will shine too brightly… There will be too many people on the Ferris wheel… There isn't a ten dollar bill available… Orange isn't quite the right color…," he rambled aloud as his pen dashed across the page.

Harold glanced at his watch and then looked down at his notes. He closed his eyes briefly. It was time to go.

He left his office and walked down the empty hallway of his office building to the elevator. He went to the first floor and greeted the security guard, "Good evening, Gus."

"Good evening Mr. McGee."

"How's life treating you?" Harold asked as he walked by.

"Life is good, sir. Oh, and, sir… it's raining."

"Normal southern California weather for this time of year… Have a good night," Harold said as he walked out the front door.

"Yes, sir."

Harold took a step outside. He opened his umbrella and looked up at the surrounding buildings. It was dark, but the city was full of life.

Another round of ineffective actions by Them. This will be easy. They only have five viable ways of killing me in the next hour. I wonder if they're even trying, he thought.

He walked about a half block up the street and stopped a passerby.

"Do I know you?" Harold asked.

"Uh… No, I don't think so," the passer-by answered.

"Oh, sorry. You look like someone I know from McCurdy's Pub."

"Yeah, I like that place," the passer-by said.

"Wish I could go tonight. I hear they're having two-for-one La Beer's. I just have too many things to do," Harold said.

"Hmm… I'm gonna go. That's good beer," the passerby said, licking his lips.

"Heh, well take care," Harold chuckled.

"You, too!"

The two parted ways.

Harold grinned a little bit as he walked away. He reflected on his knowing that the passer-by would get in a bar fight with two belligerent men at the pub. The men had already been influenced by *Them* so that they would leave the bar, cross paths with Harold, and assault him for no apparent reason. Now that won't happen.

Harold hailed an approaching cab and got in.

"Head towards the airport please," he told the driver.

The cab departed but only drove two blocks when Harold asked the driver to stop.

"On second thought, please let me out here," he said as he handed the driver twenty dollars – more than enough to cover the fare.

Harold got out of the cab and walked a little up the street.

He threw a five dollar bill in a public garbage can. He knew that in a few minutes, a homeless woman was going to go through the garbage and find the bill. She would then use the money to buy a hamburger at a nearby fast food restaurant. Her small stop at the fast food restaurant would cause a young man to get his food a few minutes later than he would have if the homeless woman wasn't there.

He knew the young man was going to get on his bicycle, drive by him, and drop a ketchup packet that he was supposed to slip and fall from. This wasn't going to happen now.

For the next hour, Harold trekked towards Frank's location; Frank was near Susie's home. Along the way, he continued taking similar actions to nullify actions meant to harm him – courtesy of *Them*. Every day was like this for Harold. Anywhere he went, he had to take such preemptive actions. His life was always in peril, but he took it all with casual stride. He accepted that it was the price he paid with his position in the never-ending conflict of *Us* versus *Them*.

Harold eventually approached Susie's home – a first floor apartment in a crumbling brownstone. The rain had stopped so Harold closed his umbrella. He smiled warmly at Susie's humble dwelling, knowing it suited her personality perfectly.

He looked down the street and saw Frank's police car a few blocks away, parked on the side of the street. Frank was sitting on the hood of his car in plain sight, staring at Susie's home. He took an occasional swig from a tall, shiny metallic coffee thermos. Although Frank was one of *Them*, Harold wasn't worried about shielding Susie from *Them*. He had plenty of *Us* nearby to help in an instant.

He looked at a car parked in front in Susie's home across the street from him. Jennifer was in the driver's seat. She looked at Harold and nodded. Harold nodded back. He then looked back at Frank.

"Rookie," Harold said towards Frank.

A cat walked up to Harold and he picked it up.

"Hey, little kitty… I've got plans for you." he said.

Harold stared at the cat and it stared, motionless, back at him. A few seconds later, the cat jumped out of his arms and ran in the direction of Frank. He knew that Frank liked cats and this one would remind him of a cat he'd had when he was a boy; Frank wouldn't be able to resist the distraction.

"Thank you, my friend," Harold said at the cat.

He then started walking in the same direction. Harold watched the cat trot by Frank's police car. Frank jumped off the hood, easily chased the cat down, and caught it – never noticing Harold approaching from behind him. Harold kept walking towards him casually, quietly.

Frank turned around with the cat in his arms – Harold was just a few feet away facing him. "Hello, Frank," Harold said with an over-the-top smile.

Frank was paralyzed, dropping the cat and his shiny metallic coffee thermos.

Harold held up his hands at Frank in mock surrender, "Here's your chance, Frank. Here's your chance to take me out."

"I'm… I'm not here for you, Harold."

"Oh? Are you here for someone else?" Harold responded looking around in all directions.

Frank blinked his eyes several times and chomped down on his lower lip before finally saying, "I'd prefer that you leave."

"You're acting rather nicely, Frank. That's uncommon for *Your* kind."

Frank didn't say anything.

Harold noticed a young couple walking towards them, talking loudly. Harold stepped forward and leaned into Frank's face. He whispered, "*You* have already lost her. Leave her alone."

"I won't let *You* kill her."

"Kill her? What has Father Crane told you?" Harold said softly with deep concern, "*Your* kind will never stop with the lies, even to each other. It's tragic. *You* will never reach your goals until *You* are able to trust each other."

They stood in silence as the chatty couple passed them. Harold took a step back and looked Frank over. "I suppose *You* are too focused on killing me to listen," Harold said and then sighed in disappointment.

Frank didn't say anything, but his body was tensed.

Harold turned around and started walking away. He stopped, turned towards Frank, and said, "Father Crane is about to text you. He will tell you that you did well against me."

Frank's phone beeped. Frank glanced down at his phone and then back at Harold.

"I don't know why Father Crane would send you here," Harold said, shaking his head slowly at Frank. "You're too new for this. You'll screw things up for him."

Harold looked towards Susie's home – knowing that she was in the middle of her weekly cleaning routine.

*   *   *

Inside her home, Susie was busily cleaning. She was innately neat, but dust did accumulate. With all of the photographs that she had about her home, it was quite a tedious chore.

She took a break and checked her email. Her eyes lit up when she saw that Dan had written her. She quickly opened his email, *How about we get together next Tuesday evening for Calculus? 8 p.m. should work for me. Cya. :)*

Susie was tickled over the happy face emoticon. He wasn't mad at her as she suspected.

She wrote back, *Sounds good!*

She clicked *SEND* and then wondered if the exclamation point was a bit obvious. Then she wondered why she was fretting over something so benign as punctuation. She closed her eyes and shook her head for a moment.

She stood up, walked over to the window at the front of her apartment, and opened the curtains. She looked outside and saw that the neighborhood was devoid of activity. There was a car parked out front and a police car parked down the street, but it was otherwise empty. It was just another night – just like last night and the night before it.

She walked over to the picture of her father and stared at it. She peered into his eyes. Susie wanted to blame her boring existence on him, but she knew she was responsible for her own feelings and choices. Still, though, she couldn't get over it.

She put the picture down and began crying a little. All of those years had gone by and yet she still cried because of that single picture. It had been a major roadblock in her life, always keeping her in the past. She recognized that, but she didn't know what to do about it. She had tried therapy for several years, but ultimately she found it ineffective because it all came down to a single vague solution: find a way to let go.

As she walked by her computer again, she noticed that Dan had already replied to her email. She opened the response and read, *Great. I'll reserve a room in the library.*

She realized that, at this very instant, Dan was probably sitting in front of his computer. She wanted to write back to him or maybe even start a chat and see what he was up to, but realized she was distracting herself. She had studying to do.

Her phone rang. She checked the caller ID and saw that it was Karen. She picked up the phone.

"Hey, Karen."

"Hey, lil' sis! How are you?"

"Fine."

"I was returning your call from the other night. I'm sorry I didn't call you right back as I promised. I got caught up in a few things with mom."

"Is she okay?" Susie asked.

Their mother wasn't always even keeled. She had been known to randomly flip out over how difficult her life had been or become overcome with anger and grief over their father. Susie knew this was another reason, an ongoing reason, why she couldn't just let go – her mother kept part of that sad fire going.

"She's fine... You know, the usual thing."

No further explanation was necessary; it was about their father. Neither sister said anything for a few seconds.

"So, what ya up to, sis?" Karen finally asked.

"Well, it's kind of something more in your department."

"Ahh... Who is he?" Karen asked with delight.

Susie laughed, "I just met him and I don't know much about him, but I think he's flirting with me."

"Is he cute?"

"Yeah... Yeah, he is." Susie hadn't thought about it too much, but, yes, she did think so right at this very moment.

"Oh, Susie! So, what's his name?"

"Dan."

"And what does he do?"

Susie sighed inwardly and thought, "Here comes Karen's materialistic checkup." She decided to cut to the chase and answered, "Karen, he would fail every test you'd have for him."

"Then he's PERFECT for you!" Karen giggled.

The two sisters continued talking for the next forty-five minutes. Susie forgot about studying and enjoyed the moment. The subject of Dan gave Susie a conversation piece with Karen, something other than the usual topics of their mother and Karen's jaded love life. But, above all, she was happy that Karen was happy for her. Susie knew that Karen worried about her finding "the right guy" and it was a relief to give her hope. Susie felt even closer to Karen by talking about Dan. Likewise, talking to her about him helped Susie immensely in conquering her fear of trusting him.

Chapter 11 – Tragedy

As planned, Susie went to meet Dan in the library the following Tuesday at 8 p.m. She found Dan – he was already in the room he had reserved. Immediately, it was obvious to her that he had been there for quite some time. Two coffee cups were next to him along with a pile of papers completely filled with handwritten notes.

"Geez, how long have you been here?" Susie asked Dan as she entered the room.

"Oh, hey, Susie!" Dan greeted her, smiling. "Oh, I've been here a few hours studying for other classes."

"I thought you didn't take notes?" Susie said, pointing at Dan's completely filled papers.

"Hmm? Oh, those. I write my own notes after class. It's just how I learn."

She had never seen so much writing on a single piece of paper before, and there was an entire stack of them. She couldn't make out any of the words; his handwriting was too illegible and it was way too small.

"How do you read those?"

He grinned at her, admitting, "It's not easy reading *Dan font* sometimes, but it's just how I write when it's just for me. And I don't like to waste paper."

"Clearly."

He quickly straightened his papers and looked around the table.

"Hey, can you hand me my backpack?" he said as he pointed.

Susie looked to where he was pointing and saw a bulging, black fabric backpack. It was sitting just out of his reach but it was right next to Susie. She picked it up and handed it to him. Dan's hand touched hers briefly in the exchange and it unexpectedly excited her.

That was nice, Susie thought.

"Let's get to Calculus," Dan said eagerly while he stuffed his papers in his backpack.

"You don't waste a second, do you?"

"Nah, this is exciting stuff."

"Exciting?" Susie asked in disbelief.

"Yeah. I love taking a class and seeing how I can apply it to the real world."

"Really?" Susie was still doubtful, thinking of Nicole's opinion of Calculus. "Most people make fun of the fact that you can't apply much of anything you learn in college to the real world – especially Calculus."

"I know, I know… But, I find that it helps me retain information if I try to apply it."

Susie felt pleasantly surprised. Dan was apparently very serious about school, but she never would have guessed it from her first impression of him. Susie looked at him closer: polo shirt, khakis, not a blemish on his face, and oddly organized, even if he did have atrocious handwriting.

"You okay?" Dan asked her.

Susie realized that she was still standing with her backpack slung over her shoulder. Once again, she found herself acting stupid around Dan.

"Oh, sorry… I was just thinking," Susie apologized as she hurriedly sat down in the nearest chair.

"Don't apologize for thinking. Most people don't do enough of it," Dan said.

Susie just smiled back at him.

"Now," Dan said, tapping his Calculus book, "Professor Gomez only has four tests and that means only four grades to count towards our final grade. We have to be sure that we hit homeruns on each exam. The first one is only a month away."

"Wow… Just a month," Susie said, intimidated.

"Ah, we'll be fine."

She exhaled, feeling comforted. Dan was right; she would be fine with him as her studymate. She was always implicitly refusing help from anybody by working hard to stay ahead of everyone else. She knew that the cost for her hard work was that study groups were her only social outlet when everyone else was distracted from their studies by their extensive social lives. But, being ahead also gave her the easy social role of tutor to fill in her study groups – a bonus on top of the reward of helping others – and made her extra effort worth more just good grades. In this case, however, she was not sure she could stay ahead of Dan. He seemed to have real enthusiasm for the subject. She would gladly accept his help to get through the horrors of Professor Gomez's class.

The study session seemed to go by in a flash. Susie knew she had learned more about Calculus with Dan than she ever could have on her own. If she were bolder, she would ask Dan if he had taken it before. After only a week of class, it appeared to her like he knew it all already. He was able to explain the details of every theorem and equation as if he had come up with them in his spare time.

They left the library together and walked in the cool night air. Only a few stars could be seen because of the surrounding city's ambient light.

"I wish I could see the stars. All of them," Susie lamented.

"Yeah, this isn't the best place for stars. Too much light."

"Yeah."

"The best places to go are the deserts here in California, Arizona, or Nevada during a new moon in the middle of the desert."

"Sounds a bit unsafe," Susie said.

"Very true, but very rewarding."

Dan stopped briefly – as did Susie – and looked up at the night sky. "It would be nice to see all the stars, to be able to visit them," he said.

Susie smiled at this, but it was quickly wiped from her face. Far in front of her, she spotted a man walking towards them. He had a lit cigarette and what appeared to be a mohawk. She bit her lip; it was the same man she saw on campus last semester. Her heart pounded a little stronger, but she felt safe knowing she was with Dan.

"Let's keep walking," Dan said without any apparent notice of the man.

Dan and Susie continued walking, but she tried to keep the man in sight. They took the next turn on the sidewalk, making their way between two campus buildings towards the parking lot. Seconds later, the man turned the same direction, following them. Susie noticed this, but didn't know if she should alert Dan to it or not. She didn't want to sound paranoid or silly to him. This man had not done anything. Besides, she wasn't sure what should she say to Dan about it.

"It's gonna be a tough semester," Dan declared.

"Uh-huh," Susie responded, not really paying attention to Dan. She was still distracted by the man. She hadn't looked over her shoulder, but she was trying to listen for his footsteps, the jingle of loose pocket change – just something – to tell her how close he was.

"How do your other classes look?"

"Uh-huh," Susie responded blindly.

Dan stepped in front of her.

"You okay?" he asked.

"Uh, yeah… Just a little…," Susie hesitated.

"That guy isn't following us anymore," Dan interrupted.

Susie turned around and saw that he was gone. She exhaled in relief. Dan had known the guy was following them after all. It was so comforting to her to see how unbothered he was about it.

"I'm sorry… I just didn't…," Susie trailed off and shrugged.

"No worries, Susie. All is well."

Susie filled with warmth. Dan's sincere, blue eyes beamed into hers. She felt safety and comfort. She sensed no wrong could happen. She almost wanted Dan to kiss her.

*   *   *

The semester continued onward. Their first Calculus test came along and Susie got an A- while Dan got a solid A. Studying together every Tuesday came to include the occasional Thursday as well. Sometimes, he visited Susie in the computer lab and brought her a coffee.

All this while, Susie wondered if Dan would ever ask her out on a date. Each day, she debated whether Dan was interested in her or not. He complimented her a lot and made her laugh, but he was never been more than mildly, though obviously, flirtatious. On campus, they appeared always together; off campus, they never were.

After a couple of weeks passed like this, Susie confessed one day to Karen how confused she was by Dan's behavior. But even Karen was stumped.

"Is he gay?" Karen asked.

"No! Well, I don't think so. He doesn't seem like it."

"Married?" she asked.

"No! Well, um, I don't think so."

"Was he in prison? How about bankruptcy? Are his parents rich? Does he have a girlfriend?" Karen asked impatiently.

"Well, you know… I don't know."

"Lil' sis, you've got more homework to do on this guy. Something is up with him. People usually talk about their lives unless they're hiding something. You've gotta ask more questions."

"Yeah, but I don't know how. I mean… all I know how to talk about is school stuff."

"You've got to try," Karen implored. "You're spending a lot of time with a guy you don't know much about."

Later that evening, Susie sat behind her desk at the computer lab. There were only a few students in the lab and they didn't need her at all. She knew she should be studying, but she was still a little preoccupied over the whole Dan thing. It had seemed to be going well for a while, but now everything had stalled. And Karen had brought up good points that made her wonder about Dan and his past.

Just then, a short, chubby, dark-haired policeman entered the lab.

"Excuse me, miss?" the policeman asked Susie.

"Yes?"

"We're looking for this woman," the policeman said as he held up a photo of Nicole.

"Nicole?" she asked blankly.

"Have you seen her lately?"

"No, I haven't. I haven't seen her for three or four weeks, I guess. She used to stop by and visit me here sometimes. Is she in trouble?"

"We don't know. She's a missing person right now."

Susie gasped, putting her hands over her mouth.

"Apparently you're the last person to see her."

"What... What about her family? Didn't they see her?"

The policeman shook his head. "She didn't appear to be very close to them. You appear to be the closest person that she had."

Susie stared aimlessly, feeling acute shame for not trying harder to be a better friend.

"I'm sorry. We'll let you know if we find her," the policeman said.

"Nicole...," Susie said softly.

She had been so caught up in Dan that she had completely forgotten about Nicole. Her shame turned into despair.

The policeman asked her a few more questions about the last time she saw Nicole and then left. Not more than a few seconds later, Dan entered the lab.

"What's that about?" Dan asked, looking back at the door that the policeman had gone through.

Susie was on the verge of crying.

"Is... Is everything okay, Susie?"

She shook her head and began crying. Dan pulled her to him and embraced her.

"My friend... Nicole... She's missing," she said with a few tears streaming down her face.

Dan didn't say anything. He just kept holding her, his silent support making Susie feel comforted. Finally, she saw Dan in a much more personal sense – he was genuinely compassionate and caring about her.

"I'm sure she'll turn up," he said. "It isn't like her to disappear."

"You... You knew her?" she asked, sniffing a bit.

"No, I just know what you told me about her."

"Oh, I didn't realize I told you much about her... But, I guessed we've talked about a lot of things."

"A ton of things," Dan said.

Dan let Susie go and looked her over.

"I just stopped by on my way out of my Economics class to see how you were doing. I'm glad I did."

"I was fine until the police stopped by. I wish there was something I could do to help," Susie replied, trying to stop her eyes from welling up.

"In cases like this, I'm afraid there isn't much that can be done except wait," Dan said.

Susie went pale, dreading the idea of doing nothing to help find Nicole. But, she knew Dan was right. She knew it was all about waiting now.

"Listen, you have to keep your chin up no matter what," Dan said with a smile of encouragement. "Negativity only brings more negativity."

"You're right. I just feel so bad that I pretty much ignored her for the past month. I didn't even realize she was missing."

"Susie, I'm sure she knows you've been busy. The best thing to do is, to keep moving. Don't stop. Don't let this bring you down. Nicole, if she were here, would agree with you."

"Yeah..."

"We've got a mid-term coming up soon. Let's get some A's on it, huh?"

Susie bobbed her head in agreement. She was glad that she had Dan's help and his encouragement. Determined to make that A, she pulled herself together.

"You're right, Dan. There's nothing I can do about Nicole. I can only worry about what's on my plate right now. If I don't, it'll just make things worse."

"Exactly," Dan said.

Susie tried her best to nod blindly. It was hard for her to stop thinking of Nicole and wondering what had happened to her.

"Hey, some friends and I are getting together tomorrow night at The Grille. You want to come along?"

Susie smiled, "Sure."

"Great. We'll be there by 7 p.m."

"I'll see you then," he said as he left.

Susie was still half-focused on Nicole. It took her a minute to realize that Dan kind of asked her out. It wasn't clear or was it? She debated calling her sister, but decided against it. She predicted Karen would likely say something like, "It doesn't count unless you're alone."

Regardless, Susie was happy that she would have an opportunity to get to know Dan outside of the classroom and library. She would get to meet his friends and maybe she would have a chance to get to know him through them.

Susie walked home almost with a skip in her step. Her jacket felt a little warmer this evening and the only thing on her mind was redoing her budget to squeeze in dinner tomorrow. Going out was a rare treat for her and she wanted to feel comfortable about her expenses. She barged through her front door and immediately examined her budget calculations. Very quickly she came to the stark realization that she only had about two dollars to spare.

"Not even enough for a soda," she said, disappointed.

Susie pondered arriving there and not ordering, wondering just how awkward that would be. She debated whether Dan would pay for her or not, still unsure if this was a date or not. She knew of one way to guarantee paying for dinner: her credit card.

She gulped at this once unthinkable solution, but she argued with herself as to how using it tomorrow was justifiable. "I never do anything. Never. I never go anywhere. I never meet anybody. I never give myself a chance. I don't know when another chance like this will come my way again."

Still, she didn't feel settled about the issue.

"I will work extra hours to make this up," she promised herself. With that, she gave herself permission to use her credit card for dinner tomorrow.

Susie went to bed with her mind racing. She tried to repress the guilt in deciding to use her credit card. She felt like a failure for deciding to use it at all.

KNOCK! KNOCK!

Susie quickly got up and walked up to the door.

"Who is it?" she asked.

"Police – please, we need to speak to you."

Susie spied through the door's peephole and opened the door. "Yes?"

It was the same policeman who talked to her at the computer lab.

"Susie, right?" he asked.

"Yes?"

"We found your friend, Nicole."

"You did?! How wonderful! Is she okay?"

The policeman shook his head and didn't say anything at first.

"Oh... Oh... Oh, no... Oh no, oh no, oh no..." Susie responded, bringing on a cry, fearing the worst.

"I'm afraid she was found dead. We found her about an hour ago," the policeman said quietly. "I'm sorry."

"NICOLE! NO! NICOLE!" Susie screamed hysterically with tears pouring down her face.

Susie buried her face into the policeman's chest, bawling uncontrollably. She sobbed and sobbed, crying out for the loss of her dear friend.

"I'm sorry, miss. I'm sorry," the policeman said, patting her on the back softly.

Susie eventually calmed down a little.

The policeman continued, "I need to ask you a few questions."

Susie nodded her head.

"You told us that the last time you saw Nicole was when she showed up at the computer lab you work at about four weeks ago. Is that right?"

"Yeah... Yeah," she sniffed, "She came by, yes."

"That was the last anyone saw of her," the policeman noted.

Susie wanted to vomit. She began sobbing again, but tried to control herself this time. Several moments later, she was able to talk.

"She... She... She came by... We talked a bit... I stepped out to make a phone call. I was... I was..." she began crying harder again.

The policeman held her and patted her back in a vain effort to comfort her, saying, "It's okay. Take your time."

She took several deep breaths and continued, "...I went outside to call my sister. I was... I was gone for only a few minutes and when I came back into the lab she was gone."

"Do you have any idea where she went?" the policeman asked.

"No. She just left a note on the computer she was sitting at. All it said was that something had come up. No details, just that something came up..."

"We need your help to do your best to think of who it could have been."

"PHIL!" Susie yelled, suddenly remembering him. "It could've been Phil!"

"Phil? Phil who?" the policeman asked.

"I remember seeing this guy down the hall that night. His name is Phil, but I don't know his last name."

"Hmm, any chance that he's about five-foot eleven or so, long, bushy dark hair, lots of tattoos, and piercings?"

"Yes. How did you know?"

"We found his body early this morning, too. We suspect foul play."

Susie's knees buckled. The policeman caught her and helped her back up. She leaned against the door's frame, crying. The policeman looked away into the sky and then made a few notes, appearing to wish he was elsewhere but more uncomfortable at leaving her so distraught. After about ten minutes of Susie crying nonstop in the doorway while he awkwardly tried to console her, the policeman helped Susie back inside her home and sat her down on the couch. After a few minutes more, Susie had stopped crying. For the moment, she was too exhausted to cry.

"If you see or hear anything, please give me a call," the policeman said as he handed Susie his business card.

Susie dropped her eyes down at the business card – it represented the last remnant of Nicole's life.

"I'm sorry for your loss," the policeman added and then left her alone, closing the door behind him.

Staring forward into oblivion, she tried her best to piece together what went wrong and why she hadn't been there to save her friend. Hours went by and Susie had hardly moved a muscle. Wide awake, she sat upright on the couch in a catatonic state.

Finally, she looked at the clock. "3:43 a.m.," she said aloud.

She had school in a couple of hours. She wasn't sleepy, but she was completely exhausted. She resigned herself to just getting up and going to school. She put herself on automatic pilot – a state where she would basically function but was without any coherent thought or emotion. She was spent.

She arrived on campus before the sun rose. Sitting on a bench at the reflection pond and ignoring the mild cold of morning, she began to nod off a bit. The birds in nearby trees began to chirp, welcoming the new day. This caught her attention and she rubbed her face to wake herself up. The chirping made her feel a little comforted. She became aware of the peacefulness of dawn and the serenity it always bestowed on her. In her state of mind, there was no better time and place for her to be.

About half an hour before class, she walked to Professor Gomez's office. He was sitting at his desk reading a magazine and sipping a mug. She was too dazed to notice what kind of magazine he was reading or anything else about his office – other than it was dark and there were piles of papers and magazines strewn about everywhere.

"Hi, Professor."

He looked up, "Hello, Susie."

"I just found out a friend of mine passed away early this morning. I'd like to be excused from class if that's okay."

Professor Gomez straightened up and frowned sadly, "Certainly, certainly... Please take care of yourself. We'll be covering chapter eight today. The midterm is Friday after next."

"Thanks," Susie said listlessly.

She shuffled away, barely maintaining a measurable pace. She had never lost a friend before. She shuddered to think that she was just a few feet away from Nicole minutes before she had disappeared and been murdered.

Uncharacteristically, Susie didn't bother stopping and asking to be excused by her other professors, even though the thought occurred to her. She just went straight home. Without an ounce of energy left, Susie fell asleep on her couch.

She woke up much later. She noticed that it was dark outside her windows and realized that she had not eaten all day long. She headed straight to the kitchen. Susie inspected her pantry to figure out what she could make for dinner. Macaroni and cheese took the winning spot.

"Isn't there somewhere else I should be right now?" Susie asked herself as she started reaching for the box.

Then, she remembered that she was supposed to be out with Dan and his friends. She smacked her forehead. But, the mood wasn't right – and she wasn't sure she would have gone, even if she had remembered. She was still in a great deal of pain from the loss of Nicole.

Her phone rang. She walked over to it and looked at the caller ID. It was labeled "Unknown" and she didn't recognize the number.

Believing it could be more information about Nicole, she picked up the phone. "Hello?" she said quietly.

"Susie! It's Dan! Where are you?! We're all here at The Grille!" Dan shouted over the very loud background noise coming from The Grille.

"Dan?" Susie asked. "I didn't know you had my number."

"What?!" Dan yelled.

Susie was a bit annoyed at having to yell to carry a conversation.

"I didn't know you had my number!"

"You gave it to me a few weeks ago, remember?!"

Susie didn't remember, but she shrugged it off.

"You coming out with us tonight?!" Dan yelled.

"No! Something important came up!"

Susie felt a bit disrespectful towards Nicole in saying that, referring to her death as merely "something important".

"Are you okay?!" Dan yelled, somehow managing to put a tone of concern into his yelling.

"I'll be fine!" she yelled back.

All Susie wanted was to be done with the call. She had no intention of hanging out with Dan or his friends. She wanted to be left alone, even if it meant cutting any romantic progress out of the picture. Emptiness dominated her being.

"Hey, I'm coming over! You don't sound too great!"

"Please, don't!"

There was a pause and the background noise went away completely.

"Hello? Hello?" she asked.

"I'm still here. I just stepped outside," Dan said. "So, you okay?"

"Nicole... You know, that friend of mine?" Susie said with strong uneasiness.

"Yeah?"

"She's... She's...," Susie gulped. "They found her dead."

Susie began crying again but more quietly than before. Dan stayed on the line and didn't say anything. After several seconds, Susie stopped briefly.

"You... You still there?" she asked.

"Yeah. I'm very sorry, Susie. I know that you cared about her. She seemed like a great friend. I wish I could do more."

"Thanks."

"Just know that I'm just a phone call away if you want to talk about this or anything else, okay?"

"Okay," Susie replied with a sniff.

"Call any time, day or night," Dan offered.

"Okay,"

"Take care of yourself."

"Okay."

Dan hung up.

Susie slowly removed her phone from her ear and rested it on her knee. She leaned back, feeling very out of kilter. She debated even bothering to make macaroni and cheese now. Her hunger was the last thing on her mind.

Susie had no idea how she was going to recover from Nicole's passing. She wondered how she would be able to move on with her life, especially with the semester moving forward.

"How selfish of me," she said herself, rebuking herself for the idea of trying to move on already.

Guilt poured into her heart. She couldn't believe that she was focused on her own problems and not more about poor Nicole. She took a deep breath and sighed. Twenty minutes had passed since Dan called, but it seemed like twenty hours.

"I need to eat something, but I don't feel like cooking. I can't afford takeout though," she thought.

KNOCK! KNOCK!

Susie slowly got up and looked through the peephole. It was a pizza delivery man. She opened the door.

"I have a pizza for Susie," the deliveryman said.

"I didn't order a pizza."

"No, uh... someone named, uh...," the deliveryman fumbled through some scraps of paper and read, "Dan ordered it for you. It's paid for, including the tip. That note on it is from him."

Susie grabbed the note. It read:

I know this isn't much but I wanted to do something to make a life a little bit easier for you tonight. —Dan

Susie smiled weakly, finding some happiness at this. Dan couldn't have done anything more thoughtful and tactful.

Chapter 12 – Paradox

The mysterious deaths of Nicole and Phil plastered the local news. This made it impossible for Susie to stop thinking about it. However, with Dan's help, Susie was able to make it through these distractions and prepare for Professor Gomez's midterm exam. She tried her best to continue writing down anything and everything that Professor Gomez had to say.

"The exam is tomorrow," Professor Gomez said with a toothy smile.

His notoriety for inflicting pain on his students and enjoying it had proven to be true so far, although Susie suspected that, somehow, he meant well.

Susie turned towards Dan to see how he was reacting to Professor Gomez's reminder of the test. To her surprise, Dan was doodling on a piece of scrap paper. She tried her best to make out what he was doodling: a picture of what looked like a horn and he had the words *Paradox of Gabriel's Horn* at the top of it. Dan was usually very attentive, but he seemed pretty detached today.

"If you've studied hard, you will do well. Before I break class, I'd like to share with you a math puzzle. You know how I do enjoy them."

Professor Gomez walked to the white board, drew a horn on it, and wrote *Paradox of Gabriel's Horn* above the picture. Susie was mystified at the coincidence. She looked back at Dan's desk, but he had already covered his doodle with a blank piece of paper. He was now paying attention, looking calm and interested.

The professor talked to the class about this math puzzle, but Susie didn't hear a word. She was busy being astounded, first, that Dan effectively predicted what the professor was going to talk about and, second, that Dan had zero reaction to correctly predicting it. She stared at the board aimlessly, hearing nothing until Professor Gomez dismissed the class.

"So, I'll see everyone tomorrow. I hope you enjoyed this puzzle," Professor Gomez said.

People started to leave the classroom. Dan collected his things, stood up, and waited for Susie. She just stared at him incredulously.

"What?" Dan asked.

"I saw your doodle. You were writing about that math puzzle before Professor Gomez even mentioned it."

Dan raised his eyebrows, paused a split second, and then said casually, "Oh, I heard he shows that puzzle every semester before the midterm. So, I looked it up."

"Oh."

She felt a bit foolish, realizing it was not such a big mystery after all and actually made perfect sense. Dan was always prepared and always appeared to know the answer; of course he would look it up if he had heard about the puzzle. She collected her things and left the room with him.

"The funeral is tonight?" Dan asked Susie, referring to Nicole's funeral.

"Yeah."

They continued walking in silence. Susie came to a slow stop.

"What?" Dan asked.

"I committed myself to writing down absolutely everything Professor Gomez says and I didn't do it with that math trick thing he did at the end."

"You can copy my notes after I write them," Dan said.

"Well, I have to write things down the way I understand it. Also, you have horrible handwriting," she smiled.

It frustrated her to have to leave Dan just because she missed some notes, but she knew that if she was to learn anything, it had to be done in real time. Straight copying from someone else's notes hardly made any impact compared to hearing it explained and taking notes from that. Right now, she wanted to make sure she was absolutely prepared for the midterm and didn't want to risk that the puzzle would be on it. She wanted to do everything she could to get an A in the class.

"I'll catch up with you later," she told Dan.

Susie immediately started marching in the direction of Professor Gomez's office.

"Call me if you need anything!" Dan yelled to her.

"I will!" she yelled back.

As she neared the office, she could see that Professor Gomez's door was cracked open. Susie lightly knocked on his door.

"Come in," he said.

Susie walked into his office. It was messy – so messy that Susie almost felt prompted to start cleaning the area. Several empty soda cans littered his desk. Shelves were filled with various books and binders. The room was dim – just a single lamp kept it from being in complete darkness – but she could make out some posters on the walls with odd titles like *Put the Fun into Transcendental Numbers* and *Be Definite About Your Integration*.

Professor Gomez was flipping through one of the many mathematics magazines that were scattered about his office. "Oh, Susie, please come in. How are you?"

"I'm doing okay, thanks."

"What's on your mind?"

"Well, I'm a little embarrassed, but I really spaced out during your last part of your lecture – during that math puzzle."

"Oh, the *Paradox of Gabriel's Horn?*"

"Yeah, that one."

"Well, you don't have to worry about that. It won't be on the midterm."

"Oh. I heard that you use that one a lot so I just wanted to make sure I was respectful of your time."

Professor Gomez curled his face, "Hmm, it's been a few years since I've put it in my lecture. I just enjoy math puzzles and tricks. I was just trying to break the ice in the room."

"Really?" Susie asked, surprised.

He bobbed his head a little.

"Oh. I'm sorry," Susie said.

"Don't apologize! I'm tickled that you cared!"

"Oh, well… thanks. I gotta go," she answered with a vague smile.

"Okay, take care!" Professor Gomez said.

Susie left his office, bewildered as to how Dan knew the puzzle would be in the lecture. She tried to give him the benefit of the doubt that somehow he had heard about it from a student who had Gomez years ago. Susie shook her head, already exhausted from the notion of attending Nicole's funeral later. She didn't want to deal with this right now, too. She was confused and tired of thinking.

Later that evening, Nicole's funeral was held. Only about twenty people showed up for the private service – mostly family members. It pained Susie to know that she was probably Nicole's only friend at school. She cried for Nicole's loneliness, and because others didn't have the chance to know Nicole the way she knew her.

Susie took the bus home; her car, Old Faithful, her "trusty" car, hadn't been so trusty these past few days. She got off the bus and began walking the couple of blocks from the bus stop to her home. As she got closer to her home, she saw a policeman – holding a shiny metallic coffee thermos – at her doorstep. This policeman was blond and thinner than the one she talked to earlier.

"What do the police want now?" she asked herself.

BANG! BANG! BANG!

Gunshots rang out from down the street. Screams echoed through the neighborhood. A man ran out from an alley. Susie looked at the policeman waiting at her door. He glanced from Susie to the man down the street – back and forth, appearing conflicted. After a brief pause, he gave chase to the man running from the shooting.

Susie stood there petrified for a couple of minutes before she finished walking home. She locked her apartment's door and sank down to the floor, leaning against the door. There had never been any gunshots in her neighborhood before. She was shaken up. She didn't feel safe.

As her nerves settled, the memories of Nicole and the violence that must have surrounded her death invaded her thoughts. Thinking about Professor Gomez's midterm was the last thing she wanted to do. She knew she needed to study, but, even when she forced herself to open her notes to do so, she was unable to focus. She scolded herself for inability to concentrate, but apathy filled her every time she tried to study.

That night and the following day seemed to pass by in an instant. Susie arrived at class for her midterm and struggled through its content. All of it looked so familiar because of Dan's help, but she had extreme difficulty piecing the information together. On the verge of breaking down at moments, Susie found ways to stave off actually doing so.

"Time's up," Professor Gomez announced at the end of the hour. "Please hand in your tests."

Susie looked down at her test. She had barely made any progress on the last question, much less had the time to double-check her work. Dan had already gotten up from his desk and was handing his test in to the professor. Susie reluctantly got up.

"How did you do?" Dan asked her as they left the classroom.

"Oh, I don't know. What about you?"

"I think I did okay."

They continued walking, not saying anything for a minute.

"Any plans for the weekend?" Dan asked.

"No."

"Well, we're all getting together again tomorrow, if you want to come along."

Susie was glad for the invitation. She felt like she needed a mental break from life. The timing couldn't have been better.

"You know, I'd love to. I need a break."

Dan smiled at her warmly. In spite of all the recent troubles, Susie felt very close to Dan and was finally comfortable around him. She was aware of his foibles, but she reasoned that everyone had some. Getting to know him better in a social setting would be nice.

The next day, Susie spent nearly an hour debating what she should wear that night at The Grille. Early March welcomed a warm up in the weather, so she was happy to ditch her jacket. She perused her closet, disappointed in what it had to offer.

"Plain jeans... Plain blouses... Plain, plain, plain... Are all of my clothes just for school? Don't I have anything nice to wear?" she asked herself out loud in frustration.

At the same time, she debated exactly how she should dress. She wasn't sure what other women wear at this place. Would Dan expect her to wear something different than what she wore at school? Should she go out and buy something for the occasion? She wondered what Dan would be wearing. She covered her face with her hands and pondered what she should do. She stood in front of her closet feeling defeated.

"I need new clothes... Just one new outfit."

She looked at her purse sitting on her bed – knowing that her credit card was the only way she could afford a new outfit.

"It's not the end of the world," she said with a smirk.

She promptly snatched her purse, marched out of her home, and caught the first bus to the shopping mall. Several hours later, she was back at home with her new outfit – designer jeans, designer blouse, and her first new pair of shoes in nearly a year.

"I hope I don't need pens for another ten years."

An hour later, Susie caught a bus and went to The Grille. She walked inside and scanned the place, trying to spot Dan. There were so many people there; she wasn't sure where to even begin looking for him. There were two bar areas in The Grille and both were crammed with people waving money, trying to get a drink. High tables took up some of the area between the bars and booths lined the back wall, but most people stood. Music blared from overhead speakers. There was a nearby area filled with guitars and a drum kit; it appeared that a live band would be taking the stage later. Susie tried to recall when she had last been in such a dynamic social setting.

Finally, on the far side of the place, she saw Dan waving at her. She started making her way towards him. There were so many people that moving through the place was literally a push-and-shove, step-by-step process.

"Sorry!" a random guy apologized to Susie when he accidentally bumped into her as she squeezed by.

More and more people bumped into her, most not bothering to say anything. The smell of sour beer saturated the air and people were yelling at each other even at close range to hear one another. Susie felt out of her element and she wasn't sure if she wanted to stay long.

She finally made her way through the crowd and saw Dan at a big booth with three men and three women. As she walked up to the table, everyone slid over to make room for her. She was relieved it was a bit quieter there, in the corner booth.

"Everyone, this is my friend Susie," said Dan.

Everyone waved and said "hi" to her, almost in unison.

"Hi, everyone," Susie responded shyly with a small wave of her hand.

"This is Brad and his wife Sarah. This is another Brad – we call him Brad Two – and his girlfriend Haley…," Dan started.

"I'm older than Brad One, by the way," Brad Two interrupted.

"I'm Brad One because I'm better looking…," Brad One shot back.

"…but Brad Two is smarter," Brad Two retorted.

"I'm sorry for my husband's behavior, Susie," Sarah said as she playfully elbowed Brad One. "I think we're all happy there isn't a Brad Three."

"Here, here!" several of them at the table said together, raising their glasses in a toast.

"Your boyfriend isn't a Brad, right?" Sarah asked.

"God, say it's not so…," Brad Two hooted dramatically.

"I don't have a boyfriend," Susie said.

"Oh… Problem solved then," Sarah said.

"Anyway…," Dan interjected and then introduced the last two people, "…this is Mike and his girlfriend Amy."

Susie waved back. She was doing her best to remember everyone.

"Brad One, Sarah, Brad Two, Haley, Mike, and Amy," she said to herself.

"Don't forget Dan, sweetie," Haley said.

"Huh?" Susie asked.

"I can see your lips moving. You're trying to remember everyone's names, right?" Haley asked with a narrow, but inviting smile.

"Who can forget Dan?" Susie said.

"Here, here!" they all cheered and held up their glasses.

They were quite the merry bunch. What caught Susie's attention the most was that everyone here – with the exception of her and Dan – was in a serious relationship. She had the preconceived notion that she would be joining a group of guys like Dan – or some variant thereof. This was quite a relief. Also, clearly, Dan didn't have a girlfriend or else she would be here.

She wondered what Karen would think of this. She imagined Karen saying something like, "Don't you think it's kind of strange that Dan is pairing you up with him? Think about it, lil' sis: you and Dan are the only ones without someone."

Still, Susie didn't know how to interpret this situation: odd or not, good or bad. She let go of over-analyzing the situation and settled on having some fun for a change – or, at least, giving herself a chance to have fun. For the rest of the evening and into the night, Susie focused on having a great time with Dan and his friends. Most of their conversation surprised her by actually being intellectually stimulating, ranging from politics to physics.

"A physics major?" Amy asked at one point.

"Yes, physics," Susie replied.

"I LOVE physics!"

"Really?"

"Yeah! So, I have to ask you your opinion on something, nerd-to-nerd…"

Susie smiled, "Okay?"

"Don't you think it's odd that quantum physics keeps adding new particles and particle attributes whenever they find a problem with contemporary theories? I mean, it started with an electron, just one equation and one variable. Then they found a problem with other experiments and they had to come up with another equation and another particle, the proton. Then more problems and they added more equations and the neutron, quark, et cetera, et cetera. Charge, charm, flavor, spin, color... Come on, what's next: mood? Anything to save their precious, tenuous theories. All of it is garbage, I think. It's just a bunch of clueless people who keep adding a new equation with a new fictitious particle or attribute so all of their other garbage still works," Amy professed.

Everyone else at the table looked at Amy seriously as if they had easily understood everything Amy said. They all turned towards Susie and waited for her reply. Susie was not quite sure what to say. It wasn't at all the sort of conversation starter she had envisioned.

"I love physics and I have more to learn, but if I'm getting what you're saying, then I'd guess you'd argue that there's a reason why we can't explain gravity, right? Because of, for example, its monopole nature?"

"Great response! Oh, Dan, she's a keeper," she said to him with a wink.

Dan just smiled back.

Luckily, Susie had read about the problems with gravity and physics in an article just last week.

"You're my new physics friend," Amy declared to Susie.

Susie laughed. At that moment, Susie looked at the great group around her and felt like it was her new home, a second family. Her face beamed from the acceptance of Dan and his friends. Finally, she had found people she could enjoy as well as embrace socially and intellectually.

"How long have you known Dan?" Susie asked.

"Me? Only for about three or four weeks," Amy answered.

"That's not very long…," Susie noted.

"Yeah. I think all of us here only met Dan within the past month or two, but it's easy to see that Dan's a great guy. We laugh all the time with him. He's always organized, he knows people, and he's hilarious. He's quite irresistible."

"He is," Susie enthusiastically agreed.

Chapter 13 – Math Trick

On the Monday after the midterm, Susie nervously sat in Professor Gomez's classroom, waiting for him to enter. With the previous exam, he hadn't wasted time in getting around to grading, so she expected her graded midterm today. Dan, who normally sat next to her, hadn't shown up yet. Susie bit a nail, wishing she could relieve some anticipation by talking to Dan.

Professor Gomez entered the room, holding a large stack of papers under his arm. She knew they were the tests. She couldn't look.

Dan walked in with a spring in his step. He made his way to his seat.

"Hey," he greeted Susie.

"Hi."

"You okay?" Dan asked her.

"No, not at all. I don't think I did that well."

"You did fine. You studied hard and you know the material."

"I've been pretty distracted lately," Susie said, biting her lip.

"Yeah… I'm sorry."

Dan looked down at the floor, appearing unsure as to what he should say.

Finally, he said, "I wasn't thinking. I guess I stuck my foot in my mouth."

"Oh, it's okay, Dan. You're a good, positive influence."

Susie turned her attention to Professor Gomez, who stood at the front of the room and was flipping through the exams.

"I have your tests graded," he said with some giddiness.

The room let out a collective groan. Even though most people believed he was sadistic, Susie believed that he just enjoyed math and enjoyed helping them learn. Grades didn't matter to him – hard tests were just his way of motivating students in her opinion.

"Just remember, everyone, that this is your midterm. It's a fourth of your grade."

He began slapping them down on the students' desks. He passed by Susie who, at this point, had her eyes closed. She was deathly afraid of her grade.

SLAP!

She opened her eyes to find her exam on her desk.

It had a C- as its grade. She frowned at it with extreme disappointment. She couldn't even remember the last time she had done this badly on any test she had ever taken. She silently panicked a bit, wondering how she could salvage her semester. Susie looked up at Dan and pointed to her grade with her pencil. Dan sighed and shook his head.

"Some," Professor Gomez began and then slapped a graded test on Dan's desk, "did better than others."

Susie craned her head up a bit to spy on Dan's score. She saw that his grade was an A. Susie looked at Dan with a slight smile of admiration. Dan, looking at Susie, simply shrugged his shoulders modestly. Professor Gomez continued giving back the tests as he made random comments. The professor, as quirky as ever, suddenly began an off-topic story, "I once had a puppy when I was a child. I loved that little dog…"

Susie blocked it out. Wanting to cry, she tried her best to think of things that would distract her enough to survive the remaining forty-seven minutes of class. She saw Dan glance at her and turn his test over to cover his grade.

Professor Gomez finished passing out the tests and headed to the front of the classroom.

"…and that's why puppies shouldn't play with kittens," the professor finished.

The professor waited for a reaction from his class, but no one seemed to know how to react to the story. Susie didn't know if it was supposed to be a joke, a fable, or what – but she really hadn't been paying attention. Other than the rustle of test papers, there was complete silence.

"Oh, well, maybe we'll go over the exam," Professor Gomez said.

For the remainder of the class time, Susie beat herself up over every mistake she had made.

"I knew that," she whispered about a question she should have got correct. "I would have gotten five more points for that one."

By the end of the class, Susie saw how all her little mistakes had added up and knew she had to accept her grade for what it was. She resolved to do better next time, no matter what.

"Okay, I guess we can leave a little early. I'll see you on Wednesday," Professor Gomez said as he looked at his watch.

Class broke and students quickly exited the room. However, Susie remained at her desk, feeling dejected and a bit hopeless. Dan stayed seated as well, appearing to intend to not move until Susie did as well.

Susie broke the ice, "An A? Why am I not surprised?"

"I was lucky," Dan replied, brushing it off.

Susie stood up, picked up her backpack, and slung it over her shoulder.

"Lucky? Luck couldn't have saved anyone on that test."

Dan collected his things as well. He said in an encouraging tone, "Susie, come on. I know you could have done better. You knew the material."

"I got caught up... I'm still upset over Nicole."

"I know. I was pulling for you. You worked so hard."

Professor Gomez interrupted, "Oh, Dan? I need to see you in my office if you don't mind."

Dan responded, "Sure, Professor Gomez."

Susie had zoned off into another world. She was tormenting herself by retracing her every move that could have caused her to make so many mistakes.

"Well, I've got to meet with the professor, Susie... Susie?" Dan asked, waving his hand in front of her face.

She snapped out of it. "Huh? Oh, um, can we catch up later and study? I still have two more grades to work on if I'm to pull out an A for a final grade."

"Sure," Dan said with a comforting pat on her shoulder.

Susie tried to smile at Dan. It was times like this that made Susie feel like Dan was truly on her side. Even at her worst moments, Dan was still Dan.

The two of them went their separate ways.

*   *   *

Dan headed to Professor Gomez's office. He got to the half-opened door and tapped lightly on it.

"Come in," Professor Gomez said.

Dan entered and patiently stood in front of the professor's desk. Professor Gomez sat at his desk reading a magazine. He looked up and saw that it was Dan.

"Oh, Dan, please sit," he told him, putting down the magazine while pointing to a chair on the other side of the desk.

Dan sat down and looked around the office some more as Professor Gomez opened a notebook and flipped through its pages.

"By the way, great job on that test," he told Dan.

"Oh. Thanks," Dan said.

The professor's eyes lit up a little, appearing to find what he was looking for.

"So, something a bit strange." He tapped the open page in his notebook and looked up at Dan, "It seems that you're not registered in my class."

Dan raised an eyebrow, "Oh?"

"No. I did some digging and it turns out your student number isn't even in the university's system."

Dan cocked his head in surprise. He wasn't sure what to say about this. After all, he had been in the class since the beginning of the semester and in many classes outside of Calculus.

"Really? I... I don't know what to think or say," he answered.

Just then, Dan received a text. He quickly read it and averted his eyes in thought.

"It could be a typo," Professor Gomez conceded. "A pretty bad one. I mean, you've been an excellent student all semester and..."

Dan stood up unexpectedly and interrupted, "I want to share with you a math trick."

Professor Gomez jolted his head back slightly in surprise. "A math trick?" he asked Dan, sounding incredulous.

Dan smiled, "Yes."

The professor put his hands across his chest and interlaced his fingers together. "Okay, but isn't this a little off topic?" he asked.

"It isn't," Dan said in monotone. "Trust me."

Professor Gomez chuckled a little. "Okay…," the professor said, captivated.

"Think of a number between 1 and 100,000," Dan asked.

Professor Gomez gave Dan a look of doubt and asked, "This isn't one of those guessing games where you're going to ask me to do a bunch of adding and subtracting and whatnot, right? Trust me, I know ALL of them," the professor said with a roll of his eyes.

"Humor me," Dan implored.

The professor closed his eyes even though Dan didn't ask him to do so. "Hehe, okay… Sure…," the professor smiled.

A split second passed.

"Your number is 32,147," Dan said outright.

Professor Gomez opened his eyes with pure shock enveloping his face. His mouth opened as if he wanted to say something, but no sound came out.

"Think of another one," Dan asked confidently.

Professor Gomez shook his head a little, as if to clear his mind and regain a sense of reality. He paused.

"Okay, you chose the same number again. Come on. Try something different. This time, choose any number you want. ANY number."

Professor Gomez, staring at Dan, sat back in his chair. He squeezed his eyes shut and sucked in his lips.

"Professor?" Dan asked with a hint of impatience, "Another number, please."

The professor opened his eyes, indicating to Dan that he had thought of a number.

Dan walked to a nearby whiteboard and wrote the number as he said it, "One hundred eighty two trillion, three hundred ninety one million, and five."

Professor Gomez's mouth opened and closed repeatedly without sound. He cleared his throat and tried to speak.

"How... How can... How are you doing this?" he asked, his mouth wobbling.

Dan walked up to the desk, planted both of his hands on it, and looked the professor directly in his eyes. "Listen carefully to what I'm about to say because after I say it, you will never see or hear from me ever again...," he began.

Professor Gomez gripped his chair's armrests tightly, breaking a sweat. Dan could almost see his heart beating through his shirt.

Dan continued, "You are very ill. You have a small, cancerous growth on the right frontal lobe of your brain. You have exactly twenty-two days to do something about it or else you will die. You must live. You are important."

"Wha... How... What?" Professor Gomez asked incoherently.

Dan ignored the professor. He simply walked out of his office.

"See a doctor. NOW," Dan commanded as he departed, closing the door behind him.

Chapter 14 – Unseen Conflict

Susie walked across the grounds of the university campus, her backpack still resting over her shoulder. It was a bit warm outside and mostly cloudy. The university grounds were canvassed with students making their way to class, but many of them were lounging about enjoying the nice weather and each other's company. The traffic from the surrounding city was drowned out by the masses of students socializing with each other.

Having just departed Professor Gomez's class, Susie was still dealing with the horror of her midterm results. But, she enjoyed the beautiful weather and seeing everyone around her – the ordinary background noises soothed her. The tall buildings of the city that lined most of the campus's perimeter comforted her with their familiarity.

She walked by a large bike rack next to a wall coated with random fliers. Between the wall of fliers and the bike rack, she noticed a UNICEF donation jar hanging on a tree. She spontaneously turned and walked to the jar, fumbling through her purse to find some change. In spite of her poor grade, she felt grateful that she could help others who were truly in more need than she was.

She made a mental note of the amount of the coins she found, put the change in the jar, and turned to walk back to her original path.

She ran into Dan as she turned around.

"WHOA!" Susie half-yelled.

"Hey, sorry," Dan apologized. "Didn't mean to sneak up on you."

"Oh, you didn't... What did Professor Gomez want?"

"Meh, he just had something on his mind... Kind of a long story."

Susie was a little puzzled by Dan's vague answer, but she decided that she wouldn't pry.

"Oh, ok," she said.

Dan noticed the UNICEF jar on the tree. "Great organization. They help millions of children," he said.

He pulled out his wallet and put two ten-dollar bills in the jar without a hint of hesitation. As he did this, the wallet opened wide enough so that Susie could tell that was all of the money in his wallet. The wallet, in fact, looked barely used.

Susie was pleasantly shocked and couldn't help saying, "Wow! Twenty dollars? I feel like a cheapskate."

Dan appeared caught off guard. He began to apologize, "Oh, I'm sorry. I didn't mean to..."

"Oh, stop," she interrupted. "It's very kind of you to give."

"Thanks," Dan said, blushing a little. "I wish I could do more, but I'm on a student's budget. You know how it is."

"Trust me, I know about that. That's why you're great."

The conversation hit a break that felt uncomfortable to Susie. She knew it wouldn't be if she didn't want even more of Dan's time. He made her feel better just by being around her.

"So…," Susie said and paused, trying to think of something to keep Dan around. "Is Mr. A+ hungry? Let's get a bite," she suggested.

Susie suddenly recognized that she didn't spend any time at all figuring out whether she could afford this impromptu meal. She wasn't sure that she had extra money, much less how much. It took her only a second to decide that using the credit card was perfectly fine.

"Heh, it was just an A," Dan said. He looked at his watch, "And I am hungry, but I have to go."

Abruptly, Dan walked away.

Susie was dumbfounded. Offering no explanation and barely any warning, Dan's departure only led Susie to believe that it was something she did or said – maybe he really just didn't want to be around her.

She thought fast, wanting to say something before Dan got away. "Call me!" she yelled at him.

"I will!" Dan yelled back, spinning around briefly to flash an affectionate smile.

Dan turned away and went immediately into deep thought. He walked and walked – unconcerned with his surroundings. He left the campus and stepped into the surrounding city.

Hours went by. The sun began to set and he was downtown during rush hour. Both the sidewalks and the streets were crowded with people and cars, funneled between buildings and advertisements. Honking, talking on cell phones, and construction noises filled the air – it was near-deafening, but Dan hardly noticed. He didn't stop to talk to anyone, look at any street signs, or even at traffic signals. He just kept walking unabated.

Nighttime fell and city lights glowed everywhere the eye could see. On a sparsely populated sidewalk, Dan's pace continued as it had for hours – almost like a mindless drone. He came across a homeless man holding a sign that read, *OUT OF LUCK. PLEASE HELP. GOD BLESS.* Dan had no money, but he noticed that the man was barefoot. He looked down towards his feet at his own sandals.

"You're about a size ten, I think," Dan said.

He removed his sandals and gave them to the homeless man.

"Thank you. Thank you, sir," the homeless man said.

"No problem."

Dan continued walking in his bare feet. He pulled out his mobile phone and typed, *No incidents. Need to…*

Before he could finish his text, he stopped dead in his tracks under a streetlight. His jaw dropped and he took in a deep but strained breath. His eyes widened and his pupils dilated. He turned and looked down the alley next to him.

A distant light in the alley created a silhouette of a man walking towards Dan. A flame appeared and a cigarette was lit. The man became close enough that the streetlight's glow allowed Dan to see the man's ominous black leather jacket, spiky mohawk, and expressionless face.

"Spike," Dan greeted flatly.

"Dan," Spike said.

Dan tilted his neck side to side, loosening it. Dan then immediately began walking into the alley towards Spike, who stopped and waited for Dan to approach. Dan narrowed his eyes and clenched his fists. His heartbeat picked up and adrenaline shot through his veins. Dan finally stopped about twenty feet away from Spike.

"*You* will not interrupt," Dan said sternly.

Spike flicked his cigarette away, grinned, and said, "Heh… Save your breath for dyin'."

Both Dan and Spike charged each other. Spike opened with a swing of his right fist. Dan ducked and countered with a swift kick to Spike's face, knocking Spike backwards but not off his feet. Spike grunted and grabbed his face – his nose was bleeding a little.

He charged Dan and tackled him to the ground, straddled him, and held him down with his weight. Spike swung a hard right elbow into the right side of Dan's face and followed with a left punch to Dan's jaw. Spike pulled his right fist back and threw it towards Dan, but Dan parried his punch and grabbed Spike's arm. He then yanked Spike's arm downward and moved upward into a hard head-butt on the side of Spike's face, stunning him for a moment.

Dan pushed Spike to the side and off of him. Dan scrambled to his feet as Spike lurched toward him again. Spike suddenly stopped short, panting. He looked towards a pile of garbage bags nearby; Dan looked in the exact same location, knowing – and certain that Spike also knew – what was underneath those garbage bags. Spike was closer to the bags and Dan knew that Spike would get to them first. Spike narrowed his eyes and gave Dan a bloody smile, exultant in his advantage.

Spike ran to the garbage bags while Dan ran in the opposite direction to a nearby dumpster. Spike reached between the garbage bags and, without any effort in searching, pulled out a crowbar. Dan, at the dumpster, quickly pulled out an old mop. Spike sneered and then charged Dan.

Spike swung the crowbar at Dan's head several times, narrowly missing each time. Dan was finally forced to block the crowbar with the mop, only to have it broken in half. Spike swung low and hit Dan in the lower leg with the crowbar. Dan dropped what was left of his mop and rolled to the ground away from Spike.

"Ahhhh!" Dan screamed, grabbing his leg in agony.

Spike strutted slowly towards Dan in a show of dominance, readying the crowbar again.

Dan's eyes lost focus for a second. He glanced to one side and saw a rat nearby. He reached for it, softly grabbed it, and looked in its eyes as if to tell it something. He then threw it at Spike. With his free hand, Spike batted the rat down from the air. The rat rushed at Spike and incessantly began attacking his leg. Spike tried to kick it, but it quickly hooked itself on his pant leg and bit down.

"Argh!" Spike yelled and he whacked the rat off of him with the crowbar.

Taking advantage of the distraction, Dan quickly lunged at Spike and clutched the crowbar. Dan tried to pull it from Spike's firm grasp, causing the crowbar to fly out of the hands of both of them and out of their reach.

Spike immediately pounded a hard left uppercut into Dan's jaw. Dan stumbled backwards and Spike quickly side-kicked him in the stomach, knocking Dan against the alley's wall and dropping him to his knees. Spike jumped on Dan and ruthlessly pummeled him until Dan was motionlessness – not capable of even reflexively trying to defend himself.

Dan watched dimly as Spike pulled out a switchblade and brandished it for a moment, grinning maniacally at Dan.

"Hey!" two passers-by yelled and began to run towards Spike. "What's going on down there?!"

Spike paused for an instant, eyes unfocused, and then hurriedly retreated in the opposite direction.

The passers-by reached Dan. "Are you okay?" one asked.

Dan was still slumped against the alley's wall and he knew he had a badly bloodied face, but he could keep his eyes slightly open and his ragged breathing was steady. He knew he looked worse than he felt, but only if he received help soon.

Dan wiggled his head slightly in response. He listened as one of them called the police and knew that he was out of *Their* grasp for now. Dan closed his eyes, grateful for his safety.

Late that same evening, Susie was cooking vegetables on the stove. Music played softly in the background. The phone rang in the living room. She quickly moved to her stereo, turned the sound down, walked into the living room, and picked up the phone.

"Hello?" Susie answered.

"Is this Susie?" a woman asked.

"It is. Who is this?"

"Susie, this is Nurse Miller at East General Hospital. We have a patient here you may know."

"Oh? Who?" Susie asked.

"There wasn't any ID on him, so we're not sure of his name. You were the only phone number that he had on him. He's in his mid- to late-twenties with short dark hair, about six feet tall..."

"Dan?" Susie interrupted.

Susie didn't know anyone else who could fit this description. Something told her it had to be Dan.

Nurse Miller paused a second.

"Well, we don't know his name, but, to be sure, I suggest you come by, if you can," Nurse Miller said.

Susie was immediately overcome with anxiety. The recent death of Nicole had already shaken her terribly, and she believed she could not handle the loss of another friend – especially Dan. She prepared herself for the worst.

"I'll... I'll be right there," she said.

She hung up the phone and ran over to her stove. She turned off the burner, leaving her food as-is, then grabbed her purse and headed out her front door. In front of her apartment, Old Faithful waited quietly for its next chore.

Susie looked at her car and pleaded, "Come on, Old Faithful. Come through for me this time. I really need you to start."

She got in her car, inserted the key into the ignition, and kissed the steering wheel. She turned the key and Old Faithful rumbled erratically, its engine having difficulty turning over.

"Please, please… PLEASE!" Susie begged.

The engine roared to a start and Susie let go of some of her tension. She put the car into gear and drove away. The hospital was only a ten-minute drive away, but Susie felt motivated to speed – something she absolutely never did. She decided against it simply because she didn't want to be delayed by a speeding ticket. Even so, she had a few close calls with red lights along the way.

Susie arrived at the hospital and looked for a place to park. All of the spots near the entrance were taken. She drove along a few rows, feverishly searching for an empty space without any luck. She ended up finding a space on the outer edge of the lot.

"I wasted ten minutes just looking for a space," she thought as she parked.

Now that she had actually arrived, she dreaded going inside and confirming her fears. She cried for a minute out of anxiety and grief. She was afraid that she would lose Dan like she lost Nicole.

"I need to pull myself together," she told herself out loud. "Dan will be fine."

She hastily wiped her eyes, got out of Old Faithful, and ran to the hospital entrance. As she walked through the front doors, Susie realized that she had no idea how to find Dan.

"What is his last name?" she asked herself.

Susie tried her hardest to remember, but she could not recall it.

"Can I help you?" a woman at the nearby information kiosk asked.

Susie turned towards her. "Huh?" she asked desperately.

"Do you need help, dear?"

"I believe a friend of mine is here, but... but I'm having a hard time remembering his last name."

"Oh?" the woman asked.

"Yeah, but I know that... Uh... Uh...," Susie tried her best to think.

"What doctor is he with?"

"He's with a nurse...um, Nurse Miller? I think...,"

"Okay, let me see what I can do," the woman replied.

She typed a few things into her computer.

"Oh, here we go," she said. "There's only one Nurse Miller on duty tonight and she can be found in A-134. That's down the hall on the right here."

"Thanks!" Susie said and rushed down the hall.

She came up to a nurses' station labeled *A-134*. No one was there. She looked around, starting to panic and wanting to yell out.

"Can I help you?" a voice from behind her asked.

Susie turned and saw a nurse with a nametag that said *Miller* and stepped towards her.

"Nurse Miller?" Susie asked.

"You must be Susie," Nurse Miller responded.

"Yes!"

"Come with me."

They walked down the hallway. Nurse Miller seemed to take her time. This only made Susie more anxious – she hoped that the patient wasn't Dan. They finally got to a room and Nurse Miller paused outside the door.

"I warn you, he's in pretty bad shape. He was beaten and found in an alley," she whispered.

"Oh my God," Susie replied with a cracked whisper.

Nurse Miller opened the door slowly and quietly. They entered the room and she saw Dan lying in bed, his face covered with small bandages. Susie gasped, overcome with emotion.

"Dan!" Susie yelled out, not able to hold back.

She ran over to Dan and grasped his hand.

He opened his eyes slightly, but didn't say anything before he closed his eyes again.

"Careful. He needs rest badly," Nurse Miller warned.

Susie was nearly hysterical at seeing Dan's terrible condition. She looked at the bandages on his head, the bruises on his body, and the swollen areas of his face. He looked completely rung out.

"Oh, Dan," Susie whispered, barely audible.

She was completely choked up, making it hard for her to breathe much less talk. First, there was the death of Nicole, and now there was this; it was simply too much for her. Still, she was relieved and thankful that Dan was alive and in good hands.

Nurse Miller gave her a few moments more before asking her, "Do you know any of his family? How we can contact them?"

Susie turned to Nurse Miller and tried to process the question for a brief moment, still distracted by her emotions. "Uh... Well... Um... No... No, I don't," she replied.

"All we found on him was an empty wallet, a cell phone, and a piece of paper with your name and number on it. His cell phone is password locked, so the only thing we had to go on was your number," said Nurse Miller. She shrugged, "It was the best detective work we could do."

To Susie, the lack of sympathy from Nurse Miller was strangely comforting; not being too concerned about Dan must mean that he would be okay.

"That's fine. I'm glad you called me," Susie responded quietly.

"I'll leave you two alone," Nurse Miller said.

Nurse Miller left the room and only returned to check Dan's vitals over the next several hours. Many hours passed by with Susie faithfully sitting next to Dan's bed.

More hours passed until it was late into the night. Susie's hair was a mess and she had dark rings under her eyes. She put her head in her hands with exhaustion. It had been a very rough couple of weeks for her.

Unexpectedly, Dan softly spoke, "Hey, you. I didn't hear you knock."

Overloaded with excitement, Susie squealed, "Dan!"

She tried to hug him.

"Ow, ow, ow... Okay, that hurts...," he said through gritted teeth, obviously trying to hold back his newly discovered pain.

Susie stopped and stepped back.

"I'm so sorry. I was just so happy to see you awake. I...," she started.

Dan interrupted with a kind smile, "Hey, no worries."

"What... What happened, Dan?"

Dan's eyes rolled a little.

"I guess someone out there doesn't like me," he gulped.

"Do you remember anything?" Susie asked.

She was mad at whoever did this to Dan and was astounded that Dan didn't seem to share her anger. He seemed indifferent, almost like it never happened at all. He wasn't worked up in the slightest.

"I remember a little, but... Well, man, am I hungry. I gotta get out of here...You know how hospital food is," Dan said.

Dan glanced around the room and tried to lift himself up.

"Oh no, you don't, Dan. You're really hurt," Susie insisted. "The nurse said you need to rest."

Dan stopped trying to get up. He looked at Susie seriously, seeming to realize the gravity of her insistence to not get up.

"Or else?" Dan asked rhetorically.

169

Susie gave Dan a stern look, indicating that she wouldn't let him move.

"Well, okay then," he said.

Dan let himself relax back into bed. He yawned, wincing as he did so. Dan looked at her with a puzzled expression, "Why are you here?" he asked.

Susie was a bit surprised by his question. It appeared to be a bit confrontational, but then she reasoned that it did seem rather odd that she was there and no one else was.

"They said I was the only contact they could find on you."

Dan's face saddened noticeably. "Oh," he said.

"We should call your family," Susie suggested. She got out her cell phone and readied herself to dial a number.

Right now, Susie was only thinking about getting Dan back home where he belonged and officially recovering from his injuries.

Dan didn't say anything.

"Who should I call?" Susie asked with her phone still in front of her.

Dan stared up at the ceiling as if to try to elicit information from thin air and didn't say anything for a few seconds. There was clearly something bothering him.

"Well, no one, I guess...," he finally answered.

Susie was curious but didn't know what to say. She had never seen Dan so sad, defeated, or lost. This was Dan, the guy who had exuded nothing but pure confidence for months, but she almost wouldn't recognize him now. He was human after all.

"No one?" Susie asked him in disbelief after a few more moments.

Dan didn't say anything. He averted his eyes away from Susie and gazed at nothing in particular. She watched him close his eyes tightly, as if holding back tears that hadn't emerged in years.

Susie felt bad – it was clear to her that she had touched on a very personal nerve.

"I'm sorry, Dan," she said.

"Oh, Susie," Dan sighed, "You're one of the kindest people I know. I wish the world had more people like you."

Susie tried to give Dan a big smile – that was the best compliment she had ever been given in her life. And, coming from Dan, it meant even more to her.

"Well, I'm staying here with you tonight," she insisted.

"Or else?" Dan asked somewhat sarcastically.

Susie smiled, almost laughing, "Or else."

When the sun rose the next morning, Susie was already up and about. She saw Dan stir a bit as the sun's beams shone brightly through the room's inner curtains.

"You're up early," Dan said, rubbing his eyes.

Her eyes lit up and she walked over to him.

"I'm fine," she said. "And, you look better. Not as pale,"

"I feel better. Very much so. But, I want out of here. I hate lounging about," Dan said with a hint of anxiety. He shifted around and stretched carefully in the bed, testing his mobility.

"I wouldn't exactly call this lounging, Dan, but, then again, you do seem to be doing much better."

Susie was happy to see that Dan was definitely better. He was already more animated and it appeared that his injuries weren't much of a hindrance on his ability to move.

Nurse Miller came into the room.

"I'm about to go off shift, you two. I just wanted to see how Dan was doing," she said.

"I'm doing great, thanks," Dan replied. "Thanks for all of your help."

"That's my job," Nurse Miller said.

"He's really looking forward to leaving," Susie told the nurse.

Nurse Miller didn't say anything. Instead, she approached Dan and looked at his injuries carefully. She flipped through his medical charts and examined them, mumbling some of the words and numbers she saw.

"He should be okay to be discharged," she finally concluded. "Just keep an eye on him for any unusual symptoms like dizziness, undue fatigue, numbness or tingling, blurred vision… Things like that."

"I will," Susie responded.

Nurse Miller removed the bandages from Dan's face, revealing numerous small abrasions, a couple of lacerations held together with a few stitches, and more bruising – a collage of black and blue covered sections of Dan's face.

"Dan, do you feel well enough to leave?" Nurse Miller asked him, looking at him quite seriously.

"How many guesses do I get?" Dan asked playfully.

Nurse Miller rolled her eyes.

"Heck, yes. Let's get out of here," Dan said. He got out of the bed and stood up easily.

Susie noticed that he was barefoot.

"Dan, where are your shoes?"

"Ah, it's a long story," he said.

Nurse Miller held up some light blue hospital slippers. "You can have these if you want," the nurse offered.

Dan cracked a smile. "That's very kind of you. Thank you," he replied.

He sat down on the bed and put the slippers on his feet.

"I hope these slippers don't come into style," Dan joked. "I just bought a whole wardrobe full of jeans and dark t-shirts. These would destroy my social life."

"You look fine," Susie giggled.

"There is some paperwork to fill out," Nurse Miller added.

A short time later, Dan and Susie emerged from the hospital and walked along the sidewalk out front. Dan had a limp but seemed otherwise okay. He looked far worse than he acted.

"Thanks for your help, Susie," said Dan, clearly sincere.

"I'm glad you'll be okay… I hope they find whoever did this to you."

"Oh, they probably won't," he sighed with resignation.

Dan abruptly stopped and looked around.

"Where are we going anyway?" he asked.

"To my car. I parked way over there," Susie said as she pointed off in the distance. "I suppose you could wait here while I go fetch my car."

"Assuming that it will start," Dan said with a sly smile.

Susie was on the verge of laughing, but then it hit her that she didn't recall Dan ever seeing Old Faithful.

"How do you know it may not start?"

"What?" Dan asked.

"How do you know that my car may not start?" she repeated, tilting her head at him and looking at him warily.

Dan raised his eyebrows and looked at her blankly for a couple of seconds. "Oh, well, I was just making a bad joke. You know, that so much has gone wrong that your car not starting would top it off," he explained, shrugging at her. "It wasn't very funny."

"Oh," she said, only halfway convinced.

She asked herself why she felt suspicious about a comment that was potentially so innocent. Then she questioned why she questioned him at all. There wasn't anything wrong with him. She wondered why she said thing that would just push Dan away. Susie closed her eyes, angry at herself for being so uptight.

"Hey, there's a diner right around the corner," he suggested. "Breakfast?"

"Can you make it?"

"Yeah, sure. I'm fine."

They began walking again, but the awkwardness of the last exchange still hung in the air.

Susie tried to keep the conversation going.

"Have you eaten there before?" Susie asked and then shuddered a little, realizing that she said yet another stupid thing.

Of course he hasn't, you moron. Who hangs out at hospital diners? she thought.

"You okay?" Dan asked her.

Susie stopped and turned towards Dan. His face told her that he wanted her to be okay, to be happy. She felt chagrined at the thought that Dan was an innocent bystander in her struggle to self-regulate what she thought and said.

"I'm sorry. I'm just a bit cranky, I guess. It's been a long couple of weeks," Susie replied.

"That's okay."

"I suppose everything happens for a reason," Susie said in an attempt to brighten the conversation up.

"Heh," Dan smirked.

"What?"

"Well, I believe...," he said while turning his head towards Susie, "That things happen because of reasons and not for them."

"What do you mean?" Susie asked.

She hadn't expected an everyday saying to be analyzed, but she was glad that Dan had changed the subject.

"Things happen because other things happen before it – a reaction, if you will. What happens next is therefore by design. Specifically, by the design of that reaction," he replied.

"Ok..."

"There isn't an inevitable future that's pulling us along certain paths regardless of anything that came before. There's always an explanation, always a cause, even if you don't know what it is."

Susie thought about this but didn't say anything. She looked at Dan and he looked back at her as they walked.

Dan drew in a deep breath, "Things cannot happen for a reason because nothing happens unless something before it happens. Thus, things happen because of reasons, not for them."

"Interesting... I guess. I mean, isn't that a bit of an over-analysis?"

Dan continued walking and didn't answer her immediately. "I suppose I have deep thoughts about meaningless things sometimes."

"That's a good thing," Susie said with warmth, "and I wouldn't call it meaningless because it's good to keep thinking and to question things."

This was something she really liked about Dan: he was definitely a thinker.

"So, you think everything is guided by fate?" Susie asked.

"No," Dan responded promptly.

"That doesn't make sense... from what you just said. Then, everything is guided by free will?"

"No," Dan responded promptly again.

Susie was confused, "Well, if you don't believe in fate and you don't believe in free will, what do you believe in?"

Dan looked to the sky and calmly replied, "I believe in...," he hesitated, "...it's best described as somewhere in-between."

"I don't understand," she said.

They arrived at the diner's front doors and entered. It was packed with people.

"Meh, don't worry about it. I'm just saying silly things," Dan said over the noise of people and plates in the diner.

Susie didn't want to drop the subject, but she didn't want to keep pressing Dan about something that he didn't want to talk about. He had been through a lot and he didn't need that. Plus, she had already put her foot in her mouth too many times with him. Sometimes she wished she could be more fun and less uptight. Dan was someone she could look up to somewhat in that he was brilliant, fun to be with, and could carry on intelligent conversations that weren't boring.

Susie glanced around the diner, which was bustling with activity. Waitresses flew by tables, handed out drinks, delivered plates of food, and took orders. A hostess greeted the two of them, glancing at Dan's bruises and bandages but appearing unbothered – obviously used to getting customers straight from the hospital.

"Two, please," Dan asked, holding up two fingers.

"Right this way," the hostess answered, motioning Dan and Susie to follow her.

She guided them to a booth and they sat down. Dan was silent and Susie debated if she had caused him to clam up. Admittedly, she couldn't think of anything to talk about anyway.

"How's your leg?" Susie asked, attempting to jumpstart a conversation.

"It's okay."

Their waitress placed menus in front of them along with a couple of glasses of ice water. Susie opened up her menu, but Dan didn't move at all.

"You hungry?" Susie asked.

"Absolutely starving."

Susie perused the menu, but she couldn't help being sidetracked with Dan still not opening the menu. She peered at him over the edge of the menu. Dan seemed completely submerged in thought and disinterested in her company. It was like he had mentally walked away, and it was almost as disconcerting to Susie as if he physically had done so.

A few minutes went by and the waitress returned.

"What can I get ya, honey?" the waitress asked Susie.

"Oh, I'll have the… uhh… the fruit bowl," Susie answered.

"Fruit bowl," the waitress repeated, writing on her pad of paper.

She turned to Dan.

"And for you, hun?" she asked.

Dan smiled at the waitress and said, "Hi, Mary. I'll have two pecan chocolate chip pancakes, large orange juice, five strips of bacon, grits, and a waffle."

"We don't have any bacon left, hun," Mary replied as she wrote down his order.

"Oh, darn it. I love bacon. Could you please check?"

"Sure, hun," Mary said and she walked away.

"Do you know her?" Susie asked Dan.

"What?" Dan asked.

"You called her *Mary* and you ordered like you've been here many times," Susie observed.

"Her name tag…"

"Oh…," Susie responded.

"…and these kinds of diners are all the same when it comes to the food," Dan finished.

Susie said nothing – she was satisfied with that answer. She decided that, simply put, Dan was brilliant. Even when it came to the tiniest things, he was observant and clever. She imagined if the roles were reversed. What would it be like for someone to question her ability to observe a simple nametag? What would it be like to be questioned about a joke that just happens to be close to the truth, like the one about Old Faithful not starting?

She really felt like a lesser person right now. She dug into herself for assuming the worst about him when he did anything that seemed even slightly odd.

I have to give him the benefit of the doubt.

Dan straightened up into a better posture and began to play around with his silverware, apparently bored. Susie still felt too awkward to try starting a conversation again and busied herself with inspecting her own silverware for spots.

"You know, Susie," Dan suddenly started, "you now know a lot about me. Tell me about you."

Just like that, Dan had opened up the conversation between the two of them to extend beyond their Calculus class, Dan's injuries, and the recent awkward questions. Susie was pleasantly surprised and welcomed the change.

"Oh, well, let's see," Susie said, a bit uncertain where to start. "I have a mother and a sister…"

"…and a father."

"What?"

"And a father, right?" Dan asked.

"Well… Um, yes and no," Susie responded.

Dan tipped his head forward, clearly interested in what Susie was going to say. Susie was flattered by Dan's sudden interest in her personal life. He had never asked before and, much as she'd rather not, she felt that she had to answer.

"Well, my father left us when I was very young…"

Susie went into a surreal state, disconnecting momentarily from her conversation with Dan. From time to time, she had been able to remember more details about his disappearance. At this moment, she retrieved a vague memory of a kind and gentle man who she believed was her father. She envisioned him walking out the front door of her house, taking a last look back, and closing the door behind him.

"I'm sorry, Susie," Dan said somberly.

"It was hard, very hard, on Mom. I don't really remember him much. But, I can tell you that his leaving really bothers me even to this day."

"He gave up? Just left?" Dan asked.

"I don't know. My mother never really told me anything in detail," Susie said, shaking her head. "I mean, she talks about it, but not ever why he left. Mostly, she gets too upset to make any sense."

"And you're still angry over this?" Dan boldly asked.

"Yes. Wouldn't you be?" Susie said defensively.

"Why?" Dan asked without hesitation.

Susie felt like this question was a borderline insult, as if he was implying that she was a fool for feeling this way.

"Seriously?" she asked. Her blood pressure bumped up a few notches. "How would you want me to react?"

"Let it go," Dan said calmly.

Susie shook her head in disagreement. She was offended by Dan's easy answer, as if it was such a simple thing to "let go". Dan hadn't been there; he didn't experience the hell that her mother went through, that they all went through.

Dan repeated, "Let it go. Life is precious. Don't waste it being angry about something you can't change. Every minute you're angry, you're taking away a minute of happiness you could have had."

After a moment of tension, Susie relaxed her defenses and relented to Dan's reasoning. She exhaled in reluctant agreement. It was hard to admit that he had the right perspective and the right attitude. Still, she couldn't picture herself just letting go of it.

"I need to go to the bathroom," Dan said as he got up. "Excuse me."

While Dan was away, Susie thought more about what he said. She knew that he was right, but she was still an emotional being. However, Dan seemed so relaxed and confident about everything in life – perhaps it was credited to his ability to let go of negativity. She found a way to let go of a little bit of her anger.

Dan returned several minutes later and sat down just as their food arrived.

"Hey, we did have bacon. How 'bout that," Mary said.

"Awesome," Dan replied. "I was hoping you had some."

Mary placed most of the plates of food in front of Dan and the single fruit bowl in front of Susie. She then topped off their glasses of water and walked away. Dan dug in with enthusiasm while Susie merely picked at her fruit bowl.

"I'm not saying letting go is easy, but I wouldn't waste another minute. Forgive him and move on. He can't hurt you or your mom anymore," Dan said between bites.

Susie found it hard to believe that someone could just let go of something so traumatic, something so hurtful.

There's no way Dan understands what it's like, she thought, dropping her fork in the bowl with a clatter.

"And what about you?" she snapped back defensively.

"Me?"

"Yeah. You seem to not have a family at all…," she said and then covered her mouth, taking a deep breath. "I'm sorry, Dan. I got carried away."

"No, really, it's okay," he calmly answered.

He took a bite of a pancake and told her as he chewed, "I was orphaned when I was three. My parents died in a fire. I was moved from foster home to foster home until I was eight. Then a monastery took me in."

"A monastery?" Susie asked, astonished.

"Yup. In fact, I was a monk," Dan said, taking another bite.

"A monk? What happened? I mean, sorry, but you don't look like a monk at all."

"Fair enough," Dan said. "Well, let's see… I was studying one day, as usual, and I asked myself if being stuck in a monastery was the best way to reach out to people," Dan said before he shoved some grits in his mouth.

Susie leaned forward in interest.

Dan swallowed and continued, "Monks only speak when we absolutely must. We can't go anywhere. We... we have very little good that we can spread. We are isolated."

"And you can't marry," Susie said.

"That, too. I thought I may want to marry someday."

Susie popped a slightly interested smile at that, indicating interest – albeit it was a bit of a fantasy. She paused and then asked, "How long have you been away now?"

"Let's see... Hmm, about five years now, I guess."

Dan took a sip of his juice and continued, "I wanted to learn more about the world. I felt I had to, in order to be effective at helping others. And, I have been better able to serve others."

"Wow. I've never met anyone like you. Not even close."

"I hope that's a good thing," Dan laughed.

"It's very good. I just didn't think people like you existed. But, you being a monk... Well, it kind of explains a lot."

"Like what?" Dan asked.

"You have the best work ethic of anyone I've ever seen. You're completely dedicated to learning. You're kind to others..."

Dan interrupted, "Please, I'm not without flaws."

"No one is."

"Well, I still live a life in many ways similar to the one I left behind," Dan explained.

"Such as?"

"I need only what I need. Anything beyond that is only what I want. I don't forget the difference. It's very serene. And, I respect those who are truly in need and look up to those who help them."

To Susie, there was nothing better Dan could have said at that very moment and in that very manner. She was entranced.

Dan took another bite of food. He wiped his mouth with a napkin, swallowed, and said, "It reflects the way I was raised and my initial calling. It really inspires me."

"Wow, Dan. You... You're a good guy," Susie said passionately.

Dan's face flushed a little. He continued to scarf down his food as if he hadn't eaten in weeks.

"What made you want to go to college?" Susie asked.

"Oh, that's easy. I needed a diverse education. I don't plan to be of the world, as the expression goes, but I have to be in it. As I said, I just don't think being locked up in a monastery is the best way to be part of humanity or serve it."

As they continued eating their breakfast, Susie reflected on the past twenty-four hours and was amazed at how much had transpired. She was with Dan as a human being – not just as a casual friend from school. She greatly admired that, in spite of his beaten physical condition, Dan persevered through it and kept a good attitude.

The waitress came by with the check. Susie snatched it.

"Hey, you can't just grab that."

"Too late," she said with a beaming smile. "Besides, you have no money. The nurse told me so."

Dan nodded his head slowly and raised his eyebrows as if coming to this realization. They got up from their table and walked towards the front of the diner to pay the bill.

Susie turned to Dan, "I understand where you're coming from – wanting to serve humanity and all – but don't you think you're just a bit too idealistic?"

"Entirely idealistic – is there anything wrong with that?"

"Nope."

They arrived at the register; Mary was attending it. She looked up at them and gave them a polite smile.

"How was the food?" she asked.

"Great!" Dan said.

Susie handed Mary the bill and some cash — she didn't think about her budget.

Mary opened the register and quickly counted out the difference. "And nine fifty-four is your change," Mary said as she handed Susie the money.

Susie took the cash and moved to put it in her purse. Dan grabbed Susie's hand, stopping it short.

"Wait. You just handed us a fifty when you should have given us a five," Dan said, releasing Susie's hand.

Susie opened her hand and, under the coins and four singles, there was a fifty-dollar bill.

Mary's eyes widened in disbelief. "Oh, my gosh! Thanks for catchin' that! It would have come out of my paycheck!" Mary spouted.

"No problem. It wasn't our money, Mary," Dan said.

"Ya know what?" Mary said as she removed a flair pin off of her uniform. "I want you to have this."

She gave the flair pin to Dan and continued, "It's my lucky shirt pin. It's yours now."

"Mary, that's very kind of you. I want Susie to have this. She could use some luck," replied Dan.

Dan gave the pin to Susie, who smiled up at Dan as he did.

He then looked harder at Mary, drawing his eyebrows together.

"You know, you look familiar," Dan said and then paused thoughtfully. "Do you have a sister named Michelle who lives in Flint, Michigan?"

Mary put her hand on her hip, cocking her head at Dan. "Why... Yes. Yes, I do," Mary replied.

"I met her years ago. She talked about you an awful lot. You look just like her," said Dan, briefly pointing at Mary.

"Really? We haven't talked in years. I guess time is just passin' us by."

"I'm sure she'd like to hear from you," Dan suggested.

"You know, I have a good feelin' about you. I'm gonna give her a call," Mary said, gushing with excitement.

"It wouldn't hurt. Besides, it could change your life." Dan smiled, "Trust yourself."

"I'm gonna do it."

Dan and Susie walked out the front, waving back at Mary. "Take care, Mary," they both said as they left.

"You two take care, too!" she yelled back.

They strolled down the sidewalk at about half the pace that Susie would normally walk – she didn't want to push Dan to walk any faster.

"That was pretty neat how you knew her sister," Susie commented. "I mean, what are the odds?"

"Yeah," Dan said with little reaction.

Susie couldn't help but notice Dan's slight limp.

"Are you sure you should be walking on that?" she asked.

"Sure. I'm just walking it off. It's really not that bad."

Susie was doubtful, but she trusted that Dan knew what he was capable of handling. She looked him over, trying her best to imagine him as a monk. She had had the preconceived notion that monks were boring introverts, but Dan was anything but that. Suddenly, it occurred to her that if Dan had only been out for five years, maybe he would someday decide to go back.

"I must know… Have you been satisfied with life since you left the monastery?" Susie asked.

"Oh, absolutely!" he emphatically answered. "It's really made a difference. I can interact with *so* many more people. That life was a bit boring, I must admit. I need to be around people – I really enjoy helping others."

Susie paused and said, "Hey, I volunteer at a homeless shelter on Thursdays. We could certainly use your help sometime, if you don't mind. You could come tomorrow if that's not too soon."

"Certainly. I would love to help," Dan said without hesitation.

Susie beamed at him and abruptly stopped walking. Dan stopped with her.

"Dan, I had no idea who you were. You just keep surprising me," she said brightly.

Susie kissed Dan on the cheek. Dan put his hand on the side of his cheek where she kissed, looking captivated by it.

"Please, you give me too much credit," Dan blushed.

"I don't think I give you enough."

They resumed walking away from the hospital, Dan seeming to silently agree that Old Faithful could wait. The weather was a little cooler than the day before and there were only a few clouds in the sky – overall, it was perfect for walking in Susie's opinion. Over the next ten minutes, Susie simply enjoyed the weather and Dan's silent company, neither seeming to feel the need to talk.

They halted at an intersection and waited for the traffic signal to change. On a lamppost there was an advertisement for guitar lessons.

Dan ripped the advertisement off the pole.

"Hmm, this address is nearby...," Dan said.

"So... you want guitar lessons now?" Susie asked playfully.

"Maybe."

Dan looked at Susie. She looked back at him curiously.

"Do you mind?" he asked.

"No! Just... wow. You just keep on moving along, don't you?" Susie laughed.

"Heh, no. I just find some things inspiring, that's all."

They crossed the intersection and made their way to the doorstep of an old two-story house with patches of paint peeling up, showing the greyed wood underneath. The wooden porch creaked with each of their steps and the screen door drooped on its hinges, its screen halfway torn off of it.

Dan knocked on the door.

A man in his early forties appeared at the door after a minute. He obviously had not shaved his greying beard in days and was holding a beer bottle.

"Yeah?" he asked as he took a swig.

Dan held up the advertisement but didn't say a word.

"Oh, that? I thought I took all of those down. No one's ever been interested."

The man seemed pretty down and apathetic. He took another swig of beer and didn't seem motivated enough to say another word.

Dan extended his hand for a handshake, "I'm Dan."

The man obliged, "I'm Kevin. Um, you okay?" He asked, finally noticing Dan's battered condition.

"I'm fine. And I'm interested, but it depends on the price," Dan said.

Kevin took another swig of his beer and scratched the side of his head in thought.

"I'd give them to you for next to nothin'. I've been out of work for some time now. The economy really stinks," Kevin responded bitterly.

"Yeah, it does stink… What is it you normally do?" Dan asked with interest.

"Upholstery," Kevin answered. "I've been doing it for years. Some years were good and others were bad. But, this past year, heh, it's the worst."

"Upholstery? Really?" Dan smiled at Kevin.

Susie glanced at Dan, befuddled, but said nothing.

"I know someone in the Midwest looking for upholsterers. Do you have a pen and paper? I can give you the contact info.

They just won a large contract with a car manufacturer, so they're hiring left and right," Dan said.

Kevin opened his mouth slightly, looking completely off-guard. Susie watched as he seemed to realize what Dan had said and what this could mean – new life appeared to fill his soul. Kevin hesitated and then disappeared behind his front door. She looked at Dan in bewilderment with a puzzled smile on her face.

Dan looked back at her.

"What?" he asked.

Susie laughed, "It seems like you know everyone."

Dan started, "Well…"

Dan was interrupted by Kevin who had returned to the front door with a pen and piece of paper. Dan wrote on the paper.

"Call this number and tell them that Dan recommends you. They'll take it from there," he said, handing Kevin the paper.

Kevin's eyes welled up with tears. Dan had clearly made his day or, perhaps, his year. Susie noticed that Kevin's hand with the paper trembled, as if his prayers of the past year had been summarily answered by this chance encounter.

"Thanks… Thanks, mister. Dan. I… I don't know what to say," Kevin said, wiping his hand across his eyes.

"You don't have to say anything," Dan said evenly. "I'm glad this all worked out."

Unexpectedly, Dan turned around and headed back off the porch without saying another word. Susie was caught off-guard by his sudden departure and was at first a few steps behind, but she followed him.

Kevin yelled, "Uh, did you still want guitar lessons?!"

"I thought you did upholstery!" Dan yelled back.

Kevin smiled and waved at him while clutching the piece of paper Dan gave him like a winning lottery ticket.

Susie caught up to Dan and put her hand on his shoulder, stopping him.

"Dan, tell me: did you even want guitar lessons?"

"Well, I have to be honest... Not really. I just saw the sign and something told me to go for it."

Susie did her best to process his explanation. It seemed too random.

Dan looked Susie right in the eyes. "Always trust your intuition. Never fail it. Never," he said with the utmost seriousness, as if reading from holy text.

Susie nodded slowly. She did invest quite a bit of trust in her intuition. Dan, however, appeared to take it up a notch higher.

Dan abruptly continued walking again and Susie, a half-step behind, caught up.

Susie was still flabbergasted by recent events. It was neat that Dan knew the waitress's sister and now he has this job for a guy he met through a flyer for something he wasn't even interested in doing. How does Dan do this? Can this really be just a matter of intuition?

Dan appeared unaffected by what had happened. "That's a good man back there," remarked Dan.

"How do you know?" Susie asked.

"Didn't you *feel* it from him? He was just so honest and upfront."

"Well, not really. I mean, you only spoke for a minute with him. He mostly just seemed like he didn't care anymore about anything."

"No, no... Not that. It wasn't anything he said. It's what you felt, what you sensed about him," Dan said emphatically, gesturing his arms like he was giving a sermon.

This was a side of Dan that Susie had never seen; it was as if he was in a different mode altogether. He had never seemed like someone who would so deeply believe in one's feelings about something. Quite frankly, she hadn't thought someone like Dan would ever entertain that kind of metaphysical conversation.

"You can get a vibe from anyone, if you pay attention to yourself," Dan asserted. "But you need to really pay attention and not talk yourself out of knowing what's right."

"Sure… I guess…," Susie answered, not really knowing what else to say.

"Well, either I felt it or I'm still on a sugar high from breakfast," he added flippantly.

She was enjoying seeing a side of Dan that was less guarded and more vulnerable. If he could talk about these things with her then he must feel comfortable around her, and this reassured her that she could do the same around him.

They arrived at a bus stop. Dan stopped walking and glanced at his watch. Susie wanted to know more of this Dan that she just now discovering, but she didn't know how to get time with him outside of studying. As she watched Dan look up into the blue sky, she could almost hear Karen's voice telling her, "Make a move, give a sign or something! He thinks you're not interested."

She took a deep breath, trying her best to muster the courage to ask him out on a real date. Although she would prefer that he asked her, she was incredibly worried that Dan wouldn't ever do so, especially after all of this time and even more so now that she knew he used to be a monk.

"Dan?" Susie asked.

"Yes?" he asked blankly, seeming distracted by something.

Susie hesitated. She stumbled over her words, "Well, I was wondering… wondering if…"

She stopped.

"Yeah?" Dan asked again, with a hint of impatience. He looked at his watch again.

He appeared to be losing interest in the conversation and she tried to rush her words, worried that the moment would pass.

"Well, I would like… That is, if you want… I'm sorry. I'm trying to form a coherent sentence… My head's a little lost…," Susie rambled.

As a bus pulled up, Dan looked over at Susie in a clueless but concerned manner. "You feeling okay? You look a little down," he said.

"No, I'm… I'm okay… I…," Susie hesitated.

Dan looked at the bus and gestured to the driver to wait for a second.

"This is my bus," he told her. "Can I borrow a few bucks to get home?"

Startled by this, Susie had no idea what to say or how to react. Whatever courage she had built up was quickly discarded and replaced with a sense of rejection. Once again, Dan was leaving for no discernible reason whatsoever.

"Oh, I didn't know you were leaving," she said after a moment, trying her best to keep from tripping over her words again.

Dan apologized, "I'm sorry. Sometimes I can be so rude. I…"

Susie interrupted, "No worries. You're fine. I'm fine. Everything's fine."

She handed Dan some money. Dan stepped onto the bus, but he turned around at the top of its stairs as he paid the fare. "You up for studying later tomorrow night?" he asked.

"Sure," Susie tried to smile, but she couldn't; she felt lost and, again, didn't know what she had done wrong.

The bus doors began to close.

"Call me if you need to or if just wanna chat!" she shouted.

Dan smiled back and waved goodbye.

"Wanna chat?" she groaned inwardly. "How dumb can I be? I bet he won't call. Why would he? God, why can't I just be normal?"

Angry at herself for being herself the whole way, Susie walked back towards the hospital to retrieve Old Faithful. She reflected on how all the events had played out only to lead Dan to disappearing again.

Uncertain as to whether Dan would ever have a romantic interest in her, Susie wondered if she should simply accept him as nothing more than a good friend. Nearly resigned to this fate, she stopped just short of accepting it. She knew that she could not bear seeing Dan with anyone else. This wasn't a matter of selfishness, but simply that she couldn't deny that she had some true feelings for him beyond friendship. Her interest in him far outweighed his occasional strange, abrupt behaviors.

She finally got back to Old Faithful and tried to start the car. The engine tried its best to turn over, but it grew weaker with each attempt. The car's battery soon died.

"Dan was right about you, Old Faithful," Susie said to her car. "You're just gonna leave me here, aren't you?"

Chapter 15 – Re-Plan

The moon shone down on a mostly empty, large parking lot. Father Crane stood there with his hands locked behind his back. His face was devoid of any emotion. His eyes were wide open, almost never blinking. He was waiting.

Father Crane watched as Spike walked into the moonlight and towards him. He stopped when he was about forty feet away. He reached into his black pants, pulled out a pack of cigarettes, tapped a cigarette out, put it in his mouth, and whipped out a lighter. He lit up and, as steadfast as ever, maintained a completely expressionless face. Neither he nor Father Crane said a word.

A moment later, Father Crane could see the silhouette of a man approaching on the edge of the parking lot about two hundred feet away. He knew it was Frank. He walked closer and stopped just in the halo of a lamppost, revealing his blond hair and policeman's uniform. Father Crane, Spike, and Frank all stood forty feet away from the other, forming a perfect triangle between them.

"Hey Spike," Frank said.

"'ello Frank," Spike greeted loudly, with an eerie smile.

"How are you?" Frank responded with a hint of nervousness in his voice.

"Can't complain. It's been a bit busy, but you knew that."

"Yeah. You have been busy. I don't know how you keep up," Frank said.

Spike bobbed his head up and down slightly to acknowledge Frank's comment.

Frank smiled back a little bit, but he still appeared wracked by the stresses of adjusting to his Polarity.

"Hey, I was wondering…," Frank continued.

"Gentlemen," Father Crane interrupted.

Spike and Frank swung their attention wholly to him.

"I brought you here tonight because we must step up our coordination. This will be the first and last time that *We* will do this for Susie. *We* are disrupting *Their* timing, but *We* must focus *Our* efforts better. Susie's time is near." Father Crane said. He stared coldly at Frank, expecting him to speak.

Frank gulped and stiffened his posture.

"*We* didn't expect Dan to escape from Spike. I was able to adjust the university's student records to get Dan removed from school, but he… he's adjusted in ways that weren't predictable," Frank said.

"Everything's predictable. Altering the university's records was marginally effective, but you're still amazingly clumsy. But, however unintuitive it may sound, your clumsiness is welcomed at the moment," Father Crane said.

Frank raised an eyebrow and opened his mouth but didn't say anything.

"Confused?" Father Crane asked him.

Frank nodded slowly.

"You've forced *Them* to take larger moves. It will make it much more difficult for *Them* to block *Us* while she's at school," Father Crane said.

Frank smiled.

"Stop smiling. It's useless," Father Crane ordered.

Frank removed his smile.

"Smiling means that you're distracted. Distraction can mean the end of you." He turned to Spike and narrowed his eyes, "Spike lost his opportunity to kill Dan in the alley because he took the time to grin at him."

Spike blinked his eyes a couple of times and gulped.

Father Crane brought his hands together in thought, interlacing his fingers. He closed his eyes to induce even deeper thought until he was nearly meditating.

After a few moments, he spoke, "Still... Dan is... He's getting too close to Susie. He's with her quite too much, I'm afraid. He's a formidable foe. Harold is using his best people," Father Crane said.

"Dan is trackin' me too closely. I can't get in. He's got all angles covered, locked up and tight as a drum," Spike said.

"Well, let's see what *We* can do about it," Father Crane suggested.

Father Crane sat down on the asphalt of the parking lot, prompting the other two to do the same. He continued, "Spike, focus on Dan. Frank, focus on Susie. I'll focus on Harold and everything else."

The three of them silently stared towards the ground into nothingness for several seconds in dead silence. Father Crane glanced briefly at them. Frank was sweating; the typical sign of a novice. Spike looked just as calm and collected as Father Crane was – he was a seasoned veteran.

Spike clutched his head in frustration, but barely had any sign of emotion on his face as he spoke, "Not good. He's got too much set up for me. Solid. Solid. Every time *We* have somethin' lined up, he counters it."

"I… I have a shot, I think. I mean, well, I know what I can do to help," Frank offered.

Father Crane placed his hand on his chin. He squinted his eyes, almost completely closing them, and spoke with authority, "Frank, you'll have to do what you can to upset Dan's plans. Shake it up a bit. Throw yourself at him if you must."

Father Crane looked both of them over. Frank blinked frequently and his fingers fidgeted. Spike kept his well-disciplined eyes squarely on Father Crane. Spike didn't move a muscle under his gaze, but Father Crane knew him well – Spike was his most valuable and universally feared asset.

"Spike, when you next have a chance to do so, kill Dan. You cannot fail again. This is coming to an end very rapidly. He's increasing protection of himself by being with Susie more often. This is certain: you don't have many opportunities left."

"It will be done," Spike answered.

Chapter 16 – An Angel

Susie was at home, going in and out of sleep on her couch with a thick book lying open on her chest. Reading books that she'd checked out from the university library was Susie's hobby of choice when she wasn't rock climbing at the university fitness center. As she was well-aware, both time and money constrained her ability to try new things.

She looked at a nearby picture of Karen and she reminisced about her most recent foray into trying something new. Over a year ago, Karen had taken her skydiving – their sponsor had been Karen's boyfriend of the moment. Susie had gamely gone through the jump training with the two of them, but she'd been uncertain how she would react when the moment to jump actually came. As it turned out, she had been fearless and loved it.

However, she couldn't afford to do it beyond that one time. Karen, being the loving sister, spent an irresponsible amount of money and bought Susie a parachute for her birthday to help her along. Susie lived with the guilt of having the parachute tucked away in her closet collecting dust. She still couldn't afford the cost of catching a ride on an airplane, or the other equipment and fees needed for the jump.

Susie sighed sleepily and settled more deeply into the couch. She pulled the book off of her and set it onto the floor. Reading gave her distance from things that troubled her. Likewise, she knew that her uncertainty over where she stood with Dan immensely distracted her from mourning poor Nicole; it filled her with guilt when she did mourn.

Susie fell into a deep sleep, deep enough to conjure a dream of her father leaving: her father was kneeling down and talking to her as a cute three-year old girl.

"...but I have to go, sweetheart," her father said, sniffing. "I can't come back."
He then walked out the front door.

The vision was contradictory, disturbing her sleep. Even while unconscious, her mind pondered the issue: Her father had seemed like a nice, kind, and caring man, and yet he had left them without any further explanation of why. His seeming kindness had never made sense with his leaving. It would have been so much easier if Susie could remember him as uncaring, selfish, or even evil. All she had was her hazy memories of him being so kind and all the memories of the troubles left in his wake.

Susie snapped out of it and woke up instantly from her distorted dream. She rubbed her face to regain her composure, turned on the TV to the evening news, and got up. Thirsty, she went to her kitchen and got a glass of water. She gulped half of it down, then paused and put her hand in her pocket, half-remembering that something was in there.

She pulled out the flair pin that Dan had given her earlier from her pocket. She smiled at the sight of it. It reminded her of Dan and her growing relationship with him. He was proving to be someone who could potentially understand her. She put the flair pin on her countertop, not quite sure where she should keep it.

* * *

Meanwhile, on the other side of the city, Dan had been wide awake for quite some time. The sun was starting to set as he leaned against the wall of a building. No one else was around for the moment; he was very good at finding privacy. Quite calm, he texted on his phone, *She has the pin Mary gave her.*

She will forget to bring it, said the returned text.

Dan closed his eyes tightly in thought. He exhaled, resigning himself to a somewhat complex plan.

I will help her, he wrote back.

Dan pocketed his phone and started walking down the sidewalk with a slight limp. He became consumed with deep thought. As usual, he ignored everything around him irrelevant to his survival, barely registering that his moment of privacy had passed. His pace was a bit slow – even considering his injured leg – and people were passing him on the sidewalk. Finally, he gave his head a small decisive nod, finalizing the details of whatever was bothering him.

His demeanor instantly changed and his expression became more bright and cheery. He looked around and took in the world about him with a deep, invigorating breath. He looked at various people going about their business and commented on them to himself.

She won't get the promotion that she deserves, he thought, eyeing a random woman passing him by.

He will finally cheat on his wife tomorrow, he thought while sizing up a man standing in front of a storefront window.

He continued making precise predictions about everyone he came across.

That little boy will make it to Congress and will be put in prison on bribery charges... Those two brothers will start a restaurant that will fail two years and sixteen days from now... The man 130 feet behind me will be mugged in slightly less than three hours; he will end up in critical condition and suffer from migraines for the rest of his life...

All of these predictions came quickly and naturally to Dan; they were omnipresent and continuous in his everyday life. They played like a thousand movies in parallel with so much momentum that little could be done to stop them. In day-to-day life, every action Dan took was deliberate – he always knew nearly everything that would happen. He spent most of his energy dealing with surprises. Surprises were rare, but when a surprise did happen – without exception – it came from *Them*.

Dan reflected a little on the stunt he had pulled with Professor Gomez. He knew he couldn't return to class or school. Susie would ask about his absenteeism and he already knew exactly what he would say to quell any suspicion. Furthermore, Dan had adjusted well by telling Professor Gomez about the cancer that would otherwise claim his life: The professor would take a leave of absence soon, the university would provide a substitute, and the substitute would be far easier than Professor Gomez. This meant that the class would be easier for Susie and that meant that Susie could spend a lot more time with Dan socially – something both he and Susie wanted.

Dan slowed his walking to a near standstill. Dan's face contorted with alarm. He increased his pace, making his limp more profound, and hurried around a street corner. A huge crowd was gathered underneath a six-story building – they were looking up at a potential jumper.

The jumper sat on the edge of an open window on the top story of the building, his legs dangling in the air. He was a tall, skinny man in his late teens or early-twenties with long, frizzy red hair and thick glasses. He looked unmistakably troubled as he stared off into nothingness as if it was the only thing on the planet he craved.

The police were on the scene and doing their best to keep the area cordoned off. One officer was trying to coax the jumper down using a megaphone. "Help is on the way. Whatever has you thinking about jumping can be solved. Please go back inside and we'll figure this out together...," the officer directed the jumper.

The jumper was unfazed. He looked down at the officer and his expression changed briefly to one of incredulity, as if asking how the officer could believe a few generalized words could somehow counteract years of torment. He continued staring at the gathered crowd below.

Dan looked up at him and devised a plan. He looked around at all of the people; they were all heavily engaged in looking up at the jumper, including the police. He paused and perfectly timed the moment in which he was able to slip by the distracted police and make his way into the jumper's building.

Dan rushed to the top of the building. He glanced at the closed door that led directly to the jumper. He knew it was locked. He passed by to the apartment door adjacent to the jumper's. He knew this door was also locked, as all of the doors in this hallway were, but he reached onto the top of the door's frame and immediately found a key – he had known the key was there. Dan unlocked the door and walked to the window that would be nearest to the jumper.

Dan opened the window and sat on the frame, hanging his legs on the outside of it. He knew the only words that would save the jumper's life.

"Crispy M&M's," Dan blurted out.

The jumper, taken by surprise, looked at Dan in shock. "What?" he asked.

"Crispy M&M's were one of my favorite candies. And then, one day, they just disappeared. They were discontinued because I was probably the only person who ate them," Dan explained.

"I loved those things," the jumper replied in a monotone voice.

"Rugby, pina coladas, cheesy horror movies... You love those, too, don't you, Thomas?" Dan asked.

"How... How did you know that? How do you know my name? Who are you?"

"I know a lot about you, Thomas. I know that you have much good you can do in the world. If you don't think so, just think about your three nieces. They love you," Dan replied.

Thomas gripped his head and began crying, "I... I can't... I can't stop the voices in my head. They... They tell me to do things that aren't right. I must stop them. This is the only way."

Dan didn't say anything. He let Thomas continue.

"The thoughts tell me that I'm a bad person and I keep telling them over and over again that I'm not... I'm not! I'M NOT! I'M NOT!" he yelled.

Dan shook his head sympathetically as Thomas wiped away his tears and rubbed his nose.

"Thomas, I am here to tell you that this isn't the only answer. Accept the love from those around you and you will find a way," Dan replied. "I know everything about you. I know what good you can do for this world."

Thomas began crying again, but then he paused and looked at Dan. "Who are you?" he repeated.

"Who I am is not important. Who you are and your purpose on this planet is important," Dan answered.

Thomas put his head in his hands and bawled.

Dan continued, "I need you to trust me. There are people who can help you. Those thoughts are not your fault. Those thoughts are only there to distract you from who you really are. You are destined to be great."

Thomas nodded his head.

"I'm coming over to visit you."

Thomas nodded his head again and sniffed several times. "I'll unlock the door," he muttered through his tears before disappearing from the ledge.

Dan went back inside and then went into the hallway to greet Thomas. Once inside Thomas's apartment, they gave each other a deep, emotional hug.

"You saved my life. I was going to do it. I was. I really was," said Thomas.

"Thomas, you will be fine. Don't worry. You will be fine," Dan said as he patted Thomas on his back to comfort him.

"What should I do?" Thomas asked, finally releasing Dan.

"First, accept that you need the help of others," Dan asked.

"I do," Thomas instantly replied.

"Second, you must seek treatment. There are fourteen places that can help you, but you must travel to them. Of these fourteen places, the one place that can help you within your budget is in Milwaukee."

Thomas didn't say anything. Dan detected that Thomas doubted him.

"Your first crush was in the first grade on a girl named Heidi. You cheated on your seventh grade spelling test and that memory still haunts you to this very day. You haven't done laundry in weeks because you keep forgetting to buy detergent," Dan said as Thomas's eyes grew wider with each statement.

Dan reached out and grabbed Thomas firmly by the shoulders, looked him straight in his eyes, and asked, "What else must I do to prove to you that I know you?"

Thomas nodded his head repeatedly, affirming that Dan had done enough.

The police plowed through the front door. They saw Thomas and Dan standing calmly and paused. Dan looked at the police and motioned them with his hand to stop and then waved at them to back away. The officers retreated to the hallway.

*　　*　　*

News channels across town quickly caught the late-breaking story. Susie's TV was interrupted to cut to the urgent story.

"Wow! What a scene! A man about to end his life by jumping from a building..." the newscaster started.

This caught Susie's attention and she looked towards the TV.

"...when a complete stranger appears out of nowhere and coaxes him away!"

The TV camera focused in and unmistakably showed Dan talking to Thomas from the window ledge. Susie gasped and put both hands up to her face in complete shock. She walked over to the TV, her eyes firmly glued.

The newscaster continued, "We understand that the man in the window is okay and is being evaluated by medical personnel. Whatever this stranger told the man must have been divine; police were trying for at least an hour before he intervened and persuaded him back inside within minutes..."

Susie sat down in bewilderment. She didn't know what to make of this. How was it possible for someone to do so much good, time after time? It didn't matter where Dan was, but he's always helping someone in some amazing manner.

"He's an angel," she said.

*　　*　　*

The next evening, Susie and Dan were working side by side at the homeless shelter, serving meals to a line of people. Full of energy and never missing a beat, Dan greeted every person and treated each plate as if there were none before it. To each recipient, it was, in fact, the most important thing in their life at that moment. Dan knew this and it reflected in his behavior.

"Thanks for asking me. This is great," Dan said to Susie.

"Thanks for coming on such short notice. We have more people to serve than usual. We would've been slammed."

"Not a problem," Dan said while doing his best to make sure the food he's serving is put neatly on the plate.

Susie grinned briefly at him but quickly turned her attention back to filling plates. As they finished serving the people currently in line, Susie turned to Dan, but didn't say anything. She just gazed at him pensively, thinking about recent events.

She didn't know what to say, but she was curious if Dan would even mention what happened last night. They had been serving for three hours straight and it had felt about the same as any other Thursday except she knew that Dan had saved a stranger's life less than a day ago. Dan had given no clue or indication to her that anything special happened at all.

He noticed her staring. "What?" he asked.

Susie didn't say anything at first. She put her hand on her hip and bit her lip, trying to figure out exactly how to bring up the topic.

"Where were you last night?" she finally asked.

"Walking about. You know… This time of year the weather is beautiful," Dan said.

"Walking about? Really?" Susie asked.

She wanted Dan to spill the beans about last night, but apparently he wouldn't. He stood in front of her looking clueless.

"Did you do anything else?" she asked.

Dan shrugged. Susie was silent, but her stare said a thousand words that all amounted to demanding to know more.

Dan relented slightly, saying, "Well, I made a new friend."

Susie said nothing. She half-playfully folded her arms and tapped her foot, showing that she demanded more.

Dan sighed and averted his eyes, "I suppose you saw the news then."

"I did," Susie replied bluntly.

Dan turned his body slightly away from her and worked on cleaning the counters in front of him as he said, "I wish they wouldn't do that." Dan sighed again and lamented, "Thomas has enough problems to deal with. He really doesn't need the attention."

With curious skepticism, Susie asked, "Thomas, is it? How do you know Thomas?"

Dan looked forward at nothing in particular. "He and I... Well, it's kind of a long story," he replied hesitantly.

Susie nodded, not prying further. Really, she had mostly wanted to see how Dan would react to his heroism and her knowledge of it. She was curious to know more, but she was satisfied for now.

"Oh, Dan... With you, it seems like everything is a long story," Susie remarked.

Dan, who was noticeably uncomfortable, replied, "Well, my life has... It has some complexities."

Susie noticed more homeless people entering the shelter for food. They had to get back to work.

"I won't pry anymore," she told Dan as she started prepping to serve again. "You have me very curious, I admit. I think what you did was very brave."

"It really wasn't much," Dan said. "I'm sure you would have done the same thing."

Susie pondered that as she prepped to begin serving again. She wasn't sure she could have done the same thing since even one wrong word might have caused that guy to jump. Even if she had known the exact words to say, she would have had to practice them a hundred or more times to be confident enough to do it. "How is it that Dan knew what to say?" she wondered.

More homeless people queued up for food – Dan and Susie picked up their pace.

As they filled plates, Dan commented, "We had a soup kitchen at the monastery not unlike this. It gave me a great sense of purpose and humility. It takes me back a little."

"It seems like you still miss the monastery."

"Heavens, yes. I mean, I wouldn't go back, but there were certainly many good things about it," Dan replied. "It was just… It was a bit outdated."

"Yeah, I can't picture you being a monk."

"Why's that?"

"I dunno. You just don't strike me as being the old, crotchety type."

Dan laughed a little, "Come on, now."

Susie looked up from the plate she was loading to the see the line getting even longer. "Well, that wasn't much of a lull. I wish more people could help here. This place can get so busy."

A homeless man approached them, looking down-trodden, and said, "I'm a proud man… I'm just outta luck… I've… I've got no hope," as he held out his plate.

"You're always welcome here," Susie replied graciously, taking his plate and filling it.

Dan pulled out a scratch-off lottery ticket and handed it to him.

"Well, I bought this earlier. You can have it. Maybe your luck is due for a change," Dan said with a wink.

The homeless man slowly grabbed the ticket, eyeing Dan suspiciously, and walked away with his plate of food without any gratitude whatsoever.

Susie stopped what she was doing. Seeing the lottery as a tax on the poor, she was mildly offended. "You really think that will help him?" she asked.

"Sometimes people just need something to look forward to... He was without hope," he said softly.

"It's false hope. The lottery is a lie to people. It promises riches in exchange for the little that they have," she rebutted.

"I agree. But, it was my money that I spent and I bought it strictly for fun. Giving it to this gentleman simply seemed to be the right thing to do," Dan answered.

Susie was silent. She didn't want to say the wrong thing. She had finally found what she saw as an outward flaw in Dan and she had to remind herself that no one was perfect. Dan clearly had the right intentions, but his execution was counter-productive.

Dan continued, "I think the best way to help is to..."

He was interrupted by joyful yelling coming from the eating area.

"HOLY SMOKES!" the homeless man bellowed out, looking at his lottery ticket.

Everyone in the shelter looked at him.

"HOLY SMOKES!" he yelled again, running outside.

"And, sometimes things like that happen," Dan commented, slowly nodding at the door that the man just ran through.

Susie was awestruck. Dan had just changed that man's life with one small act of kindness. She wanted to write it off as luck, but she couldn't. Once again, things had worked out too perfectly. Dan was too lucky to be lucky. Conflicted, she tested Dan from a different angle. "Heh... That was your ticket. That would have been your money," she said.

Dan bobbed his head a little but didn't seem bothered by it. "Yeah, but who knew, right? I think I used it in the best possible manner at the time, don't you?"

"I guess so...," she assented after a moment, too astounded to argue. He showed no remorse for what could have been his, but, instead, seemed like the richest guy on the planet in that instant; he didn't need the money and clearly only felt good about what had happened.

She served a few more people before she felt motivated enough to say to Dan, "Nothing... Nothing seems to bother you. Why is that?"

Dan filled another plate with food and answered, "This is life. Good things and bad things will happen. I've found that everyone's attitudes rub off on each other." He handed the filled plate of food back with a friendly smile and then continued, "Just have a good attitude no matter what and watch what happens."

Susie could agree with the sentiment, but that kind of perspective seemed like the run-of-the-mill platitude that no one was ever serious about. In practice, there were just too many people who acted differently. She didn't believe having a good attitude explained how these things just work out.

"Yeah, but you always seem to be at the right place, at the right time, and do the right things to help random people," Susie pointed out.

Dan chuckled a little. "The past few days have been unusual," he said with a shrug. "But, it is what it is. It certainly has been interesting."

Susie spent the next couple of hours thinking over recent events, Dan's actions, and his explanations for it all. By the end of the evening, she was even more enthralled by him and wanted to know more about him badly.

Chapter 17 – Timing

The following Monday, Dan and Susie were studying math at The Grille. Mondays were quiet at the restaurant, so they could easily talk and work without much distraction. Dan and Susie sat very close to each other. Dan wrote down equations, circled numbers, and pointed at different diagrams as Susie leaned in to watch and take notes.

"Remember, Calculus will get you if you don't look out for divide by zero situations," he said.

Susie was doing her best to absorb what he said as she wrote it down. He explained things so fast, she couldn't keep up. She finished writing down a few more words and took a sip from her drink. Many papers were strewn about their table and it wasn't even close to being a date, but she took it.

She sat back and stretched her cramped hand. "Oh, by the way, why did you miss class last Friday and today?" Susie asked.

"Well... I probably won't return this semester."

"What? Why not?!"

"For some reason, the university doesn't have a record of me in their computers. They told me that until things were cleared up, I can't go back."

"Seriously?" Susie asked, completely floored.

"I'm afraid so."

"But you've been a student for, what, a couple of years?"

"Yup," Dan answered tersely.

Susie could tell that talking about this was upsetting him and wondered why he was even bothering to study with her. She decided to shift the subject. "That's odd... Professor Gomez took a medical leave and he won't be back either," Susie told Dan.

"Really?" Dan asked.

"Yeah. Well, thanks for helping me even though you don't need to study," Susie said, looking at Dan with affection and uncontrollably smiling.

She was smitten and knew it. Susie believed Dan was probably the right guy for her. She anxiously wondered if Dan could ever come to feel the same way.

Their food arrived and they cleared the papers off the table.

"Ah, this looks good," Dan said.

"It sure does," Susie agreed.

Dan's plate contained only a plain hamburger, consisting of nothing but the bun and patty, and he was only drinking water as a beverage. Susie looked down at her iced green tea and her salad with no less than fifteen different fruits, nuts, and other plant-life.

"Wow, our meals are so different," she said.

"Yeah, it's kind of funny," Dan agreed. "So, Susie, what do you like to do for fun?"

Finally, Dan had asked her a social question – something that she knew could lead to a real date – but Susie was not quite sure how to answer. Her life was pretty boring to her. She didn't want to turn Dan off, but she couldn't think of anything else to say. In a very strange, counterintuitive way, Susie nearly wanted to return to talking about Calculus.

"Well, I think I'm pretty boring," Susie responded.

Dan dismissed this, "Nah. There's more to you than that. You have too much gumption about life. You don't have to be a rock climber or a skydiver to have an interesting life."

Susie laughed.

"What?" Dan asked innocently.

She continued laughing.

"What?" Dan asked again.

"Well, I like to rock climb and skydive," Susie answered, laughing throughout her response.

"Seriously?" Dan laughed with her. "Wow... Wow... See, there ya go. I would be scared to death!"

Susie laughed a little more, "Oh, you should try them."

Dan shook his head in playful fear.

"I rock climb at the fitness center on campus," Susie explained, "which isn't real rock climbing, I guess... But, it's still a lot of fun and it's a good workout."

Dan nodded his head, "Oh, yeah, there is a rock climbing wall there."

"And I haven't been skydiving in a while, but I do love it," she said between bites. "I even have my own parachute."

Dan laughed out of nowhere.

"What's so funny?" she asked.

Dan laughed a little more and explained, "Oh, I always wondered what it'd be like to board an airplane with a parachute as your carry-on luggage... Just to mess with people."

Susie giggled, "You could sit in the emergency row..."

Dan finished her sentence, "...holding onto the emergency door handle really nervously!"

Susie added, "You would definitely freak out a bunch of people!"

Dan dropped his voice, pretending to be that fictional passenger, "If anyone needs me, I'll be just outside this door!"

They laughed together.

"Oh… Oh… Oh my goodness… I'm gonna choke on my food!" Susie nearly yelled, laughing.

Hours later, they left The Grille with their backpacks full of papers and books. It was a gorgeous night. The temperature was just right and there was just enough wind to be refreshing. Susie and Dan walked along a brightly lit sidewalk. Tall buildings surrounded them.

"I've spent my whole life in this city. I've always loved it, but I've wondered what it would be like to get away," she said.

"Why's that?" Dan asked.

"Hmm… Just for something different I guess. Sometimes I wonder if I've hindered myself too much by staying here. I guess it's kind of like your story in why you left the monastery."

Dan nodded a little. He bit his lip and said, "I understand, but this city is a world apart from what the monastery is like. Why would you need something different?"

"I don't know. I just wonder sometimes. Something just tells me that my place isn't here."

"This city... It's the only place you want to call home, right?" he asked.

"Most of the time. When I think about leaving, it would also mean that I leave my family. I don't want to do that – they're all I have."

"I understand," Dan said as he looked at his watch. "Whoa. It's pretty late."

"Yeah. I better get home."

A taxi was approaching from down the street. Dan hailed it. The taxi pulled up beside them and Dan opened the door for Susie.

"Thanks for a great night, Dan," she said.

Dan, smiling, replied, "No. Thank you."

"You gonna be okay getting home?" she asked.

Dan looked around and returned his attention to Susie.

"Oh, I'll be fine. I'm gonna catch a bus," he answered.

"Goodnight, Dan."

"Goodnight."

Dan closed the door of the cab behind Susie and the cab drove away.

Several minutes later, the taxi drove up Susie's street and stopped in front of her home. As she paid the fare and tip, she realized that it wasn't within her budget. She ignored the thought and walked into her apartment. Closing the door behind her, she took a deep breath and smiled. It had been a great night for her.

She put her backpack down and walked towards the kitchen. Along the way, she passed by the many framed pictures she had on the wall. Once again, she picked up the old picture of her father holding her when she was three. She thought about what Dan had said at the homeless shelter and decided to do her best to apply it, however minutely she could at this moment.

"Dan makes it seem so easy and effortless," she said to herself, grumbling just a bit.

She focused on how her father was lovingly holding her. It made her angry. Then she looked at the expression on her younger self's face: It was that of a happy child. She realized that she had loved her father deeply back then and something told her that his leaving wasn't something he wanted to do. She suddenly saw that the little girl in the picture had her hand on his face, a strikingly loving gesture that somehow she had never really noticed. She let go of her anger just a little bit.

*　　*　　*

Elsewhere in the city, Dan continued walking along the street alone. He had already walked for quite some time and he was now in a very different part of town. There were run-down and dilapidated buildings nearby, but he was not concerned for his safety. He knew that no one would bother him. He didn't detect any of *Them* either. He had been very careful to avoid *Them*, and he felt at ease at the moment. *They* had help, but so did he. He predicted he wouldn't have any problems for at least the next hour. He approached an intersection and stopped to decide where he should walk to next.

Suddenly, his face became aghast. He spun around and shock enveloped his body. Spike was running towards him from about two hundred feet away.

"How?! How did *They*?!..." he yelled out, questioning why he hadn't seen even a chance of this in advance.

He began to run away, limping hard and on the verge of crying from desperation. Everything was unfolding very quickly and he had little time to plan, let alone act. Since each side could exactly predict what will be, "what will be" had to be constantly changed to gain any advantage. Dan was very much aware that, physically, he was extremely predictable because of his injuries. If he wasn't injured, he would have a better chance of survival against Spike. In his current state, he was certain to perish. He knew he had to defeat Spike indirectly, by changing events around him.

Spike closed in quickly and did not relent in his pursuit in the slightest for even a moment. Dan had been caught off-guard and he knew Spike had the perfect opportunity to kill him.

As they ran down an abandoned street, Spike pulled out a gun and fired off a succession of shots. Dan already knew that

Spike had a gun and he knew exactly where Spike was going to shoot. Dan ducked and weaved, each shot missing him by hundredths of an inch. His face contorted as stabbing pain emanated from his already injured leg.

Dan turned a corner, ran up to a stray dog, placed his hands on its head, and briefly but deeply looked it in the eyes. He let go of the dog and continued running.

The dog snarled and ran in Spike's direction.

Spike turned the corner and was merely thirty feet behind Dan. But, the dog jumped on him, attacking him as if it were rabid. Dan glanced around briefly to see Spike fending off the dog's attack, but he kept running as fast as he could with his limp.

The dog will keep him busy for 11 more seconds, Dan thought in panic, *I need more time.*

With difficulty, Dan climbed an embankment to a busy ten-lane highway with only a low concrete barrier separating the two sides of traffic. He got to the top and blindly bolted across the highway, completely unconcerned about any danger. Cars narrowly missed him and swerved violently.

Dan looked back for a split second and saw that Spike was already up the same embankment and was about to charge into the same lanes of traffic. Dan realized that he had to change something in this very microsecond; Spike would catch him and Spike would, in fact, kill him if events weren't altered this instant.

Dan abruptly stopped in the middle of the innermost right-hand lane. An SUV veered hard to the right to miss him and clipped the front of a car in the lane next to it, causing it to waver and skid. The driver panicked and slammed on the brakes; the car spun around and was broadsided an instant later. A van right behind them swerved hard to avoid them and slammed into the side of the car next to it. The van bounced off and rammed the original accident while the car crossed the next lane and sailed off the highway, flipping when it crashed down on the embankment.

Dan could tell the pile-up had confused Spike and forced him to simply dodge the immediate threat. Even after he reassessed his plan of attack, the multiple-car accident was a significant obstacle now and would cost a few extra seconds to negotiate.

Dan ran along the barrier, far ahead of the site of the accident, and – with shooting pain – swung over the concrete barrier. Dan ran into the other half of the highway without pausing, sensing that Spike had resumed his pursuit.

He knew timing was everything – he had quickly developed a plan, but it required him to wait several seconds. He stopped in the middle lane of the five-lane highway – knowing that cars would safely swerve around him. He then turned and casually watched as Spike worked his way over the tops of the front line of crashed cars and hopped down next to the concrete barrier. Spike immediately crouched down.

Swerving and braking to avoid the pileup on the other side of the highway, a car hit a large piece of debris from the accident, flipping up and over the concrete barrier and the crouched Spike. It flew into oncoming traffic on Dan's side of the highway. Several cars braked suddenly and spun out of control, trying to avoid the rogue car. Spike had jumped up and was running full tilt along the barrier before the first car hit it.

Dan remained motionless in the middle of the five lanes, calmly watching the scene. Spike crossed the barrier where Dan had and stopped in the innermost lane of traffic, leaving only one lane separating them.

Dan knew he couldn't safely move from his spot without being struck dead by a car. He also knew that Spike couldn't move either for the same reason. Dan calmly sat down on the concrete highway. He didn't flinch as cars and trucks flew by him, narrowly missing him at high speed only to crash seconds later. A piece of twisted metal flew far from the wreck and whizzed above Dan's head – he knew with certainty that it would have hit him if he had been standing up.

Spike took an occasional step or two back and forth to dodge the cars and trucks, but was completely unable to progress towards Dan.

The two looked at each other with utmost contempt – both unable to move from their immediate area for the moment – outwardly oblivious to the carnage around them. They both were forced to wait for an opening in this lengthy chain-reaction wreck.

Spike's expression changed to a look of defeat. Dan smiled – he knew he would escape Spike and he knew that Spike was riddled with frustration.

A huge tractor-trailer screeched to a twisting halt and flopped over between Spike and Dan, cutting them off from each other. Dan ran away and off the highway, leaving Spike behind – still standing and unharmed.

Father Crane looked off into the distance outside his window of the monastery, reading a text from Spike, *Unless something changes that was my last chance.*

Motionless, without even the most minor movement of any muscle, he sat for a minute thinking, planning, and scheming.

He eventually wrote a text to Frank, *Do what you think is right and do not hesitate to act regardless of how ineffective it may seem.*

Chapter 18 – Veil Lifted

Susie walked out of the bathroom, having just taken her morning shower. She had a towel wrapped around her head and she was wearing a worn bathrobe. She walked over to her cell phone, playfully hoping that Dan had called while she was showering.

"No messages," she said. "I already miss him."

Her phone rang in her hand. The caller ID showed it was Dan. Her face lit up.

"Hi Dan!" she answered.

"Good morning! I hope I didn't call too early?"

"Nope."

"I was wondering if you wanted to study math right now?" Dan asked.

Susie was disappointed and surprised – she didn't know what to say.

"I'm kidding! I'm kidding!" Dan laughed.

Susie laughed with him in relief.

"So silly," she said, trying her best to contain her excitement.

She had seen so much of Dan's serious side recently that she had almost forgotten that the guy was exceptionally popular and funny.

"Actually, a friend of mine just left me two tickets to the botanical gardens in town. They're only good for today and I know it's short notice, but do you wanna come?" Dan asked.

Susie quickly thought about what her day looked like. It was a Tuesday and she had the afternoon free. Normally, she would study during any free time, but she was not going to pass up this opportunity. She really enjoyed her time with him.

"I'd love to," she said.

Later that day, Dan and Susie walked through a large park filled with the many lush trees and plants that made up the botanical gardens. Everywhere, flowers were in bloom and the humidity made it feel as if they were in a tropical forest. They took a short break and talked on a bridge that crossed a small stream.

"The beauty of places like this never ceases to amaze me," Dan said.

"It's so peaceful. So serene," Susie added, nodding.

Dan pointed to a nearby patch of plants.

"Yet, all of those plants over there are carnivorous," he said. "They look and act innocent, but they are simply patiently awaiting their prey. It's ironic that, among all of these plants chosen for their tranquil beauty, those plants are included."

Susie couldn't tell exactly which plants he was referring to, but she trusted him that they were there. To her eyes, it was just a bunch of plants of varying sizes, shapes, and colors. She quickly gave up trying to find them.

"Yeah, it is a bit ironic," she agreed anyway. "Who would ever think that so many vicious creatures can blend in and seem just as nice as all of the others?"

"Those plants are vicious. The giant pitcher plant over there can actually eat rats. It doesn't move; it just waits for its prey to haplessly fall into its trap."

"I'm sure there are people like that."

"It can be confusing to know who is truly good or who is truly bad based on looks alone," Dan said.

"True," Susie said. "I think people should…"

She stopped talking and choked unexpectedly. She became increasingly dizzy with each passing second. Her vision slightly blurred. Her knees began to buckle a little and she grabbed her mouth, wanting to vomit.

"What's the matter?" Dan asked, sounding a little surprised.

Susie was too confused and light-headed to give an intelligible answer.

"I… I don't know… I just feel weak. My head… spinning… I… I…," she stumbled.

Dan's eyes widened, he visibly tensed up, and he turned around. He grabbed Susie and held her close to him. About twenty feet away was a man dressed in a plaid button-down shirt and blue jeans.

"Frank," Dan whispered.

Frank panted a little and blinked frequently, as if he was losing his sight as he slowly walked towards them. With each step closer, he seemed to be growing weaker. He stumbled and vomited on the spot. He was within twelve feet of Dan and Susie when he collapsed to the ground. Dan tried to hold Susie in his arms, but she fell to her knees and began hyperventilating.

"What's… What's going on?" Susie cried.

Staring at Frank, Dan sternly replied, "Just keep still, Susie. Don't move."

Frank didn't get any closer. He reached out his hand towards Dan and Susie, but he kept his eyes shut – he was writhing in pain.

Frank struggled to speak. "You... You... You...," he whispered as he frothed at the mouth.

Dan commanded, "You MUST leave! You are NOT welcome here, Frank!"

Franks shook his head violently. "You! You! You!" he hollered, gasping between words.

Susie sat on the ground completely disoriented. She panted, "It's... It's... It's overpowering."

Dan turned his body towards Susie but didn't take his eyes off of Frank. "Stay strong," he told her.

He then pointed at Frank and snarled at him, "Leave NOW!"

Frank cried out and thrashed in pain. Scooting backwards, he turned around, staggered to his feet, and ran away.

Susie's panting slowed, but she remained sitting on the ground.

Dan sat down next to her to comfort her. "You okay?" Dan asked Susie, continuing to look in the direction that Frank ran.

"I... I think so. I... I don't know what to think. I've never felt that way before."

Dan was silent.

Susie was quickly regaining her usual self. "You called him Frank... You seemed like you knew him. Do you?" she implored.

Dan looked to the ground, still silent.

"What happened, Dan? Tell me! WHAT HAPPENED JUST NOW?!" she yelled.

Dan took a deep breath. His face flushed a bit and he gulped.

"Since I was young, I have been blessed in certain ways...," Dan began. He looked at Susie for a second and then stood up. "Let's walk."

He helped Susie up to her feet. They continued their walk on the same path as before, but much slower. Susie could tell that

Dan was struggling to find words. She was okay with him taking his time – after all, he did protect her from that terrible man.

Dan continued, "I've been very attune to keeping things peaceful. It… It gives me peace in return. Conversely, I'm very attuned to sensing things that disturb that peace."

Susie kept her face stern, demanding more information.

Dan looked at Susie, appearing troubled. "It's also why I always seem to be in the right place at the right time to help others," he explained. "I sense it. I sense where I should be and what I should do once I get there."

Dan waved his hand behind them and said, "That man back there… He was a bad man. I sensed it. You sensed it. Nothing was right. He was out to harm us."

"He was… He made me feel like I was going to implode on myself. I've never felt anything like it before," Susie said.

Dan didn't say anything in return. He resumed walking and Susie followed.

"But, you knew his name… and you got him to leave us alone somehow," Susie noted.

Dan shook his head, but didn't say anything.

"Why aren't you saying anything?" Susie demanded.

"It's a little complex."

Susie narrowed her eyes in dissatisfaction.

"I'm trying my best to put words together. Sometimes weird things happen," Dan explained.

"Things like this… They just don't happen," she asserted.

"Oh, yes, they do. Trust me. It's simply that when they happen, no one else seems to be around or they aren't paying attention. These things happen all of the time," Dan said.

"I don't understand. I've never seen you… I never knew that you…I've…," Susie struggled.

Dan finishes, "You haven't seen me like this?"

Susie nodded with fervor. She had seen so many sides to Dan that she didn't know what to think anymore. He acted like nothing happened at all. He wasn't shaken up in the slightest. It appeared to be – and quite literally – just another day in the park for him.

"I don't know what to say," Susie said.

Part of her wanted to run away, but she felt safe with Dan. She had no idea who that guy was back there and she surely didn't want to come across him again.

No words were exchanged for the next few minutes as they walked through the park and turned onto the walkway around its perimeter. Susie kept hoping that Dan would offer more information on his own, but he seemed content just to walk.

As they began to pass by a tall beige house on the border of the park, Susie grabbed Dan's shoulder, abruptly stopping him. She was tired of waiting for answers and she wanted them now.

"Aren't you going to say anything?" Susie asked.

"Well, let's see, this goes back a few years...," he began but stopped.

Susie saw his eyes shift and stare to the right. Then, he was walking briskly away from her, leaving her behind.

"Hey! Where are you going?!" she yelled after him. "You just can't walk away like this!"

Dan didn't say a word. Instead, he walked to the tall beige house and around to its front. A woman faced the house, avoiding the wind while she tried to light a cigarette. Dan approached the woman, violently grabbed her arm, and pulled her towards him.

"HEY! What are you doing?! Let me go!" the woman yelled, with the cigarette still hanging from her mouth.

She began beating his arms, but Dan ignored her. He dragged her a few more feet and finally gave her one good yank towards him as hard as he could; she stumbled a few feet in his direction.

She screamed, "HELP! HELP!"

A half second later, a car came out of nowhere, narrowly missing the woman and plowing into the side of the house – demolishing the spot where she was standing. Dust filled the air. Debris from the house and car was everywhere. The car's horn produced a loud continuous honk.

Dan let go of the woman. Dumbfounded, she let her cigarette drop from her mouth and just stared at the wreck in awe. Dan walked away without saying a word, without giving any overt clue as to what just happened. Susie followed in close pursuit and caught up.

"Hey! HEY!" she yelled. "Stop! Just stop!"

Dan stopped with his back still to Susie. She gripped his shoulders and spun him around to face her. She poked him in the chest and insisted, "Tell me everything. No more 'oh it's a long story'. No more ambiguities. Just the complete truth!"

Dan let out a long sigh. "You got a C- on your test," he said.

Insulted, Susie responded, "Yeah, we both knew that already."

"You got it because you didn't have time to study the night before," Dan explained.

Susie was silent, but looked at him curiously.

"I know you told me that you were upset about Nicole, but the reality was that, on the night before the midterm, you spent hours on the phone comforting your sister in her latest relationship crisis."

Susie's eyes narrowed, "Have you been spying on me?!"

Dan shook his head.

He continued, "You have exactly three sticks of chewing gum in your purse right now. You always leave at least one stick in case your mother asks you if you have gum. Your mother loves gum."

Susie was petrified.

Dan looked around. He pointed towards a nearby office building. "The light on the top corner of that office building…," he said while pointing, "…will turn on… NOW."

A light in an office at the top corner of the building turned on at that exact moment.

Dan continued on, "That jogger is about to trip," he said while pointing at a jogger.

The jogger tripped on cue.

He turned to Susie and pleaded, "You will talk to your sister later about this… But, I ask you to not do so or talk to anyone at all about this or else I will disappear forever."

Dan's face filled with sadness.

Susie was speechless.

Dan continued, "It's hard, knowing things before they happen… Knowing lots of things before they happen… And trying to live a regular life in spite of it."

Susie asked softly, "Are you… Are you…"

Dan looked earnestly at Susie, "There's nothing special about me. There are many others just like me."

"You're… an angel?" Susie asked, feeling a bit foolish in doing so.

But, she had to ask because it would somewhat explain things to her.

Dan let out a brief laugh, "Ha! Oh, no… At least," he frowned and said solemnly, "I don't think so… And, I'm not a psychic either. There is nothing supernatural involved. It's all quite natural."

Susie looked blankly forward, not knowing what to say, but badly wanting to know everything.

She finally asked, "So, there are others then?"

Dan said, "Yes. Several."

"Do you know them?"

"Some of them," he answered and then briefly paused.

He looked at Susie, his eyes welling up. She felt a stab of guilt – she didn't want to make him sad.

"*We* sense each other," he explained. "*We* rarely talk to each other."

"Why?"

"Well, there really isn't much to say when you already know what will happen. It's like everyone is watching the same movie they've all seen a thousand times together. Everything, regardless of how amazing it may seem to other people, is very boring and mundane to…," he hesitated, "…*Us*."

Susie wondered if she was dreaming. None of this can actually be happening. Even though it answers why Dan is always at the right place at the right time, this opens up so many other questions.

Susie was consumed in thought. She decided to sit down at a nearby bench so she could think more clearly. Dan sat next to her, slumping a bit with his arms folded. She decided that she should test him, but she had to think of a good challenge.

Dan blurted out, "In about thirty seconds, you're going to test me by asking me how much change you have in your purse. The answer is one dime. A single dime. The very same dime that you thought you lost when you went grocery shopping at the end of last semester."

Susie lost her breath in wonder at his knowing about that silly incident with the dime, but then she realized that he was wrong. "Um, no… I don't have any change at all. And, I spent that dime," she insisted.

"It's between two business cards at the bottom of your purse. One business card is from a pet store, which you picked up last year when you went to the mall with Karen. You briefly considered getting a parakeet as a pet. The other is a business card from your cell phone salesman and you got that card 19 months, 4 days, 22 hours ago."

Susie rummaged through her purse. Dan was right: the dime was exactly where he described.

"*We*, uh…," he paused uncomfortably, "People like me can see into the future… and the past… perfectly."

Susie was now convinced that this had to be a dream. There was no other explanation that she could accept. She was waiting to wake up and laugh about it with Dan later on.

"Can you read my thoughts?" Susie asked, wondering if Dan read them just now.

"Nope," Dan replied. "That isn't part of the gift. *We* can only see events that have unfolded and events that will unfold later. When it comes to reading thoughts, well, *We* don't have to. Whatever you don't say, you will eventually say with actions."

Susie bit at her finger in silence. She doubted the reality of the moment.

Dan said, "Let me put it this way: do you ever come across people that you seem to click with?"

"Yes," Susie said.

"And sometimes you come across people you don't click with? You know, ones you get a creepy feeling about?"

"Of course."

Dan got closer to her face and looked hard at her.

"Now then, *why* is that?" he asked emphatically.

Susie hadn't really thought about it before. She shrugged, "I don't… I don't know."

Dan went on, "Everyone experiences it. They come across people they do or don't like instantly and – for no obvious reason and without ever knowing them – they don't know why."

Susie's breathing picked up a little, worried that Dan could actually be speaking the truth. She knew precisely what he was talking about and it was one of those inexplicable things in life that she took for granted. But, she wasn't sure where he was going with this and it didn't explain why Dan had the abilities he exhibited and described.

"Everyone, and I mean everyone, has the ability to feel this about other people and they don't know why," Dan repeated. "The reason is the same as why people like me exist, except that our ability is much more extreme."

"Wow," Susie said under her breath.

Dan took a deep breath and resumed, "It all depends on what *We* call our Polarity."

"Polarity?" Susie asked.

"Yes. Like the north pole or south pole, like positive or negative, like left or right, like up or down, like from one extreme to another: it is two-sided."

"I... I...," Susie stammered.

"I'll try my best to explain. There are some old refrigerator magnets in that garbage can over there," he said, pointing at a group of cans nearby.

He got up from the bench and walked over to a particular can, reached into a bag inside the can, and immediately pulled out a couple of magnets – spending no effort in searching. Susie was amazed at how easy he made it look.

"These refrigerator magnets...," he said while holding them up, "They are nothing more than metal. Metal is everywhere, but only a very small fraction of it is magnetized. Likewise, there are people everywhere, but only a very small fraction of them have their full Polarity."

"True," Susie said, "but that doesn't explain..."

Dan interrupted, "Of course, Polarity has nothing to do with magnets. I'm just using them to illustrate a point."

Susie blinked her eyes several times, trying to understand what Dan was saying.

"You have some degree of Polarity, your sister does, your mother does, and so on. Everyone does. This allows everyone to often sense the good or bad in people, remember some things with clarity, and occasionally predict future events to a small degree. These are things that everyone can do no matter who you are. What's interesting is that people have tried for centuries to explain why humans can do these things. It is usually dismissed – most often as luck or intuition or some other generic, meaningless word."

"I guess... sure... I mean, I've never thought about it. It's true that humans have these abilities but no one fully understands or agrees about why we have them."

Dan continued, "When a human gets their full Polarity, it's just like metal becoming a full magnet: it's an extreme transformation in ability. The magnet was once just metal, but it now has an amazing power – so is the case in humans with Polarity."

"Polarity...," Susie whispered.

"The simple power of sensing good or bad is just your ability to construct small pieces of the future – anyone can do it. With your full Polarity, this is taken to an extreme so that you know and see everything in the past, present, and future tenses. You are clairvoyant in that regard."

"This strangely makes sense to me," Susie said. "It does explain a lot. It's... it's just coming at me too fast."

Dan sat back down on the bench next to Susie and fiddled with the magnets in his hands. "Just like a magnet, Polarity with humans comes with two sides, however cliché that sounds. One pole is completely dedicated to destruction, instability, and, well... evil. The other pole is focused on stability, peacefulness, and, um... good."

Dubious, Susie commented, "That is cliché. Good versus evil. Old story."

"I only use those words because they carry the most meaning to you. I could have said chaos versus order or complexity versus simplicity. The 'evil' side...," Dan said while putting his fingers in a quotation gesture, "...does not believe *They* are evil. *They* believe that *They* are only bringing out what's required for mankind to progress. *They* believe that instability and destruction are the mechanisms to force mankind to progress. Death forces you to examine your own life. Pain forces you to seek pleasure. Destroying a building forces the next one to be built stronger," Dan said with increasing passion.

"It seems that you...," Susie began.

"It makes me sad...," Dan interrupted, "...very sad to know that people would do such horrible things. I embrace and make it my only purpose in life to foster stability and peace. I believe mankind will progress, but it will do so with a foundation of doing good to one another," Dan said, smiling. "Destruction, by definition, destroys progress."

"I've never really thought about these things in this way before," Susie said.

"Well, why do people get angry?" Dan asked.

"Because something didn't work out the way they wanted it... They get mad."

"And that anger results in wanting change so badly that you examine ways to force that change to happen. Anger and outrage make issues important. People – however proactive they want to believe they are – are almost entirely reactionary," Dan said.

"True... So, these two sides... How do they deal with each other?"

Dan held up the two magnets, "Magnets have a positive side and a negative side, right?"

"Yes."

"Just like magnets, depending on which side you're on, you'll either repel each other...," Dan demonstrated by holding the magnets so that they repelled each other and would not touch,

"…or you will attract each other," he said as he flipped one the magnets so that they pulled together with a click.

"I guess nature has a way of making two different sides appear everywhere," Susie commented.

"Humans aren't an exception," added Dan.

"Abilities like this are right in front of our faces and we don't question it. Even if I don't believe in Polarity, it's true that these things do happen – it has to be called something," Susie said.

Susie looked briefly at the ground, trying her best to piece together the information as skeptically as possible. This did explain the amazing things Dan was able to do, but it was still too surreal. She needed more details.

"Well, this doesn't explain how you know so much about everything. You talk about knowing about the past and the future. How does Polarity add up to that?" Susie bluntly asked.

"The world is nothing more than a countless number of events: each creates one or more other events, which also create one or more and so on," Dan said.

Still sitting on the bench, he leaned over and picked up several small pebbles from the ground, pointed at a large nearby puddle of water, and tossed a pebble into it. The water rippled on impact. He clarified, "Each event has a ripple effect in causing other events to happen. Everything, down to the tiniest level, is nothing more than a giant chain reaction."

He threw another pebble into the same puddle of water. He then threw about ten more into the puddle. Ripples were everywhere, intersecting with each other; some built higher, some were negated.

"Like the butterfly effect?" Susie asked.

Dan cocked his head.

"You know: If a butterfly in China flaps its wings, it will cause a tornado in Kansas? Because everything is connected?" Susie explained.

Dan laughed, "Heavens, no! Well... That is, not exactly."

Susie gave him a sour look – she didn't appreciate Dan's laugh. She wanted to know.

Dan tossed the rest of his pebbles into the puddle. He pointed to the ripples in the water, "When you have your full Polarity, such ripples in life are easy to predict. Just as it is easy for you to blink your eyes, it is nearly effortless to predict the future. If you know all of the events going on now, you can play them out a few seconds, minutes, hours, days, months, years, and so on into the future – all in an instant."

Susie looked at the hundreds of ripples.

Dan continued, "You can go as far forward or backward as you wish. You can predict anything in perfect detail and you can recall any event, even if you weren't there, in perfect detail. It's nothing more than just a bunch of events."

"It just seems like it's too much for a human to do," Susie said.

"Remember: it's the same mechanism that lets you, me, and everyone else sense good or bad in people or places we don't know anything about. You do get those feelings. You are using your small amount of Polarity and you don't even know how or why. It's automatic."

"Wow," Susie whispered, still trying to take it all in.

Dan laughed a little, quipping, "Butterflies have been known to also prevent tornados in Kansas."

Susie didn't react to his attempt at a joke.

Dan wiped the laughter from his face.

"Having my Polarity is second nature to me. It's woven into everything I do. It's with me whether I want it or not," Dan said.

Dan stood up, gesturing passionately as he spoke.

"Because of this, *We* are able to manipulate the events to change the outcomes as *We* need. *We* wouldn't care about butterflies causing tornados unless it interfered with *Our* goals," he said.

He paused and stared out into the distance, seeming almost regretful.

"Really, *Our* only limitation is that *We* are still human and, individually, *We* cannot track everything. There's just too much."

"I don't know what to say," Susie said. She still sat on the bench, trying to absorb these revelations.

Dan sat down next to her again and cracked an understanding smile. He told her, "It's okay. I don't expect you to understand it or even believe it at this point."

Susie became thoughtful about the question of belief. She wanted to give Dan the benefit of the doubt. She had seen the good he had accomplished. She had seen how many lives he'd already touched.

"You only manipulate events for good…," she began.

Dan finished, "Yes. And, for *Them*, they manipulate events for evil. There is no in-between. It's based entirely on your Polarity."

Susie took a deep breath.

"Dan, why did you tell me all of this?" Susie asked.

Dan averted his eyes away from Susie briefly. "Well, Susie, it's pretty clear that *They* are not just after me, but *They* are also after you, it seems."

"They…," she starts nervously.

"*They* want to kill you, yes," Dan finished.

"W-w-why?" Susie probed, almost crying.

"I'm not sure."

"I thought you knew everything."

"Fair enough," Dan answered. "I know what will happen, but so do *They*. If you have your full Polarity, you can change the events of now to affect the events of later. The future is always changing where *We* or *They* are involved."

"What…," she said.

"Think of *Their* plan as many dominoes carefully arranged in a line. Each domino is an event that may involve a person… like you. If one domino is knocked down then all others ahead of it will eventually get knocked down also. The last domino will be whatever ultimate goal *They* seek."

"Just like the chain of events you talked about," Susie said.

"Exactly. However, if one domino is out of place then all other dominoes ahead of it won't fall down and *Their* plan will fail. Each domino must be lined up just right. Any degree of unpredictability comes from events intentionally changed by *Us* or *Them* – kind of like moving a domino out of place. Make sense?"

"Yeah. I think so."

Dan stood up.

"Walk with me, please," he asked politely. "We shouldn't stay here any longer."

They strolled aimlessly along the city's streets.

"It's possible that you're a threat to *Them*," Dan remarked. "You are kind-hearted. You help others. You are counter to everything *They* stand for. Heh, you may even get your full Polarity, too. Who knows?"

This made Susie's stomach churned. She stopped walking.

"Get *my* full Polarity?" she asked.

Dan smiled sympathetically, "Yes. No one starts life having it. You just get it one day."

Susie was intrigued – this curious power was accessible to anyone. Dan spoke of Polarity so casually and mundanely. Her mind filled with wonder.

"How… How does it happen?" she asked.

"Well, it has everything to do with you – only you. You have positive intentions and you have negative intentions, right?"

"Yeah, everyone does."

"Not everyone. Not those with their full Polarity," Dan said solemnly. "Once you are completely rid of any negative intentions, you are polarized to what I'm generically calling 'good'."

Dan paused and beamed a smile at her. Susie felt a rush of excitement.

"Or, once you are completely rid of any positive intentions," Dan said with visible uneasiness, "you are polarized to evil."

"I… I don't know how that's possible. Humans are emotional beings. We cannot control ourselves to such an extreme level," she said.

"Why do you think serial killers always seem to be one step ahead of the law? Why is it that people like Mother Teresa knew exactly what to do to help people? They are commonly on the cusp of getting their full Polarity," he said nonchalantly. "But, who knows if you'll ever get it. Many come close, but never do."

"You can't see that in my future?"

"I don't know if you'll live long enough to…," Dan began but quickly stopped.

Susie's eyes welled up in tears; Dan spoke too confidently to be lying. She came to a standstill on the sidewalk, overcome with emotion.

Dan hung his head in shame.

"Oh Susie, I'm so sorry. I'm so so very very sorry. I… I'm not used to talking so candidly with someone who doesn't have their full Polarity."

Tears streamed down her face and she kept silent. Even through her weeping, Susie could see that he didn't mean to be so insensitive. She knew what kind of person he really was.

"Don't… Don't worry about it," she finally said.

Dan grasped Susie firmly by the shoulders and looked her straight in the eyes. "Susie, I swear that I would die before I would let *Them* get you. Mark my words as a solemn oath," Dan said. "*They* make predicting future events very difficult… that was all I was trying to say. Instead, I managed to put both feet in my mouth."

He released her and started pacing back and forth.

He continued, "Because *We* are being targeted, *They* are constantly changing things. *We* must do the same. It's the only way to counteract."

"So, why don't you change things?" Susie asked.

Dan quickly answered, "Oh, I am and I have been constantly, but the fact that you're in the mix now makes it even more difficult. Most of the time, each side makes lots of very small, subtle changes that gradually lead to a big result. Those are harder to detect. But lately, *They* seem to be willing to take risks and act more directly."

Dan stopped pacing. Without a hint of emotion on his face, he looked to his left and then towards the sky. "We need help," he announced.

Dan whipped out his phone and started typing a text message. He explained while typing, "Since *We* can't get too close to anyone with the same Polarity, *We* use things like texting to communicate."

"Why can't you get close to each other?"

Dan stopped typing and sent his text. He sat down on the curb and motioned for her to join him.

He explained, "Oh, well… Like the magnets, those with the same Polarity repel each other. It's pretty painful, very disorienting, and extremely uncomfortable. Put two of us with the same Polarity next to each other and we'd be completely incapacitated, and we would both die within a minute or so."

"And those with opposite polarities?" Susie asked.

"Nearly uncontrollable attraction… But, it's in a *very* violent, cataclysmic way. The urge to annihilate the other is insatiable," Dan said, his nostrils flaring out slightly.

"Annihilate?" Susie asked.

"Kill."

Susie pointed out, "But, I thought those who are good wouldn't want to kill."

"It's uncontrollable," Dan said. "Besides, it's seen as the only way to keep *Them* suppressed. *They* cannot be reasoned with. *They* are deceptive. *They* are the ultimate wolf in sheep's clothing."

"Hmm," she spouted, shifting uncomfortably.

"Would you kill someone knowing that, if you didn't, they would kill a thousand others?" Dan asked.

Susie straightened her posture. "No. Absolutely not. I wouldn't. Killing is never right," she affirmed.

Dan retorted, "It isn't a question of right or wrong. It's a question of effectiveness. Remember, *They* are otherwise unstoppable."

"There are other ways to get the same result," she said bluntly. "There must be."

Dan sighed and clenched his fists a little. "Before I got my full Polarity, I shared the exact sentiment you do right now. I was afraid to step on a doodlebug. Now that I have my full Polarity, I can see just how unrelenting *They* are. It's exceptionally difficult to have *Them* caught as criminals and have the law take care of things. *They* leave no discernible trace of their deeds that can be used as evidence. *They* make accidents happen. *They* influence people to do things that *They* would never do *Themselves*," Dan explained.

Susie was unfazed by this. She stuck firmly to her belief. "We'll have to agree to disagree," she said.

"In any case, it's uncontrollable. I don't make the rules, but I am stuck with them."

Susie could see how conflicted Dan was. But, she shook her head, not budging on the issue. Still, she couldn't picture him hurting anyone. His heart was always in the right place. How can he believe that this was the right thing to do?

Dan shrugged. "Many times I really don't have a choice. *They* attack me directly and if I don't defend myself then I will die by *Their* hand."

Susie remained silent.

"When you found me in the hospital, it was because I was attacked by *Them*," Dan admitted.

Susie gasped and sat up a little.

"*They* sent Spike after me. I was half a second from getting my throat slit," Dan said, choking up a little.

Susie's heart melted. She saw now that, truly, he was in a predicament that he didn't chose and couldn't change. He had his Polarity and he had to live with it.

"Spike?" she asked.

"A ruthless killer," Dan answered. "He kills without a speck of remorse. He's killed so many that it's second nature to him. You will never see an ounce of emotion on his face other than pure, sinister, evil."

Susie dropped her gaze – the truth behind Dan's hospital visit made everything very real to her.

"Spike is the guy who's been following you recently," Dan said.

Her eyes shot to Dan, "What?!"

"Do you remember the night on campus after your World History final and you saw a man light up a cigarette on your way back to the car?"

"Yeah... Yeah, I remember that."

"That was Spike. I knew he planned to attack you and that's why I made sure to be there that night. I was there to protect you from him. You were moments away from really bad things happening."

Susie's jaw dropped.

"He's followed you several times actually, whether you knew it or not," Dan revealed. "Each and every time, he would have killed you if it hadn't been for intervention from *Us*."

Susie dropped her head slowly in disbelief. She wondered how she could have been so stupid as to not see this before: The same mohawk silhouette, the same lit cigarette, and the same posture – it was all there. Dan was always there for her. He had protected her every step of the way and she hadn't even known it.

"It's getting dark," Susie said as she looked around, noting the twilight.

Chapter 19 – Hanging Out

As night fell, Dan and Susie were eating in a sparsely populated fast food restaurant. They sat in a booth, occasionally taking bites of food, as Dan patiently handled Susie's torrent of questions.

"If they want me dead, why don't they just barge into my home and kill me?" Susie asked Dan.

Dan took a sip from his drink and replied, "Ah, because it's too easy for *Us* to lead the police to *Them*. Even being detained for questioning is a major disadvantage because it wastes time. So, *They* prefer to do their deeds indirectly. *They* simply cause events to set in motion other events – just like falling dominoes – that will ultimately yield the same result."

"Another thing…," Susie started.

"Yeah?"

"Why do you emphasize *they* and *us*?"

"Now that is a very long story," Dan answered.

"Never mind then. I was just curious."

"In short, these are just the names we give each other. *They* refer to *Us* in the same way."

Susie was still skeptical but open to learning more. She mentally reviewed experiences that could possibly support what Dan has told her.

"Déjà vu?" she asked.

"What about it?"

"Is it like this?"

Dan gazed at Susie for several seconds.

"What?" Susie asked, seeing that Dan was hesitant.

"Oh, sorry. Yes, of course, déjà vu is actually your tiny little bit of Polarity spouting out from time to time. You have the déjà vu moment and you're astounded by it. You distinctly feel that you've experienced that particular moment before, but you can't remember when, right?"

"Yeah," she said.

"You try your hardest to decide if you saw it in a dream, if you're re-living a past life, or if it's a form of divine inspiration, right?" Dan asked.

Susie didn't answer Dan's rhetorical question.

"None of that is what déjà vu is. When you have déjà vu, you are quite literally chaining together the events a microsecond before they happen. Your brain processes the information and puts it in your memory. Your brain will then process the information from your eyes and instantly recognize it as something it already knows. You truly remember it, but you truly don't know how or why. And then you get that 'Oh this is so cool!' feeling. You tell everyone around you that you had a déjà vu moment, and people are collectively excited for a few moments."

"Yeah…"

"Polarity agrees with science," Dan said with a degree of reverence. "Polarity is just as natural as sight, touch, and hearing.

Everyone has it and uses it in their everyday life to some degree… And there are some who are masters at it."

Polarity was clearer to Susie now. Being able to effortlessly predict future events could give such people infinite power, riches, fame, or whatever they wanted, unimpeded. She decided to turn the questioning to a larger scale. "So, do you do things like control who the president is going to be, other world leaders… that kind of thing?" she asked.

Dan shook his head emphatically. "No, things like that are too easy for *Them* to counter because it's so narrowly focused. Besides, controlling world leaders is inefficient; it's the people who count. Both sides prefer to influence entire populations en masse at various levels and at the same time. Over time, things change one way or the other until, eventually, the change is irreversible."

"Oh… But, that seems so slow. You could do so much good in such a short amount of time," Susie argued.

"No, not really. *They* won't let such easy things happen. No matter what *We* do, *They* will make it difficult."

"It still seems slow," Susie repeated.

"Yes, but it's the only effective way of making the changes that are sought. The First World War is a great example," Dan said.

"How so?" Susie asked with keen curiosity to finally hear something specific.

"Well, how did it start?" Dan asked.

"Some guy got shot or something… History isn't exactly my strong suit," Susie said shyly.

"That's quite alright. That 'some guy' was Archduke Ferdinand. He was assassinated in 1914 and the world was in just the sort of position to set a massive war into motion for no apparent reason. And that's about as deep as anyone can really go."

"Yeah. All I remember is that some guy got shot," Susie said.

"The fact is that no one really knows why or how World War One started. There are theories and explanations but the actual web of events are so complex that it's incomprehensible unless you have your Polarity. I can tell you that most of the 16 million who died across the world couldn't have cared less who Archduke Ferdinand was."

"16 million died?" Susie rhetorically asked, sickened.

"The truth is that, for well over a hundred years before, *They* caused many small, seemingly inconsequential changes. These led to greater conflicts and disagreements that ultimately altered relationships between the major empires and other countries in the world. Tension built up and no one really knows why or how. There are theories and explanations, but, at best, they only cover the most superficial levels that were influenced. All anyone says is that 'some guy got shot'."

"I'm curious," Susie said as she drew out her phone. "I'm gonna look it up."

Dan waited patiently as Susie read through several websites.

"Hmm," she said with an agreeing smile as she put away her phone. "Strange. No one really knows."

"Yeah, strange." Dan continued, "The next thing everyone knew, the world was at war. I have to admit, *They* were very clever to make that happen."

"What did, uh, *They* do to start it?"

"Sadly, it was a well-orchestrated plot involving 732 mostly mid-level ministers between the warring states over many years. By the time *We* caught onto it, it was too late," Dan said.

"Well, it all worked out in the end. *They* did lose after all," Susie noted.

"Are you sure *They* lost?" Dan asked, "16 million people died."

Susie didn't answer. She felt stupid for suggesting that either Polarity would side with politics or nations as a whole. She had not even considered that the death toll could have been an end in itself. She knew she had no business with notions like winning or losing when she was still grasping the depth at which Polarity was used.

"I'm sorry for sounding so sanctimonious," Dan apologized. "Again, I'm not used to sharing details like this with anyone."

"It's okay."

"Anyway, *We* think of progress as the sum of lots of little things. Some are so small that you wouldn't pay attention to them."

Susie buried her face in her open palms. Retracing her steps, she had no idea what she would have done differently if Dan hadn't been around. She wondered what little things were changed to keep Spike from getting to her – especially when Dan wasn't around.

"What can I do... to protect myself?" Susie asked calmly.

"Trust your instincts. Listen to them. Follow what they tell you. When evil is nearby, you will feel it. This is why Frank couldn't get to you."

"Frank?"

"The man who approached us at the botanical gardens and tried to attack."

"Oh, yeah... He's one of *Them*?"

"Yes," Dan replied. "He's new to his Polarity. He doesn't know his full power yet. He's too awkward and too reckless. He's still in a stage of confusing the near future with the present. I'm a bit shocked that *They* would send him to do anything."

"He was... so normal-looking," Susie reflected.

"Yup, he certainly was. Don't expect evil to look evil," he said as he looked at his watch. "It's getting late."

Susie didn't want Dan to leave. She wasn't tired and she knew she wouldn't get a wink of sleep tonight.

"Dan...," she started.

"Don't worry, Susie. You'll be fine. *We* have kept you safe so far and *We* will keep you safe tonight. "

Susie was unsure. The complexity of the situation made her feel vulnerable.

"I'll stay with my mother tonight. Would that be safe?"

"*We* already knew you would ask that," Dan answered with indifference. "Go ahead and stay with her, if it makes you feel more comfortable."

"It would. Let's get together tomorrow..."

"Nine o'clock?" he asked.

"Sure."

Within an hour Susie was at the doorstep of her mother's house. She knocked on the door and her mother answered – a sweet, plump woman with long, mostly grey hair and a withered face.

"Honey, what's the matter? Are you okay?" her mother asked at seeing Susie's anxious and weary face.

"I'm fine. I'm just feeling a bit under the weather. School has been stressful," Susie answered quietly.

"Susie, Susie, Susie," her mother repeated lovingly as she gave Susie a big warm hug and welcomed her inside.

Her mother's home was filled with relics from the fractured years that had gone by and would be, at best, considered eclectic in style. None of the furniture remotely matched and most of it, Susie knew, was in disrepair. Susie took a nostalgic glance around the living room and saw a familiar couch whose cushions were faded and speckled with stains, a chair with a stack of books in place of a missing leg, and a bookshelf that looked as if it was about to collapse under its own weight. In fact, Susie suspected that one of its shelves was actually being supported by two tall books on the shelf below it. The dining room table was covered with piles of junk mail, empty boxes, and newspaper clippings.

Her mother would occasionally buy damaged but once-expensive items at garage sales in a vain attempt to make her home more upscale. Sitting on top of the bookcase was a Tiffany lamp that her mother must have had just bought because Susie didn't recognize it. As she got closer, she could see that it was cracked from top to bottom, but, from a distance, it wasn't noticeable.

Susie noticed that, as usual, her mother was wearing several pieces costume jewelry; she knew it was her mother's attempt to feel more glamorous. This is the result of a woman left scraping by most of her life who was just trying her best to give whatever she had to her two daughters.

"Karen is here, too, by the way," her mother said.

"Oh, why's that?"

Her mother shrugged her shoulders and fiddled with a sparkly bracelet on her wrist, "I don't know. She comes over here pretty frequently... I lose track of why."

"Oh."

Susie followed her mother as she walked into the kitchen. Nothing much had changed in here for as long as she could remember. The kitchen décor was outdated by decades, the laminated countertops were chipped on every edge, and Susie wasn't sure if the ice maker had ever worked, but it looked and felt like home.

"You want some tea, sweetheart?" her mother asked.

"No, thanks, mom," Susie said.

Susie rested against the kitchen counter, watching as her mom filled a mug with water and heated it in the tiny microwave. She was glad to be home, amongst the people and things she grew up with. It distracted her a little from the events that had unfolded with Dan.

"Do you have any aspirin? I have a headache," Susie asked.

"Yes I do!"

Her mother quickly searched through her cupboards. As Susie expected, nothing was organized – her mother dug out bottles, cans, and cartons of various items that had no business being together.

"That's where the bubble bath soap went," her mother mumbled to herself. "Ah! Here it is!" she proclaimed, as if finding a long lost treasure.

Her mother handed Susie a bottle labeled aspirin and piled things back into the cupboards haphazardly. Susie filled a glass with water from the sink and tapped a few tablets out. As she swallowed them, she noticed that the bottle had expired over a year ago. She wasn't surprised.

Karen walked into the kitchen.

"Hey, sis!"

"Hi, Karen," Susie said, smiling ear to ear.

She wondered if she would be as safe as Dan had led her to believe. Not wanting harm to come to her mother and sister, she quickly pulled out her mobile phone to write Dan a text. Instead, she received one from Dan, *You, your mother, and your sister will be fine.*

Susie smiled and felt strangely comforted.

"Something up, sis?" Karen asked. "You're smiling. I mean, you're smiling really, really hard," Karen goaded.

Susie hesitated.

"Who is he?" Karen asked, putting her finger in her mouth, still smiling.

"Susie has a boyfriend?!" her mother yelled.

"I think so!" Karen yelled back.

"Hey!" Susie yelled. "We're in the same room here. Don't need to yell!"

"Tell me it's not true!" Karen laughed.

"When can I meet him?!" her mother shouted over her shoulder as she scooted into the living room with her mug of tea.

"Oh, mom, I told you she would find someone in college. I told you!" Karen cheered, plopping down on the couch nearest the chair her mom was settling into. "She just needed to…"

Susie interrupted, "Hello?! I'm still here!"

Karen stopped talking, and they both looked at her and waited for her to speak.

The problem was that Susie didn't know what to say. She didn't know if Dan was actually her boyfriend. She wasn't sure if it was even possible now.

"The truth is… um…," Susie started.

Karen and her mother leaned in – literally on the edge of their seats.

"The truth is that I don't know."

"You don't know?" Karen asked incredulously.

"How can you not know?" her mother added. "Sit down… Sit down, Susie," she insisted, motioning Susie with her hand.

Susie sat down next to Karen on the couch.

"Well…," Susie said, "we get along great and we have the same kinds of passions and…"

"And?" her mother asked impatiently.

"And…," Susie tried to continue.

"Have you kissed yet?" Karen interrupted.

Susie playfully hit Karen on her leg.

"That's a yes," Karen laughed.

Susie froze. She and Dan hadn't kissed and weren't even close to a relationship that went beyond friends. Susie halted her logical thought process and gazed at the endearing faces of her beloved mother and sister; they looked so hopeful. It appeared that they had been hoping for this moment for a very long time. She didn't want to take this away from them.

"Let's just say that we hung out all day today and we'll hang out all day tomorrow, too."

Her mother put her hands up to her face in glee. Her face was brighter than ever.

This made Susie very happy. She glanced at Karen and sensed some envy, but in a loving way. Susie sympathized – even though Karen was more experienced in relationships, Karen was still single and had never found a guy with whom she would spend all day, much less two days in a row.

"What about school, sis? Are you gonna miss classes?"

"School?" Susie asked herself aloud, dropping her gaze to the floor. "School?" she repeated, looking at Karen.

Susie had completely forgotten about school. She had a full day of classes tomorrow, but it had completely escaped her mind. She would have to figure something out. For now, she tried to be casual about it. "Yes, of course. School. Don't worry about that."

"Well, I am worried, dear," her mother said. "You're the only one in our family, from any generation that I know of, to ever go to college. Please don't stop."

"Mom, I won't. It's okay. It's a long story."

Susie wouldn't be able to live with herself if she let her mother down. The thought was too much to bear.

Suddenly, it occurred to her that she had used Dan's common adage "it's a long story" on her own mother. She now realized why Dan must say that so often; there wasn't an easy way to ever explain the complexities that he experienced. She could finally empathize with him on his tendency to be vague, at least to some degree. She couldn't possibly summarize the events of the past couple of days in any meaningful manner.

The three of them chatted into the late hours of the night. Susie fell asleep on the living room couch and awoke the next morning feeling more refreshed than she had thought she would. Dan's words had comforted her. She did feel safe.

Chapter 20 – Dominoes

Later that morning, as Susie's English class proceeded without her, Dan and Susie were in an art gallery.

"I especially like that one because there isn't any blue in it at all," Dan said, pointing to an abstract painting of a lake under an empty sky.

"Why do you like it because of that?" Susie asked.

"It's during the middle of the day. What artist in their right mind would paint a sky and lake at that time of day without blue?"

Susie looked at it again. "That is interesting. It gives more depth and character to the art."

"Yes," Dan said and continued enthusiastically, "Part of the fascination of abstract art for me is trying to figure out why the artist made it abstract by seeing how it was created. In this case, the artist may have been avoiding blue because he wanted to portray a world that was free of depression."

Susie tested Dan, "But… If you can see into the past, can't you tell me why he painted it without blue?"

Dan briefly closed his eyes and replied, "This artist is Italian. I don't know Italian, so I can't understand a word that he said. I can see everything else that went into this painting, all of the hands through which it was exchanged and so on."

He paused and took a deep breath.

"But I really don't want to analyze art in this way. I'd rather just appreciate it for the way I see it at this moment."

She enjoyed this side of Dan that she knew; it made him human. Of course, Susie knew that he was just as human as she was, but his gifts dominated the way she saw him now.

As they walked to the next painting on the wall, Susie said, "Coming here was a good idea. It's nice to get some variety. Also, it helps me get my mind off of...," she faltered, "...the things we talked about yesterday."

Dan looked at her and said, "I brought you here to talk specifically about that."

"Oh?"

"Yes."

Dan stopped and looked the room over.

"Look around. There are several people here, right?" he said.

"Yes," Susie answered, afraid of what Dan would say next.

"In many ways, it is harder to protect yourself in public places such as this," Dan said, turning to her. He repeated quietly, "Look around."

Susie studied the people walking about. There was a group of middle-aged women talking to each other as they walked by pieces, a few couples standing and staring at particular works, two men in suits wandering around a bit aimlessly, a young woman with a little boy who were both fixated on a painting of a horse, and one guy sitting on a bench reading a book. Susie grew nervous as she realized that she couldn't watch all these people at once. She couldn't be sure she was safe or if someone was going to suddenly attack her.

Dan pointed, "That boy will sneeze."

The boy sneezed.

He pointed elsewhere, "That lady in blue will spill her purse."

The lady was bumped by someone walking by, knocking her purse off her shoulder and spilling its contents out onto the floor.

Dan yawned, crossed his arms, and told Susie candidly, "Anything can happen in an environment like this. There are too many things to keep track of. I can see many things unfolding, but it's a bit risky, probably too risky, to stay here much longer. *They* could have influenced any of these people," he said, sweeping a pointed finger across the room.

He turned towards Susie and continued, "*They* could have convinced any of these people that you must die."

Dan looked around rapidly in an exaggerated manner to accentuate his point. "Who's it gonna be?" he asked rhetorically.

Susie shivered.

"I'm getting creeped out," she whispered, hugging herself for a sense of security. "Can we get out of here?"

Susie rocked her body a little, in a vain attempt to give herself more comfort.

Dan stared at her briefly before answering.

"I understand. We are safe, though. *We* do have people helping us here."

"Where?" Susie asked while looking around.

"You see that nicely dressed lady on the other side of the room with the large man next to her?"

Dan pointed at a woman, perhaps in her early-thirties, with a very large, muscular man in tow. They were both nicely dressed in designer clothing. Susie thought the woman looked a bit unnerved. The man cautiously looked about and didn't seem interested in the art at all.

"Yes. Uh, is he her bodyguard or something?" Susie asked.

"He is. Her fabulously rich ex-husband has fled the country on criminal charges. She believes that he's out to kill her because she has information that could convict him."

"Okay... So?"

"Well, she was tipped off by *Them* that someone fitting my exact description is going to try to whack her sometime this week. *They* even told her what clothes I would be wearing."

"Why don't we leave?" Susie asked quietly.

"It wouldn't accomplish anything," Dan answered. "But, don't worry. We'll be okay."

"What's gonna happen?" she asked.

"Once the bodyguard sees me, he's going to try to kill me," Dan answered casually. "He has a nine millimeter gun on him."

Susie's heart pounded. She was petrified.

Dan patted her on the arm reassuringly, saying, "Just watch. We will be fine."

Susie watched the bodyguard out of the corner of her eye as he diligently inspected the room. His eyes made contact with Dan's eyes. Dan waved and smiled at him. The bodyguard's eyes widened quickly and, without hesitation, he started to run at Dan. Susie jumped a little, but Dan had no discernible reaction. Within a couple of steps, the bodyguard was tackled by police who seemed to come out of nowhere. They handcuffed him. Everyone in the gallery moved aside and watched.

"Andrew Maya, you're under arrest for murder. You have the right to remain silent...," a police officer barked.

Susie's tension released a little.

"What just happened?" she asked.

"*We* tipped off the police that Andrew Maya, who has many warrants out for his arrest, would be here today."

"But... But, this was so close. If the police had been even a few seconds late, you could be dead," Susie pointed out.

"True, but a few seconds is an eternity. These kinds of things happen to me several times a week on average. Since you've been in the mix, it's been a few times a day. This is a tiny bit of the struggle that's been going on for thousands of years between Us...," he turned towards Susie, "...and *Them*."

It occurred to Susie that if this "struggle" had been going on for so long then it could mean that there was no foreseeable end to this for her. She wondered if she would have to depend on Dan to save her life every day by mere seconds.

"I know what you're going to ask, so I'll go ahead and answer it because otherwise you're just going to fret about it for the next eight and a half minutes before asking," Dan unexpectedly blurted out. "*They* only want to kill you to influence a future event. It's not personal. So, if *They* can't kill you within the timeline to affect that event then *They* will move on. *They* are evil, yes, but *They* are not without a plan."

Susie scrunched her forehead in thought.

"It's like a domino being out of place... remember?" Dan said

"And what is that event?" Susie asked. "I'm so insignificant in this world."

Dan gently grabbed her hand.

"Susie, you're not insignificant. No one is. Everyone has a part. Most people have a huge part and never know it." He paused in thought before continuing, "The event you speak of... It's hard to put a finger on it. You could just be a decoy. *They* are expending a lot of energy on you, but it could be to distract *Us* away from other things. To be honest, I don't know."

"So, you don't know how long this will last?"

"No, but *They* will move on eventually. In the meantime, we must keep moving. Let's get out of here."

About an hour later, Dan and Susie were sitting on a bench facing a beautiful lake. Ducks were swimming nearby and the water had a light chop from a mild breeze.

"Not many people here," noted Dan.

"It's safer for us here?"

Dan shook his head and said, "Our influence isn't just with people. It goes much further."

Dan turned his head to his left and towards a lone stray dog sniffing a tree about fifty feet away. He called to the dog, "Here, boy! Come here, boy!"

The dog happily came and Dan lovingly petted it with both hands.

"You ever notice that most dogs are happy all the time?" Dan asked her.

"Yes… Well, mostly, I guess."

"When they are around happy people, they, too, are happy. When they're around mean people, they, too, are mean. Generally speaking, this is true," said Dan.

Susie nodded her head in agreement. Although Dan's assessment seemed anecdotal in nature, she accepted it.

"All animals are surrogates of Polarity. This means that they temporarily take on whatever Polarity they come into contact with; they will emulate the behavior of the humans around them," he said.

"Why's that?"

"They are hardwired this way because they do not naturally comprehend right from wrong – they don't have their own Polarity but, instead, adopt it from whomever they're in contact with. In that sense, animals are able to instantly take on one side of Polarity or the other."

Dan petted the dog some more. Susie moved to scratch the dog's head. He growled at her.

"Whoa!" Susie jumped back.

"Careful," Dan said. "He is still a dog."

"I guess so," Susie said, feeling a little rejected.

"Pets are very good at sensing when their owners are sad, happy, and so on due to this trait," Dan added. "As I said, everyone has a slight degree of Polarity one way or the other. What people don't know is that they are directly influencing their pets' behavior without doing a thing."

"I wouldn't know. I always wanted a pet growing up, but we couldn't afford one. I always wanted to have one just to have a friend... of sorts."

"Animals are perfect friends, especially if you have your Polarity in full. When animals come in direct contact with those who have their full Polarity, such as myself, there is temporary but strong bond that occurs between the two. His Polarity becomes one with mine. We do not repel because we are one. His goals are my goals. His commands are my commands. I don't have to say anything. He will do anything I think of without delay."

Susie smirked a little with doubt. There wasn't a reason to not believe it, but she didn't fully understand how this could be.

She tried to pet the dog again. It growled again.

"He sure doesn't like me," she said.

"I think it's because his brain can't comprehend your relationship with me. He's just being a dog," said Dan. "Watch this."

Dan knelt down to the dog, putting his hands on its head. The dog remained motionless, focusing on Dan even though he didn't speak. Dan kept holding the dog's head for about ten seconds and then let him go.

Without hesitation, the dog ran to a nearby house across the street from the park. The dog barked and scratched incessantly on the door until the homeowner came out. The dog bit down on the homeowner's pant leg and pulled. Not sure if the dog was attacking him or not, the man was confused and tried to pull back. The dog growled louder and pulled harder. The man slowly moved with the dog, obviously trying to think of how to stop or get away from the dog without being bitten. The dog dragged the homeowner until they reached the sidewalk.

BOOM!

All of the sudden, the house exploded and knocked the homeowner to the ground. Susie jumped and involuntarily shrieked, but Dan didn't even twitch. The dog let go and ran away.

"Whoa!... Wha... Um, is... Is he alright?!" Susie asked, completely unnerved but concerned for the man.

Nonchalantly, Dan responded, "He's fine. He'll have some permanent minor hearing loss, but he's fine. He had stayed home from work because of a sinus infection, but a gas line had ruptured in his home early this morning. With some help from our dog friend there, he was saved."

"But... But he has no home now. Why didn't you tell him about the gas leak?" Susie asked.

"His house was infested with termites and he didn't have the money to repair it. He'll get insurance money and will move to the east side of town. In two weeks, he'll meet the woman of his dreams and will get married on May 15th next year."

Susie was floored. It was so compelling to her that Dan did all of these nice things and no one ever knew. She was sure that Dan never got anything close to the full thanks he deserved.

"Thank you, Dan," she said.

"For what?"

"For being you."

Dan smiled, "Please don't. It's really nothing. It happens all the time. I'm sure you would do the same if you could."

"It seems like a lot of responsibility," she said.

"Anyway, the point is that sometimes – like just now – *We* will call on animals to help. You hear stories about animals that seem to know when an earthquake or bad weather is about to hit? It's not a coincidence. Animals can also play events forward and see into the future, but they are severely limited on how far they can go and what they can do because they lack the intelligence."

Dan slowly stood up and stared into the sky.

Susie could hear distant sirens, heading towards the burning house next to the park. She watched as neighbors from the surrounding block gathered around the wreck, some comforting the distraught man.

"So, I'm not safe anywhere?" Susie asked, also standing.

"Yes and no. It's not the place that keeps you safe. It's the plan that keeps you safe. Speaking of which, we should go."

By the time evening arrived, Dan and Susie were walking along a busy street in the city.

Susie felt clammy. Minor things were making Susie a little nervous – from a car honking to a pedestrian walking by. She wasn't sure who or what might pop out and attack them. As they walked by several storefronts, Susie's eyes were glued to them, watching whoever walked out of the doors.

"On occasion, *We* talk to people directly. To influence them… To change events in order to change some other outcome near or far into the future," said Dan.

Dan looked around.

He pointed at a van driving by and said, "That van will run out of gas tomorrow at 5:32 p.m. during rush hour." He paused and they watched the van drive by.

Dan continued, "I could chase the driver down and warn him. Or…," Dan looked up blankly towards the sky for a moment and then added, "…or I could call his cell phone."

"How do you know his cell phone number?" Susie asked.

"By chaining together the events that would lead me to get his number," Dan said.

He pointed to a car that was parked nearby and told Susie, "I could take that car and follow him home. That car has its keys in the ignition… I know this because I played out the events of checking every car parked along this street."

Dan then looked at the ground with an expression of deep thought and continued, "I could follow him home, sneak into his house while he is in the bathroom, find his phone, and call my phone from his phone. Caller ID gives me his number. I can see this as clearly as if I had done all of that."

"That seems like a lot of work…," Susie commented.

"It is, but you asked and I answered. The point is that just about anything is possible as long as you could do it in time… Timing is everything."

"It just seems like a lot."

"Not really… Hey, do you mind if we stop and pick up a few groceries?" Dan asked.

"No, not at all."

A little bit later, Susie and Dan were casually browsing in a grocery store. Susie pushed a cart, leaning against the handle, as Dan walked alongside her.

"Because *We* know almost everything, everything *We* do is deliberate. Everything is planned," said Dan.

"And there are others like you… Doing the same thing?"

Dan nodded ardently.

"Yes. If *We* have conflicting goals, it becomes a tough fight. The best I can do is to set in motion many small events to confuse *Them*. However, I expect *They* will do the same."

Dan picked up a bag of coffee from a shelf and took a big whiff of it.

"Ah, this is the stuff," he said, smiling at Susie.

"I love that blend," Susie remarked as she smiled back at him and reached for the bag.

Dan winked and replied, "I know."

It dawned on Susie that Dan probably knew everything about her. He could see anything in the past from anyone's perspective, including hers. She realized that he probably knew how much she had talked about him, how much she liked him, and so on.

"It's kind of embarrassing... how much you probably know about me," she said slowly with uneasiness, placing her hands back onto the cart's handle.

Dan smiled and reassured her, "Well, Susie, I don't know everything. I only know what I need to know. Remember, *We* can't keep track of everything. There's just too much going on."

Susie was unconvinced. She cocked her head at him, frowning a bit.

He tried again, "To be honest, Susie, I never look into your personal life. I keep on the periphery. I knew you were about to comment on the coffee and I made a bad joke. Others of *Us*, however, have looked a little bit further. But, think of them as doctors: there is nothing that they haven't already seen and they are taking care of you objectively."

Susie remained defensive and tense, but she was listening.

Dan continued, "Personally, I don't want to look into your personal life, Susie. It's more enjoyable getting to know you straight from the very beginning. It makes me feel more normal, I guess. I've truly enjoyed getting to know you, from you, directly."

Susie cracked a small smile at that. "That's very kind of you, Dan," she said. She shook her head and sighed, "Getting to know you has been a bit confusing, but, at the same time, enjoyable as well."

Dan handed Susie the bag of coffee and she placed it in their grocery cart. They kept strolling through the aisles. Dan threw a few items here and there into the cart: a six-pack of sodas, candles, steel wool, a flood light, 14 boxes of paperclips, and so on.

She looked down at the contents of the cart with an overtly puzzled look on her face.

"I'm buying some things that will be needed soon. *They* keep me busy," Dan explained.

"*They* are watching?" she asked.

"In some form or another, yes. Probably all of the time. You are very important to *Them*."

Dan's expression on his face changed to worry.

"Which reminds me," he said as he stopped walking and turned towards Susie, "*They* will try to influence you indirectly."

"Indirectly? What do you mean?"

"*They* will try to turn you against people you love. *They* are very effective in causing confusion through deceit. It's caused countless problems," Dan explained.

"You mean *They* will have my mother try to kill me?"

"No, no... Not that obvious. It will be along the lines of your loved ones accidentally leading you into a trap of some kind. You won't know what hit you," Dan said.

"What can I do then? How would I know?" Susie asked.

"If something doesn't feel right or seems awkward then err on the side of caution. My advice to you is to go with what you know now and don't waver. Your life depends on it."

Susie grimaced, not finding this helpful. "I'm not sure..."

Dan looked her straight in the eyes, "Look at me. Trust me. Trust yourself. You are now aware that when you get an uncomfortable feeling that you should avoid whatever it is that's giving you that feeling."

"Okay."

Dan paused thoughtfully and closed his eyes briefly, appearing a little distracted.

"Is… Is everything okay?" Susie asked.

"Yes… Sorry about that. *They* are changing things constantly and I'm thinking about how to adjust. For every one hundred things *They* change, ninety-nine of those changes are meant purely for distraction. It can make it a challenge for *Us* occasionally."

"We're gonna be okay, right?"

"Sure," he said.

Susie's anxiety climbed at Dan's short response. His face showed no sign of concern, but Susie couldn't help but wonder if Dan wasn't hiding something. She wondered how often he became distracted like this and if she would be safe with him when he seemed so distracted.

They checked out and walked outside of the grocery store. Dan was carrying all of the bags of groceries.

"Do you mind carrying a few of these bags?" he asked Susie after a few minutes.

"Not at all," Susie replied as she took two of the bags from Dan.

Dan immediately pulled a can of soda out of a bag, opened it, took one sip, and then set the can on top of a car that was parked next to them. He then continued walking. Susie followed.

"You forgot your can," Susie pointed out.

"Yup," Dan replied, still walking away.

Susie looked back at the can, falling a half-step behind Dan, but she quickly caught up.

"The world is full of many coincidences," Dan blurted out. "Things happen because of reasons, not for them."

Susie listened carefully, looking up at him in curious bewilderment. She wondered what he was up to.

"Everyone is a tool," he said. "Everyone has a purpose that is integral to mankind whether they know it or not."

They were about halfway up the block when they walked up to a tall, skinny man with neatly groomed, light brown hair and wearing a light jacket – he was waiting to find a break in the traffic to cross the busy street.

"Excuse me, sir, what time is it?" Dan asked the man.

The man looked down at his watch and jerked his head back. He looked closely at his watch, shook his wrist wearing the watch, and then put the watch next to his ear. While he did this, Dan slipped a hundred dollar bill into a front pocket of the man's jacket; part of the bill dangled out slightly.

"I don't know. I think the battery's dead," the man responded.

"Oh, that sucks," Dan said.

"Yeah," the man said.

"Thanks anyways."

"Sorry."

Dan and Susie walked about a hundred feet farther up the street. Neither of them said a word. He appeared consumed in thought.

Dan stopped to re-tie his shoelaces. When he did, he took out some steel wool from a bag and placed it next to him on the sidewalk. He stood up and continued walking.

"Why… Why did you leave that steel wool there?" Susie asked.

"Because the wind won't blow it away, it looks too scruffy for people to take, and…," he turned towards her, "Because it's flammable. Most people don't know that."

"Yeah… but… but…," Susie stammered.

"Don't worry," Dan said, smiling at her, "It will be fine."

Susie briefly looked back at the steel wool. It lay on the ground featurelessly. Other people didn't notice it as they walked by.

"Susie, please, timing is everything. We must keep walking," Dan asked calmly.

"Oh, sorry," Susie answered.

Dan stopped in front of a tall, stone building at the end of the block. He looked around carefully from side to side. Susie tried her best to notice anything of interest, but there was nothing.

"I need you to stand against the wall of this building," Dan told Susie.

"What?"

"Please, quickly. It's important. Just stand against that wall and don't move, okay?"

"Dan?"

"No time for questions. An event is unfolding and you'll be fine right here. I have everything set up perfectly," Dan implored.

"But Dan…"

"Please."

Susie walked over to the building and leaned against the wall. She put her bags down on the ground.

"Thanks, Susie. I'll be right back."

"You're leaving?" Susie asked, hinting fear.

"You'll be fine. This will be over with before you know it. You will never be in any danger and I will never leave your sight."

Susie was speechless.

"Trust me, Susie. I won't let anything happen to you."

Susie nodded.

"I'll be right back."

Dan walked back the direction they came. Other than the tall man with the broken watch, there didn't appear to be anyone else around. Susie stood there silently and wondered if she felt too dependent upon Dan. This was a stark contrast towards the life that she was so diligently building. She could do nothing but watch Dan casually walk down the street, still going in the same direction they had come from.

Her eyes wandered to the ground and she saw a quarter beneath her. She squatted down to pick it up. She examined the quarter, realizing that its date is the same year as her mother's birth. "Wow," Susie thought, "That quarter is as old as mom."

Still squatting, she looked up to check on Dan. She saw him almost halfway up the block. She looked further up the street and noticed what appeared to be an intense exchange between the tall man with the broken watch and a much shorter man wearing a baseball cap. The shorter man was holding what appeared to be money in one hand and a small gun in the other.

"My God, that poor man is getting mugged," she said to herself. "Why isn't Dan doing anything about this?"

Instead, Dan was waving to get the attention of a familiar car slowly driving by – Susie could see the car still had Dan's soda can on top of it. Dan made motions to the driver to stop, pointing to the soda can he put on top of the car. The car stopped and an older, heavyset man smoking a cigarette got out. He grabbed the can and tossed it indifferently to the ground, not bothered about littering. He then flicked his cigarette indiscriminately towards the sidewalk, which landed on the steel wool. The heavyset man got back in his car and drove off.

Within a few seconds, the steel wool was ablaze. Susie saw that Dan just stood there, motionless. A short moment later, a shopkeeper popped out of a nearby store holding a fire extinguisher. He aimed it at the fire and sprayed its contents, smothering the steel wool.

Susie noticed that this distracted the mugger and, as a consequence, the tall man grabbed for the gun. The two struggled and the gun went off as Susie heard a loud snap above her head and then the high-pitched ping of a ricochet on the stone wall behind her. The sounds jolted Susie into action and she dropped from her squatted position to lying flat on the pavement.

She looked up and saw that the shopkeeper had noticed the struggle between the tall man and the mugger. He ran up and swung the fire extinguisher into the back of the mugger. The shopkeeper and the tall man quickly subdued him.

"Someone call the police!" the shopkeeper yelled.

Dan walked back over to Susie. She was still lying flat on the pavement, scared witless.

"It's over, Susie, we can go now. You're safe," Dan said.

"I... I... I can't move!" she yelled. "I almost got shot!"

"Yes... But you're okay."

Dan traced his fingers in the small pockmark left behind by the bullet in the stone wall of the building. He looked around in all directions, not appearing too concerned.

"Dan?" Susie asked.

"Yes?"

"Did...? What...? Who...? I...," Susie fumbled.

"That guy with the gun was following us. *They* have been influencing him since yesterday and he was led here. He was going to try to rob you and accidentally shoot you. I saw an opportunity to stop him and I took it."

Susie stopped breathing.

"He failed. It was close for you, but, trust me, you were far from danger."

Dan turned his attention back to the dent of the bullet again, lost in thought. He traced his fingers in the dent again, looked towards where the mugging occurred, and then looked in all directions.

"Is everything okay?" Susie asked.

"Yes... Yes... Fine."

"Are you sure?"

Dan regained his full attention towards Susie. "Absolutely. You were brilliant, Susie. You followed everything precisely as I told you to."

"I don't feel safe. I feel... I feel uneasy. I almost died."

"But you didn't. You were far from danger."

Susie wanted to get upset, but she wasn't sure why.

"You should go home now. There is a plan unfolding right now," he urged.

Susie's face tensed. "How... How can you expect me to just leave when something like this just happens?"

"Don't worry. You are safe. Remember what I told you: Go with what you know now and don't waver. You'll be fine. I have to take care of a few things. Trust me now like you trusted me before. No harm will come to you."

"Call me tonight, please," Susie quietly asked.

"I will... A taxi will be passing here in about twenty seconds," Dan said.

He reached in his pocket, pulled out his wallet, and handed her eighteen dollars. Susie crumpled the money in her hands, already feeling alone even though Dan was still there.

"I've got to keep moving: timing is everything," Dan said.

Susie watched Dan walked away. He turned and said with a wink, "Taxi coming."

Susie turned her head and, sure enough, a taxi had just taken a turn and was approaching her. She hailed the taxi and it stopped. She got in and felt increasingly despondent with every step Dan took away from her. The taxi began moving.

Dan picked up his pace – almost to a jog – and rushed into a hardware store a block away. He rested at its storefront and then glanced at his watch. He waited a few seconds and then walked inside.

Dan's entrance was announced by a ringing metal bell affixed to the door. The store was filled with a variety of tools and home improvement goods. With the exception of the checkout clerk who was casually reading a newspaper, the store was devoid of people.

The clerk was an older man, wearing thin bifocals. He briefly shifted his eyes up at Dan before going back to reading the newspaper. "Let me know if I can help you with anything," the clerk offered, clearly engrossed in his reading material.

"Thanks," Dan said.

Dan grabbed a shopping cart and marched judiciously down a nearby aisle. He pored over the various wrenches on shelves, then summarily gathered up all of the ratchet wrenches that were there. He dumped them into his cart and quickly went to the checkout counter.

The clerk looked down at the pile and then looked up at Dan.

"Son, why do you need so many ratchet wrenches?" he asked with a slight southern accent.

"It's a long story," Dan replied.

The clerk chuckled a little and began scanning each of the wrenches, tossing them into bags one by one. Dan watched each ratchet wrench as it passed through the scanner.

As the clerk grabbed a particular one, Dan suddenly stopped the clerk and took the wrench from him.

This wrench is defective. It will be perfect, Dan thought.

"I'm going to put this one back," Dan explained to the clerk.

"Leaving me with one, are ya?" the clerk quipped.

"I can't be completely selfish," he joked back.

Dan went back to the aisle he came from and placed the ratchet wrench back onto the shelf where it came from. When he got back, he saw the clerk had finished ringing up the order.

"That will be $498.72, please," said the clerk.

Dan gave the clerk five hundred-dollar bills. The clerk held them up to the light to check for watermarks and the security strips. He completed the transaction and handed Dan his receipt and change.

Dan walked out the hardware store's front door with several bags in his arms, struggling to carry them because their weight. He hurried desperately to make it around the corner of the hardware store. He rounded the corner then peeped around back at the store's entrance. A moment later, a truck pulled up and parked in front of the store. A man wearing a mechanic's uniform got out of the truck. He was a bit dirty and ruffled his hands through his hair – clearly panicked about something.

Dan nodded and said to himself quietly, "You've lost your ratchet wrench and I've left you the one you should buy."

Chapter 21 – A Friend

Susie sat at home quietly, not knowing what to do with herself. She sipped some hot tea from a mug, gripping it with both hands tightly. Curled up in her chair, she waited anxiously for time to pass. Being without Dan was more painful than she thought. She couldn't think of anything that would help calm her – everything would just make it worse. Turning on the TV may drown out any noises that she wanted to be alerted to and reading a book would be too distracting. Knowing that *They* were out to kill her was eating her alive.

"I'm gonna drive myself nuts," she said aloud.

Her phone beeped – she had received a text message. Susie got up to retrieve her phone. The message was from Dan, *Don't answer the door.*

KNOCK! KNOCK! KNOCK!

Susie immediately looked up at her front door, completely stunned.

KNOCK! KNOCK! KNOCK!

She was catatonically stricken with panic. Each knock seemed more amplified than the previous one. Each knock felt like a cut slicing through her body.

There was a pause. Susie relaxed slightly.

KNOCK! KNOCK! KNOCK!

"Susie, it's Karen! Are you home?!" Karen half-yelled.

Susie perked up and took a step towards the door, but then she stopped. She received another text from Dan, *It's a trap. Don't answer the door.*

Susie stood petrified, just feet away from her door.

"Hey, Susie, are you home?!" Karen yelled.

Susie slowly backed into an empty corner of her living room floor. She sat down in the corner and hugged her knees to her body. Tears quietly streamed from her eyes.

"What are *They* doing to her?" she whimpered.

She then got another text from Dan, *Carefully look out the window and see who Karen is talking to.*

Susie crawled on the floor – not knowing why exactly, but it did make her feel safer. She approached the bottom of her front window, slowly moved a small section of the curtain aside, and looked out the window. She saw Karen talking to a policeman. At first, Susie didn't think anything of it. Karen then stepped aside a little and Susie could see the face of the policeman – it was Frank, the man who had attempted to assault her at the botanical gardens.

Susie fell backwards onto the floor and began crying profusely, wondering what would become of her beloved sister. She already blamed herself for whatever would happen to her. She imagined what horrors might have happened to her friend Nicole and what would now happen to Karen.

Susie's phone rang. It was Dan.

"Dan?" Susie answered with a shaken voice.

"Hey," he responded calmly.

Susie didn't say anything.

"You there?" he asked.

"I'm… I'm scared," Susie cried.

"You did the right thing, Susie. I know it was hard, but you did the right thing."

"It was Karen…"

"Yes, it was. But, she was tricked by *Them*," Dan explained.

Susie struggled to breathe regularly.

"Will *They* hurt her?" she asked, partly not wanting to know.

"I don't think so," Dan said.

"You don't *think* so?! We have to warn her!" Susie demanded.

"No," Dan sternly replied. "The best thing to do is ignore her. *They* will move on. *They* want us to be drawn to her."

Susie cried helplessly, "I didn't do anything to deserve this! Now my family is in danger! Why?!… Why?! I have nothing but my mother and sister, and *They* are taking them from me!"

"I know… I know," Dan said evenly.

"What are we going to do, Dan?!" she pleaded.

"Well, we have more help and I have a car now. I'll pick you up tomorrow morning at 9 a.m."

"I can't stay here tonight!" Susie yelled. "I'm helpless!"

"You are safe, Susie. And, *We* will protect your family. Please, trust me."

Susie didn't say anything.

"Trust me, Susie."

"Okay… Okay, Dan. I do trust you. This is all just so disturbing, and it's all happening too fast."

"The hardest part of this is that it happens too fast, faster than any single person can handle. This is why *We* work as a team, Susie."

She was silent.

"Try to get some sleep, Susie. I'll be there at nine. Try to relax until then."

For hours, Susie laid in bed trying to sleep and failing miserably. Around 5 a.m., she finally gave up on sleep and curled up on her living room chair. Only being with Dan could make her better, she was convinced.

Susie awoke from her couch the next morning to a knocking on her door.

KNOCK! KNOCK!

She jumped from her couch, disoriented, and fell to the floor.

KNOCK! KNOCK! KNOCK! KNOCK!

"Susie, it's me," Dan's voice said loudly at the door. "It's not a trap. If *They* were nearby, I wouldn't be knocking on your door; I would be too busy fighting for my life."

Susie opened the door slowly. Dan looked her over. She drooped from physical and nervous exhaustion and was even without the energy to greet Dan.

"You poor thing," Dan said.

Susie hugged Dan deeply. Never had anyone's touch comforted her so much. She felt safe with him. The warmth of his body felt like a cozy fire. She would kiss him if she had the courage to do so.

Shortly afterwards, Susie freshened up a bit and they got into Dan's car – a small, white, four-door sedan. Susie glanced at the interior of the car and noticed some rips in the seat fabric and a crack in the dashboard.

"This car is old, yes, but it won't break down for another 42,344 miles," Dan said.

Dan drove as Susie sat in the front passenger seat next to him, rubbing her temples.

"Dan, how long will I have this awful headache?"

"Seriously?" he asked.

"Yes, please."

"Twenty-three minutes after you drink some water."

Without another word, Dan stretched his arm into his backseat and grabbed a bottle of water – almost as if it had been brought specifically for this moment. He handed it to Susie.

"Thanks," Susie said after taking a deep swig of it.

"Sure."

She took another swig. "So, what are we up to now?"

"We will need help," Dan replied. "I can't be everywhere at once."

Dan paused, and Susie got the sense that he was carefully choosing his next words. "It isn't clear if *They* are after me, you, or both of us. *They* could just be trying to misdirect *Us* about *Their* intentions," he finally said.

Susie didn't react. She was too tired to do so.

"Don't worry. There are others of *Us* who will help you more directly now. You and your family will be safe," he said

Susie took a deep breath and exhaled, seeking some relief. "God, I'm so tired," she whispered, rubbing her eyes. She turned to Dan and looked at him warmly, "I'm so glad you're here."

Dan smiled at her briefly then returned his attention to driving.

"Susie, I would never forgive myself if *They* were ever after you because of me. The world really needs people like you," he said.

As they stopped at a red light, Dan's phone went off; he had received a text. He read it pensively.

"Hmm… Okay, we're just a few minutes away," he announced.

"Dan?" Susie asked abruptly.

"Yes?"

"If you know what's going to happen in the future, why do you even bother with texting? I mean, don't you just know what you'll read?"

Dan grinned. The traffic light turned green and they began moving again.

"What?" Susie asks.

"Oh, just that you're probably going to ask a lot of questions like that. The funny thing is that I've never had to explain Polarity before. It's become strangely fun for me."

Susie just kept looking at him expectantly. He glanced at her and nodded, "Okay... Nothing is certain until it actually happens," he answered. "Each of *Us* have hundreds or thousands of events that *We* are each tracking. Sending a text or actually spending time talking to each other, one on one, indicates that certain key milestones have been hit. When a milestone is hit, it cues those of *Us* involved to begin another set of actions. It makes it easier for *Us* to collectively work together."

Dan glanced at her and continued, "Meeting in person is the most effective way because we can talk more. But, it requires extra space because we can't get too close to each other. Whereas texts, unlike phone calls, won't disturb those around us. *We* prefer texting these days and so do *They*."

"What was it like before texts?"

"It was a lot harder to divide up the work between people. There were more mishaps on both sides. Of course, *We* knew when texting would be invented and *We* already knew exactly how *We* were going to use it."

"What other things will be invented?" Susie asked. "Will we find a cure for cancer or AIDS or other diseases?"

Dan stiffened. "That kind of knowledge is never safe with those who don't have their full Polarity. I'm sorry, but I won't answer those kinds of questions."

"Well, if you got cancer, wouldn't you want to know how to cure it?"

"We do know how to cure some forms of cancer, yes. With each day we know more and more that will be. It depends on how badly *They* meddle with the present to alter the future," Dan said.

Susie sat up. She was somewhat offended that Dan has this knowledge and refused to share it with the world when so many people were dying.

"Dan, why not? Why not save people? Why not end suffering?"

Dan appeared a little bothered by the question.

"Fine, I'll answer this one question, but after that we need to drop the subject and get back to focusing on what needs to be done. Remember, the whole 'kill Susie thing' going on right now?"

"Fine," Susie agreed.

"I'll first answer from *Our* perspective: Intervening with the natural progression of mankind is directly counter to the stability that *We* fight to foster. Death is a part of life; it is natural. Mankind improves itself by keeping itself focused on real problems and not the massive distractions caused by *Them*. If *We* just gave mankind all of the answers, there wouldn't be any impetus for mankind to improve on its own. *We* know what will be, but *We* also know that this can change because of overt actions by *Us* or *Them*. Most important, the future is constantly changing because of *Our* conflict – especially with important discoveries and events. Ultimately, there really isn't much to be told."

"Alright," Susie responded.

"Now from *Their* perspective, the last thing *They* want to do is give mankind tools that will help. *They* don't want to end mankind; *They* just want to keep it in a constant state of chaos and disarray – forcing mankind to suffer and, by suffering, forcing it to improve itself. Suffering is an amazing form of motivation. When someone dies in a weird and tragic way, mankind generally overacts and overcorrects. Giving mankind the answer wouldn't produce the overaction and overcorrection. Also, however misguided *They* are, even *They* aren't dumb enough to trust mankind with knowledge it doesn't understand on its own."

"Hmm," Susie pondered aloud.

"So, you can see, the struggle between *Us* and *Them* only uses mankind itself as the catalyst."

"It's a waste," Susie opined. "It's such a waste to avoid helping so many people who are suffering. I thought that helping out at the homeless shelter could make a difference, but you... well, you alone can make a huge difference."

Dan pointed out, "Yet, I still choose to help at the homeless shelter because I believe that it's best for mankind."

Susie shook her head in disagreement.

"Anyway, back to the events of now," Dan said abruptly. "Things will get more complex from this point on. *They* are clearly desperate. Even though you will have more of *Our* help, you have to stay vigilant. You don't want to be caught by *Them*."

"What should I do?" Susie asked.

"Never, ever let your guard down. *They* are very persistent. We can't even afford any more conversations such as the one we just had – it distracts me."

"I'm sorry," Susie apologized.

"Don't apologize. Just remember that your life depends on your constant attention as well."

"How will this end?" Susie asked with shakiness interwoven in her voice.

"People are going to die," Dan answered plainly. "It's the only way it can end. *They* cannot be reasoned with."

Susie gulped. She knew this was true. Hearing it again made it even more real, but she didn't want anyone to die. She recognized that her life was in peril, but she had never really explored what she would do if confronted. The only thing Susie was certain of was that killing was never right, no matter what.

"There is always some form of reasoning for every conflict; it is always calculated," Dan said out of nowhere. "Part of that calculation is predicting your own response. But, how you plan to respond will affect how *They* will fight you. Word of advice: Don't roll over and curl up in a ball – always fight."

A few minutes later, Dan pulled over to the side of the road and parked. He pointed to a convenience store about a half block away on the right. "In that convenience store is an ally of *Ours*. His name is Rich." He turned to Susie, "He will help keep you safe while I take care of other things."

Susie looked at Dan a little confused. She didn't know why Dan wasn't dropping her off. She was so tired.

"You have to walk over there," Dan insisted.

"Why can't you..."

Dan interrupted, "Since Rich and I are of the same Polarity, *We* cannot get close to each other. *We* have to keep our distance of no closer than forty feet or so or else, well, it's not pleasant."

Susie didn't want to leave Dan's side again – he was her rock.

"How will I know what he looks like?" she asked.

"Don't worry about that. It's already planned so it will look like a coincidence to those around him. This is a necessary tactic to keep him hidden. He will find you. All I can tell you is that he is in the store. I won't tell you anything more because the progression of events must look natural," Dan explained.

Susie hesitated, not wanting to leave the car.

"Okay... Will I be safe getting there?" she asked, seeking reassurance.

"I don't sense *Them* in the area, but *They* do mask *Themselves* well. My advice is to ignore everything around you. Go straight to the store. You never know who has been influenced," Dan said.

Susie would have preferred a guarantee that everything would be fine, but she was getting used to Dan's matter-of-fact yet ambivalent descriptions. She knew she should follow his instructions, but she felt – oddly – colder when she was away from him. She wished he could pull up just a bit further, but it was obvious that he wasn't going to budge.

Susie slowly got out of the car and stepped out onto the concrete sidewalk. She closed the door and took a few steps forward, doing her best to muster courage in spite of her uncertainty. She paused and looked back at Dan. He nodded his head in encouragement, and she resumed walking.

She stopped sharply. There was a group of six boys between the ages of ten and twelve coming around the block's corner. They were walking directly towards her. One bounced a basketball while the others laughed and joked around.

"I'll race ya!" one yelled.

They all start running towards Susie. She was motionless, frozen by the possibility that they were going to kill her somehow. The image of the attacking bodyguard at the art gallery was at the forefront of her mind.

She backed into a nearby fence and the kids harmlessly passed her by. She spun around, watching them go, and lifted her gaze to look at Dan. Susie could only see a silhouette in his car, obscured by the glare on the windshield. She turned back and marched toward the store.

SQUAWK!

She jumped. Badly startled, breathless and heart pounding, it took her a few seconds to realize it was only a bird overhead. She re-gained her composure quickly but felt foolish.

What am I doing to myself? I'm a mess. The longer I stay out here, the more of a mess I will be.

She hurried blindly to the convenience store and quickly entered. She felt safe but definitely had adrenaline pumping through her. In an odd way it was welcomed because it made her feel a little more awake.

There were several customers browsing and a few others were lined up at the checkout counter. A woman was carefully picking her numbers at a lotto machine. A little kid dropped his candy bar. Susie stood in place, got up on her toes, and searched the room for Rich – no one seemed to especially notice her. She walked slowly about, looking down each aisle in the hope that someone would make friendly eye contact with her.

She overheard the checkout clerk talking to a customer at the checkout counter.

"Credit or debit?" the clerk asked.

"Debit," the customer responded.

"Okay, go ahead and enter your PIN," the clerk instructed.

Susie got a good feeling about the checkout clerk. Dan had told her to trust her instinct and go with what she felt, so she headed towards the counter. As she got closer, she could see his nametag read *RICH*. She smiled with giddiness.

She randomly grabbed a bag of chips from an aisle's end-cap nearby and got in the line. She was looking at him, smiling with hope, as he was tending to customers in front of her. She was finally next. She gave her item to the clerk. He scanned it, just as he would scan any other item.

"That will be a dollar forty-nine," he stated mundanely.

Susie cracked a bright, friendly smile at him. He didn't respond other than politely smiling and looking a little puzzled.

"So, you're Rich?" Susie asked enthusiastically.

"Do I know you from somewhere?"

Susie hesitated. "Um, well... No, I guess not," Susie answered with obvious embarrassment. "Uh, how much was it again?"

"A buck forty-nine," the cashier told her.

Susie was searching for cash in her purse when the clerk suddenly held up the chips to show Susie.

"You know this is expired, right?" the clerk said.

"Uh… No," Susie shook her head. She hadn't really looked at what she grabbed, much less the expiration date.

"Let's get you another one," the clerk suggested.

The clerk got up on his tip-toes to look over her shoulder at the end-cap where she had grabbed the chips. He then looked around in general before finally yelling out, "Hey, Rich!"

A head popped up from an aisle near the back of the store.

"Yo!" a man yelled in response.

Susie spun around and saw an obese, jovial-looking man in his mid-twenties with thick, messy, dark hair.

"Can you help this young lady?!" the clerk yelled back.

Rich walked towards Susie, smiling ear-to-ear. He was the epitome of overly happy.

"Absolutely!" he responded back gregariously.

Rich walked up to the checkout counter and gave Susie a quick wink. Finally, Susie felt at ease; this was the Rich she had been looking for.

The clerk explained to Rich, "This is expired and there's not another on the shelf there. Can you help her get another one? We should have gotten a box of these in the shipment yesterday. Check the back."

"Not a problem, boss," Rich said.

He took the chips from the clerk.

Susie found it strange that Rich, who should have all the amazing powers that Dan had, was in such a low-level job. He can be anything. He can do anything. He doesn't have to listen or take orders from anyone. But, instead, he's a stock boy in a convenience store.

Rich instructed Susie, "Come with me, please."

Susie took a few steps but stopped suddenly. She got a baffled look on her face, inexplicably feeling a little troubled.

"Hey, you okay?" Rich asked.

281

"Yeah. I guess so," Susie answered quietly. "I just feel a little weird."

Rich told her quietly, "It's because I'm new to you and you are putting blind faith in me in a life-or-death situation. You have nothing to worry about. Dan and I go way back."

"I guess so," Susie responded.

"Come on, let's go to the stock room."

They made their way into the stock room in the back of the store. It was full of boxes, some opened and some closed. There were a few lockers on one of the walls. Rich went to his locker and opened it, revealing a large stash of snacks. Rich snatched a box of powdered donuts, opened it, took out one of the donuts, and shoved it halfway in his mouth as he set the box on a nearby chair. He chewed the donut while he took off his smock, threw it into the locker, and closed the door, locking it. Some crumbs fell to the ground.

He swallowed and told her, "Hey, I know this is scary, but everything will be okay."

He stuffed a second donut into his mouth.

Susie raised an eyebrow. She was a little saddened at Rich's gluttonous eating. It pained her to see someone at the mercy of an addiction. She couldn't care less about Rich's weight problem, but she did care about how others may judge him.

"Oh, I'm sorry, where are my manners? You want a donut, too?" he said as he shoved the box towards Susie's face.

"I'm okay, thanks," she politely responded.

Rich shrugged and took another donut for himself.

"So, anyways, I'll take care of you while Dan is elsewhere. Any questions?"

Susie looked around and couldn't help but ask, "Why do you work here?"

"Huh? Oh, yeah, this," he said with a chuckle. "The proverbial question of 'Why don't you win the lottery?'".

Susie tilted head her to one side, implying agreement.

"I don't need it. It's really that simple," he answered.

"But, you could be spending your time somewhere else doing much greater things," she suggested.

"You'd be surprised how much I can do here."

"You could do things on a grander scale…"

"Not true," he interrupted. "Once people pick up that you have money or power, they change and that complicates everything you want to do, that you need to do. I don't care who you are, they change."

"You don't have to tell people you have it."

"The last thing *We* want to do is draw attention to ourselves. *We* really don't worry about material possessions, so money doesn't mean anything. *We* just want to be around people, so *We* can help," he explained.

He stretched out his arms, indicating the store around them. "This… This is ideal," he finished.

Suddenly, Rich stood at rigid attention and lost all expression on his face.

"Uh, you okay?" she asked, surprised at his shift in demeanor.

"You have five bucks I can borrow?" Rich asked, somewhat distracted.

"Sure."

As Susie pulled the money from her purse and handed it to Rich, it vaguely occurred to her that she no longer even thought about her budget at all. She shook her head, dismissing the thought.

Rich set down the box of donuts, then looked around and walked to a nearby box. He picked up a box-cutter sitting on top of it and walked calmly to the door that led back into the store. Susie followed him out of curiosity. Rich rested against the frame of the open door, watching and apparently waiting for something.

A nicely dressed man walked by about fifteen feet away. He was wearing a pressed suit and tie, his hair was slicked back, and he was clean-shaven. Susie was too far away to smell it, but this man looked like he was slathered in cologne. He was on a cell phone talking loudly, obnoxiously so. He had a coffee in his other hand.

"You see that guy in that fancy suit?" Rich quietly asked Susie.

"Yeah."

"He's one of the most unethical, deplorable, and just plain mean people you can ever meet. He cheats on his wife." Rich looked at Susie, "He also cheats on his girlfriend. He fires people for his own mistakes. He even killed someone in a hit-and-run accident, but he was never found."

"So, is that important?" Susie asked.

"Not for what's about to happen. I just thought I'd give some background on the guy before I intervene."

"Intervene?"

"Yeah. Just watch." Rich said with disappointment lining his breath, "*We* even help people who aren't so nice."

The man approached the hot dog machine – it had several dogs slowly turning and heating on its long rollers. He leaned to look at the hot dogs, doing his best not to spill his coffee.

The man yelled, "Hey! Can I get some help over here?! I thought this place was a convenience store!"

Everyone in the store noticed the belligerence of the man but otherwise ignored him. The clerk at the front counter also ignored him and continued serving customers.

He waited a few seconds and yelled again, this time with pronounced anger, "You people are just terrible, incompetent, morons!"

A couple customers looked like they muttered something under their breath and briefly glared at him, but most dismissed him, including the clerk who was pointedly carrying on with business as if he had heard nothing. It was becoming a very uncomfortable situation for everyone.

The man in the suit inaudibly mumbled a few more things and put his coffee on the table supporting the hot dog rollers. He peered at the machine, determining how he could get to the hot dogs by himself.

"I can't believe I have to do this myself!" he yelled haughtily.

The man opened the protective dome over the hot dog machine with impunity, grabbed a nearby set of short tongs, and leaned over the rollers to select a hot dog.

Rich rolled his eyes and let out an exhaustive sigh.

He turned to Susie and calmly said, "Well, I gotta do the right thing."

He walked casually into the store towards the man, taking his time and holding the box-cutter point downward. Susie perked up, not sure why Rich had the box-cutter.

Within a matter of seconds, the man's tie got tangled in one of the hot dog rollers. It began to draw the man into the machine.

"What?!" he yelled. By now, everyone was deliberately ignoring him and avoided looking his way at all.

The man tried to pull his tie out, but it was useless. He was slowly being pulled into the hot dog machine. He grunted with effort as he braced against the table, yanking back to no avail. With his face inches from the hot rollers, he began choking. With each passing microsecond, the choking got worse and worse.

Suddenly, Rich walked up and, with one pass of the box-cutter, he cut the man's tie, freeing him. The man stumbled backward as he gasped for air, his face deep red and tinged with purple.

After a few moments, he looked down at his cut tie, looked at Rich, and yelled "Hey, moron! That was a two-hundred dollar tie. It's designer. You're gonna pay, so help me God!"

Rich coolly put the box-cutter down on the table and picked up the cut portion of the tie. By now, this incident had drawn the attention of everyone in the store and most had crowded around both him and the man.

"You got this tie at a discount store. It was on sale for five bucks," Rich announced, just loud enough for everyone to hear.

Rich held up the tie for all to see. He then held up its tag. "It says TIES FOR LESS, MADE IN MEXICO."

The man was instantly quieted, but he showed no signs of embarrassment.

Rich handed the man the five-dollar bill Susie gave him. The man pocketed the money and strutted out of the store with strident arrogance dominating his posture.

Rich walked back towards Susie.

"Let's keep moving," he told Susie as he passed by her.

Susie followed him back into the stock room. She could see that Rich was clearly just as gifted and generous as Dan. Most of her tension and anxiety melted away, but she was curious. "What would have happened if you didn't intervene?" she asked.

"He would have choked," Rich responded flatly.

"To death?"

Rich took a deep breath.

Despondent, he answered, "No. The machine would have broken his neck with the tie first."

"Not many people would have even bothered with that guy... Why are you sad?"

Rich shook his head, closed his eyes, and softly replied. "He'll be dead soon anyway." He paused and opened his eyes again.

He continued, "He'll be on his cell while driving from his office. He will get angry at the person he's talking to, causing him to run a red light. He'll be broad-sided by an ice cream truck coming from the left. What's sad is that he'll actually see the ice cream truck coming – it's bright orange, hard to miss – but his arrogance will make him think he can beat it across the intersection."

Susie was silent.

"*We* can't handle everything. There's just... too much," Rich explained.

Susie patted him on the back, trying to comfort him as he was obviously distraught over this. The incident had given her a good taste of the complexities that both Dan and Rich faced all of the time. She could see now that there were a countless number of events going on and that *They* could not save everyone.

"I think it was very kind of you to give him a little more time," she said with warmth. "You're a good man, Rich."

Rich smiled shyly and even blushed a little.

"Well, tell ya what. Let's get out of here. My shift just ended," he said.

He went back to his locker got out a bag of taffy and what appeared to be an open can of soda. He stacked these on top of the mostly full box of donuts from earlier and picked it up.

"You good?" he said, waving the snacks in front of Susie.

"I'm fine," she said.

They left through a back door that led outside and behind the store.

"That's my van," Rich said as he pointed to a big, white van parked nearby.

Susie stopped walking.

"*They* are nearby. Are you okay?" Rich asked Susie.

Susie wasn't sure. She felt muddled in her thoughts and her adrenaline was wearing off, letting her feel her full exhaustion.

Wishing that Dan was there to help her sort through her feelings, she resigned herself to the care of Rich.

Susie replied with a clear, unsure tone, "Yeah... Yeah... I just feel..."

"*They* are nearby and that's why you feel uneasy, but we are okay right now. Let's go. We must hurry," he said.

Rich didn't seem to Susie to be the type of guy who would ever be in a hurry. The fact that he was pressing to move quickly motivated Susie to keep going with the flow. She worried that any further pondering might cause too much hesitation and allow *Them* to close in.

They got in his van and Rich started the engine.

"The rest of the day will be interesting and most likely a bit fast-paced. *They* are desperate and *They* will try desperate things. *We* have to be on constant alert," Rich said.

Susie still hadn't got used to the overly-emphasized pronouns: *We*, *They*, etc. She had started getting used to it from Dan, but hearing them from Rich made everything seem that much more real. Rich spoke in these terms as though it was natural; for Susie, this brought her closer to the reality that these two factions – *Us* and *Them* – had been around for quite some time.

Rich stuffed another donut in his mouth and took a sip from the open soda can. He began driving away and, within minutes, they were driving through downtown.

He told her, "We're going to go to the mall to hang out for a bit, but I have a small errand I have to run first. *They* are nearby, but I'm not sure what *They* are up to."

"That's not very comforting," Susie said lethargically – she was trying to keep herself awake.

"*We* are constantly changing our course. *They* are changing theirs. It makes it difficult to know what will happen next," Rich explained. "I'm sorry, but it's the truth."

He stuffed another donut in his mouth and quickly followed it with some taffy. He paused, chewing. "When *We* help each other, it makes it even more difficult for *Them*."

"But, can't *They* help each other, too?" Susie asked.

Rich nodded emphatically. He chewed for a few more seconds.

"Definitely," he said after he swallowed what was in his mouth. "In fact, that guy, Frank, who was about to attack you at the botanical garden?"

"Yeah, Dan told me about him," Susie said.

"He's works with that other guy, Spike."

"Yeah, Dan told me about Spike, too. He said he attacked Dan a few days ago, but," Susie reflected, "I didn't think *They* were working so closely together."

"Every single step of the way, yes," Rich quickly said.

Susie, tired as she was, made the effort to collect her thoughts.

"Who else is helping *Them*?" she asked.

"You know, *We* don't know. There are probably a few involved, but *We* don't know to what extent. *They* are good at distractions," said Rich, glancing at her.

She felt down and worn out. She rubbed her temples some more, soothing her bad headache. Susie lamented, "Just a few days ago, my life was very different, very simple. The problems I thought were big then are nothing now."

About twenty minutes later, they had left the city and were in a suburban neighborhood across town. Rich parked his van near a sidewalk and under a tree. He left the keys in the ignition, got out of the driver's seat into the space between the two seats, and, hunching over, stepped towards the back of the van. Susie only now noticed that there was a cage-like door separating the front of the van from the back of it. Rich opened the door and headed into the back.

"Why do you have a door there?" Susie asked as he went by.

"Great question," he called back. "You will see very soon. I have to take care of something."

Susie turned around to watch Rich. Everything he did intrigued her – just as it was with Dan.

Rich opened the van's right-side sliding door and sat down on its edge. Then, he took out a handheld game and began to play it.

"What are you doing?" Susie called to him.

"Shh…," Rich shushed her. "Just wait."

Susie waited, but she couldn't help but wonder why they were in such a rush before. Rich was just sitting there playing video games.

A moment later, Susie saw in the distance – through the van's opened door – a small boy, about nine years old and wearing a Yankees baseball cap, turning the corner onto the sidewalk. He wandered slowly down the sidewalk, hardly paying attention to where he was going as he headed in their direction. He, too, was playing a handheld game. When the boy was about fifteen feet away from the van, Rich yelled out, "Darn it! This game is too hard!"

The boy looked up, curious, walked closer. Rich was still focused on the game and seemed to not notice the boy.

"What game are you playing?" the boy asked.

Rich was startled, "Huh? Oh, hi. It's Rocket Blaster 2."

Cocky, the boy sneered, "Oh, I'm good at that! I can beat it with no problem."

"Really?" he said. "Can you help me?"

"Uh-huh," the boy answered proudly.

"Hey, that's awesome!"

"Oh, wait... The batteries are going dead," Rich said. He got up and searched aimlessly in his pockets, as if he forgot something. "Let me get some more."

Rich went back into the van and started rummaging around.

After waiting about ten seconds, the boy hopped up into the van to see what was going on. Rich quickly shoved the door closed and darted through the cage door, closing it behind him. He twisted its lock and sat in the driver's seat, immediately pushing the LOCK button for the van's side doors. He turned the ignition, hit the gas hard, and drove off. The boy lost his footing in the van and fell to its floor.

"What are you doing?" Susie asked.

Rich didn't answer Susie. Instead, he picked up a wireless microphone out of the driver's side door pocket. Using a deep, terrifying voice, Rich yelled into the microphone, "I'VE GOT YOU! YOU FOOL! YOU'RE MINE!"

The boy screamed and pulled in vain on the van's side door handle.

"WHAT ARE YOU DOING?!" Susie yelled.

Rich, again, ignored her.

"I'M GOING TO HURT YOU! I'M GOING TO MAKE YOU BLEED! HA HA HA HA!" Rich screamed into the microphone.

The boy grabbed his head and belted out a blood-curdling scream. Rich pressed a red button on the van's console. Susie heard a loud barking come from the back of the van. She turned around and saw a large black box in the front corner of the van's back shaking violently with very loud barking coming from it. The boy scrambled away from the black box and huddled in the back corner of the van, crying and screaming.

"MY DOG IS GOING TO RIP YOU APART!" Rich yelled.

Susie cried and begged, "STOP! STOP! STOP! PLEASE, STOP!"

She slapped Rich's arm repeatedly, but it didn't affect him.

The boy screamed, "PLEASE, DON'T HURT ME! PLEASE, PLEASE, PLEASE!"

Susie watched in shock as Rich casually took a bite of a donut and continued driving the van as if nothing unusual was happening. Other than yelling in the microphone, he seemed completely at ease and undistracted.

"IT'S TOO LATE FOR YOU, BOY! YOU'RE GONNA DIE!" Rich yelled and then calmly popped the remainder of the donut in his mouth.

Susie didn't know what to do. She didn't know what was going on, but she was overwhelmed with panic and horror.

"I knew it! I felt it when I first met you! You're horrible. You're evil!" she shrilled.

Rich looked at her, shook his head, and then he yelled in the microphone, "THIS IS WHAT YOU GET FOR GETTING IN A CAR WITH A STRANGER!"

The boy screamed, "NO, NO, NO! NO!"

Rich yelled back, "DO YOU WANT TO DIE?!"

The small boy yelled, "NO! NO! NO!"

Rich stopped and parked the van. He picked up the microphone and, in a serene voice, said, "Never get in a car – especially a van – with a stranger, okay?"

The boy cried out, "OKAY! OKAY! OKAY!"

Rich pressed a button and the sliding door of the van opened, allowing the boy to escape. The boy immediately jumped out and ran away for dear life.

Susie was without words, feeling a potent mixture of anger, awe, and disapproval. Rich smiled at her and chomped at his taffy. Susie frowned at him.

Rich tried to explain, "Look, I know that was a bit extreme..."

Susie interrupted, screaming, "EXTREME?! THAT BOY WILL NEED THERAPY FOR THE REST OF HIS LIFE!"

Rich tapped the steering wheel, appearing to doing his best to think of something to say.

"Look, you have to trust me," he said after a few moments. "The boy's parents never taught him the dangers of getting in cars with strangers. Very shortly, the boy will be faced with that very real decision. I had no choice but to do this to ensure his safety," he said.

Susie crossed her arms in disapproval. "You couldn't have just simply TOLD HIM NOT TO?!" she yelled.

"I went through nearly seventy different scenarios in advance. None of them worked. I even predicted what would happen if I gave him a thousand dollars," Rich answered, pulling ten one-hundred dollar bills out of his pocket.

Rich rubbed his face a little, looking a bit flustered.

He continued, "That little boy... Nothing worked... Nothing at all except this. And he had to learn immediately."

Rich went through the cage door and to the black box. He flipped a couple of latches and lifted it up, revealing to Susie that it was just a mechanical device.

"Even this was necessary," he insisted.

"Is it right to play God?" Susie challenged.

Rich, contrite, responded, "*We* don't. *We* can only influence. *We* can't do magic."

Susie could feel her outrage dying down and she knew it wasn't just Rich's explanation that was convincing her to accept his justification. This incident had only added more stress to Susie's life – she had little energy to care anymore. In the past few days, her life had been turned upside down, but she was trying her best to keep her head in spite of it all.

"The boy was in immediate, dire trouble and it could be prevented. There are so many people out there who we simply can't help because there are too many of *Them*," Rich tried to explain as he settled himself back in the driver's seat.

"Why NOW?" Susie challenged.

"It was now or never," Rich answered.

*   *   *

A short distance away, the boy was still running at full speed. He stopped to catch his breath and was wiping tears from his face. Just then, another white van pulled up beside him. A man yelled out his window, holding a handheld game.

"Hey, kid, can you help me with this game?!" he shouted.

A dog popped its head out of the driver's window.

The boy screamed, "Wahhhhhhh!" He continued yelling at the top of his lungs as he ran away.

*   *   *

Susie scrutinized Rich. "So, why this particular boy? You really went through a lot of trouble," she said as she motioned at the big black box housing the faked dog.

"Time means nothing to Us. Timing, however, means everything to Us. Effectiveness and influence means everything to Us. The effort to build that thing…," he said as he pointed to the black box, "…was nothing compared to the effect that it had."

"But, why that little boy instead of someone else?"

Rich winced, apparently struggling to give an answer that would make sense to Susie.

"Well… he is necessary for many other good things to come," he answered quietly. "It was worth it. He will play a very small role for a much greater good later. He will influence an important person later. The boy has to live."

Susie relaxed a little as she began to think more about Rich's point of view. She could see that she was not in a position to judge when she understood so little.

Rich continued, ranting, "There is so much pain in the world. I don't like it. All the time... All. The. Time. Dan, me, all of *Us* are constantly intervening. You saw firsthand how often Dan finds himself miraculously helping complete strangers."

Susie nodded slowly.

Rich hit his steering wheel in frustration. "Every minute, I'm aware of horrible things that happen to people. I see it. I feel it. It's almost as if I live it," he said gruffly, choking up. "What I do, what *We* all do... It goes on all the time. It's been going on since mankind existed. The only difference for you is that now you're aware of it."

Rich paused, popping another donut in his mouth, and they sat in silence for several seconds.

Susie looked at Rich sympathetically. It was clear to her now that he did think about the welfare and well-being of others.

Rich swallowed the donut and continued, "Most of the time, *Our* influence is simple and non-intrusive. This...," he said, smacking the cage door, "...was just an extreme case that required extreme influence."

"I'm sorry," Susie said. "I can't imagine what you go through. What you... What your life is like. I know you don't have to do anything. You could just let things happen without resorting to extremes like this, but then the suffering would be more than it is. You must be sad all the time."

Rich flashed her a big smile, although it seemed a little forced to her. "Me? Noooo. I love to laugh. I love to eat. I love music!"

He turned on the radio to a rock station.

"Let's go!" he said, starting up the van and driving off.

Chapter 22 – Short Drive

Susie and Rich were driving back into the city. Rich tapped to the beat of a song on the steering wheel. He seemed happy and back to the person that Susie remembered when she first saw him at the convenience store.

"All of this could be a little tricky," Rich said out of nowhere.

"What are you talking about? What will be tricky?"

"It occurred to me that I have a little more time to explain about the dynamics of Polarity," he said.

"Oh."

"Hmm, it's coming up on eleven o'clock. You hungry?"

Soon, they were both sitting in a fast food restaurant. Rich had a double cheeseburger, large chili-cheese fries, some chicken fingers, a large cola, and a brownie in front of him. Susie had small yogurt and a large coffee.

"Why will this be tricky? What do I need to know?" Susie asked, breaking the stride in Rich's eating.

Rich dabbed his face with a napkin.

"Well…," he started and grabbed the salt and pepper shakers at their table, "…suppose that *We* are the white salt shakers and *They* are the black pepper shakers."

"Okay."

Rich got up and moved to an empty table next to them.

"We're attracted to each other. To the death," he said, pushing the white shaker and black shaker together on the empty table.

"However…," he said, grabbing the white shaker from their table, "…the catch is that those of the same Polarity can't get close to each other."

Rich put the second white shaker next to the first white shaker and knocked them both over.

"The same is true for *Them*," he said, putting their black shaker next to the black shaker already on the table and then toppling both.

He moved the extra shakers back to their table and stood up the original white shaker and black shaker. "So, what you're left with is a situation that will always be one-on-one."

He grabbed a ketchup packet. He held it up.

"This means that you…," he said, pointing to the ketchup packet, "…can only have one of *Us* with you at any point in time."

He put the packet of ketchup next to the white shaker.

"I got that, but why does it make it tricky?"

"Well, if something should happen to me while we're together, don't expect help too quickly. *We* cannot gang up on *Them* and vice versa. It is always one-on-one," he said.

"I see," Susie said with trepidation.

"We should eat now," Rich told her as he sat back at their table. "Gotta get back on the road soon."

Shortly thereafter, Susie and Rich were back in the van, driving through the city streets again. "The one-on-one issue is always problematic. But…," Rich said happily, "…*We* have a plan that just may work."

Susie chuckled a little. Rich turned to her.

"You can laugh?" he asked playfully.

Susie laughed a little more.

"Okay, I like laughing, but I don't know what you're laughing about," he asked.

"When you say *We*, you mean that it involves me, too, right?"

"Yeah, of course… How's that funny?"

"You could have let me in on the plan," Susie said.

"I can see where you're coming from. I'm sorry. I'm not used to talking to people about Polarity."

"Well, so, what is the plan?"

"Well, it just changed again," Rich answered.

"Just like that?"

"Yup, just like that."

"Let me guess… It's a long story," she said.

Rich laughed, "You got it!"

He looked at his watch and then tossed a piece of taffy in his mouth. He turned down the music in the van slightly – his eyes changed to a direct stare forward.

"We'll take care of you," he blurted out.

"You seem so certain," Susie responded cynically.

Rich shook his head and grinned, "*We* always have the advantage over *Them*. Always."

Susie briefly thought of how Dan was almost killed by Spike. Dubious, she asked, "Why's that?"

"It's always a close call between *Us* and *Them*. Those who use their Polarity most effectively always win," explained Rich. "If you've had it for a long time and you're a quick thinker, you have the distinct advantage. It doesn't matter which side you're on."

Rich paused as he turned onto another street.

He continued, "However, *They* get too distracted by anger – and emotion from the anger gets the best of *Them*. For example, both sides mock each other – it can be a very effective weapon. When it comes to mocking, *They* are more susceptible because of *Their* emotions attached to *Their* anger. So, *They* avoid one-on-one contact with us, if *They* can," he said with an odd hint of excitement.

"Interesting," Susie commented. "Just how much of an advantage is it?"

"A very small one. It doesn't seem like much when *We* do have one-on-one contact. But, over the long run, it equates to a significant advantage," Rich said. "Still, it's best to eliminate people before they get their full Polarity – before someone becomes one of *Them*. It saves a lot of hassle later. You never want to allow more on *Their* side."

"I dislike how casually you use the word 'eliminate'."

"I got ya," Rich said, nodding. "If you had your full Polarity, you would understand without a second thought... But, that's just me talking and you having to believe me."

Rich perked up, as if something new caught his attention. He looked from the side mirrors to his rearview one.

"Hmm..." he said with a little grunt.

"What?" Susie asked.

"Well... *They* were trailing us and now *They've* stopped."

"What?! Why didn't you tell me *They* were trailing us?"

Rich, smiling as always, answered, "I didn't need to. No need to cause you to worry, but..."

Rich didn't finish his sentence. He just stared intensely into his rearview mirror.

"But, what?" Susie asked. "But now I should worry?"

"Kind of," Rich answered slowly, clearly distracted.

Susie didn't respond and decided to wait until he was able to sort through whatever had his attention.

"Okay!" he shouted. "We're good!"

Rich turned onto another street and sped up.

"*They've* set something in motion against us, so *They're* now keeping their distance," he explained.

Susie grabbed her face in vexation. She sighed and with resignation asked, "So, what's going to happen?"

"Meh... We'll be fine. Probably best to close your eyes, though."

Susie's eyes widened, "What?!"

At that very moment, Rich took a sharp left turn that threw Susie into her door. A police car popped out of an alley and pursued them. Rich stepped on the gas.

Rich calmly laughed a little bit as he weaved through traffic. He told her, "When I was growing up, I used to wonder what it would be like to be in a high-speed police chase."

Susie was gripping her armrests for dear life.

"Kind of funny how it's happening now," Rich casually commented.

He took another very sharp turn, tilting the van up on two wheels momentarily – nearly flipping over – before it slammed back down.

Susie's eyes bulged and she screamed. Rich giggled. Susie looked at Rich and he looked back at her.

"This is NOT funny! Keep your eyes on the road!" Susie yelled at him while pointing forward.

Rich shrugged and resumed weaving through traffic, narrowly missing cars – it seemed effortless for him.

They approached a red light with a line of cars stopped in front of them. Rich didn't hesitate and careened into the empty on-coming traffic lane, bypassing the stopped cars. The van barreled through the intersection, shooting between cars coming from the right and left.

Susie screamed at the top of her lungs.

"I CAN'T LOOK!" she yelled as the van dodged back into their lane on the other side of the street.

"Yeah, you don't have to," Rich said.

He hit the accelerator as he chewed some taffy.

"Hmm," he mumbled.

"WHAT?! WHAT?!" Susie yelled.

"Here comes some more."

Rich passed through another intersection. Police cars appeared from both sides of the intersection and pursued them. Rich pulled out a thick pillow from behind his seat and handed it to Susie.

"Here ya go," he told her.

Trembling, Susie took it from Rich and held it out in front of her, wondering why she had been given a pillow. Just then, a man on a bicycle dashed out in front of them, causing Rich to hit the brakes. Susie's upper body slammed forward. Her head smashed into the dashboard, but it was protected by the pillow she was holding.

"Sorry... Guy on a bike back there," Rich said to her, accelerating again. He then took a sip of soda and added, "Oh... and the uh... seat belt doesn't work right all the time."

Susie looked at Rich in disbelief, a bit dazed from the impact.

"You can keep that pillow, if you want to," Rich suggested.

"I will," she panted, hugging the pillow tightly.

"The hard part about this, of course, is to make sure no one gets hurt," Rich said as the van cut through a parking lot.

"Then why don't we STOP THE VAN?!" she yelled.

Rich laughed a little, "Oh, we can't do that. The police will apprehend us and *They* will get you."

Watching Rich narrowly miss several cars and pedestrians in the parking lot, Susie yelled, "I don't care! I don't care!"

Rich took another bite of taffy as he missed another pedestrian by inches.

"Oh, you say that now," he said. "But you'll thank me later. *They* would torture you in ways that you cannot imagine. Remember that *They* will know exactly what to do to maximize your suffering. *They* wouldn't kill you immediately, no. *They* would just make you wish you were dead."

Rich made a hard right out of the parking lot and an immediate left down another street.

"I'm gonna throw up," Susie said, pale and nauseated.

Rich winked at her and smiled, "Nah, you won't."

Police cars, with sirens blaring, spun into the street behind them and were closing in fast.

"You know what we need?" Rich asked rhetorically.

"A helicopter?" Susie asked weakly.

"A helicopter? Oh, that's good! Funny!" Rich laughed. "No, what we need is some good car-chasin' music."

He pushed a button on the van's CD player in the console. "Born to Be Wild" started playing as they zipped through another red light. Rich started humming along with the song. Oddly, this did quell Susie's fears a bit.

"It's strange how you get used to this," said Rich. "When I first got my Polarity, it was pretty disorienting. Looking at you now, it really brings me back."

Susie barely caught any of that, grabbing her mouth in nausea.

"What I'm doing right now is probably the most harrowing moment of your life."

"Yeah…," Susie said nervously, "…it's definitely up there."

Rich nearly hit a car pulling out of a parking space.

"AHHH!" she yelled, "Dear God, this is like a Disney ride from hell!"

"Disney ride! Ha!"

Rich turned the van so hard that it spun 180 degrees, while he smoothly switched gears into reverse. He immediately

302

accelerated and resumed driving without looking behind him. The police were now facing him.

Susie screamed at him and hit him on the shoulder, "Look where you're driving!"

Rich replied, "Well, I suppose I could if it makes you feel any better. I mean, I really don't have to. I could do this with my eyes closed. I already know what's going on, remember?"

Susie started hyperventilating.

"I sense an enormous amount of good in you," Rich said suddenly. "It's not a surprise that *They* are after you."

Rich reached and grabbed a cup from behind Susie's seat.

"These nails should come in handy," he said. He tapped the switch to lower his window and tossed the nails out.

Several police cars' tires blew out, causing the cars to skid and twist in the street so that they completely cut off the cars behind them. Rich swung the van back around to facing forward again, immediately switching back into drive and accelerating. Another police car popped out from a side street and started pursuit.

"Is the fancy driving really necessary?!" Susie yelled.

"It's not fancy; it's efficient," Rich answered, swerving briefly through oncoming traffic and onto the sidewalk.

"You've got a handle on ALL of this?!" Susie hollered.

"Oh, heavens, no, not completely," he said, taking a hard left onto a busy one-way road, going the wrong way. "I'm only human. But, this is pretty easy."

He dodged around the honking cars with ease and took a left onto another road. Suddenly, Rich acutely turned the steering wheel so that they were heading down a wide alley. About halfway down, he blindly turned again, promptly pulling into an open garage directly on the right. He slammed on his brakes and immediately put the van in park. The police cars turned into the alley and passed them by.

"Oh, my God, this isn't happening," Susie said loudly. "Are we safe?!"

Rich tapped the steering wheel in thought. "Hmm? Oh, no. Not yet," he said.

He put the van in reverse, quickly backed out of the garage, and came out the way they came in the alley. As they were pulling back out into the street, the police cars appeared down at the other end of the alley again and resumed their pursuit. Rich accelerated down the street, further widening the gap between them and the police. He took a left turn down a street and quickly decelerated until he was at the speed limit.

"Why are we slowing down?!" Susie demanded.

"I don't want to draw any attention from those around us," Rich answered. "We'll be okay."

"What?!" Susie tried to yell, her voice now hoarse.

Rich slowly made another turn, pulled the van up to the curb, and neatly parallel parked in one of the few gaps between cars. He pulled a hairnet out of his pocket and hurriedly put it on. Rich then pulled a blond wig out from behind his seat and put it on as well, quickly making sure its ponytail was straight in the back. He then added a baseball cap and some glasses. Police sirens were quickly approaching. He opened his door and got out.

A second later, police cars came around the corner and, just as they passed by, a semi passed by Rich's van, hiding them from view. The police continued onward.

Rich asked Susie, "You coming out?"

Susie was in shock, still clutching the pillow. She asked him, "Why... why aren't we driving?"

Rich didn't answer. Susie turned and saw him go to the back of the van. She got out and followed him. He removed some black and white stickers from the license plate to change the lettering from *TS1831* to *18 S8T*, then went around and did the same to the front plate. He opened Susie's door and, from behind her seat, pulled out a big magnetic sign labeled *YOU'RE LOOKING FOR US* in large font; underneath this, in a smaller font, was *PEST CONTROL.* He then slapped the sign on the side of the van facing the street.

"We'll be fine," Rich said, beaming proudly at his handiwork.

Susie cocked her head at the sign.

"Hey, you gotta have a sense of humor in this world," he said with a laugh and a playful slap on Susie's shoulder as they went around the van and onto the sidewalk.

The semi pulled away. Having circled back, the police were driving up the street towards them again. They slowed down briefly, comparing a picture of Rich to the man with the long blond ponytail, glasses, and baseball cap. They then looked at the license plate and they continued on.

"Let's keep moving," Rich said, still in disguise.

"Where are we going?"

Rich pointed vaguely, "Food court. There's a side entrance to the mall just up here. I'm a little hungry."

They walked into the mall together. Rich walked with a confident stroll while Susie was still shaking from the car chase ordeal.

"I'm hungry again. You hungry?" he asked her.

She thought a moment and then shrugged. "Why ask when you already know?" Susie answered indifferently.

"Fair enough. You were going to respond with 'How can I think of food after that?' right?"

Susie tried to smile but she could not conjure one.

Rich said, "Well, I'm going for hamburgers."

"I wonder what it's like in your world. There aren't many surprises, are there?"

Rich turned to her and, with a very serious face, told her, "Hey, I've been blessed. I'm honored to have this gift. But," he sighed sadly, "I will admit that it is a bit lonely."

Susie felt sorry for Rich. She knew how terrible loneliness could be. He was a bit out there and maybe not exactly in touch with those around him, but he was a nice guy and had good intentions. At the very least, he was definitely the life of the party.

With stern compassion, Susie responded, "Rich, I may not entirely understand how you do your work, but you are a good and honest man. You and Dan are two peas in a pod."

Rich blushed.

Rich and Susie were soon sitting down in the food court with their food. Rich buried his mouth in a hamburger while Susie sipped a coffee.

"Would it sound strange if I said that I'm getting used to this?"

"Used to what?" Rich asked with his mouth half-full.

"You and Dan have opened this whole new world to me very quickly. You kind of threw me in the deep end and forced me to see it up close and personal."

Rich nodded, "Yes, it was part of our plan. You will see there are far more extraordinary things to come. What you've seen so far was just a tutorial."

"Polarity seems somewhat... well, natural," she casually commented and then took another sip.

Rich stopped eating.

"Susie, it is as natural as sight or sound. It could be scientifically tested, if one of *Us* or *Them* allowed it. It is a part of life, a part of physics, and a part of every creature. There isn't a rational reason why it isn't possible to chain events. It's just as certain as cause leads to effect."

"I understand, but there is just so much going on. It's incomprehensible how much information you have to process," Susie said.

"Humans only use about twenty percent of their brain. There's plenty of potential processing power there. Plenty. That extra eighty percent was built in, through evolution, for those who get their full Polarity. It's a mystery to most people, but not to *Us* or *Them*."

As she considered Rich's words, it made sense to Susie why Dan and Rich would choose to remain hidden. Susie could only imagine how exploited they would be by the rest of the world if they allowed it. There were no surprises with Polarity. It was like Christmas, but you already know everything you're getting in advance for the rest of your life. She reasoned that there was little reason to feel special when there was no mystery.

"I see things… differently. I guess that's what I'm trying to say," Susie expounded to Rich.

A mother and her three-year old daughter, holding hands, walked by Rich and Susie. The girl stopped in front of Rich and stared.

Her mother said, "Honey, it's not polite to stare."

"Why are you fat?" the girl asked Rich with no reservation.

Her mother gasped, "Stacey!"

Rich smiled and loudly told the girl, "Because I LOOOOOOVE FOOD!"

"I'm so sorry," the girl's mother apologized. "I'm so embarrassed."

"Hey, it's not a big deal," Rich laughed. "She's adorable."

"Why are you funny-looking?" the girl then asked Rich.

"Stacey, stop!" the mother said, flushing red.

"So I can make little girls laugh!" Rich said, laughing and not missing a beat. He made a funny face at Stacey.

She giggled nonstop. Her mother grabbed her and pulled her away.

Rich laughed a little and took another bite of his hamburger.

Susie was impressed.

"Wow, you handled that so well," she said. "I'm actually more impressed with that than all of the stunt-driving you pulled off earlier."

Rich brushed it off, "She's a child. She doesn't know any better. She won't even remember this. She is adorable, though."

"Other people would have reacted very differently."

Rich took a sip from his drink.

"Well, she doesn't know the difference between right and wrong yet," he said. "Once she does, then it's different for me. It will also be different for her because she will remember what she does."

Susie raised an eyebrow.

He explained, "Everyone has the ability to chain events together to some degree. Remembering things from the past is exactly that." Rich paused briefly, "The thing is, you don't get that ability until you know the difference between right and wrong."

Susie started, "I…"

Rich interrupted, "Do you remember anything from when you were her age?"

Susie thought back to when her father left. She reflected for a second and then answered, "Only an ambiguous memory of when I last saw my father. Other than that, no."

"Well, once they know the difference between right and wrong, everyone gets some small degree of Polarity. Once they do, they can chain events in the past or sometimes in the future."

"So, I can't remember things when I was young…," Susie began.

Rich finished, "…because you can't remember anything until you know the difference between right and wrong. However, any mix of good and evil will screw up your ability to see into the past or future clearly. This is why your memories get fuzzy. Many people can't even remember things that happened literally yesterday. They joke about getting old, but the reality is that their memories are fuzzy because their Polarity is, well, fuzzy."

"Oh."

"When someone fully gets their Polarity, seeing things in the past and future is easy and VERY exact."

Susie challenged this, "I thought children can't remember things because their brains aren't fully developed."

Rich agreed, "That's true. And they can't tell the difference between right and wrong because of it."

He stuffed some fries in his mouth and asked her as he chewed, "Why do you think you only really remember the good and bad things? And, well, everything else is just merely forgotten?"

Susie sat back in her chair to think while Rich continued munching. While she could recall times that weren't really one way or the other, she had to admit that most of her memories, especially her clearly detailed ones, were of the particularly good or bad events of her life.

Rich shoved more fries in his mouth and explained further, "Like I said, there's nothing supernatural about this. Some people can chain events to see into the future to some degree."

"Like psychics," said Susie.

"Well, their ability to see precisely into the future is about the same level as your ability to remember precisely what happened in the past."

"Kind of fuzzy sometimes," Susie said.

"Yeah, or extremely generalized – better than nothin'. But, it is there. It does exist. Science just writes it off because there are many frauds out there," Rich said with a hint of frustration.

"What about people who believe they are prophets? Like Nostradamus?"

"I won't comment on anyone in particular, but, yes, there were some legit ones out there. The ones that go public are ostracized by both *Us* and *Them*. We push them away because it puts both groups at risk. It's really the only alliance, of sorts, that *We* have with *Them*. *We* and *They* ensure that the predictions of these so-called prophets are imperfect enough to be ignored."

"Why ostracize the ones trying to do good with their predictions? Why not help them?" Susie asked.

Rich laughed. "Remember that the words like good and evil aren't really the best way to describe *Us* and *Them*. It's more like very stable and very unstable. Those who go rogue are against everything stable, which excludes them from *Us*. As for *Them*, well, *They* keep a tight ship. *They* want destruction and chaos, but, ironically, *They* have to be organized to accomplish it and don't tolerate insubordination. Often, it's simpler to just eliminate the self-styled prophets than discredit them."

"I still think there could be a way to help them as opposed to… eliminating them," Susie said.

Rich scratched his head, "You would only know if you had your Polarity."

Susie smirked.

Rich shook his head slowly at her, sighed, and scooped the last of his fries into his mouth. Mouth full, he told her, "I've been where you are right now. I wouldn't have believed that my thoughts would change so dramatically either."

Chapter 23 – Executive Meeting

Dan walked into the lobby of a tall office building and strolled up to a large portrait hanging for all to see. Underneath the picture was a name, *Harold I. McGee,* and title, *Chief Executive Officer.*

"That's a good picture of you, Harold," he said.

He walked over to the elevators and pressed its call button. People gathered around him, waiting as well. Dan's ears perked up at a conversation between two women. He glanced at them out of the corner of his eye. One was a tall, good-looking, well-proportioned brunette wearing an elegant, perfectly fitted outfit; the other was much shorter, a bit stocky, plainly dressed, and wearing glasses.

"You really screwed up. Your incompetence has hit a new low," the tall brunette scolded the shorter woman.

"I'm sorry... I'm sorry...," the shorter woman pleaded.

The elevator dinged on arrival and the doors opened. Dan, as well as everyone else waiting, entered it.

"'Sorry' won't fix this. I don't know why I still have you. A brain-dead monkey would do a better job. It's embarrassing," the taller woman berated her as they entered the elevator.

Dan could tell this exchange had everyone else feeling awkward. Most looked sorry for the woman being chewed out; a couple of people were simply annoyed that this was going on in public.

The shorter woman broke down in tears.

"Cry then, why don't you? That will fix it. Ridiculous. Simply ridiculous," the taller woman scoffed, clearly not caring how her domineering and crass behavior was disturbing everyone else stuck in the elevator with her.

Dan decided to intervene. He turned to the taller woman and, with warmth, asked, "Kristy?"

The brunette woman, Kristy, turned her head towards him. She briefly looked Dan up and down. Annoyed, she asked in an irritated, snobbish tone, "I'm sorry, do I know you?"

Dan cocked his head back and acted puzzled. "Well, yeah. Sort of...," he answered.

"And what does *sort of* mean?" she asked as the elevator stopped at a floor and some people hurriedly got off.

"A couple of years ago, you worked at a daycare. You were watching a friend of mine's son," Dan said.

Kristy shifted uncomfortably. She shook her head at Dan a little.

"I wasn't working at...," she started.

Dan interrupted, "You're last name is Reilly, right? Well, I know you go by Kristy Benton these days..."

Kristy was silent and averted her eyes from Dan.

Dan continued, "...but you have a sister and a brother, both older, and I remember that tattoo you have on your lower neck."

Without hesitation, Dan tugged her blouse's high collar down to slightly reveal a tattoo.

Kristy slapped Dan's hand, "How dare you!"

Dan quickly responded, "Whoa, you've come a long way since Hooters."

The shorter woman piped up, "Hooters?!"

Dan looked at the shorter woman, "Yeah, she left the daycare to work at Hooters... Maybe like a year ago in New Mexico." He turned back to Kristy, "You bragged about making three hundred a day in tips – pretty sweet."

The elevator stopped again, but no one made a move to get off. Everyone stared, in captivation, at Kristy. She was still silent as the doors closed and the elevator moved again.

The shorter woman peered into Kristy's face and said with renewed confidence, "Daycare? New Mexico? Hooters? You said you went to Harvard and worked in investment banking for five years after that in New York."

Kristy gulped a little.

The shorter woman raised her voice, "And to think, I took all of that CRAP from you for the past six months!"

The elevator doors opened on Dan's floor and he stepped out. "Well, this is my floor. It was good seeing you again, Kristy!" he said brightly as he waved back.

He saw Kristy look at the shorter woman nervously. As if years of injustice were instantly vindicated, the shorter woman kept her eyes zeroed in on Kristy. Kristy turned her head away. The people standing behind them in the elevator just watched silently in shock.

"You caused me so much pain. You were ruining my life and you're nothing but a fake, a charlatan, a cheat...," the shorter woman said with vehemence as the elevator doors closed.

Dan started walking through the office space and he opened a door. The door closed behind him and he stopped. At the other end of a long hallway was Harold.

"Everything is moving along?" Harold asked.

"Yes, but I've predicted complexities in the next thirty-one hours."

"I see," Harold said. "This will need to be all over with by then."

"Yes."

Harold put his hand on his chin, thinking deeply.

Dan added, "*They* have been increasing their attention towards Susie, but *They* are doing so with less conventional means."

Harold commented, "Yes. The new one, Frank, is practically throwing himself at her. Very odd."

"At the botanical gardens, Frank just walked up to us with no apparent plan – it was reckless. What was he going to do? Shake my hand? I've never seen *Them* do that before."

"Well, it did force you to reveal who *We* are to Susie."

"That possibility was already planned for," Dan said.

"Yes, but it is not the ideal path – you know that. It upset many things *We* already had in place."

Dan nodded, "True, but it's just so bizarre. Also, to have someone like Frank – so new and inexperienced – work with a seasoned veteran like Spike is very... unusual for something of this importance."

Harold exhaled deeply and raised his eyebrows. "Dan, you are one of *Our* best, but I have to ask...," he started.

Dan interrupted, "The relationship that I've developed with Susie will not affect the outcome. She is my responsibility and *They* will not get to her."

"...and she's with Rich," Harold asked.

"Yes. For the next forty-seven minutes."

Harold shifted his gaze to the ceiling and said, "This will be close. *We* need to protect her more."

"There's at least Frank and Spike on *Us*, but there are probably a couple more that I'm not aware of," Dan said.

Harold told him, "There are three directly involved. Frank and Spike, yes – but the third is a priest."

"A priest?"

"Yes," said Harold. "A priest who was in your monastery. He knows you well and, because of that, he has been able to evade you."

"Father Crane," Dan said under his breath, shocked.

"Yes," Harold said sternly. "*They* have the powerful Father Crane on this personally."

Dan remained silent. Although surprises were rare, Dan was aware of the enormous skill and effort it must have taken for Father Crane to remain undisclosed to him for this long. However, Father Crane, like Harold, was a true master of his Polarity; if Harold hadn't told Dan, Dan knew he never would have picked up on Father Crane.

"Father Crane knows you so well, Dan, that he could walk up to you in plain daylight, shake your hand, and slash your throat before you even realized who it was," Harold chided.

Dan didn't respond. He knew that Harold is digging into him to make a point: Be more aware. Dan could see that he had been careless, not seeing far enough or broadly enough. He wondered what he could have done differently. He wondered if he had been too distracted, too social with Susie.

"Are you okay?" Harold asked.

"Yes... Yes, I'm just shocked that he's involved. At the monastery, he was always so self-serving and high on himself. He enjoyed making me feel small. He did so whenever he was given the opportunity. I never picked up on his Polarity back then."

"Dan, you may have your full Polarity, but just like everyone else, no one convinced you to ignore everything. You unknowingly chose to ignore this. People unknowingly choose to ignore things all the time – and it has nothing to do with Polarity. Being too close to someone can hide your better judgment,"

Harold said gently. "You gradually let him in without knowing. He is clever."

"The best way to get close is to earn trust...," Dan started.

Harold added, "...slowly from a distance...,"

Dan finished, "...until you get close enough that the person doesn't sense anything."

"Yes," said Harold. "Even *We* aren't immune to that. He earned your trust and you never saw what he really was."

Dan, remorseful, answered, "No."

He looked at Harold. He wanted to say more, but stopped himself.

"You're distracting yourself, Dan," Harold said calmly. "Focus. *We* need your focus."

"I understand."

"Moving on, *We* know what *We* are facing. Expect it to become more interesting with Father Crane in the mix, along with Frank and Spike."

"I understand."

Chapter 24 – The Destination

Rich and Susie were still at the mall – they had finished their meal and had been sitting quietly at the table for a while. Rich pulled out his phone and read a text.

"Hmm... okay. Time to go," Rich said while standing up. "Right now. Gotta move."

"What? Now?" Susie asked.

"Yup. Sorry, no time to explain. Please, we must hurry."

Susie and Rich rushed out of the mall's food court and headed to the van.

*   *   *

Elsewhere in the city, Father Crane was quietly standing next to a newspaper stand, waiting for events to unfold. His phone beeped. He looked down at it and read a text, *Time to move.*

Father Crane bit his lip a little bit in thought. He then looked up, pocketed his cell phone, and began walking quickly, almost running, towards downtown. His face was uncharacteristically stricken with anxiety.

Rich and Susie were speeding through the streets. Susie tried not to cringe in the passenger's seat whenever he swerved between cars.

"Susie, the only way to end this is through you," Rich said.

"What? What do you mean?" she asked, knowing she wouldn't like what he was about to say.

Rich took a deep breath and said, "You are going to face one of *Them* by yourself."

He looked at her, accentuating his seriousness. Fear overcame Susie like a landslide, "I can't do that! Are you nuts?!"

"Trust me, you will be alright. Okay?"

Susie's heart raced and her breathing picked up. She had troubled constructing her thoughts – she was exhausted and nothing made sense.

"Hey... Okay?" Rich implored, nudging her.

Susie turned to Rich and said, "I... I don't feel right. Something's wrong... really, really wrong."

"Listen, I know you're scared, but *We* are certain that if you go through with this...," Rich began.

Susie screamed, "STOP THE VAN! STOP! STOP IT!"

Rich quickly pulled over to the side of the street and brought the van to a stop.

"I'm sorry, Susie. I didn't mean to freak you out," he said.

Susie's mobile phone rang. The caller ID showed that it was Dan. Susie picked up the phone.

"Susie, forget about it," said Dan. "We'll do something else. I'll meet you at your house in ten minutes."

Susie broke down crying, overwhelmed. She was beside herself with the stress of the danger that she and her loved ones were in. She had not expected Rich to ask so much of her. She couldn't keep up with Dan or Rich. It seemed like they had forgotten she didn't have Polarity like they did. She was lost, her mind spinning.

Susie bawled into the phone, "I'm... I'm just so lost!"

Dan comforted her, "I know. I know. There are other ways. Please, come see me."

Susie inhaled deeply and, sniffing, answered, "Okay." She knew she would feel better once she saw Dan.

Almost ten minutes later to the second, Rich's van pulled up outside Susie's home and stopped to let her out. As soon as she closed the van's door, Rich backed up the van, turned it around, and drove off in the direction it came. Susie saw Dan ahead on the sidewalk and began to run to him. Dan ran to meet Susie, arms opened wide. They embraced.

"Ohhhh, Dan!" she cried in joy, feeling safe with his arms wrapped firmly around her, "I feel so safe with you. Please don't leave again!" she pleaded.

Dan patted her on the back, still holding her.

"It will be okay," he said softly.

After a minute, Dan and Susie went into her home. Susie walked into her kitchen to make some tea to help soothe her frazzled nerves. Dan casually walked around her living room and wandered into the kitchen.

"Oh, you still have that flair pin from Mary?" Dan asked, pointing to the pin sitting on the countertop.

"Yeah," Susie answered.

"You don't wanna lose it, do you?"

"No," Susie said.

She walked over to the pin, picked it up, and dropped it in her purse. She then grabbed a mug and started filling it at the sink.

"So, what are we going to do?" Susie asked.

"There are many possibilities. But, *We* have determined why *They* are only after you," Dan said.

Susie's heart stopped. She had always thought *They* were also after Dan since Spike had attacked him. She watched as the mug overflowed and she clumsily turned off the water.

"But... Just me? Why?" she asked, her hands trembling too much to hold the mug any longer and she set it down in the sink

"It has to do with your father."

Susie's face filled with disbelief. "No... I mean... What?" she said with dumbfounded amazement.

Dan explained, "Long ago, your father left you and your family, right?"

"Yeah."

"Why?" Dan asked.

"Don't know," Susie answered. "Pretty sure not even my mother knows. He just left one day."

Dan didn't move a muscle.

"You... You know, don't you?" Susie asked.

"Yes."

"Tell me," Susie tersely demanded.

Dan shook his head, "I can't. Your father must tell you. He will tell you from his heart, something I cannot do for him."

"Can't you just...," Susie started.

Dan interrupted, shaking his head, "No. Please, trust me. You have to see him. *We* know where to find him. He's in Detroit."

Susie stumbled to a chair and sat down. She took a few deep breaths and then asked, "When should I go?"

"Now," Dan said.

"Now?"

"Now." Dan said as he handed Susie her itinerary. "Well, you can pack, of course. Your flight is already booked; it leaves in three hours."

Within a couple of minutes, Susie had hauled out a medium-sized black suitcase and was packing in her bedroom. Her bedroom was neat and, like the rest of the house, a bit sparse. Dan stood nearby as she packed.

Dan, with regret, said, "I really wish things could be different for you. I've never seen anything like this before."

"You know," Susie said, pausing briefly in her packing, "I feel this is the right thing to do. So, I'm okay with it."

She smiled at Dan, feeling pretty cheerful.

"Really?"

"Yeah," she replied with a grin.

Susie looked around, trying to think if she had forgotten anything.

"Hmm… Oh, can't forget the picture," she said.

She left the room momentarily and returned with the small, framed picture of her younger self and her father.

"Why bring that?" Dan asked.

"It's the only shared memory we have together that I'm sure of. I want to know what he remembers from it," she said.

"Oh."

Susie looked around her room again, searching it for anything else she may have forgotten.

"Well, I'm packed I think," she declared after a moment.

"Okay, I'm parked around the corner," Dan said. "I'll go get my car."

"I'll meet you out front. Just want to look around again."

Dan left the room.

Susie stood there in thought. She raised her eyebrows and looked up to the ceiling, once more trying to make sure she hadn't forgotten something. Not being someone who traveled much or even at all, she was concerned about what she may have forgotten that she could possibly need.

A couple of minutes later, Susie headed outside with her luggage. Dan had brought his car around and he helped Susie put her black suitcase and a light blue backpack in the trunk. They got in the car and were soon driving to the airport, which was about an hour from Susie's apartment.

Excited as she was, Susie was still very tired. It was hard for her to think straight. At this point, she was more than willing to let Dan do the thinking for her. He appeared well-rested and well-organized – the same old Dan.

"Hmm…," Dan mumbled after they'd been on the road about an hour.

Susie, half-dozing, turned to Dan and sighed, "Whenever I hear that, I know it's not good."

Dan glanced at her briefly.

"So, what is it?" Susie prodded, rubbing her eyes a bit. She looked around and noticed that they were nowhere near the airport but in the middle of the city. "Wait, why are we…," she began.

"I was trying to avoid this," Dan interrupted. "I will have to drop you off up at a corner up here. From there, you must go to the airport alone," he said.

Susie gave Dan a look that said, "You've got to be kidding," and rolled her eyes.

"I'll do my best to simplify what's going on. If *We*… Well, if I or anyone of *Us* gets any closer, *They* will attack *Us* directly. *They* are desperate and willing to be reckless now. If *They* attack, you will miss your flight and we'll have to start all over again."

Susie closed her eyes. She didn't want to go through with this anymore. She wanted this to end quickly, but her thoughts were muddled by sleep deprivation and exhaustion.

Dan pressed, "Don't worry, Susie. *We* have you protected from this point forth. Use the advice I've given you before: Don't allow yourself to be distracted. Trust your instincts."

Susie, resigned, agreed, "Okay."

Dan gave her a playful smile, "This will all be over soon and we can go back to studying, okay?"

Susie smiled back at Dan.

Dan pulled his car up to a curb. It was early in the rush hour, but traffic was beginning to get heavy. Several pedestrians hurried by on the sidewalk and a few cyclists zipped through the bike lane. Dan got out of his car, as did Susie. They both walked to his trunk and Dan unloaded her luggage.

Dan handed her luggage to her and said, "Well, this is it. Take a cab from here. You can catch one a block over that way." Dan pointed up the street, indicating a right turn. He slammed the trunk shut.

"Okay, thanks."

"Call me when you get there."

"I will," Susie answered softly.

Dan looked deep into Susie's eyes, leaned in, and gently kissed her on her mouth. Susie flushed and her heart skipped a beat.

"I'm sorry, but I've gotta go," Dan said, sighing.

He got in the driver's seat and closed his door.

As he drove away, she whispered aloud, "I love you."

Susie grabbed the handle of her black suitcase and extended it so she could pull it on its wheels. She stacked her smaller, light blue backpack on top of the black suitcase. She took several steps forward and instinctively felt that she should look further down the street – she didn't know why. Almost a block away, she saw a Catholic priest – he wore a fedora hat and glasses. He was standing with his hands behind his back and was staring directly at her through the many people.

Susie got a strange inkling that she should approach him, but she noticed a homeless man off to her left about thirty feet away and next to a building. He held a sign reading, OUT OF LUCK. PLEASE HELP. GOD BLESS. Susie decided to give him whatever change she had. She moved closer to him and noticed his sandals – they looked familiar somehow.

Suddenly, she heard a loud screech of a car throwing on its brakes from up the street in the direction she had just been looking. This was quickly followed by a loud crashing noise. Susie returned to the street's curb and looked. There appeared to be a terrible accident at the same location where the Catholic priest had stood – a bright orange ice cream truck's front end was badly smashed in. The Catholic priest was nowhere to be seen and a small crowd of people had already gathered in that area. She wondered if the priest was okay.

She received a text from Dan, *Avoid distractions and keep your course.*

She stopped walking and turned around. "I have to be focused," she said to herself.

Susie squinted down the street and spotted a cab in the traffic that was heading her way. She hailed it and the cab turned on its blinker, indicating that it would pick up Susie. The cab stopped in front of her, but she stopped as well. She didn't move for a second, but then she fell on her knees to the ground. She was wracked with a sudden sense of frailty – gravely disturbed and locked frozen where she was.

Within a few seconds, a familiar-looking small boy wearing a Yankees baseball cap and holding a handheld game ran to the cab's door.

"Let's take this one, mom!" he yelled.

The boy's mother ran up to the boy. She was toting many bags from various nearby stores.

She chided him, "You CANNOT just take someone else's cab! This cab was for this nice lady here."

"It's… It's okay," Susie said weakly.

"Are you okay?" the mother asks, seeing Susie on her knees and hearing her feeble voice.

"I'm fine… Thanks."

The boy's mother shrugged off Susie's condition as the small boy jumped into the cab and immediately started playing his game. She rolled her eyes at him.

"I'm so sorry," she said to Susie.

Susie quietly responded, "Really, it's… It's okay."

The mother of the small boy looked into the cab and, with a raised voice, said, "Driver, I need to put the bags in the trunk."

The cab driver got out of the cab. Susie's heart ceased to beat – it was Spike. She wasn't able to speak, overcome with rarified fear. She staggered backwards, scooting on the ground away from the cab. Spike stood there sweating profusely, but he didn't move.

"Driver?" the mother of the boy asked.

Susie was able to muster up the courage to get up and run away.

Dan texted her, *Well done Susie.*

This text comforted her in this time of need – a sign that everything would be okay. Susie quickly found another cab and was once again on her way to the airport.

She received another text from Dan, *You're doing great.*

Susie smiled at the text, wishing he could be with her.

After several minutes, the cab pulled up at the airport departure area and Susie got out, paying the driver as he handed over her luggage from the trunk.

The area teemed with people and cars rushing about their business. Susie looked confident and felt oddly happy that she would see her father soon. She still harbored some anger towards him, but she felt much more at ease about him, more than she ever had before. She hadn't quite forgiven him, but she was looking forward to doing so, if she could.

She walked through an entrance and immediately went to the flight information board. She saw her flight to Detroit was on time. She smiled ear to ear. She made her way further in, toting her bags, and walked confidently to the check-in kiosk.

She pulled her itinerary out of her purse. When she did, the flair pin from the diner flew out of the purse and fell to the ground behind her. Susie turned around, smiled slightly at it, and bent down to pick it up. As she stood up, she saw the back of a policeman in the distance – he looked familiar.

"Frank?!" she thought, with adrenaline shooting through her body.

It was Frank – he began to turn towards her, but she sidestepped behind a nearby pillar, hiding herself from his view.

Stay there. Count to ten and then continue on your way, a text from Dan said.

Susie inhaled deeply and, as Dan had instructed, she counted to ten to herself, "One, two, three…,"

As she counted to herself, she felt more and more calmed. When she finally got to ten, she peeked around the pillar and Frank was nowhere to be seen. She stepped back to the check-in kiosk, punched in her flight data, and printed her boarding pass. She knew she was completely safe, sensing that Dan, Rich, and others were protecting her.

Susie approached the security line and patiently waited. She took a step forward, but she stumbled to the ground, rapidly becoming ill. Her head began to spin a little and she was slightly short of breath. She turned around and, before her eyes, was Frank.

Susie gasped, "You…"

She passed out.

Susie came to with a TSA agent hovering over her.

"Hey, are you okay?" the agent asked.

She looked around. There were a few people standing around, but she didn't see Frank. A medic arrived shortly.

"Are you okay?" the medic asked.

Susie, still confused, answered, "Yeah... Yeah, I'm fine. I guess I'm just a nervous flyer... I guess."

"Well, you just passed out," the TSA agent pointed out. "You sure you want to fly?"

The medic shined a light in and out of Susie's eyes and continued assessing her for a few minutes.

"Well, she appears okay," the medic said. "This kind of thing does happen from time to time."

Susie assertively stood up – proving to them that she was better.

"Oh, I'm okay. I'll be fine. Thank you," she said gratefully but still feeling a little embarrassed.

"Okay, then," the TSA agent said with a smile, "I'll need to see your boarding pass and ID."

Within minutes of finding her gate, Susie's flight began boarding. She shoved her purse into her small black suitcase, put her light blue backpack on over her shoulders, and walked up to the gate agent.

"Boarding pass?" the agent asked.

Susie got her boarding pass out of her bag and handed it to the boarding agent. She received a text from Dan, *No need to worry now. All is clear.*

Susie smiled in relief. She made her way into the plane and stood in line to get to her assigned seat. Within a few minutes, she found her seat and stuffed her black suitcase in the overhead bin. She put her light blue backpack under the seat in front of her and sat down.

Unexpectedly, Professor Gomez stood next to her in the aisle. "Excuse me, but I think you're in my seat," he said.

Susie, surprised, exclaimed, "Professor Gomez?!"

"Susie? Wow, what a surprise!" he said, just as jolly as she remembered him.

"Yes," she said. "How are you doing?"

Susie suddenly remembered that Professor Gomez was on medical leave. She felt awkward.

"I've got some health issues to deal with," he explained. "I'm going to the Mayo Clinic in Minnesota, so I'm in the best hands possible. I'm just transferring planes in Detroit. What about you?"

"Wow, I'm sorry. I hope you'll be okay," she replied.

Professor Gomez smiled warmly, but he looked nervous.

"What about you?" he asked, trying to change the subject.

"I've had some personal things going on. It's kind of a long story...," she trailed off.

She looked at the seat indicated on her ticket and moved over a seat, next to the window, shifting her backpack over as well. Professor Gomez sat down.

"My father lives in Detroit," she said, deciding to talk about it. "I'm going to visit him."

"That sounds wonderful," Professor Gomez said.

Susie was about to say more to the professor but, unexpectedly, she saw Mary, the waitress from the diner who gave Dan her flair pin. Mary was planted in the walkway, waiting in the line of people getting to their seats. Her eyes drifted towards Susie.

"Hey, I know you!" she merrily shouted. "You're that great gal that saved me from my fifty-dollar mistake!"

"Wow, this is like a reunion of people from my recent past! How cool is this?!" Susie said.

Mary said joyfully, "Hey, I called my sister like your guy friend suggested. Oh, I tell ya, we hadn't talked like that in ages! I'm off to see her now."

"So, she lives in Detroit?" Susie asked.

"No, in Flint, Michigan. It's nearby," Mary explained. "She paid for my ticket, too!"

"I'm so happy for you both!" Susie said brightly.

Passengers waiting in line behind Mary were getting impatient with the dialogue, wanting to get to their seats. Susie saw their looks of disgust spread across their faces. Mary looked back and rolled her eyes.

"Okay, okay, hold your horses, people," Mary told the people behind her. She turned back to Susie, "Hun, I gotta go sit down. I'll see ya when we get there!"

Susie was thrilled that Dan had had an immediate impact on that nice woman's life. It warmed her heart that, even when he didn't have to intervene, he took the opportunity to help whenever he could.

Her thoughts of Dan were quickly overrun with her tiredness. She found herself almost dozing while waiting for all of the passengers to be seated. As the last of the passengers settled into their seats, it occurred to her that she didn't bring a book or music to help time pass while flying. She needed something to occupy her mind and the only thing she had was the picture of her father. She apologetically scooted past Professor Gomez and retrieved the picture from her bag in the overhead bin. She sat back down just as the flight attendants started checking that everyone was buckled in.

As the airplane taxied around onto the runway, she was holding the picture of her father, reflecting on it.

The captain spoke on the intercom, "Ladies and gentlemen, we are next in line for takeoff…"

Susie peered into the picture deeply, blocking out the captain's voice. She focused on her father's eyes. She found herself in a dreamlike state and then, all at once, she remembered everything.

"Susie, my dear little Susie, I will miss you badly. You'll never have a chance to know me, I'm afraid," her father said, wiping tears from his eyes.

He knelt down next to her and planted a kiss on her head.

Young Susie had no idea why he was crying, but she wanted to comfort him. She stood beside him, holding her stuffed teddy bear.

"Don't cry, Daddy," she said and then hugged him.

Her father cried uncontrollably.

"Don't cry, Daddy," she repeated, hugging him harder.

"I have to go, sweetheart," he sniffed. "I've been accused of things I didn't do. I don't have a choice. It's either I leave or I go to prison... Either way, you will never know me. But, try to remember that I love you."

The young Susie handed her father the stuffed bear she was holding.

"Here, Daddy," she said.

Susie's father kissed her on the head once again, stood up, walked over to a nearby table, and grabbed the framed photo that adult Susie knew so well. He took the picture out of its frame and wrote something on the back of it.

Susie snapped out of her memory and returned to the present. With excitement, she took the picture out of the frame and flipped it over to reveal a handwritten note:

My little Susie, know that I will always love you with all my heart, no matter what. You will always be with me in my thoughts.
Daddy

Susie cried a little and bit down on her knuckle, trying to deal with her overwhelming emotions. She looked out the window to hide her tears from those around her. She could see the houses below get smaller and smaller as the plane left the ground.

"I forgive you, Dad," Susie said with a sniff.

Instantaneously, Susie's vision went completely dark for a fraction of a second and then everything was enveloped in pure, bright light. She went rigid, consumed with it. The light dimmed slowly until she could make out objects in her surroundings. Everything around her gave off rays of white light and had a slight blue sparkle. She could hear echoes of people's voices around her.

Susie had gained her full Polarity. She recognized it as if she had always known it.

She looked around and, without any apparent reason, people started moving in fast forward and then in rewind, as if someone else was controlling a movie and couldn't decide which direction to go. Repeatedly, people momentarily returned to normal motion, only to be returned to skipping forward, then backwards again.

Susie couldn't bring herself to speak. She gripped her chair's armrest like vise grips. She blinked her eyes hard several times in a vain attempt to get back to reality.

She calmed down finally. The speed of her surroundings returned to normal, although voices were still a little echoed and the small sparkles of blue light still emanated from objects.

"Professor Gomez?" she asked him.

No reaction was given from the normally talkative Professor Gomez.

"Professor Gomez?" she asked again, tapping his shoulder this time.

The instant she did this, she saw no less than twenty different reactions of Professor Gomez at the same time. She tapped him again. She saw twenty different – and new – reactions from before and, again, all at the same time. This time, however, people in surrounding seats appeared to be involved for most of those reactions. It was too hard for Susie to make out.

She decided to stop tapping Professor Gomez. All of the reactions stopped and he acted as if she had never touched him at all. It was as if she simply saw all of the many different possibilities that could result from the simple act of tapping of his shoulder.

The world stopped around her. Nothing moved except for her. She stood up and looked around. She saw Mary the waitress two rows directly behind her. She was seated next to and talking to Kevin, the same guy Dan had helped to find work as an upholsterer.

Susie then looked further back and she saw Thomas, the would-be jumper she saw on the news with Dan. Time started again, but it was about at half the pace of normal. Voices echoed – she knew what she saw wasn't real.

Thomas looked very annoyed. He was getting angry at the person next to him. He then stood up and began to yell at the top of his lungs, "I'M NOT! I'M NOT! I'M NOT!"

He gripped his head with both hands and his body convulsed violently. People all around him were scared and began to panic. In the row behind Susie's, a man sitting in the aisle seat jumped into the aisle and drew a gun. "U.S. Air Marshal! Get to the floor!" he commanded.

Thomas ignored the air marshal, continuing his screaming and frantic jerking.

Kevin got up from his seat and moved to tackle Thomas, but he was tripped up on one of Mary's feet. Immediately, Thomas grabbed and shoved Kevin down the aisle towards the air marshal.

The air marshal was pushed backwards and stumbled over Professor Gomez's leg, which he had put out into the walkway when he had turned around at the ruckus. The gun flew out of the air marshal's hands and towards the front of the plane. Thomas jumped up onto Kevin's chest and then jumped over the fallen air marshal, snatched up the gun, and ran up the aisle towards the cockpit.

Everything froze to a dead stop, but Susie was still in motion and had another vision. This time, it was of an event that had happened a short while ago:

> *The mechanic left the hardware store after having bought the last ratchet wrench. He was next seen on an airplane doing maintenance. His supervisor noticed that bracket supporting the lock on the cockpit door was loose.*
>
> *"Hmm... This locking bracket is a little loose," the supervisor noted. "Tighten its bolts, will ya?"*
>
> *"Sure thing," the mechanic said.*
>
> *He attempted to tighten the hinges, but the ratchet wrench immediately broke. The mechanic pondered what to do. He tested the lock several times, struggling to make the lock engage properly.*
>
> *"Well, the lock catches most of the time... sort of," the mechanic said.*
>
> *"Hmph," the supervisor grunted. "Forget it. Let's make this Detroit's problem."*

Everything unfroze and Susie returned to her previous vision. Thomas grabbed the cockpit door, cleanly opening it. He rushed into the cabin. Gun shots went off.

Susie snapped out of her vision. She was back in real world at the current time. People were moving around normally and the echoing was gone. No longer were sparkles of light coming out of the surrounding objects.

She could tell that no time had passed during her vision – since the instant things had gone dark. She was unsure what to think about this when, all of the sudden, screaming filled the cabin.

"I'M NOT! I'M NOT! I'M NOT!"

Susie pressed against the back of her seat. She realized that the vision she just had was unfolding now, that this time it would be real. The plane was doomed.

*   *   *

Many miles away on a green hilltop, Dan watched the airplane fall out of the sky. It dove sharply, disappearing behind some trees in the distance. A second later, a great fireball erupted, followed by a huge black cloud of smoke.

Dan had no expression on his face as he watched the smoke rise. Then, his eyes narrowed slightly and he cracked a devilish smile. He felt a presence. Dan turned to his right, brimming with pride. He saw Harold standing about forty feet away.

Harold smiled, "You did good work, Dan. Fabulous, really. You should be proud of what you've accomplished."

"Oh, I am, Harold," Dan said. He smiled hard, barely able to contain himself. Dan turned to his left and saw that Rich was there, about forty feet away.

"Danny boy, you are one sneaky guy. I mean, you actually went the extra mile and got her to love you," Rich said with an envious smirk.

"Well," Dan chuckled, "I had to make it fun for me."

Rich yelled at the wreckage far away, "SAYONARA, YOU GOODY-TWO-SHOES WHORE!" Rich's fist pumped up and down a few times.

Dan cackled a little bit at this. He started to take a deep breath but stopped short. His face wiped clean of any expression. Suddenly, anger ravished his face.

"*We* have failed," he announced, "and it's my fault."

He recalled the series of events that had taken place, that he wished had never happened:

...*At Kevin's house, he had told Susie, "Always trust your intuition. Never fail it. Never."*

He realized that this stuck with her.

...*While at the restaurant, he had joked, "Oh, I always wondered what it'd be like to board an airplane with a parachute as your carry-on luggage... Just to mess with people."*

He realized that this, too, stuck with her. Now, rewinding events, he saw what had happened when he left Susie to get the car to take her to the airport:

"I'll meet you out front. Just want to look around again," she said.

Dan left the room.

Susie stood there in thought. She raised her eyebrows and looked up to the ceiling, once more trying to make sure she hadn't forgotten something. Not being someone who traveled much or even at all, she was concerned what she may have forgotten that she could possibly need.

She looked towards her open closet and saw her light blue parachute – so similar to a backpack – sitting up high on a shelf. She stared at it briefly and then swiped it from the closet. She felt she had to take it, but didn't know why.

Dan concluded to his great dismay that not only had Susie survived, but that he was the one who gave her the events she needed to chain together her survival – long before she got her full Polarity. He had even handled the parachute without recognizing it for what it was, too caught up to bother taking the time to see what role a seemingly useless piece of luggage might play.

"She's a tougher adversary than I thought…," Dan sullenly said to himself under his breath, "… maybe even more so than Father Crane."

Dan, Rich, and Harold simultaneously parted ways without saying a word.

*   *   *

The crashed plane smoldered near a river running through an open field lined with trees. The smell of burning fuel, fire, smoke, and death permeated the air. There were no survivors except one.

Over the wreckage, a light blue parachute streaked by. The parachutist landed safely and struggled to get out from underneath the parachute's canopy. Susie emerged.

She cried out, expressing every possible form of sadness a human could conjure in a lifetime. She collapsed to the ground, having no ability or will to stand up. She beat her fists repeatedly on the ground in anguish. She suddenly stopped crying and looked up to her left. There stood Spike, about forty feet away. He was expressionless.

"Susie, you are safe," Spike said.

Susie strongly nodded her head in agreement. Still in tears, she answered, "Yes… Yes, I know that now."

Spike cracked a smile. Susie perked up and looked around her. As far as she could see, people were appearing on the other side of the river, spaced out about forty feet from each other. Some waved to her.

Frank was on Susie's right, also about forty feet away. He gave her a concerned but happy smile.

"Susie," a man's voice from behind her called out.

Susie turned around.

"I am Father Crane. *We* are honored to have you with *Us*."

The End...
...For Now

Made in the USA
Charleston, SC
13 February 2014